GOT YOUR NUMBER

by STEPHANIE BOND

a humorous romantic mystery

You can run, but your past will always catch up with you...

Cover by Andrew Brown at clicktwicedesign.com

ISBN: 0989912779
ISBN 13: 9780989912778

CHAPTER ONE

ROXANN BEADLEMAN'S scalp roasted, and she realized with a start that she was still wearing the red wig. Puffing out her cheeks at her carelessness, she yanked off the remainder of her disguise as she wedged her van Goldie into a parking space at Rigby's Diner, home of the Big Daddy Crab Plate. Rigby would fire her for sure. Waiting tables had never been her favorite gig, but the job had great benefits (Rigby's brother-in-law sold health insurance), and the schedule was flexible enough to accommodate her obligations to the Rescue program. Until this morning.

She jumped out and bent at the waist to give her real hair—short and dark and plastered to her head—a lick and a promise with a vented brush. Biloxi, Mississippi, was celebrated for its sweltering heat, but she'd sort of expected a break by the twelfth day into the month of October. She slammed Goldie's door twice before it caught, then sprinted to the employee entrance of the diner.

Shuttling the Lindberg family to the bus station had taken longer than she'd expected, mostly because the twin five-year-old boys had stripped down to their skivvies and tossed their clothes out the van windows. Twice. According to her travel watch (two faces to accommodate dual time zones), she was exactly one hour late.

"You're an hour late," Helen, the head waitress, confirmed when Roxann slid into the kitchen.

"Car trouble." Not the first lie she'd told for a good cause.

Helen clucked and balanced a third plate on her arm. "Imagine that, a twenty-five-year-old van giving you trouble." Helen was sixty, with the wit and legs of a coed.

"Is Rigby angry?"

"Yeah, but I covered for you. Still, you'd better get shakin'. I need a couple of étoufée platters." Helen disappeared, then stuck her head back in, winking a mascara-laden eye. "And I almost forgot—there's a Steve McQueen type at table nine waiting to see you. Been here goin' on a half hour."

Anxiety twinged low in her stomach. She peeked around the divider between the blistering kitchen and the crowded dining room, but her view was obstructed by the weekly gathering of the Morning Glory Ladies, sporting straw gardening hats and lingering in the aisle to say their farewells. Roxann ducked back to dish up the étoufée for Helen, her stomach growling at the tangy aroma of shellfish and cracked pepper.

She didn't have a clue who the man might be. That one call Melissa Cape had made to Roxann's cell phone still had the potential of landing them both in the bayou if the woman's private investigator ex-husband made the connection. But in truth, any of the men in Roxann's life would have elicited the same gut-clutching response as Frank Cape.

Her father? The sole reason Walt Beadleman left his La-Z-Boy in the tiny living room of the tiny house in Baton Rouge was to cast for channel cats in the Mississippi River. He'd never think of floating on down to Biloxi to see his only child who was such a monumental disappointment, unless someone in the family had dropped dead.

Her most recent lover? The last time she'd seen Richard Funderburk, he was spitting mad that she'd dare to confront him about his drinking. Then he'd simply disappeared—to a twelve-step program she'd hoped. Wasn't there a step about seeking forgiveness from those you'd wronged? He still owed her fifty bucks, the mooch. And at least as many orgasms.

Her neighbor? Mr. Nealy had been hovering ever since her roommate and Rescue coworker Elise had wigged out, forcing Roxann to ask Elise to *move* out. Roxann cringed when she imagined what the old man had picked up with his hearing aid pressed against the kitchen wall. Any doubts that he'd overheard Elise's stunning proclamation of passion had been erased when Mr. Nealy had "run into" Roxann at the trash Dumpster and proceeded to spin an unlikely tale whose moral seemed to be that just because a woman was a tomboy, it didn't mean that all her neighbors thought she was "you know."

Of course, none of those men resembled Steve McQueen even if she'd swallowed the worm at the bottom of a bottle of Mezcal.

At last the chatty garden ladies dismantled, giving her an unobstructed view of the dark-haired stranger sitting alone at table nine. Relief pulled at her shoulders—according to Melissa Cape's description, her ex was a slim blond. This fellow was fortyish and brawny, with a jutting profile. His blocked jaw was clean-shaven, and his hair well shy of his collar. His khaki shirt was J. Crew sturdy and dry-cleaner-starched. An unlit cigarette dangled between his lips as he moved the saltshaker and aluminum napkin dispenser, probably looking for an ashtray. Finding none, he frowned and settled back against one of the hard wooden bench seats Rigby's teenage son's shop class had made over the summer, and opened a worn paperback. An obscure thriller that she'd already read—quite good.

Helen reappeared at her shoulder. "New boyfriend?"

"No."

"*Old* boyfriend?"

"No." And not at all her type—although granted, she could barely remember her type.

"So where do you know him from?"

Her memory for names wasn't keen, but she was certain she'd never seen this man's pensive face. And the agency always let her know when to expect a client—not that this guy looked as if he needed help from anyone. In fact, he looked about as approachable as a Doberman. He might be a reporter who'd tracked her down from that *Clarion-Ledger* expose of the Rescue program—one failed relocation in the hundreds she'd facilitated over the years, and she'd made the front page. Or rather, the description of her disguise had. She squinted. Frankly, though, the man didn't look like a reporter.

Then one side of her mouth slid back in a wry frown. Of course—he was a cop, chock-full of questions for her about something or someone having to do with the Rescue program. Nervy, considering the organization would gladly dismantle if the police would do their jobs.

"Roxy?" Helen probed.

"I've never seen him before."

"Want me to tell him you won't be in today?"

"No—he'll just come back. I'll see what he wants."

"Holler if you need backup." The older woman spoke casually as she rang up a sale, but Roxann knew Helen had noticed the handful of nervous women who had shown up with shaky kids in tow, asking to be seated in Roxann's section.

"You running some kind of charity?" Helen had ventured once.

"I don't know what you mean," she'd said, and Helen hadn't pressed.

Roxann slipped around the divider, instantly bombarded by the low roar of diners talking with their mouths full. Forks clinked against stoneware plates, and glasses scraped against wooden tabletops. Zydeco music jostled out of mounted speakers in far corners.

When she saw the man at closer range, she was tempted to keep walking—she didn't need the hassle of a cop on her back. Still, she'd danced around a herd of lawmen over the years. And in her experience, they weren't nearly as bright as they looked, although at least this one didn't move his lips while he read.

"Good afternoon," she offered. "What can I get for you?"

Still chewing on the unlit cigarette, the man scanned her slowly from her dubious hairstyle to her red polyester blouse and skirt to her bare legs and sensible black lace-up shoes. At his slight grimace, she bit back the retort that she had better-looking shoes at home, because she wasn't sure she did. His hair was dark auburn, as thick as a pelt, and touched with silver above his ears. His skin was tawny, his eyes brown, his lashes pale—unusual coloring for a redhead. Striking, but a scowl short of good-looking.

He yanked out the cigarette. "You Roxann Beadleman?"

No Saint Christopher's medal. No academy ring. No badge. Still, she'd bet a week's pay that he was a uniform. "Yes. And you are?"

"In need of an ashtray." He spoke with enough of an accent to betray him as a home-grown Biloxi boy. He wore faded Levi's and black Tony Lama boots. The only question that remained was whether his king-cab pickup truck was a Ford or a Chevy.

"You can't smoke in here, sir."

"Hell. Trying to quit anyway. How about coffee?"

"Just coffee?"

"Black, hi-test. And make it quick."

Roxann bit her tongue at his tone and walked to the coffee station. She certainly wasn't in danger of the man *charming* information out of her.

Rigby rounded the corner, his big face purple. "Where the heck have you been?"

She pulled an apologetic face. "Car trouble. Sorry, it won't happen again."

He wagged a finger. "I got girls lined up wanting to work here, Roxy. I don't have to put up with you coming in late." He looked down. "How come you're not wearing black panty hose?"

"Rigby, it's two hundred degrees."

His head periscoped. "The *hose* are *part* of the *uniform*—customers don't like bare-legged women serving them vittles!"

She didn't dare laugh. "It won't happen again."

"I'm warning you, the very next time—"

"I'd better get back to my customer," she cut in, holding up the coffeepot.

He frowned, then snapped his fat fingers in succession. "Well, don't just stand there—can't you see we're swamped?"

The things a woman put up with for major medical. She returned to her mysterious customer and filled the white mug in front of him. "One black coffee."

He drank deeply and swallowed hard. "Not bad."

"Will there be anything else?"

He set down the cup. "I need to ask you some questions, Ms. Beadleman."

She glanced around at hungry customers who shot daggers her way. "Unless it's about the menu, sir, I'm a little busy at the moment."

"What time do you get off?"

She frowned. "I'm not interested."

His frown mirrored hers. "I'm not hitting on you."

"Then who are you and what do you want?"

"Detective Capistrano, Biloxi PD." He gave her a sardonic smile. "I'd show you my badge, but I'd hate for the people you work with to think you're in some kind of trouble."

Despite the spike of her pulse, she manufactured a plausible laugh. "*Am* I in some kind of trouble?"

"Could be. I'm looking for Melissa Cape."

Two weeks had passed since she'd escorted Melissa and her daughter to the airport—all along she'd had a bad vibe about the case, but she'd finally started to relax.

"Roxy!" Rigby jerked his thumb toward a six-topper waiting to be served.

She looked back to the detective and shook her head. "Sorry, the name doesn't ring a bell. And I really have to get back to work."

His hand snaked out and encircled her wrist loosely before she could react—a fact that distressed her much more than his gesture of intimidation. "Not before you explain why the last call Melissa Cape made before she disappeared was to your cell phone."

Roxann wet her lips. "I get lots of wrong numbers on my cell phone. Now, Detective, unless you want your hand amputated, I suggest you let go."

His casual smile belied the pressure of his wide fingers. "Not until I get a straight answer."

Having worked most of her life with bullied women, she conceded that she was a tad more sensitive to being manhandled than the female population at large...but it was one of her character flaws that she could live with. Roxann returned his smile and dumped the "not bad" contents of the coffeepot in his lap.

He did indeed let go, punctuated by a howl that silenced the entire diner. Roxann called upon one semester of high school drama to feign innocence. "Oh, I'm *so* sorry."

Rigby trotted over and gawked at the man's wet pants. "You're fired, young lady!"

"But he grabbed me." She looked at Capistrano. "Tell him."

But the detective was frozen in a half-standing, half-hunkering position, his face a mask of agony.

"Get out!" Rigby yelled at her. "And don't even *think* about filing a dental claim."

Roxann glanced at a tearful Helen, then turned on the heels of her sensible shoes and walked out, fighting a rare attack of tears herself. Over the years, she'd worked almost every kind of job imaginable to accommodate her commitment to the Rescue program—tutoring college math, selling mortgages over the phone, delivering flowers, modeling for art students—but she'd never been fired. Graduated top of her class at Notre Dame, and she'd just been sacked by a fat guy with one name.

A too-clean, too-new black Ford Dooley pickup in the parking lot caught her eye, and she smirked—Detective Capistrano's ride, no doubt. She indulged in a half second of victory before surrendering to the spiraling sensation in her gut as her situation sank in. No income, no insurance, no prospects.

Bad memories plucked at her—estrangement from her father, the nasty breakup with Richard months ago, the bizarre encounter with her roommate Elise. The only good thing she had in her life right now was her work with the Rescue program, but lately...

She climbed behind Goldie's steering wheel, her mind spinning in a hundred directions. Turning the key, she cajoled the van to life with a series of thumps on various surfaces that had nothing whatsoever to do with combustion, but usually worked. Sure enough, the engine sputtered to life and, as a bonus, she received a face full of singed air from the vents. Goldie had been retrofitted with air-conditioning circa 1995, but the blower had pooped out one week after the two-year warranty expired, and Roxann hadn't gotten around to having a new one installed.

"I'm getting too old for this," she murmured, hating the unease that stirred in her empty stomach. Thirty-two and still trying to fix the world one broken family at a time. Ironic, considering she hadn't seen a member of her own family in...hmm. A long while. In fact, some might look at her involvement with the Rescue relocation program and label her a fake. Or worse, a fake fighting an unwinnable battle.

Some things just can't be fixed, Roxann, no matter how much glue you put on 'em.

At the age of eight, holding the teacup her mother had given her, now broken into a dozen pieces, she'd tearfully fended off her father's cynicism with an entire jar of Elmer's paste and a roll of Scotch tape. But lately she'd begun to wonder if she were fooling herself. After all, she hadn't been able to drink out of that cup again.

A lifetime ago—sixth grade, to be precise—a school counselor had asked what she wanted to be when she grew up. "A judge," Roxann had answered without hesitation. Wearing a black robe and wielding a wooden mallet to protect the good people from the bad people had seemed like the most perfect job imaginable. But somewhere between puberty and maturity, she'd decided to bypass the flawed legal system and put her summa cum laude political-science degree to no good use whatsoever by driving around the deep South, whisking fleeing women and their children to their next checkpoint.

No black robe, no red cape, no laser-firing gold-plated bracelets. Just a woman, a van, and a suitcase full of wigs. *This is your life, Roxann Beadleman!* Applause, applause. Not exactly what she'd had in mind in middle school.

So what am I doing here?

Everything in her body quieted, like the stillness after an echo, but no response materialized. She angled the rearview mirror and studied herself—wide-eyed, pale, and still sporting rebel hair. The last time she'd worn her hair long was 1980, B.D. (before divorce). Before her father's lawyer had wrangled her away from her mother. The day of the custody judgment, she'd cut a lock of her long hair to give to her mother, and the gap in the dark mane her father adored struck her as so wickedly satisfying, she'd simply kept whacking. Her parents had been appropriately horrified, and she'd kept her hair short ever since. As if she had something to prove—then and now.

Roxann bit down hard on the inside of her cheek, attributing her bout of self-doubt to the heat and to the newspaper article and to being fired. What she needed was time to think. She pointed Goldie in the direction of the Y. Maybe a cathartic run on the track would help her work through the mess that had become her life while she was otherwise occupied.

In college, her plans had seemed so simple and so right. Devote her time to a worthwhile cause, make enough money to get by, share her life with a righteous man...then again, in college, there had been Carl.

Dr. Carl Seger, professor of theology. She hadn't seen him since graduation, but over the years his face had had a way of floating into her mind when she needed to remember that goodness did exist. He was uppermost in her mind because he'd left a message on her machine a few weeks ago—a shock. Her foolish heart had fluttered, then zoomed back to earth when he explained in a businesslike voice that he was calling because her name had come up during an alumni board discussion about this year's recipient of the Distinguished Alumni Award. But they didn't want to draw undue attention to her if it would somehow compromise the program or her anonymity. Then his voice had changed—he had his own selfish reasons for wanting her to come back to the Notre Dame campus to accept the award during Homecoming week. He...missed her.

She'd left the message on her recorder for days and replayed it, oh, about two dozen times. But in the end, she hadn't returned the call—as much as she yearned to see him again, she couldn't very well do it under the guise of accepting an award that she didn't deserve, even if she was only one of two people who knew why.

Dr. Carl...a renaissance man. Handsome. Wise. Noble. And in the end, his nobility meant they couldn't be together. Deep down she knew she'd always measured the men in her life and, to some extent, her own behavior, up to Carl, the moral compass. And suddenly, sadly, she remembered—*Carl* was her "type."

She offered polite nods to familiar faces as she walked through the gym, but stopped short of engaging in conversation. With her mobile lifestyle, she usually didn't go out of her way to form friendships—girlfriends were complicated, and goodbyes were messy. A blast of laughter from a corner of the bustling locker room caught her attention—smiling women with normal lives, normal loves. How enviable.

She'd sacrificed so many everyday trappings that other people took for granted, although she'd never missed those mundane attachments. Until lately. Swathed in a fog of rising panic, Roxann changed into running gear. Where had the last ten years gone, and what did she have to show for them? A twenty-page resume, a gas-guzzling van, and a few dozen acquaintances scattered to the ends of the map.

She hit the footpath at a fast jog, sucking in fresh air, then exhaling forcefully. A quarter of a mile flew by quickly, then a half mile. The comforting *thunk, thunk* of her running shoes hitting the packed dirt lulled her into a more peaceful place, where women and children didn't have to be rescued from abusive spouses, where fathers and daughters cherished each other, where families lived intact and happily ever after.

"So, what are you going to do now?"

At first she thought she'd spoken aloud to herself. Then she jerked her head around to see Detective Capistrano jogging calmly behind her, still wearing his stained pants.

Roxann bit back a groan. This day did not appear to be improving anytime soon.

CHAPTER TWO

WITHOUT BREAKING STRIDE, Roxann looked back to the running path. "Did you come to apologize for getting me fired, Detective?"

He caught up with her in two strides and fell into a lazy jog. "Apologize? I'm the one who got the lap full of hot coffee." His eye contact was fleeting, his tone dismissive. "I ought to arrest you for assaulting a police officer. That's a federal offense, you know."

"You're not limping, so you must be okay."

He almost smiled. "Still, I'm going to let you make it up to me by answering a few questions."

"I told you, I don't know the woman you asked about."

"Think hard—Melissa Cape. Blond, back side of forty, daughter named Renita."

She dug in deeper for more speed—she would at least make him work for it. "No, sorry. What did this woman do?"

He had no trouble matching her pace, even in his ridiculous boots. "She disappeared."

"Disappearing isn't a crime in Mississippi."

He turned to face her while jogging backward. "No, but disappearing with a child to thwart court-ordered visitation with the father *is* a crime."

All that without stopping for a breath. She lurched to a halt and dragged her forearm across her sticky brow. "Why are you here, Detective?"

He stopped and leaned one hand against a tree that had been planted there twenty years ago for his convenience. "I have reason to believe that you work for Rescue."

"Rescue?"

He smiled patiently. "You know, the underground network that helps women escape from violent spouses?"

She shrugged. "Sounds like a good cause."

"Are you denying knowledge of the program?"

"No. Are you hassling me for being a knowledgeable citizen?"

He pulled his mouth down with his hand. "The sooner you answer my question, the sooner you'll be rid of me."

"What *was* your question?"

"Are you familiar with the operations of the Rescue organization?"

Roxann chewed on the inside of her cheek while she chose her words. "I've heard of Rescue, and I support its mission. Any reasonable person would."

"Ah, but do you play an active role in carrying out its mission?"

She crossed her arms. "If you know anything at all about the program, Detective, then you know that if I were involved, I would never tell *you*."

"You make it sound as if I'm the enemy here."

"It's my understanding that the program helps women the legal system have already failed. Maybe this Melissa Cape is one of those women."

He angled his head. "If so, then according to the exposé in the *Clarion-Ledger*, your organization would have relocated the Cape woman and her daughter, and given them new identities."

"It isn't *my* organization. Besides, I was told that particular article contained inaccurate information."

"Well, it must have because the description of the woman who apparently talked this lady into leaving her husband sounds like you, only with red hair."

She seethed. Nanci Harmon was a confused woman whom Roxann had tried to get into counseling because she hadn't seemed committed to cutting ties with her violent ex-husband. Sure enough, the woman had reneged on her relocation and returned to the guy, who then exposed the Rescue program as a man-hating gang of vigilantes. "From what I've heard about the organization, no one gets talked into anything."

"If you say so. Now, how do I go about finding Melissa Cape?"

A hollow laugh escaped her. "You must be joking."

With one blink, his mood changed—for the worse. “I'm deadly serious, Ms. Beadleman. I intend to find the woman, and I intend for you to help me.”

Panic licked at the nape of her neck. This man was someone to be reckoned with. “If Melissa Cape disappeared to escape a psycho, then what does that make the man who would send her back?”

A rueful smile curled his mouth as he shook his head. “I think that people like you believe you're doing the right thing, but pardon me if I believe the police are in a better position to help Melissa Cape than a bunch of bra-burners.”

Quiet anger sparked in her belly, but she knew he was trying to get a rise out of her, hoping she would let something slip. “If Melissa Cape turned to Rescue for help, she obviously thought different.”

His chest ballooned out with a deep inhale, then he rubbed his shoulder, as if it were bothering him. His knuckles on his right hand were scabbed—she hoped that whoever had been on the receiving end of his punch had actually deserved it.

“Look,” he said wearily. “Your little secret do-good organization is a burr on the ass for people like me, but right now, I couldn't care less about the father's visitation. The Cape woman has knowledge of a crime that can't be prosecuted without her testimony.”

“What kind of crime?”

“An armed robbery, during which a police officer was critically wounded. We suspect her husband pulled the trigger.”

“All the more reason the louse shouldn't have been granted visitation with his daughter, and all the more reason for him to want Melissa dead—to keep her from testifying.” She shook her head. “I can't help you.”

He frowned. “I didn't finish my coffee, so I'm a little cranky.”

“I was just fired, so *I'm* a little cranky.”

A muscle ticked in his neck, red with razor burn. “At least tell me if the Rescue people relocated her.”

“I know enough about the organization to know its clients are promised confidentiality.”

A mocking light flamed in his eyes. “I guess I could hope that the Cape woman has a change of heart like the lady in the newspaper article.”

Roxann lifted her chin. "If Melissa Cape sought refuge through Rescue, she must've had reason to believe her life or her child's life was in danger. By pursuing her, you could be making things worse."

"That doesn't change the fact that I have a comatose cop on my hands."

"Better a comatose cop than a comatose cop and a dead witness."

He opened his mouth, then wiped away whatever he'd been about to say and sighed. "Ms. Beadleman, the best way to keep Melissa Cape safe is to put her ex-husband behind bars, but we can't do that without her testimony."

"And she'll have your personal guarantee that he won't get off on a technicality?"

His neck muscle ticked.

"And even if the man is convicted of armed robbery and attempted murder, he faces what—a few years?"

"Six to ten."

"So what happens when he gets out early due to prison overcrowding? He'll kill her for sure."

"We'd protect her."

"Right." Roxann shook her head. "Detective, what makes you think I would help you even if I could?"

He pursed his mouth, then shrugged. "I guess I'm counting on whatever sense of duty drove you to work for this organization in the first place." Then he angled his head. "Unless you're a fake."

Without knowing it, he'd hit a nerve. After the legal system had deprived her of her mother, an innate sense of judiciousness had embedded itself in her belly. She rooted for the underdog, adopted the strays, gravitated toward the outcasts, and in general, tried to build her life on the foundation of doing what was right. And except for a couple of deviations—

"Come on, Ms. Beadleman, I'm running out of patience."

She blinked, then looked him over. A big man with a badge whose loyalty lay with a fellow uniform. She admired his allegiance, but she wasn't about to betray Melissa Cape out of sympathy for the wounded officer. Melissa was safe, and she deserved to be left alone to start a new life for herself and her daughter.

"Goodbye, Detective. I have an appointment with the want ads." She pivoted and attacked the path with her trusty blue Adidas.

"The next time I see you," he shouted, "I just might arrest you for assault *and* obstruction of justice."

She didn't look back, but her skin burned from his gaze. Had she seemed as vulnerable as she felt? When she looped around the quarter-mile path, she half expected to find him lounging by the tree again, but he was gone. Had he retreated to watch her? To follow her? The police had come sniffing around the organization before, but usually to follow up on a missing-person report, not because the client was wanted for questioning.

Filling her lungs with the perpetually fish-scented air of Biloxi, Roxann forced herself to slow down, to finish her five-mile run at her normal pace. Afterward she showered and launched Goldie on a winding route toward 255 Amberjack, Unit B, checking occasionally to make sure she wasn't being tailed by the cop—again.

Few people knew her address since the duplex was leased through the agency's network. She had lived all over the southeast, although over the last five years she'd migrated back toward the Mississippi Valley—guilt over her father, she presumed, which was alleviated somewhat by being on the same page of the atlas.

She received her mail through a post office box, and her phone was unlisted. She relied on pay phones to conduct most business with Rescue, whom to meet and where, setting up details of a relocation, arranging transport. The only people who knew the number for her cell phone were her father and her Rescue supervisor. In a desperate attempt to contact her, Melissa Cape had obtained the number from a friend who worked for the wireless company. Roxann hadn't recognized the number on the display, and should've known better than to answer, but she'd been afraid not to. Afraid something had happened to her father, afraid...

She sighed. Maybe she would take this opportunity to visit her father. Try to reconnect. An outlandish notion, considering they'd never really connected in the first place. Disparate relatives, sharing a roof, both longing for a black-haired woman long gone.

Perhaps her recent restlessness was rooted in the shakiness of the relationships with the people she should be closest to. Working odd jobs and operating covertly didn't lend itself to forging intimate liaisons. She thought she'd found a friend in Elise, who also worked for Rescue, but that had ended disastrously. Other facilitators in the organization who worked in tandem were often hundreds of miles apart, communicating in as streamlined a manner as possible. The women she helped she never saw again. It was the perfect pursuit for a loner.

But lonely.

Leaving town for a few days might throw Capistrano off her scent for a while. Or maybe it was time she moved again, although she rather liked Biloxi and had even fancied living here for a while. Make friends, look for a permanent job—something more challenging than waitressing or retail or temp work. She'd even painted her bedroom, a first. The thought of moving again put a stone in her stomach she'd never felt before. Loading all her worldly possessions onto a U-Haul trailer and looking for a new place to live had seemed so romantic in her twenties. Now she fretted about finding a new gynecologist and if the neighbors had a noisy pet.

Wrestling with her decision to take a roadtrip, she stopped at her post office box to retrieve a week's worth of mail. Bills, junk mail, two Notre Dame University alumni newsletters, both dated and forwarded many times, and—she squinted at the thick ivory-colored envelope and held it up to the light. A *wedding* invitation?

Very curious, considering most of the women she knew were trying to *escape* marriage.

CHAPTER THREE

THE INVITATION ORIGINALLY had been sent to her post office box in Atlanta, then forwarded to the one in Montgomery before being forwarded on to Biloxi. The return address, written in black slanting script by a calligrapher, read "Mr. and Mrs. Jackson Ryder, One Portobello Place, Baton Rouge, Louisiana." Her address, oddly, had been scribbled in blue ink in a different, and less princely, handwriting that seemed vaguely familiar.

Roxann smirked. Her cousin Angora was finally getting married? It seemed likely since she was the only child of Jackson Ryder and Dixie Beadleman, Roxann's father's sister. Of course when Dixie had caught the eye of *the* Jackson Ryder, heir to the Ryder Hotel empire, she'd shortened her name to Dee. More fashionable, and more appropriate, considering all the wonderfully wicked *D* names Roxann had made up for her.

She slid her nail under the flap of the grubby envelope—a little worse for the rounds—and pulled out the origami-like invitation. Impressive. Extensive. Expensive.

Mr. and Mrs. Jackson Ryder request the honor of your presence as their daughter, Angora Michele, is united in marriage to Dr. Trenton Robert Coughlin...

Leave it to Angora to snag a doctor. A little late, considering she was approaching thirty-two, but Roxann assumed the man was just getting his career underway. By now Angora would be the perfectly schooled society wife. She'd been born to it, the upper-class life. Unlike Aunt Dee, who'd had to finesse her way into the Baton Rouge Junior League, Angora was groomed from toddlerhood to look and behave like a white-gloved debutante. When they were in college together, though, even the sweater-wearing tennis players preferred the girls who put out, so Angora and her lily-white virtue had gone ignored. The debs who wised up were engaged by graduation, but Angora had clung to her virginity.

Roxann shook her head. The girl could never please her parents, no matter how hard she tried. Born pretty, and made beautiful through braces, jaw surgery, and rhinoplasty—all before the age of fourteen—she'd had the self-esteem of a leper. True, Angora wasn't the sharpest pencil in the drawer, but she wasn't a bad person. Infuriatingly feminine and a bit of a fibber, but not a bad person.

Their parents, Roxann's father and Angora's mother, hated each other. Well, maybe *hate* was too strong a word for brother and sister, but they certainly maintained a resilient aversion to one another. Walt Beadleman thought his sister had gotten above her raising, and Dee thought her brother was a clodhopper. (During a rare visit when Roxann had overheard her aunt say as much to a neighbor, she'd evened the score by peeing in Dee's bottle of Chanel No. 5.)

Proximity and class distinction had effectively separated the girls until they were seniors in high school. Roxann had been working part-time in an upscale dress shop, and in marched Dee followed by Angora, shopping for a graduation dress. Dee had proceeded to trot Roxann from rack to dressing room for two hours before buying a dress worth what Roxann earned as a shop girl for an entire year. In between fittings, however, she discovered that she and Angora had both applied to Notre Dame. She'd been praying for a scholarship; Angora had confided she was dreading the entrance exam. After that, Angora dropped by the dress shop often to chat—she'd been a prim little thing, and Roxann had felt sorry for her, caught under Donkey Dung Dee's thumb.

They'd both made it into Notre Dame, and signed up to room together, against Dee's wishes. It was the first and last time that Angora had defied her mother, but with good results. The girls had become fast friends—Angora was a neophyte in all things wicked, and Roxann had been happy to tutor. But when Angora had been busted for low grades, her parents had pinned the blame on Roxann (even though she herself was a straight-A student), and whisked their little princess into a chaperoned sorority house.

Subsequently, the girls' paths had crossed only when necessary, although she sensed that Angora missed their late-night pajama powwows consulting the Magic 8 Ball as much as she. After graduating with a liberal arts degree, Angora had returned to Baton Rouge to work for a stuffy art museum. Roxann hadn't seen her in seven—no, *nine* years.

Oh, well, she was sure her cousin would be happy with Dr. Trenton. If not, Dee would be happy enough for both of them to have a titled man in the family.

She turned her attention to more pleasurable reading—the university newsletters. Occasionally, Dr. Nell Oney, the ethics professor who'd mentored her and suggested she become involved with Rescue, wrote a feature column. And sometimes Carl Seger's name was mentioned within the pages since he was active in coordinating alumni activities. Roxann rolled down Goldie's windows and scoured the newsletters while loitering in the United States Postal Service parking lot.

Homecoming week was just around the corner, with lots of activities planned to raise money for a new student counseling center—a brick sale, a bike-a-thon, and a bachelor auction. Her heart skipped a beat when she spotted a black-and-white candid of the man who hadn't been far from her thoughts today.

Dr. Carl Seger, theology professor and coach of the varsity soccer team, will be the guest bachelor auctioned off as part of the Homecoming fund-raising events.

The man still had all of his glorious salt-and-pepper hair. She rubbed her finger over his handsome face, his winning smile, and nostalgia warmed her limbs. Assuming the picture was current, he'd barely aged a day in the decade since she'd seen him. The fact that he was still single surprised her, since the man wasn't exactly short of admirers. If his classes were still eighty-percent female, he'd probably fetch a hefty sum at the auction.

She'd counted herself among the smitten. Dr. Carl had held her spellbound from the first moment she'd walked into his freshman theology class. Handsome, thoughtful, articulate. In comparison, most of the college boys were hopelessly immature. She and Angora had attended his class together as freshmen and whiled away many pajama powwows spinning fantasies about the man.

But because Angora had moved out of the dorm, she wasn't privy to the relationship that developed between Roxann and Dr. Carl during their senior year.

"After you graduate," he'd murmured once in the library stacks, "we won't have to hide our feelings." The unrealized sexual energy between them had been palpable, and had left her damp and sleepless more nights in the dorm than she cared to recall.

But mere days before graduation, Nell Oney had paid her a visit. Carl was being brought before the Board of Regents to defend allegations of impropriety with a student. He was, after all, a professor of theology, and a deacon of the university church. Knowing she herself was the student in question, Roxann agreed to leave until things settled down.

At Nell's urging, she'd joined the Rescue program, and moved to Memphis, where a facilitator was needed, but remained poised to leave as soon as Carl called. Except when he'd called, it was to beg her understanding for choosing his job over her. If he were ruined, he'd told her in a tortured voice, he'd have nothing to offer her, and honor dictated that he stay. Of course she understood. She'd cried for a month, then thrown herself into her volunteer work, determined to prove something to Carl, even if he never knew.

Seeing his picture brought all that pent-up longing flooding back to her. Everybody had one person in their past, one person who evoked questions of what might have been. Other men had come and gone, men who on the surface appeared to be concerned with the state of the world but, when it came right down to it, were unwilling to do more than write a letter or don a T-shirt for the cause.

Her former lover Richard Funderburk fit that category—he made the bar circuit with his guitar and his backpack, singing about the indulgences of man, then took his pay in Canadian beer. She would lie in bed after cryptic sex and wonder if she would ever again meet someone who moved her as much as Carl had without even touching her.

She closed the newsletter, then blinked her eyes wider at an old photo of herself on the back page under a caption that read "We Remember." In the dated photo, her mouth was open, delivering a yell, and she hefted an unreadable protest sign. *In 1994 political-science student Roxann Beadleman led a protest against modesty discrimination in the art department that resulted in policy change.*

Roxann smiled wryly, remembering the rally. The art department had sponsored a show of nudes drawn from live models, but the drawings of the male models had featured little flaps of canvas over their privates that observers had to lift for a peek. The drawings of the female models, on the other hand, were free of the "modesty flaps." Roxann had been outraged at the discrepancy and led a march to have the flaps removed.

When political cartoons in national papers began to parody the issue, school officials caved. But her newly won notoriety made it difficult to see Carl on the sly. Then the allegations against him had ensued and she'd left South Bend to embark on what now seemed a fairly aimless path.

Roxann drove toward her apartment wrapped in a swirl of bittersweet memories, trying to ignore the clench of yearning in her stomach. The road not taken taunted her—marriage, family, a permanent address, Sunday pot roast. Maybe she hadn't fought hard enough for Carl. She'd told him countless times that she didn't believe in marriage. No wonder he hadn't put his career and church appointment on the line...

She hadn't given him reason to believe she was commitment material.

And how could she be? Then or now. Between her parents' fiasco of a marriage and her exposure to the underbelly of relationships through Rescue, she was much more familiar, perhaps even more comfortable, with dysfunction.

Feeling prickly, Roxann parked in a multilevel garage, then walked two blocks before slipping between two houses. After veering right, she tramped through high grass to get to the backyard of her duplex. With one last look over her shoulder, and Capistrano's threat running through her head, she climbed the small stoop and removed her door key from her bag.

"Hi, Roxann!"

She nearly swallowed her tongue before she realized that Mr. Nealy was standing at the rear entrance of his side of the duplex, leaning on a broom. "Hello, Mr. Nealy."

He doffed his plaid flop hat—which might have matched his pants if they'd been the same color. Or the same plaid. "You're home early."

She nodded and smiled, loath to engage in a drawn-out conversation.

"Has your roommate come back?"

She shook her head—another land-mine subject.

"Never liked her myself," he said.

Not sure how to respond without encouraging more trashing of Elise, she said nothing.

"I was thinking that since you're alone now, er, perhaps you'd like to join me for dinner tonight?"

At the jaunty set of his chin, she realized incredulously that the old man was hitting on her. The people who had shown a love interest in her lately were a lesbian and a senior citizen.

"Thank you, Mr. Nealy, but I can't." Even though she was hungry enough to eat his hat.

"You know, Roxann, if you ever need anything, anything at all, you can call on me." His voice was spookily wistful. His wife had died in the flower bed a year ago, before Roxann had moved in.

"Th-thank you, Mr. Nealy. Have a nice evening."

He winked and disappeared into his unit. Sighing in relief, she inserted her key into the lock, surprised when the door swung open with no resistance.

Somebody had been there.

Objects overturned, drawers upended. She froze, her ears pricked for any sound that would indicate the intruder was still inside, but only silence greeted her. As a precaution, she reached into her gym bag and withdrew a can of pepper spray. For a split second, she considered yelling for Mr. Nealy, but then thought better—she might have to save them both. With her heart pounding, she moved toward the TV room, her weapon poised, her muscles twitching in case she had to unleash a few well-placed kickboxing moves: *kneecap, groin, nose.* She suddenly regretted missing class the last two weeks.

Motives swirled through her mind. Burglary? If so, the perp would have been mightily disappointed. Apart from a broken strand of pearls, she had little worth stealing. In the living room, cushions were turned and books scattered. The TV had been tumbled, probably because the thief had been irritated to find an unimpressive nineteen-inch model with a garbage bag twistie for a knob.

Had the person been looking for something in particular? She gingerly rounded the corner to Elise's former bedroom, which sat empty except for a box of clothes for Goodwill, now thrown helter-skelter.

The sight of her own bedroom made her ill, the Terra-cotta Summer wall paint notwithstanding. Her closet door stood open, and clothes had been dumped on her bed. Bureau drawers hung open, the rug was upturned. From her desk, the blue monitor of the aged computer glared at her, and her initial relief that it hadn't been stolen was replaced by apprehension when she saw from the doorway that words had been typed on the screen. Only after she checked the bathroom and under the bed did she concede she was alone, and made her way back to the computer.

I'VE GOT YOUR NUMBER, YOU FAKE.

The blinking cursor was a silent exclamation point. She stumbled backward and fell hard on her tailbone. Warm blood oozed around her teeth from having bitten her tongue, and her mouth sang with pain. She scrambled to her feet, still staring at the screen. The words were personal, not the mischief of a random intruder.

I've got your number.

Was the message literal, meaning the person knew her unlisted information? Or figurative, meaning they had damning information about her? Her mind raced, sifting through the list of people who could have broken in and taken the time to leave an enigmatic calling card.

Frank Cape? He might have tracked down her address hoping to scare her into revealing Melissa's whereabouts. In the newspaper exposé, the thwarted husband had used the word *fake* a half-dozen times. *Those Rescue people are a bunch of fakes.* Frank could have simply borrowed the wording.

Richard Funderburk? When she and a few of his friends had confronted him about his drinking, his reaction had stunned her—ugly, vengeful, and defensive. *I'll get you back, you self-righteous fake.*

Elise? Roxann had asked for the key when she moved out, but Elise could've had a spare. During their argument following Elise's shocking announcement, hadn't Elise used the word *fake? You led me on with your fake friendship.*

Detective Capistrano? He hadn't bothered to hide his disdain for her and the program. *Unless you're a fake.* Maybe he was desperate enough to search her place for clues about Melissa Cape and make it look like a break-in.

Or—she swallowed hard—was the past catching up with her? A dirty little secret that sometimes jolted her awake from a deep sleep to remind her that the venerable life she'd built had been the fruit of a poisonous tree. But no one knew about those circumstances except Angora, and it didn't seem likely she'd be terrorizing Roxann when she was on the verge of getting married. Besides, Angora had just as much to lose if the truth were revealed...maybe more.

She shook away the useless train of thought, forcing herself to deal with the immediate situation: call the police and report the break-in. But halfway to the phone she stopped. And tell them what?

That a man might be after her because she helped his ex-wife disappear, oh, and by the way, the woman is a material witness to a crime in which a cop was shot, but no, she can't reveal the woman's whereabouts.

And did she mention that her former roommate might be out for revenge because she had rebuked the woman's advances?

Or that her former lover had threatened to teach her a lesson for embarrassing him with an intervention?

Plus she'd talked just this morning with one of their detectives who might have taken the law into his own hands to get the answers she wouldn't give him?

The police would show up all right—with a net.

She performed a cursory search to see if anything was missing, although it was hard to tell. Her scant costume jewelry had been rifled, but her broken pearls were safe in the glue-bound teacup she'd kept all these years. Her personal files were in disarray, but it was policy not to keep Rescue records at home—she even shredded names and phone numbers scribbled on scratch sheets of paper. The contents of her shredder had been strewn, which led her to believe that either the intruder hadn't been searching for anything in particular, or had simply given up. Somebody had wanted to scare her, to send her a message.

A quick check of the windows showed no signs of forced entry, and the door hadn't been jimmied. Someone with a key, or a good lock-pick. She yanked out a duffel bag and stuffed in clothes as she found them, along with a few personal items. On the way to the back door, she noticed her land-line phone-message light was flashing—a rarity.

Holding her breath, she pressed the button. Two hang-ups, then some heavy wheezing that sent a chill up her spine, then another hang-up. She erased the messages, then nearly lost the contents of her bladder when the phone rang. It took her three rings to find the cordless receiver. She hit the talk button, heart leaping in her chest. "Hello?"

"Last chance—I'm thawing a rump roast."

She closed her eyes and asked herself *why* she'd given the man her phone number. "Thanks, Mr. Nealy. Really." She winced at the rhyme. "But I'm going out of town for a few days."

"Is something wrong, dear? You don't sound like yourself."

"No, nothing's wrong. Mr. Nealy, you didn't happen to see anyone outside today, did you?"

"No. Why?"

"I've been expecting a package, that's all."

"Oh. Shall I water your plants while you're gone?"

"No, that's not necessary." She had no plants.

"Well, I'll keep an eye out for your package."

"Thanks. But don't open your door to a stranger."

"Oh...kay."

No need to take chances if the culprit was some kind of neighborhood gang. She promised to join him for dinner when she returned, and he seemed satisfied.

She slung the duffel over her shoulder and headed for the door, her mind spinning. She'd pick up Goldie, alert the home office that she was being harassed, and hit the road while she considered whether she needed to find a new place to live.

Her mail was scattered across the kitchen floor where she'd dropped it in her haste to arm herself. She scooped up the envelopes, stopping at the sight of the wedding invitation on top. An idea bloomed.

The nuptials were to take place tomorrow afternoon in the showiest cathedral in Baton Rouge. She could get a hotel room tonight, be in her hometown by noon tomorrow, catch the highlights of the wedding, then swing by to argue with her old man for a while. It might even be fun to see Angora again, and to check out her doctor man. Heck, it would be worth it to drop in without an RSVP just to piss off Aunt Dee.

And, in truth, it would be nice to take a break from reality, to peek in on her cousin's charmed life until she could clear the cobwebs in her own head.

Minutely cheered, Roxann slipped out the door and locked it behind her.

CHAPTER FOUR

"ON THREE, LADIES. One...two...three."

Angora Ryder strained not to blink, but from the photographer's post-click frown, she suspected she had. Her first childhood memory was of being posed and photographed, but today she couldn't stop blinking for some reason. A nervous tic?

"Let's try it again," he intoned. "On three."

Her mother stood beside the camera pointing to her own cheeks and mouthing, "Watch the laugh lines."

Watch the laugh lines. Dee's mantra. After thirty-two years, Angora realized it was the closest thing to motherly advice she was going to get. Well, today was her wedding day, darn it, so she was going to smile. Some. If only she could keep from blinking.

"Let's try it again," the photographer bellowed, eyeing her.

October thirteenth, at last. She was minutes away from marrying an intelligent, handsome doctor. Then she would embark on a three-week honeymoon to Hawaii, and upon return, Dr. and Mrs. Trenton Robert Coughlin (she loved the way that sounded) were moving to Chicago. Trenton had landed a spot with a prestigious podiatry practice, and she had snagged a position with the number one art agency in the Windy City. So what if the owner's passion for Notre Dame and its progeny had cinched the offer?—she would prove her worth when she discovered the next Kandinsky. She just needed a chance. And maybe a brilliant secretary.

Goodbye, cataloging exhibits at the Baton Rouge River Walk Museum. Goodbye, overbearing mother. Goodbye, Angora Michele Ryder. Hello, Life.

"I think I got it that time," the photographer said. "Okay, ladies, I need for you to turn sideways and move in as close as possible so I can get the fountain behind you."

Twenty-four bridesmaids in primrose pink. Angora inhaled as the girls on either side squeezed in closer. Not an easy feat to round up twenty-four girls from the club who weren't pregnant or who hadn't already ballooned up because they'd been married too long to care, but she'd done it. True, three of the girls she barely knew, but they came from very good families, and twelve maids on each side of her would look splendid in the photos.

She'd wanted to ask her cousin Roxann to be a bridesmaid, but her mother had vehemently refused. Dee detested Roxann, which was a shame since she was Dee's only flesh-and-blood niece, but things were what they were.

"Angora, darling, stop frowning," her mother called.

She smiled, which triggered the pantomimed reminder about laugh lines, so she tried to fix her face into the nonsmiling, nonfrowning expression her mother had patented.

If truth be known, Dee hated Roxann because Roxann was smart. Smarter than anyone Angora knew, and certainly smarter than anyone in the family, including Dee with all her conniving talent, so devious at times it bordered on admirable.

"Your cousin is a beatnik lesbian and I won't have her at the wedding," her mother had declared when Angora proposed the idea.

She had nearly burst out laughing. Roxann, a lesbian? Her cousin had taught her how to give a blowjob on a tube of toothpaste. Roxann could recite verbatim entire chapters from *How to Make Love to a Man,* and had been working her way through the positions illustrated in *The Joy of Sex.* When Angora had been forced to leave the dorm, Roxann and her poet grad-student boyfriend were up to "the Figure Eight." She always wondered how that one had turned out.

"Mother, what makes you think Roxann is a lesbian?" she'd asked.

"She's so *odd.* Besides, she's not married."

"I'm not married."

Dee had made an impatient noise. "It's not the same thing. Roxann has always worn her hair short."

She'd dropped the dead-end conversation with Dee, but she'd asked the calligrapher for one blank invitation and addressed it using the post office box she'd wangled from Uncle Walt last Christmas.

She'd even started a couple of letters to Roxann several months ago, but the words had seemed forced and boring. With the exception of her engagement, her life was much the same as it had been ten years ago. Same people, same parties, same gossip. In comparison, the details she'd gleaned from Uncle Walt about Roxann's life were beyond exciting—her exotic cousin was living on the fringe of the law as some sort of top-secret bodyguard. Uncle Walt had been evasive and a little bewildered, but button-busting proud. Angora would have given her second-favorite pair of diamond stud earrings if she thought she could make her parents proud.

Not that she actually expected Roxann to come to the wedding—she couldn't be sure, but to an outlaw, country club events were probably a bit passé . Besides, Uncle Walt said Roxann had to keep moving around, so she might not even have received the invitation. She cringed when she realized if the invitation was returned, Dee would know she'd sent it.

"Darling, *why* are you frowning?"

She rearranged her face and bugged her eyes at the lens.

"Got it!" the photographer said.

Oh, well, she would consider it payback for Dee insisting that she invite Darma Walker Lowe, Trenton's former girlfriend. Her mother practically fell to her knees any time one of the Walkers entered a room—their real estate empire and influence were far-reaching. Trenton and Darma had dated years ago, but she'd left him for a man higher up the food chain, a plastic surgeon. They'd been ill-suited anyway, Trenton had assured her. She believed him, because no two people could be more suited than she and Trenton. They liked the same restaurants, listened to the same music, drove the same model of BMW. They understood each other.

"Okay, just the bride and her parents."

The bridesmaids squeezed her hand and wished her luck. She squeezed back and kept an eye on her train to make sure it wasn't trampled. The twelve feet of crystal beads and iridescent sequins had doubled the cost of the white silk dress, but she was marrying a doctor, after all.

"You look beautiful, sweetie," her father said, touching her tiara—the most stunning of her crowns, Miss Northwestern Baton Rouge, 1987. She only got the chance to wear it two, three times a year at the most, so her wedding was the perfect occasion to remove it from her crown case.

"Stand up straight, dear," Dee said. "And hold in your stomach."

Angora tilted her head to accommodate her mother's hat, an enormous fuchsia creation designed by a famous gay clothier in New Orleans. Her mother didn't mind exploiting the talents of gays, she just didn't want them in attendance at the wedding. Of course, she didn't know about Mr. Fenton and Mr. Johnston, the "widowers."

Her engagement ring glittered from this morning's ultrasonic cleaning. One-and-a-half-carat solitaire diamond, emerald cut, platinum setting. Dee stressed that Angora let Trenton know from the start that she expected a quality lifestyle. In fact, one of Dee's shower gifts to the couple had been a subscription to the *DuPont Registry,* which listed only the most expensive estates in the country.

"Not for your first home, of course," her mother had told Trenton, "but certainly the next."

"On three, everyone."

Angora thrust back her shoulders and sucked in her stomach to the point of pain. She'd existed on carrots and popcorn for six weeks to get into this gown, but it'd been worth it. As a bonus, the carotene had put a nice ginger cast on her skin.

"The bride keeps closing her eyes," the photographer whined.

Dee poked her in the ribs, causing her to exhale abruptly. "For heaven's sake, Angora, keep your eyes open. How lazy can you be?"

"The girl is probably tired, Dixie," her father said, which elicited a glare from her mother. She hated to be called "Dixie."

"On three," the photographer yelled.

"Watch the laugh lines," Dee murmured in her ear.

She inhaled, arched her back, diluted her smile, and bugged her eyes.

"Got it!"

"Looks like rain," her father said, nodding to the charcoal-colored clouds rolling in from the west.

"Shush, Jackson, it simply can't rain today."

"If you say so, dear." He winked at Angora.

She grinned back, laugh lines or no. Her father was a saint to put up with her mother.

"Now just the bride and the father."

Her dad stepped in and put his arm around her shoulder. "I'm proud of you, honey, for turning out to be such a good person."

She wasn't such a good person, but she was relieved her father thought so. Relieved and a little guilty.

"I hope you and Trenton will be as happy as"—he shot a glance toward her mother, then cleared his throat—"will be happy."

"We will be, Daddy."

"Now the bride and the mother."

Dee hummed with disapproval. "Really, Angora, you have the most confused look on your face."

"How would you like for me to look, Mother?"

"Don't be snide, young lady. For another hour, you still answer to your father and me. Stand up straight."

Angora bit her tongue so hard that tears clouded her eyes.

"Okay, that's it," the photographer said. "I'll see everyone at the front of the church after the ceremony."

Which couldn't come soon enough. But she had to endure another layer of hair lacquer and a makeup touch-up under Dee's supervision, all the while standing because the gown could not look creased. Her feet ached, her stomach churned, and she was light-headed with anticipation. This must be how a prisoner felt just before being paroled—the incarceration was at its most suffocating moments before freedom.

Her mother sighed. "I'm not sure the chignon was a good choice, but it's too late now. You look a little puffy, dear, did you use Preparation H under your eyes like I suggested?"

She nodded, realizing it was the remnants of the anti-inflammatory cream that were making her blink. She'd probably go blind during the ceremony.

"I took the liberty of having Dr. Henry prepare a little care package for your trip, dear. You'll find it in your purse."

Dr. Henry, her gynecologist? "What kind of care package?"

"Oh, you know, precautionary implements. I know you and Trenton will be having children, but it's considered gauche these days to become pregnant on your honeymoon." She sniffed, then walked away.

Angora blinked. Her mother had never talked about birth control before, or even sex for that matter. At age nine when she'd asked for specifics, Dee had declared sex a messy business that Angora was better off not knowing about. "Your husband will take care of everything," she'd promised. "Just keep a towel handy."

Her wedding gift to Trenton was her virginity, and she couldn't wait to part with it. Dee had been holding it over her head since her first period. There had only been one man who had tempted her to thwart her mother's orders, but Carl hadn't wanted her...

"Places, everyone," the wedding director announced, clapping her hands.

Thank God. Dee reappeared to give the gown one more pat, then marched out of the dressing room. No words of wisdom, no sentiment, no nothing.

The bridesmaids filed out next, atwitter about which one of the groomsmen was escorting them, which everyone knew was the greatest perk of being a bridesmaid. She'd met Trenton five years ago when they were both in the Wilcott-Stanton wedding party. Beth Stanton had had only eighteen bridesmaids, poor dear.

"And now the bride," the director said with a sweeping gesture toward the door where her father stood, his hand extended.

She glided toward him, then tucked her arm in his.

"This is it, baby. Are you sure?"

"I'm sure."

And when she reached the back of the chapel and saw Trenton standing at the altar, she'd never been more sure of anything in her life. Tall, blond, handsome. Everyone said they looked like Ken and Barbie. The years ahead unfolded in her mind: a spacious home, tow-headed children, a weekend home, successful careers, Little Miss beauty contests, a chalet, anniversaries, grandchildren, a yacht. Just an aisle's walk away.

The church was brimming, and the guests were on their feet, staring at her expectantly. She knew if she tripped, Dee would sprint down the white aisle runner and strangle her with it, so she stepped carefully. On the last pew, a slash of bright orange caught her eye. When she connected with the person's face, she grinned. Roxann! Her cousin wiggled her fingers in a little wave. Warmth flooded Angora's chest—Roxann would see how well she'd done, the man who'd chosen her, the life she was about to embark on. She was getting a late start, but after today she'd make up for lost time. Maybe they would get a chance to catch up at the reception, before she and Trenton left to catch their overnight flight to Maui.

She moved on down the aisle, making eye contact with friends of her parents, coworkers from the gallery, and extended family from her father's side. She caught sight of Darma Walker Lowe, now a redhead and dressed in Givenchy black—fabulous frock, but an odd choice for an afternoon wedding. To her great relief, the woman didn't make eye contact. Angora turned her attention to her destination.

The bridesmaids in pink, and the groomsmen in dark gray fanned out from the altar like the petals of an enormous flower waiting for the center to arrive. Reverberating organ music, white satin curtains draped over the altar, dozens of candles ablaze—it was almost too much to take in. This was *her* day, the first time in her life when she was in the spotlight instead of playing second fiddle to Dee. If she never did anything else in her life to garner fame, she would always have this lily-scented day.

And speaking of Dee, she actually looked happy as they passed by her pew. Happy and relieved. As if her job was done, and now she could concentrate her energies elsewhere, such as redecorating Angora's old room.

At last Angora focused on Trenton, her beloved. Dear, sweet, handsome Trenton, who had picked her among all the still-eligible Baton Rouge belles.

He would declare his love for *her* before this enormous crowd. He would vow to cherish *her* until death parted them. Her heart swelled at the sight of his shining blue eyes.

The priest was bent and elderly, with a monotonous voice. Both sets of parents had insisted on a full mass, so the ceremony became an exercise in stooping, kneeling, and standing again. When she had envisioned her wedding, she imagined she would be riveted on each holy word, savoring its meaning before tucking it away in her heart. Instead, her senses were so hyper-stimulated, the words flew by her. Before she knew it, she was saying, "I do." Then the priest was delivering to Trenton his charge as a husband. Her skin tingled in anticipation.

"I...can't."

For a full ten seconds, she didn't comprehend Trenton's answer. Behind them, someone guffawed into the stunned silence, and the organist leaned on the keyboard, blasting them with a cacophony of sick notes.

"Excuse me?" the priest said, cupping a hand behind his big veiny ear.

Trenton shrugged. "I'm sorry, Angora, I can't go through with this."

Her jaw loosened, and her mouth moved, but no words came out. She was paralyzed. A murmur surged through the guests like a swarm of bees.

Dee's best fake laugh rang out. "Everyone, this is just a little misunderstanding. The children are under a great deal of stress." Angora didn't turn around, but she knew her mother was on her feet, directing.

"Yes," the priest said, recovering. "Perhaps we should take a little break."

Angora began to shake violently. The single most important day of her life was being shattered because Trenton was stricken with a lousy bout of cold feet? "Why are you doing this to me?" she managed to squeak in his direction.

"I'm in love with someone else."

She swallowed hard. *Oh, Gawd.* "Who?"

"It doesn't matter—"

"Who?"

He sighed. "Darma. When I saw her walk into the church, I knew I couldn't marry you, Angora."

No one had ever accused her of being smart, but some things were obvious even to her. “Trenton, Darma’s already married.”

He shook his head. “Her husband died two weeks ago. Cut himself with a scalpel and gangrene set in.”

Ergo the black dress. Damn, if fate didn’t have a fiendish sense of timing. “What are you saying, Trenton?”

“The wedding is off,” he said, his voice loud enough to carry. Silence burst around them. “But feel free to hock the ring.”

CHAPTER FIVE

THANKS TO THE MICROPHONES suspended around the altar, Roxann heard the groom's declaration just as clearly as Angora probably had. *Feel free to hock the ring?* Someone needed to rearrange the man's wedding tackle.

Old feelings of protectiveness roused in her chest. Despite Angora's silver-spoon upbringing—or maybe because of it—she seemed to always have an emotional bull's-eye painted between her wide baby-blues. During the drive to Baton Rouge, Roxann had divided her time between looking over her shoulder, and wondering how much her cousin had changed over the past decade. But as soon as Angora glided into the church sporting the crown and a nerve rash, Roxann realized Angora was still the insecure daughter of Dreadful Dee. And Roxann's hopes that Angora was marrying a kind, sensitive man with a good bedside manner now seemed far-fetched at best.

Everyone stood rooted to the spot, as if waiting to be told how to diplomatically dismantle a wedding party. *Run*, she urged her cousin silently. *Get out before the vultures descend.*

But Angora stood frozen, her pink mouth slightly ajar. Sensing that pandemonium was about to erupt, Roxann stood and sidled to the end of the pew, compromising a slew of expensive shoes along the way. Then she dashed up the aisle and grabbed Angora's hand, a cold limp thing, with a strange orangish cast to the fingers.

"Angora? It's me, Roxann."

Her cousin turned toward her, but her eyes were so full of tears, Roxann doubted she saw her.

"Come on, I'm getting you out of here."

Angora nodded dumbly.

"Hey, who are you?" the groom had the nerve to ask.

"The black sheep of the family," Roxann said, and made a snap decision, no matter how unfair, that pretty Dr. Trenton would bear the brunt of her pent-up male-directed frustration. "How do you do?" Forgoing a round-off kick in deference to her skirt, she balled up her fist and popped him square in the nose. He reeled backward like a windup toy, blood spurting, and fell off the altar. The wedding party scattered and the guests lunged to their feet for a view.

Roxann shook her stinging hand while she yanked Angora forward. "Let's go."

"Wait just a minute," screeched a voice she recognized as her aunt's. "What do you think you're doing?"

Roxann turned and the sight of her father's sister put a crimp on her intestines. "Hey, Dixie, what's shakin'? Besides your chin, I see."

Dee gaped and the fuchsia monstrosity on her head bobbed. "What are *you* doing here?"

"Rescuing Angora."

"Take your hands off her, you, you, you...dyke."

Gasps chorused around them. Roxann lifted an eyebrow. "Dyke? Did you say dyke?"

Dee took a step backward. "Y-yes."

"You got a gay radar under that sombrero?"

Her aunt pulled herself up, her face mottled. "Get out!"

She saluted. "Gladly." She tugged on Angora, who seemed to be in shock, staring straight ahead, her bouquet hanging from her arm by an elastic strap. Roxann sighed, then gathered the absurdly long train, threw it over her shoulder, and herded Angora toward the exit The climate outside the church looked even less promising than inside. Clouds rolled overhead, and thunder boomed, drowning out Dee's screeching behind them.

Roxann urged Angora to hurry, but they were only halfway across the parking lot when lightning slashed and the sky unleashed sheets of rain. At least the dousing seemed to revive Angora—she needed only a little shove to tumble into Goldie's passenger seat. Getting the train in was another matter.

When Roxann finally slammed the door, two feet of beaded and sequined fabric hung out, but it couldn't be helped. She ran around to the driver's side and threw herself into the Naugahyde seat, slammed the door twice before it caught, and heaved a sigh of relief. Her hastily tossed-together outfit—black skirt and orange pullover—were glued to her skin. She looked over at Angora slumped down in the seat, then gave in to the inappropriate laughter welling in her throat.

Angora pivoted her head. "What could possibly be funny?"

"You look like the casualty of a carnival dunking booth."

"Thanks a million."

"Hey, I'm kidding."

Angora's bottom lip trembled. "This is the worst day of my entire life."

When dealing with traumatized women, Roxann had learned to forgo "enabling" small talk. "You escaped marrying a bum. I'd say it's the luckiest day of your entire life."

"I suppose." Angora sniffled. "Thanks for punching him."

"No problem." No need to mention she'd decked him as much for her own satisfaction as for Angora's defense. "Who's Darma?"

"A girl he used to date. She dumped him and married someone else."

"The gangrene guy?"

She nodded, sniffling again.

"Why the heck did you invite his old girlfriend to the wedding?"

"It was Mother's idea."

"Oh, that's classic."

Angora laid her head back, and a fat tear rolled down her rain-soaked cheek. Her hair hung in wet globs around her face. Her face was striped with mascara, eye shadow, and blush. The dress was a droopy disaster.

Roxann looked up. "What's with the crown?"

Angora reached up to touch it, then cried harder. "My Miss Northwestern Baton Rouge tiara."

Of course.

"I'm a mess," Angora blubbered. "What am I going to do?"

Roxann fished a purse-pack of tissues from the center console and handed them over. "I don't suppose you have any clothes to change into at the church?"

She shook her head against the seat and blew her nose. "My trousseau is at home."

"How do I get to your place?"

"I...still live with Mom and Dad. And I can't go back there."

"Where do you want to go?"

Angora was quiet for so long, Roxann repeated the question.

"I don't know...s-somewhere D-Dee won't f-find me." Her teeth were chattering.

Roxann turned on the air-conditioning, which, in Goldie, was the same as turning on the heat. "We could go to my dad's. Your mother wouldn't go near there."

"W-will Uncle W-Walt mind?"

"He might not even be home."

"He doesn't know you're in town?"

Roxann squirmed. "No, but I was going to stop by after the wedding anyway."

Angora gave a lethargic shrug. "Anything to avoid D-Dee for a few hours. Maybe you can help me figure out what I'm going to d-do now." Angora pulled the stained seat belt over her sodden dress and clicked the buckle home. She sniffed mightily, then sighed. "Let's g-go."

Roxann surveyed her bedraggled cousin with wonder—Angora still had a talent for sucking Roxann into her melodrama. Just yesterday she'd been dogged by a cop, the victim of a break-in, and the object of a subtle threat. Yet her potentially life-threatening situation had just been upstaged by Angora's jilting.

"Did I mention it was good seeing you again?" she asked sarcastically.

For the first time, Angora offered a watery smile, and Roxann knew her cousin was going to be all right. Eventually.

CHAPTER SIX

ANGORA HAD CRIED HERSELF to sleep before they reached the part of town where Roxann had grown up. Roxann was glad, partly because Angora needed the rest, and partly because she wanted to experience the old neighborhood privately.

The rain had slackened to an aggravating drizzle. Only the driver-side windshield wiper worked, slapping a clear path of vision every few seconds. The houses, the streets—everything seemed smaller and bleaker, if possible. River Hills was a postwar development that had fallen out of favor with realtors when a power plant was erected at its boundary in the late 1960s. Property values plunged, and many residents fled inland.

Walt and Ava Beadleman had stayed put to show their support for her father's employer, RTC Electric, so Roxann had had a close-up view of the rapid degradation of the area. Homes were turned into rentals, then abandoned altogether, and drug dealers took over the ballpark. Government housing brought in kids from broken homes with too much time on their hands. Graffiti spread from one end of River Hills to the other. And she had her own theories about the glowing power plant's effects on the residents' health—physical and otherwise.

Her mother's discontent with the area had been the beginning of the end of her parents' marriage. Her father detested change, and refused to leave his circle of friends and his favorite fishing hole. The first day Roxann had come home from second grade and her mother wasn't waiting by the front door remained vivid in her memory. She'd sat in the front-porch swing, terrified, until her mother arrived, flushed and apologetic, making Roxann promise not to tell her father.

The disappearances became more frequent, then her mother gave her a key to let herself in the house after school. A blue car would drop her mother off in time to get supper started before her father came home from work. It was only a matter of time, though, before Walt discovered his wife was keeping company with another man. One day he'd torn the seat out of his work coveralls, and had come home for a change of clothes to find Roxann alone. He was there when the man dropped off her mother. He'd thrown a loose brick from the front steps through the back windshield as the blue car raced away, and he'd made her mother leave.

The next few months were a painful blur, with the exception of the phone conversations she'd overheard. The ugly, ugly things her father had called her mother still stung. After the custody hearing, she rarely saw her mother. Her father hired a woman in the neighborhood to cook and clean, but Mrs. Holt was a dour person who didn't like to be bothered while she watched television.

Emotion crowded her chest as she slowed to turn onto the road where her father still lived. Braeburn Way seemed too pretty a name for an overgrown, shabby street. When she pulled into her father's driveway, sadness plucked at her. The pale green bungalow looked tired and tucked into itself, the eaves sagging, the clapboard siding in desperate need of a fresh coat of paint. The yard was a tangle of ivy and weeds, strewn with limbs from a wild apple tree that hadn't borne fruit in years.

The gravel driveway and covered carport were empty, so she assumed her father was out fishing or drinking. Or both. She pulled under the carport so they could enter the house without getting wetter. Lurching over the uneven ground roused Angora, and when Roxann turned off the engine, her cousin opened her eyes.

"We're here," Roxann announced.

Angora groaned and moved slowly, lifting her head to squint out the window. "Where?"

"My dad's, remember?"

Her cousin winced. "Oh, yeah." Her crown sat at a precarious angle.

"Come on, Queenie, let's get you into some dry clothes."

She swung down, then walked around to collect Angora, who practically fell out of the van after she unhooked her seat belt.

Angora cried out when she saw the part of the train that had been flapping against the van for the past twenty-some miles. "It's ruined."

"Were you planning to wear it again?" Roxann asked wryly.

"No, but..." Angora burst into tears again, and fell against Roxann, who hustled her to the side door.

The key on Roxann's ring still worked, as she'd expected. She led Angora into the musty kitchen, flipping on lights before depositing her into the only chair at the table that wasn't stacked high with newspapers—her father was a voracious reader. A fishy smell permeated the air, and dust motes floated lazily, disturbed by the opening of the door. The old brown linoleum popped and cracked under her feet.

A crucifix adorned the wall next to the kitchen table, testament to the fixation on morality Walt Beadleman had developed after the divorce. At every chance, but especially when he drank, her father sermonized the virtues of chastity and honesty. Look at what her mother's deceit had done to their family, he would rail, and how it had led to her untimely demise.

I'VE GOT YOUR NUMBER, YOU FAKE.

Shaking off the heebie-jeebies, Roxann glanced around the cramped space, her heart squeezing at the clutter and neglect. Old feelings of shame resurfaced. She'd hated other kids knowing that she lived in River Hills, and her father was so slovenly, she'd been too embarrassed to have friends over. Angora had never been there—God only knew what she must be thinking.

"I'll get my bag so we can change clothes." Roxann trotted outside, and after two grunting attempts, slid open the van door.

"Who's there?" an elderly voice called.

She looked out to see her father's neighbor standing in the weedy driveway, his neck craned.

"It's me, Mr. Sherwood. Roxann Beadleman."

The man's face rearranged into a smile. "Roxann! Child, it's good to see you."

"Good to see you, too, Mr. Sherwood. Do you know where my father is?"

He nodded. "Him and Archie Cann drove to Gramercy for a fishing tournament. Going to be gone all weekend long."

"I should have called," she said, harboring mixed feelings. Although she felt an obligation to see her father, it was never a wholly pleasant experience. And with Angora in tow, the visit would have been doubly awkward.

"You going to be staying a while?"

"I'm not sure," she hedged. "If I have to leave, I'll write Dad a note."

"He'll be sorry he missed you."

She managed a smile as she hauled out the bulging duffel bag. "Thanks, Mr. Sherwood. You take care."

She slid the van door closed and waved, then reentered the house. Angora stood at the sink that was piled high with dirty dishes, running water into a dented teapot. "I thought we could use some tea," she told Roxann primly.

The incongruity of a bride in full regalia making tea in her father's dilapidated house was almost incomprehensible. Personally, Roxann was craving a beer, and she was almost certain her father didn't have any teabags, but she said, "Sounds good," then nodded toward her duffel. "Dry clothes."

"You'll have to help me get out of this dress." Then Angora proceeded to scare the crap out of Roxann by trying to light the ancient gas stove. The flash melted the sequins on Angora's bodice and left Roxann's eyebrows feeling crackly.

"Let's see if we can find my old bedroom," she urged, then crossed the kitchen into the shabby living room, a throwback to the Harvest Gold and Burnt Orange decorating era. Books and magazines occupied every vertical and horizontal surface, including the floor. The faded carpet was footworn, and the familiar cabinet-model television squatted under the window, taking up too much room. A naked bulb in the center of the ceiling cast a garish glow that blinded while leaving the corners dark. More or less, everything was the sa—

Roxann came up short at the sight of her college diploma hanging over the couch like a prized piece of artwork. Professionally matted in Fighting Irish Green and framed in satiny cherrywood, the piece was fantastically out of place against the peeling wallpaper. Getting a degree was the only thing she'd ever done that had pleased her father, but the precious piece of paper had led to an even bigger rift between them when she'd "thrown away her education" to become involved with Rescue. Her father had had his heart set on her attending law school—

"Are you okay?" Angora asked.

"Sure." She made her feet move and picked a path across the living room. "I'm sorry—Dad's a slob."

"He's a lonely bachelor."

Her cousin had always had a soft spot for Roxann's father. Probably because she only saw him at his best once a year at Dee's Christmas shindig.

"When was the last time you were home?" Angora asked.

"Dad and I communicate best over the phone." Besides, she couldn't recall.

She led the way down a narrow hallway and pushed open the door to the bedroom that used to be hers. She blinked. The room hadn't been changed since she'd last slept there. Though the yellow comforter was faded, it was neatly made, topped with two denim pillows that she'd made in sophomore home ec. True to the Craftsman bungalow style of the house, the ceiling was low, and the room compact, large enough to hold only the bed, a bureau, and an upholstered chair. A small green braided rug lay at the foot of her bed. She used to leap out of bed and hit that rug, then jump to a fuzzy mat in the bathroom so her feet wouldn't touch the cold wood floors.

Step on a crack, you'll break your mother's back. And the wood floors had had so many cracks to avoid.

On top of the dark judges paneling that encompassed the walls, she'd hung panels of corkboard, which were still dotted with curled, yellowed clippings and snapshots of long-forgotten acquaintances. An eight-by-ten of her high school senior portrait sat on the headboard in a dated frame. She hadn't been smiling. Roxann glanced at Angora—the Spartan little room was a far cry from her cousin's wonderland boudoir, with a walk-in closet and sitting room with phone and TV.

"Looks like your dad is hoping you'll come back home to live," was all she said.

"Yeah, right, at my age?" Too late, she remembered her cousin's housing arrangement. "Oh—sorry. I'm sure you have a good reason for living at home."

"Not really. Where do you live?"

"Biloxi. For now."

"Oh." Angora stepped out of her shoes, losing three inches in the process, but settled down to a respectable five feet and six inches anyway. They were identical in height. "If I don't get out of this dress, I'm going to kill myself."

No wonder—she looked as if she'd been poured into the gown to begin with, and it had surely shrunk from the wetness. Roxann tackled the zipper, recalling that Angora had always struggled to keep her curves at bay, with Dee breathing down her neck at every meal. When the zipper gave way, her cousin practically groaned in relief. She peeled the wet silk from her shoulders and stepped out of the gown, revealing a strapless elastic bodysuit that extended from armpit to knee, and looked painful as hell.

"The bathroom's through there," Roxann said, pointing. She dropped to sit on the foot of her bed, instantly reminded of the creaky springs. "But it's just a tub, no shower."

"A bath sounds like heaven."

To her, too, but she'd give Angora first crack. The girl had had a bad day.

Angora pushed open the door, then stopped. From her vantage point on the bed, Roxann saw her cousin's eyes widen at her disheveled hair and makeup reflected in the wavy mirror on the opposite wall. Her chin began to wobble. She slowly lifted the rhinestone tiara from her head and placed it on the avocado-green sink, then removed what pins were left in her sodden hair. The look in her eyes scared Roxann—hatred?

"Let me get the water started," she volunteered, and slipped past Angora into the bathroom. "I remember the stopper was a little tricky."

The old porcelain tub was dusty, but otherwise still in good shape. She turned on the water, which ran rusty for a few seconds, then swished her hand around the sides. The rubber stopper nestled into place just fine and the water ran warm almost immediately. She checked the medicine cabinet and found some gel bath balls that were stuck together from age. After tossing a handful into the water, she turned a smile back to Angora, who was still staring at herself in the mirror.

"In you go," she said cheerfully.

Angora's shoulders started shaking, and her face crumbled. She let out a wail that Roxann was sure would have Mr. Sherwood looking out his window. Roxann caught her before she fell. "Let's get this scuba suit off so you can relax." Stripping the elastic suit from Angora while half supporting her weight was a feat, but she finally managed it.

Angora's breasts and hips sprang out to their normal proportions—generous. The suit, which was doll-sized in its original form, had left angry marks on her skin.

"Did you jump out of a two-story window into this thing?"

"It was worth it—my dress was a ten instead of a twelve."

Roxann looked back to the heap of soiled silk on her bedroom floor but said nothing. She helped Angora climb into the tub, then turned at the sound of the teakettle whistling. "I'll get that—yell if you need me."

Angora nodded miserably and lay back in the tub.

Roxann sighed, then walked back through the house to turn off the burner. She opened a few cupboards looking for tea, but found little except canned ravioli and chili. Her heart squeezed—her father wasn't taking care of himself. And she wasn't taking care of him, either.

She scrounged up a box of garbage bags and went through the cabinets, tossing out anything that looked or smelled dangerous. Then she poured the kettle water into the sink and washed dishes, and took a shot at cleaning the counters. In the living room she cleared as much clutter as she could and ran the old canister vacuum, giving special attention to the crumbs and stains around her father's La-Z-Boy.

She peeked in on Angora, and as she suspected, found her cousin fast asleep—and snoring like a bear. A by-product of the nose job, Angora had insisted when Roxann complained in college. Roxann sighed. Sitting in an old tub in a seedy part of town probably wasn't what Angora had envisioned when she rolled out of bed this morning. Poor little rich girl.

Roxann returned to the hall and glanced toward her father's bedroom. She didn't want to intrude on his privacy, but neither did she want him living in squalor. The door was ajar, so she poked her head inside, pleased to see the bed passably made. Clothes were stacked on a straight-backed chair, but they appeared to be laundered. She picked up a couple of towels in the bathroom and rehung the sagging shower curtain. On her way out of the bedroom, though, she stopped, her heart in her throat.

CHAPTER SEVEN

A COLORIZED PHOTO OF HER MOTHER sat in a silver frame at her father's bedside. Roxann remembered the photo because she'd thought her mother looked so glamorous with her flip 'do and her off-the-shoulder dress. The photo had once sat on the fireplace mantel, but had disappeared, along with other photos of her mother, after the divorce.

"Where are all the pictures of Mommy?" she'd asked.

"Gone," he'd said, and not nicely.

"I want to live with *her*."

"Well, you can't. Go get me a beer."

When her mother had been killed in a car accident four years later, she'd longed for a photo, but had to settle for the pictures in her head. Soon, though, the impressions of her mother's scant visits had been overridden by the image of her mother lying in a casket. For the past few years, she'd been unable to conjure up her mother's face at all. Seeing the photo now was a bittersweet gift. Her mother had been so beautiful, with full lips and expressive eyes. Roxann bit back tears, grappling, as always, with her father's inexplicable behavior. When had he forgiven her mother enough to remove the picture from his hiding place?

"Roxann?" Angora called.

She replaced the picture, wiped her eyes, and returned to the bathroom. Angora was still in the bathtub. "Would you help me rinse my hair?"

Roxann had taken plenty of baths in that tub with no help rinsing her hair, but granted, Angora wasn't used to making do, and she had about a hundred times as much hair as a normal person.

"Sure." She used the cup that once held her toothbrush to capture warm water from the faucet and pour it over Angora's bent head until the soap was gone. "Feeling better?"

Angora sat back, immersed to her shoulders. She looked younger and more delicate without makeup. "A little."

"So this guy was the love of your life?"

Angora studied a clump of dissolving bubbles. "I thought so."

She had that wild-eyed look again that made Roxann shiver. "Do you want me to call someone—your mother?"

"What time is it?"

"Around five-thirty."

"Maybe later."

Make them suffer a little longer. She couldn't blame her. "Do you want to spend the night here? Dad's at a fishing tournament, so we'll have the place to ourselves."

"I don't have anyplace else to go." She had regressed to a little-girl voice.

Roxann sat back on her heels. "You'll have to face them sometime. Besides, this situation wasn't your fault."

"Yes, it was—I should've stood up to Mother when she wanted to invite that woman to my wedding."

Blame everyone but the guilty. "And what would've happened two months from now when Trenton ran into his old girlfriend at the airport?"

"He wouldn't have," she said miserably. "We were moving to Chicago."

"Really?"

"I was going to be an art agent for a big important firm." She knuckled away a tear. "Now that's all down the drain."

Roxann frowned. "Why?"

"Well, because now I'm not moving."

"Why not? Go without the goon."

Her laugh was rueful. "Mother and Father would never allow me to move there alone."

"So don't ask them."

Roxann knew that look—Angora had always struggled with her desire for independence versus the burden of being cut off from the goodies. Suddenly she brightened. "Maybe I can live with you."

"Uh...I don't think that's such a good idea. You'd better get out of the water before you wither away. Besides, it's my turn."

Angora nodded and sat up. "I could really use that tea."

Roxann shook her head as she rummaged for the least threadbare towel under the tiny vanity. "Sorry, I couldn't find any tea. But help yourself to anything in the fridge that isn't rancid. If you're hungry, we could go out and get some dinner. Or I could order a pizza."

Angora's eyes lit up for just a second, then she patted her stomach. "I'd better not—I'm on a diet."

"What kind of diet?" she asked suspiciously, remembering the harebrained gimmicks Angora had used to lose weight when they roomed together.

"It's a food-combination plan."

"What foods?"

"Um...popcorn and carrots."

"Popcorn and carrots? Is that why your skin is the color of a pumpkin?"

"I think it looks nice."

"Christ, Angora, you're *orange*."

She snatched the towel. "Could I please just have those clothes you promised?"

Roxann frowned, then went into the bedroom and unzipped the duffel bag. She fished around, wishing she'd taken more care when she'd packed her bag. The nicest thing she had to offer Angora was a pair of faded jeans and a tie-dyed T-shirt.

"You're kidding, right?" Angora asked, looking over her shoulder.

"Sorry, I sort of packed in a hurry."

She held up the T-shirt. "Good grief, when was the last time you went shopping?"

"For clothes?" Roxann pulled at the hem of her orange pullover self-consciously.

Angora sighed. "That's a horrible color for you."

She smirked. "Maybe I'll start eating carrots."

Angora picked up the bottle of pepper spray. "Is this what all the well-dressed women in Biloxi are wearing?"

Roxann grabbed the pepper spray before Angora could spray herself, "Just a precaution."

Her cousin sighed. "I'll never be able to get my butt into those jeans—don't you have anything stretchy?"

"Just these." Roxann held up a pair of red thong underwear.

"Now I know you're kidding."

Remembering Angora's penchant for girdle granny panties, Roxann grinned. "They're not so bad once you get used to them." She left Angora studying the underwear, then ran her own bath. She stripped, indulged in a few seconds of envy over Angora's curves next to her own boyish figure, then slid into the water up to her shoulders. A groan escaped her as the warm water caressed her calves, still tender from yesterday's run. Unbidden, Capistrano's face popped into her mind, his expression mocking as he perused her ugly shoes. Maybe she should have called him yesterday to report the break-in. Maybe he would have—

She scoffed. Maybe he would have helped her? Help her what? She couldn't be sure that Frank Cape was looking for her. Besides, Detective Capistrano struck her as the kind of guy who would expect something in return—like the whereabouts of Melissa Cape.

No, the more she thought about it, the more she suspected that Elise had been behind the trashing of her place and leaving the bizarre message. Elise was a computer buff, and had spent hours on Roxann's desktop, mostly surfing chat rooms. Which is where, Roxann believed, Elise had gotten the idea that her repeated failed relationships with men meant that she was gay. But if that was the case, Roxann thought wryly, most of the female population would be gay. Elise had always been wound tight, so Roxann suspected that the woman's newfound gayness was justification for the things she perceived to be wrong in her life. And the break-in was probably retribution for Roxann's not jumping on her bandwagon—from Elise's stories, she knew the woman had done some pretty wacky things to men who had wronged her.

The fact that Rescue would hire her was testament to their desperate need for staff.

Roxann inhaled deeply, then exhaled, relaxing her back and shoulder muscles. For now, she'd simply lie low for a few days, and maybe look for a new place when she got back to Biloxi. Although she really liked the color she'd painted her bedroom...

She must have dozed, because Angora's voice startled her so badly she klonked her head against the unforgiving porcelain. "Ow!" She looked up to see Angora, wearing only the T-shirt and the tiny panties, holding a bottle of something. "What did you say?"

"Sorry. I said, look what I found. Tequila."

Roxann winced, rubbing her head. "Don't tell me you want to drink that stuff."

"But I do."

"Have you become a hard drinker since we last partied together?"

"I like margaritas."

She laughed and pushed herself up, then reached for a skimpy towel. "It's not the same."

"Come on, I deserve a drink."

"I won't argue that point, but there's truth to the adage about drinking tequila 'to kill ya.' You'll have to mix it with something just to get it down."

"I saw some tomato juice in the fridge."

She grimaced. "If you're determined."

"You look great," Angora said, nodding in the general direction of Roxann's nudity.

"Uh, thanks...I guess." A stupid flush climbed her neck as she tucked the ends of the towel between her breasts.

"You were always so nice and thin."

"You were the one with the great figure."

"Great figure? I'm considering swallowing a tapeworm to get rid of these extra pounds."

"You're letting Dee get to you. I'm ordering pizza and we're going to enjoy it." If she could find a pizza parlor that would deliver to this neighborhood. "How are those thongs?"

Angora frowned. "Invasive."

Roxann laughed, padded into the bedroom, and picked through the hodgepodge of clothing spread out on the yellow comforter. She stepped into underwear and a pair of denim shorts, and pulled on a pink tank top.

"Can I borrow a horsehair brush?" Angora asked, running her fingers through her nearly dry golden hair. "I can't afford to get split ends."

"There should be a brush in here," Roxann said, opening the top drawer of the bureau. "But I can't promise horsehair." She rummaged through miscellaneous items that resurrected memories: key chains, dog-eared paperbacks, her name badge from the dress shop where she'd worked during high school, her Notre Dame tassel. Why hadn't she taken it with her when she left home?

Why, indeed.

"Our Magic 8 Ball!" Angora lifted the vintage toy—a pajama powwow prop—from the clutter with a squeal. "Wonder if it still works?" She placed her hands on the ball and closed her eyes. "Am I a big loser jilted bride?" She opened her eyes and consulted the "magic" window. " 'Yes, definitely.' " She looked up. "It still works."

Roxann laughed, relieved to see her cousin's sense of humor returning. "If memory serves, the thing is broken—it only says 'Yes, definitely.' "

"Is this a college annual?" Angora asked, removing a bound book embossed with "1992." She squealed again, and Roxann was reminded of her cousin's annoying habit of squealing. Angora's split ends were forgotten in her glee to locate her picture. "Here I am. Oh, that jacket is dreadful, isn't it?"

Roxann looked over her shoulder. "Who can see the jacket for that big hair?"

"Okay, let's see your picture, smartie." She flipped back to the Bs, then frowned. " 'No picture available.' "

Roxann grinned. "Sorry to disappoint."

Then from the pages of the annual, an envelope fell and twirled to the floor. A memory chord stirred as Roxann bent to retrieve it.

"A love letter?" Angora teased.

"Yeah, right." Neither she nor Carl had dared to write down their feelings for each other.

"Open it."

She slid her finger under the envelope flap, and pulled out several sheets of yellow legal-pad paper. When she unfolded them, she was swept back through a time tunnel. "You won't believe this."

"What?"

Roxann held up the sheets for her to see the writing on the top of the pages: my life list.

"Our life lists?" Angora murmured. "Omigod."

Oh my God was right. What more torturous exercise to face during an early-life crisis than to be reminded of all the things you'd planned to accomplish at the ripe old age of eighteen? "Let's break open that tequila."

CHAPTER EIGHT

ROXANN DECIDED tomato juice and tequila was quite possibly the most noxious combination of liquids ever concocted. Thank goodness the pepperoni pizza overrode the taste. "Do you remember what we were doing the night we made our life lists?"

Angora tucked her legs beneath her on the comforter Indian-style and pulled the T-shirt down over her knees. She was wearing her tiara, and her eyes were already bright from only half a glass of the "tequato" juice. "I was smoking my first and only joint." Angora leaned closer. "I don't suppose you have any marijuana on you right now?"

Roxann cracked a wry smile. "Uh, no. Sorry to tell you this, Angora, but I grew up. Besides, you were sick for a week after you smoked that joint."

"I don't remember that."

A convenient trait of Angora's—selective amnesia to go along with her penchant for embellishing the things she did remember. "I suppose you don't remember where we'd been the night we made our lists?"

"No."

Roxann studied her cousin's face, wondering how much of their college experience Angora had managed to block out. Roxann had thought her cousin would be thrilled to be away from Dee, but instead she had suffered from bouts of depression and homesickness, even anxiety attacks. Four torturous years. "We were at a memorial service for that girl who was run down in front of the Science Building."

Angora bit into her lip. "Tammy Paulen."

"Right," Roxann said, turning to the senior class where she skimmed the thumbnail black-and-white photos. "Here she is—Tammy Renee Paulen, philosophy major." On the page, Tammy was an attractive blonde with a wide smile, frozen in time in a big shoulder-padded blouse and permed hair. When she'd posed for the picture, Tammy probably couldn't have imagined she wouldn't live to graduate.

Steeped in melancholy, Roxann leaned against the headboard with a denim pillow at her back. "Tammy was in one of my classes. I remember walking by her empty seat for the rest of the semester. It was so weird. Didn't you know her?"

"No," Angora said, then took another drink from her glass.

"It says here she was a member of Delta Zeta." Angora's sorority.

She shrugged. "I knew who she was, but I didn't know her. Seniors didn't associate with freshmen."

Angling her head, Roxann said, "I thought you saw her the night she was killed."

Her cousin pulled back, then lifted her shoulders in a slow shrug. "Maybe. My memory is fuzzy."

Roxann turned back to the girl's photo, wondering what Tammy Renee Paulen would have done with her life if she'd been given the chance. Something better than separating dysfunctional families? "They never found out who did it, did they?"

"A couple of students were questioned...I think."

"The memorial service was so sad."

"Her mother wore a green suit," Angora said, nodding.

More details crowded Roxann's mind, too. Red-eyed students. Skittish university officials. Frightened gossip. Angora's ashen face...

Angora had been especially upset when someone had whispered that Tammy's injuries prevented an open-casket viewing. So upset, in fact, that they had left the service early. Back in their dorm room, Roxann had offered Angora a hit from a joint to help her calm down. The scene came flooding back so strongly, Roxann's nostrils twitched. "We were smoking and started talking about what we wanted to do with the rest of our lives," she recalled.

"And you suggested we make a list." Angora smiled, seemingly relieved at the change in subject.

Roxann closed the annual, contrite for mentioning the troubling incident—she was supposed to be cheering up her just-jilted cousin.

Angora rifled through the sheets of paper lying on the bed between them. "But why do you have both lists?"

"I found them after you moved out."

"Oh, right. Mother was sure you were corrupting me."

"I was."

Angora leaned in. "I have to ask—how was the Figure Eight?"

"Huh?"

"The Figure Eight. You know—*The Joy of Sex* and that long-haired poet?"

Roxann smiled. "Oh, yeah. I don't remember that position specifically, although I did have a soft spot for the Modified Spoon."

Angora sighed dramatically. "God, I was so bored after I moved into the DZ house."

The dizzy house, as it was known on campus. "You were involved in... things."

"Nothing inspiring," Angora said, tossing her glorious blond hair, which still hadn't been brushed. "You were the one always making headlines in the campus paper."

"I was going to change the world, all right."

"So what do you do, exactly? Uncle Walt said you had a top-secret job."

Roxann nodded. "And if I told you, I'd have to kill you."

Angora's eyes widened.

"I'm kidding." She laughed at her cousin's gullibility. "I help women who are in trouble."

"Like me."

Roxann smiled wryly. "Except the women I deal with are usually in danger of more than being jilted at the altar."

"Everything's relative," Angora said with a sniff, then frowned into her glass before taking another drink. "But I always knew you'd do something good with your life."

I'VE GOT YOUR NUMBER, YOU FAKE.

Roxann fidgeted and downed another mouthful of the drink. "Everyone has their own opinion of what's good."

"Was helping women on your life list?"

"I don't think so, not specifically. I honestly can't remember."

"How many things are on your list?"

Roxann picked up the papers and flipped to the last page. "Thirty-five. You?"

"Thirty-six. What's your number one?"

"Let's see...'Backpack across Europe.' "

"Have you?"

"Not yet." Not on the meager salaries she commanded, and the tiny stipend she received from Rescue went straight into a money market account. She smoothed a finger over her double-faced travel watch. It was 1 a.m. in London. "But someday. What's number one on your list?"

Angora grinned sheepishly. "To be Miss America."

Of course.

"It could still happen," she insisted.

"Don't you have to be twenty-five or under?"

"Hey, I could squeak by, but you also have to be single. Oh, I forgot—I am single." She misted up.

"You still have—what is it? The Miss Uptown Baton Rouge title?" The alcohol was bleeding through her limbs like menthol.

"Miss *Northwestern* Baton Rouge."

"Oh. Well, with a big honking crown like that, I'll let you count it."

"Thanks." Angora sniffled and put a mark on the page with an "RTC Electric" ink pen. "My number two is 'Fly a plane.' "

"Fly a plane?"

Angora shrugged. "Why not?"

"Because it's a big hunk of metal that hurtles through the air."

"Are you saying I'm not smart enough to learn how to fly a plane?"

"No."

"Good, because I'm going to someday. What's your number two?"

" 'Learn to speak French.' For when I went to Paris, of course."

"Is that why you used to wear that ugly beret?"

Roxann frowned—Carl had said it was chic.

"Did you ever learn French?" Angora asked.

"Just the Cajun I picked up around here, but I doubt if it would get me very far outside of Louisiana. Maybe I'll take a class someday. Number three?"

" 'Have a cameo on General Hospital.' "

"Wow."

"Luke and Laura were all the rage." Angora sighed. "Now *there* was a match made in heaven."

"*There* was a match made during a writers' meeting. How were you going to wangle your way onto a soap opera?"

"Well, I figured once I was Miss America, I could go on any TV show I wanted to."

"Good thinking." Either that, or the tequila was grabbing hold of her. "My number three is 'Write a screenplay.' "

"And?"

"And I couldn't tell you the last time I even saw a movie."

"Why did you write down things that were so hard?"

"Because I had big plans." At eighteen, nothing had seemed beyond reach. World renown. Global peace. True love. "Number four?"

" 'Meet the president.' "

"Of the United States?"

Angora bit her lip. "I don't know."

"Well, since you didn't specify, you can be creative."

"Thanks. What's your number four?"

" 'Be valedictorian.'"

Angora bounced up and down on the bed. "You were, so you can cross off that one."

She did, but her stomach churned from the foul drink—so of course she drank more of it.

"Next I have 'Drive a nice car.' " Angora smiled smugly. "Cross off."

Roxann's return smile was wry. "Which makes my 'Ride a horse' pale a little in comparison."

" 'Design a line of clothing.' "

" 'Read the entire works of Shakespeare.' "

" 'Learn to swim.' "

Roxann lifted an eyebrow. "You can't swim?"

"No."

"But your parents have an Olympic-sized pool."

"Mother wouldn't let me use it—she was afraid I'd drown."

Dee's logic was nothing if not consistent. " 'Learn to play the piano.' "

Angora's eyes welled up.

"What?"

"The next thing on my list is 'Marry a doctor.' "

Roxann winced. "You were close. I'll let you count that one."

"Thanks," she choked out, "but I don't think that would be fair."

"By the way, what kind of a doctor was he?"

"A podiatrist."

"A foot doctor? I don't think that counts anyway—a bunion isn't life-threatening."

"You're just trying to make me feel better."

"Angora, you don't have anything to feel bad about."

Her cousin started crying in earnest. "I couldn't keep my man."

"Oh, God—are you going to sing a country song?"

She blew her nose on her sleeve. "No—that's number thirteen on my list."

"Hey, watch it, that's my favorite T-shirt."

"Sorry." Angora sighed. "I wouldn't expect you to understand about Trenton."

"Why not?"

"Because you don't need a man."

"Don't tell me you believe your mother."

"I didn't mean you don't need a *man*, I mean you don't *need* a man."

Roxann shifted, ashamed to admit she'd been the tiniest bit envious watching Angora walk down the aisle. "Yeah, well...yeah."

Angora gestured to the ruined dress heaped on the floor. "Daddy spent a fortune on that dress, the florist, the caterers."

"If you feel bad about it, pay him back."

"With what? The allowance he gives me?"

She blinked. "You still get an allowance?"

"Just for extras."

Roxann was starting to remember how high-maintenance Angora could be. "So sell the rock like Trenton said and give the money to your folks."

Her cousin stared down at her enormous ring, and a new wellspring of tears erupted. "But look at it—it's the perfect ring."

"And will scare off every eligible man in the state."

Angora hiccupped. "The ring goes back. Next?"

" 'Get a postgraduate degree.' "

" 'Get a gold credit card.' "

" 'Go parasailing.' "

" 'Go on a round-the-world cruise.' "

" 'Become proficient at chess.' "

" 'Become a famous painter.' "

"Angora, I didn't know you were an artist."

"I'm not, but I've seen enough of that abstract nonsense in the museum to fake it."

You fake. Roxann peered over the top of her list at her tipsy cousin and considered telling Angora about the break-in and the message left on her computer. She chewed on her impulse, testing the story in her head. Maybe it was the distance, or maybe it was lying on her childhood bed, but the threat of danger now seemed more perceived than real. She changed her mind and swallowed the rest of her drink, closing her eyes to ward off the bitter sting at the back of her throat.

Angora, who seemed to have acquired a taste for the mixed drink, refilled Roxann's glass under protest. By the time they were nearing the end of their lists, they were both feeling the effects of the alcohol—and from the items rounding out their lists, Roxann realized they must have been feeling the effects of that joint years ago.

"Number thirty-one," Angora slurred, "is 'Get a tattoo.' "

"Mine is 'Become a prosecuting attorney'—ha. The legal system is a joke."

"Thirty-two is 'Enter an amateur strip contest.' "

"Which explains why my number thirty-two says, 'Watch Angora make a fool out of herself in an amateur strip contest.' " They laughed hysterically, but Roxann sobered when she saw the next item on her list.

"What is it?"

"Well...remember Dr. Carl Seger?"

"Do I ever."

"I had a wild crush on him." An understatement.

"And?"

"And number thirty-three on my list is...well..."

" 'Sleep with Dr. Carl,' " Angora finished.

Roxann frowned. "How did you know?"

Angora held up her list. "Ditto. I had a wild crush on him, too. And so did every female on campus."

"I suppose you're right." Roxann stewed in the juices of old memories—the first time Carl had kissed her, the nights they'd stayed up late putting together research for his presentation, the special looks he reserved for her during his lectures. She'd adored him, all right.

"He's still single, you know." Angora wagged her eyebrows. "The newsletter I got a couple of months ago said he was going to auction himself off for a fund-raiser during Homecoming."

"I saw that issue."

Angora sighed. "Wonder what a man like that would go for?"

Roxann opted for silence again, but computed the amount in her IRA.

Angora yawned. "The rest of my list makes no sense—what's a 'spebanker'?"

"I have no idea."

"Well, I wanted to own one."

"You wanted to own one of everything."

"What are your last two?"

Roxann looked at her list, then swallowed hard. *Have a daughter. Be a good mother.* "Uh...mine are unreadable, too. I guess we fell asleep."

Angora laughed. "Or passed out. You know what we should do, Roxann?"

"I'm afraid to ask."

Her cousin's jaw seemed a little loose, and her eyes were bleary. "We should take a vacation and mark off some of the items on our list."

Roxann laughed—go on vacation with Angora? "You're nuts."

"Why not? I'm supposed to be on my honeymoon for three weeks." Her face lit up. "Hey—we could go back to South Bend for Homecoming!"

Her heart thumped faster. "I don't think that's such a good idea."

"Oh, come on, wouldn't you like to see Dr. Carl again and see how he turned out?"

More than anything. "I still don't think—"

Angora's snore cut her off. Her cousin had fallen asleep sitting up, holding her glass and wearing her crown.

Roxann nudged herself up slowly to prevent a head rush. She retrieved Angora's drink, then made her stretch out on the bed. Angora emitted little sounds of protest and refused to relinquish her crown. Roxann gathered up the remains of their meal and tiptoed from the room—although she was sure her cousin wouldn't have heard a plane land on the roof.

She walked to the old phone mounted on the kitchen wall and, after consulting directory assistance, dialed Angora's parents' home. Of course, Dee answered.

"Hello?"

"Dee, this is Roxann."

"*Where* is my daughter?"

"She's with me, at my dad's."

"You kidnapped her."

"She's an adult."

"You always were a bad influence on her."

"Angora's fine, thanks for asking."

"Why, you—"

"I'll bring her home in the morning, but don't worry, I won't come in. Bye, now." She hung up the phone, wondering why people had kids at all if they didn't give a damn about them.

Nine thirty-five p.m.—what a day. She stuffed the pizza box into the trash. Fatigue pulled at her limbs, but her mind raced, refusing to shut down. Yesterday's events in Biloxi...today's events at the church...being home where the memories were relentless. The alcohol should have numbed her, but instead, seemed to have keened her senses, magnifying the panic, the anxiety, the sadness.

An alien sound sent fear bolting through her, until she recognized the ring of her father's phone. It was probably Dee calling back, so she wasn't about to answer it. After three rings, though, an answering machine kicked on in the bedroom. She had sent the machine to her father for Christmas, although she was sure he wouldn't use it. In fairness, though, she hadn't called enough to know.

Curious as to what her aunt would say for herself, she walked into the bedroom and leaned against the door, arms crossed as her father's raspy voice trailed off and the tone sounded. But instead of Dee's unbearable high-pitched whine, a man's voice came on the line. A *familiar* man's voice.

"Mr. Beadleman, this is Detective Capistrano from the Biloxi Police Department. I'm looking for your daughter, Roxann. If you've heard from her or seen her in the last twenty-four hours, please call me back at—"

She snatched up the phone and fairly hissed into the receiver. "How dare you call my father's home."

"Good, you're there. Saves me a heap of paperwork."

She squeezed the phone, wishing it were his red neck. "What the hell are you talking about?"

"I went by your place a while ago to finish our conversation. Remodeling?"

"Funny."

"Do you know who did it?"

"You came to mind."

"I'm much neater when I break and enter."

"Why are you calling?"

"When I saw the mess, I started thinking maybe Frank Cape had dropped by to bully you into giving up his wife's hiding place."

"You're the only bully I've encountered, Detective."

"Then you're unharmed."

"Unemployed *and* unharmed."

He sighed. "Is that why you're in Baton Rouge? To look for a job?"

"That's none of your business. How did you find me?"

"I took a chance that you would run home to Daddy if you were frightened."

The gross misinterpretation of her relationship with her father made her want to laugh...and cry. "I'm not frightened."

"You should be. Has it occurred to you that if I could track you down in a single phone call, Frank Cape could do the same?"

"You're assuming, Detective, that he's the one who ransacked my place."

"You have other enemies?"

She certainly didn't want to get into the other suspects—Elise, Richard. "It might have been a random crime."

"Then you should consider moving to a better neighborhood."

She smirked. "I'll do that, Detective, as soon as I get a job."

"That 'got your number' message on your computer screen—does it have something to do with the break-in?"

"You went inside?"

"How else was I going to make sure you hadn't been stuffed in the refrigerator?"

Oh. "Yes, whoever broke in left the message, but I don't know what it means."

"Old boyfriend?" He sounded dubious.

Roxann frowned. "It's possible, but not likely."

"Did you file a police report?"

"No. Because I thought it might have been you."

He scoffed. "Have you changed your mind about cooperating?"

"No."

"I can protect you from Cape."

"I can protect myself."

"Is your father home?"

"He's gone for the weekend."

"Don't tell me you're alone."

"My cousin is here."

"In the event Cape drops by, is your cousin a big strapping guy?"

"No, but she could talk him to death."

"Christ. Do you have a gun?"

"No. I have pepper spray."

"Christ. I have your father's address, I'll be there by daybreak. Stay put."

"Don't—" But he'd already hung up. Roxann cursed and flailed for a full minute before she realized it was just the kind of hysterics that Capistrano would have expected. She counted to ten to calm her thinking, then used her cell phone to call Tom Atlas, her supervisor at Rescue.

"Roxann, I was just about to call." His tone was rushed, elevated. "Where are you?"

"At my father's in Baton Rouge."

"Get out of there, pronto."

"What's wrong?"

"After you called me about the break-in, I left a message with Melissa Cape's sister. She just called back to tell me that Frank is on the warpath. Said he was going to find you and make you take him to Melissa. He has a dossier on you—where you live, where you work, where you grew up." Tom paused to take a breath. "He was making threats against your family, Roxann."

Her throat convulsed—if something happened to her father because of her, she couldn't bear it.

"Unfortunately, there's no money for a hotel. Do you have someone you can stay with for a while? Somewhere Cape wouldn't find you?"

Her sluggish mind chugged away until Dr. Nell Oney's sweet face materialized. "I have a friend associated with the organization I can call. I'm sure she'd put me up for a few days."

"Good. Keep me posted on your whereabouts."

Roxann disconnected the call and extinguished all the lights, then with heart racing double-time, checked every window in the house to make sure they were locked securely. She flipped on the outside lights, irritated to discover that most of the bulbs were out. Frank Cape would be glad to know he had her completely spooked, although she was slightly relieved to know who was behind the break-in. Pure luck must have kept their paths from crossing at 255 Amberjack, Unit B.

With a shaky hand, she punched in Dr. Oney's number by the glow of a flashlight, weak with relief when her voice came on the line.

"Dr. Oney, it's Roxann Beadleman. Do you remember me?"

"Roxann? Of course I do. I've been hearing such good things about you through Rescue. Are you coming to South Bend for Homecoming?"

Her chest welled with emotion at the warmth in Nell's voice—she hadn't realized how much she missed her. "Not exactly," she hedged. "Although I could use a place to stay for a few days."

"Are you in trouble?"

"Just a disgruntled ex-husband of a woman I relocated a couple of weeks ago."

"Ah—been there. Usually the bullies are more bark than bite, but there's no reason to take chances. And I'd love to see you again—why have you stayed away so long?"

"I've...been busy."

"Are you married?"

"No."

"Kids?"

"No. I'll be coming by myself." She glanced toward the bedroom. Once she got rid of Angora, that is.

"When can I expect you?"

"I'm not sure—I might avoid the interstates."

"Good idea. Don't hurry, I'll see you when I see you. Do you remember where I live?"

"Yes." The few times she'd been to Dr. Oney's cozy little home, she hadn't wanted to leave.

"I'll put a key under a flowerpot. You've been on my mind lately, Roxann—I saw an old photo of you in the alumni newsletter."

"That rally seems like a lifetime ago."

Dr. Oney laughed. "It was. I can't wait to see you and catch up."

Roxann smiled into the phone, immensely cheered. She thanked Dr. Oney and hung up, then sank into her father's indented recliner, oddly comforted by its contours even as her body twitched to be on the road. But she'd have to wait until the alcohol wore off. At least she'd be gone by the time Capistrano arrived. Bothersome fool. She'd let him drive to Baton Rouge in case he crossed paths with Cape—better him than her father—but the detective needn't know where she was headed.

She sighed and sat back in the dark, pulling her legs up under her. How strange that she and Angora had spent the evening reminiscing, and now it looked as if she were bound for South Bend, Indiana, after all. Back to Carl—number thirty-three on her life list. Maybe this would be her opportunity to satisfy her burning curiosity about the man who had inspired her to make a difference in the world.

Roxann closed her eyes and conjured up his face. With the situation she was in, and the slump she'd experienced lately, she could certainly use a little inspiration. She'd never believed in premonition, but she had the queerest feeling of being pushed in a certain direction, as if she were careening toward the rest of her life. And that Carl Seger was destined to play a major role.

CHAPTER NINE

ANGORA SMILED AND WAVED to the crowd. Thousands of bulbs flashed. Here she was, Miss America. The first woman to break the age barrier. Who needed a husband and a career when you had a sash and a crown?

"Congratulations, Angora. Angora...Angora..."

"Angora?"

She opened her eyes and blinked her cousin Roxann into view. Why was Roxann in Atlantic City?

"Angora, something's come up. I have to leave."

She squinted. "Hmm?"

"Wake up, Angora. We have to go."

She moved her tongue, only to discover that someone had deposited something foul in her mouth. "*Ugh*. Where am I?"

"You spent the night at my dad's. Can you sit up?"

"Why wouldn't I be able to sit up?" She sat up, and a bomb exploded in her head. "Ohhhhhh."

"I brought you some aspirin."

"Shhhh!"

"Take deep breaths."

On the third deep breath, her stomach vaulted to her throat. She barely made it to the bathroom before everything she'd ingested the night before came surging toward daylight. Oh, God, she'd never eat pepperoni pizza again. In fact, she might never eat again, period. The Hangover Diet. Maybe she'd finally shed those ten pounds that had eluded her since puberty.

Roxann handed her a cool cloth, and she buried her face in it. Then yesterday's events came flooding back to her—the shame, the disappointment—and she wanted never to lift her head again. The next few years of her life, so carefully planned as late as yesterday, now stretched before her...empty...lonely... not rich. She would be damaged goods in the eyes of the families that belonged to the club, forever referred to as "the jilted one." And Dee would never let her live down this fiasco.

"Try to swallow these aspirin," Roxann urged. "It helped me."

"If I die," she whispered, "don't let the coroner take a picture of me like this."

"Don't worry—I'd fix your hair first. Can you make it to the bed?"

"Only if you bring the bed into the bathroom."

"Come on, up you go."

Angora groaned as she became vertical again. The bed was a mile away, but she finally reached the end of it and eased down to a sitting position. "Why do I feel like hell and you don't?"

"Because my body is used to processing more than carrots and popcorn."

Roxann was right, of course. Roxann was always right. Her cousin's duffel bag sat on the floor, zipped and ready to go. "Did you say you have to leave?"

"Yes—as soon as possible. I found a pair of Dad's sweatpants for you to wear, and a flannel shirt."

Angora peered at the darkened window. "What time is it?"

"Four-thirty."

"In the morning?" She hadn't been up at four-thirty in the morning since... wait—she'd *never* been up at four-thirty in the morning.

"Sorry—I really need to get going."

"Back to Biloxi?"

"Eventually. I have a few stops to make first."

"Take me with you."

Roxann shook her head. "I can't."

"Please, Roxann? I can't face everyone, not yet." And not like this.

"I called your parents last night and told them you were all right."

"Thanks." She bit into her bottom lip. "Were they worried?"

"Absolutely."

A sliver of happiness cut through the disappointment that cocooned her heart. If they were worried now, think how much more worried they'd be if she didn't come home right away. "I don't want to go home."

"Okay, then I'll take you to a friend's."

Her mind wasn't operating at top speed, but she had the feeling that even if she weren't hung over, she wouldn't be able to come up with a name.

"Angora?"

"I'm thinking."

Roxann sighed. "How about your maid of honor?"

"Amanda Whittaker? We're not that close."

"Then why did you ask her to be your maid of honor?"

"Because she asked me to be hers last year."

"Come on, Angora—there must have been twenty girls up there with you."

"Twenty-four. You know, I wanted to ask you to be a bridesmaid."

"I'm...flattered."

"Dee had a fit, though, and I was pretty sure I'd never get you in a pink dress anyway."

"I guess you were the one who sent me the invitation?"

She nodded. "I wasn't sure you'd get it, but I'm glad you did."

"So am I. I think. Angora, you're not close to any of the women in your wedding party?"

"To Trenton's three sisters, I thought. But I heard them saying nasty things about me in the bathroom at my bridal shower." *She's not very bright, is she? No, and she's chunky. I don't know what Trenton sees in her.*

"What about a coworker?"

"The only person I associate with outside of work is my boss, and that's only because he's a friend of Dee's." Her coworkers had made it clear that since she'd gotten the job because of her connections, they weren't about to include her in their art-uppity circle. They seemed to enjoy talking over her head, discussing artists and paintings that she had to look up during her lunch hour. She was sure they had come to the wedding for the shrimp cocktail.

"There must be someone."

"Maybe I should just go with you."

But Roxann shook her head. "Sorry."

She lifted her arms and allowed Roxann to pull off the hideous tie-dyed T-shirt. "I won't be any trouble."

"Angora, you can't help but be trouble."

"I know." She sniffled.

"Don't start crying, your head will hurt worse."

"It can't hurt worse," she mumbled as she shrugged into the flannel shirt Roxann held behind her. "And these thongs of yours make me feel like I had a wedding night after all."

"You'll feel better once you can rest in your own bed in your own underwear."

Angora relented, knowing that her cousin didn't want to be bothered with her on whatever exciting adventure she was off to next. No one wanted to be bothered with her. She choked back a sob, and tugged on gray sweatpants that swallowed her, tummy bulge and all. She looked like a bum, but her only alternative was to wear her wedding gown home, and she wasn't about to try to get back into that torture garb. "What will I do for shoes?"

"I have an extra pair of sneakers."

"But you wear a size six and a half, and I need at least an eight."

Roxann frowned. "You remember my shoe size?"

She remembered a lot about Roxann. In fact, from those few months rooming together, she probably knew more about her aloof cousin, and had revealed more of herself to Roxann, than anyone else on earth.

"Well, I might be able to find a pair of Dad's house shoes."

"Never mind," she said, standing and holding on to her head to keep it from flying apart. "I'll wear my pumps. Might as well get one more wear out of them, considering they cost as much as the plane tickets to Hawaii." Dee wouldn't be up anyway, to be scandalized by her appearance. She wadded up the dress that she'd spent so many hours searching for and stuffed it under her arm. "I'm ready." Not really, but she was trying to prove to Roxann that she could be brave, too.

Roxann picked up her duffel and led the way back through the cramped little house, which seemed much neater and smelled a little nicer than the previous evening—for that, her stomach was grateful. When had Roxann had time to clean? As always, she seemed capable of doing everything at once. Envy barbed through her—was there anything her cousin couldn't do?

Roxann turned when they reached the side door. "Stay here until I tell you to come out."

Angora frowned. "Why?"

"Because...this isn't the best neighborhood. Sometimes homeless people sleep under the carports."

She watched as Roxann slipped out, her hand inside her duffel bag, probably on the pepper spray can. Her cousin was so brave. In the dim light of a naked bulb, Roxann walked all around the van, then signaled her to come out.

Angora stepped down onto the uneven concrete and promptly twisted her ankle in the high heels, but recovered adequately. It was still dark out, the air wet and cool. The tang of garbage from a nearby Dumpster burned her nostrils and toyed with her unsettled stomach. Still, the lights in the small houses across the road, silhouetting people moving around in their kitchens, probably getting ready to go to work at the electric plant, was somehow comforting. Living in a tight-knit neighborhood must have been so fun growing up, with kids everywhere, and fire hydrants opened wide in the dog days of summer. Since she had no friends of her own, she'd always hoped Roxann would invite her over to play with hers. Dee wouldn't have agreed, of course, but she'd wished anyway.

She opened the creaky door to the van and pulled herself up, wincing against the pain in her skull, then tossed the wedding gown in the backseat. The vehicle had a peculiar odor, raising questions about what kinds of exotic things had taken place inside. Stakeouts with lots of take-out food? Sleeping on an air mattress, hiding out from the law? Transporting entire families and their belongings?

Roxann opened the sliding door of the van and set a box on the floorboard.

"What's that?"

"Some of the junk from my room—I thought it was time to get it out of Dad's way." Roxann set the duffel bag on the backseat, then closed the door and swung up into the driver's seat.

"I'm sorry you didn't get to see your father."

"Maybe next time."

Even through her headache fog, she detected a measure of insincerity in Roxann's voice that perplexed her. Sure, Uncle Walt was messy and poor, but he was an adoring father who thought enough of his daughter to maintain her girlish bedroom. Dee had already hired an interior designer to change *her* bedroom into a day spa. Twice she'd come out of the shower to find people measuring.

She watched as Roxann cranked the engine and launched into some kind of strange hand-slapping routine on the dashboard. Then a shot rang out, sending Angora at least an inch off the seat. "What was that?"

Roxann gripped the wheel and pivoted her head to the side, her eyes wide. Then she relaxed and sighed. "The van backfired."

Angora managed a little laugh. "For a minute I thought someone was shooting at us."

"Well, that's pretty unlikely, even in this neighborhood."

But her cousin seemed genuinely spooked as she backed out of the narrow driveway and onto the quiet street. "Maybe it's just my weak stomach," Angora said in an attempt to lighten the moment, "but I don't remember the van vibrating this much yesterday."

"You were a little preoccupied yesterday," Roxann offered wryly.

"No offense, but this is a wreck."

"I don't have a need for a BMW."

"How did you know I drive a BMW?"

"Lucky guess. Don't worry—Goldie might seem a little rickety, but she runs like a deer."

"Goldie—is she your undercover car? Does it have a race-car engine under the hood so you can outrun the Smokies?"

"The Smokies? Angora, you watch too much television. And the van is a regular old eight-cylinder."

"But you do use it for your...work?"

She nodded.

"Can't you tell me anything?"

"My work's not nearly as glamorous as you might think."

Probably more glamorous than disinfecting the headsets for audio tours of the Baton Rouge River Walk Museum. "How do you find out about women who are in trouble?"

"There's a network of counselors and social workers all over the country who know about Rescue."

"Rescue? Is that what it's called?"

Roxann nodded. "It's a last resort for women who want to get away from abusive partners."

"What do you do for them?"

"Help them and their children relocate. And, in some cases, help them establish new identities."

"Is it legal?"

"In most cases," Roxann said, nodding. "But there have been a few times when a woman's ex had visitation rights despite evidence that he was a threat to the children."

"And?"

"And in those cases, the woman is thwarting court-ordered visitation by denying her ex access to the children."

"So she's kidnapping her own children."

"As far as the law is concerned, yes."

Angora pursed her mouth. "Can you get in trouble for helping them?"

"It's possible to be brought up on obstruction-of-justice charges, or maybe contempt charges...but not likely."

"But it's still dangerous."

Roxann glanced in the rearview mirror. "The greatest danger is if the ex-spouse finds his wife. And some of the exes have been known to go after the Rescue volunteers who helped their wives disappear."

"Isn't all that kept secret?"

"It's supposed to be, but leaks are bound to occur. That's why the facilitators sometimes wear disguises or use bogus names when they transport a family. And we move around a lot."

Angora leaned close. "You're a facilitator?"

"Uh-huh."

"Wow. Have you ever been threatened?"

"Um...nothing serious." Roxann glanced in the mirror—probably a reflex, Angora decided.

She herself had no reflexes, unless the urge to match her lipstick and fingernail polish counted. "Do they pay you?"

"A little, but I work other jobs for my primary income, and for benefits."

"What kinds of jobs?"

Roxann shrugged. "Anything flexible. Lately I've been waitressing in a diner."

"You're joking."

"Nope."

"Oh, God, that's so exciting—a waitress by day, and rescuer by night."

"Not so exciting, just exhausting."

Angora crinkled her nose. "I'll bet you have to wear ugly shoes."

Roxann laughed. "Not anymore, I was fired."

"Fired? Why?"

"Because a relocation took longer than I expected, and I was late."

"Don't the people at the diner know what else you do?"

"No. It's better to keep a low profile."

Angora wet her lips—this was better than the movies. "Last night did you get called about a...what do you call it?"

"A relocation? Yes."

She sighed and eased back her aching head—oh, the drama. Meanwhile, life was passing her by as if she were one of those statues in the wing of the museum that only school kids visited, and then under protest.

"How are you feeling?" Roxann asked.

"Lousy."

"At this hour of the day, I'll have you home in no time."

She grimaced at the pre-dawn scenery flying by. "Don't hurry on my account."

"Hey, today can't be as bad as yesterday."

"Oh, yes it can. By now Mother will have identified everything I should have done to keep Trenton from standing me up at the altar, and she'll have devised a plan to save face with everyone who attended the wedding."

"Dee is...meticulous."

"And still in bed, I hope. If I'm lucky and the maid cooperates, Mother won't even know I'm in the house until dinnertime."

But it was not to be. When they pulled up to the huge brick home that her father had built to her mother's specifications twenty-five years ago, nearly every light was blazing.

"I'd forgotten your house was so big," Roxann murmured.

Angora swallowed. "I don't think I can do this."

Then the front door opened, silhouetting her mother in a voluminous muumuu. She did not look relieved to see her only child home safe and sound.

"Correction—I know I can't do this."

Roxann scoffed. "What's the worst thing she can do?"

Shake her head. Roll her eyes. Call me names.

"Oh, I almost forgot." Roxann twisted and lifted the box lid. "Here's your crown. And your life list."

Angora set the crown on her head, comforted, as always, by its weight. Then she unfolded the sheets of paper with shaky hands. "Everything seemed much simpler when we made these lists."

"Everything *was* much simpler."

"Have you ever wished you could turn back time?" she whispered through a haze of tears.

Roxann averted her eyes. "There are some things I would do differently, sure."

Angora looked toward the house. Even from this distance, she could see that Dee was tapping her foot. "Will you come in with me, Roxann?"

"I don't think—"

"Just for a few minutes. She won't go completely berserk if you're with me. Please?" She wasn't above giving her cousin the pitiful look that had won her over in the past.

Roxann sighed. "Just for a few minutes."

"I owe you one." At her cousin's pensive expression, she wondered if Roxann was remembering another pact they'd made. They owed each other.

After a deep breath, Angora gathered her soiled gown and slid down from the vinyl seat. She felt ridiculous wearing men's sweatpants and high heels, but she forged ahead, up the elaborate stone sidewalk, toward her fuming mother. As always, some small part of her still harbored the hope that Dee would throw her arms wide and offer her comfort. But when Angora was within arm's reach, her mother spun on her feathered mules and marched into the house. Angora had no choice but to follow. Roxann was a few steps behind.

Dee glided into the parlor, then turned for dramatic effect, fabric fluttering. "Well?"

"Well, what?" Angora asked.

"Well, what do you have to say for yourself?"

"Um...I'm sorry for being jilted at the altar?"

"Don't be smart, young lady. You left me and your father in an extremely awkward situation, running off like that with—" She glared at Roxann. "With *her*. Really. And Roxann, what a waste of your good education you've turned out to be."

Roxann said nothing, only blinked lazily and offered up a small smile.

The disappointment in Dee's eyes when she looked at Roxann—it was so intense, like the disappointment of a mother looking at a disobedient but favorite child. Angora had always suspected that deep down Dee had wished she'd given birth to Roxann, the smart one, and, in truth, the one with more natural beauty. The fact that Roxann chose not to enhance her looks had been a curious obsession of Dee's.

"I'm sorry for leaving so abruptly, Mother," Angora murmured. "I just wanted to get out of there."

Dee's eyes cut back to her. "And let someone else clean up your mess."

"Trenton was the one who changed his mind."

"The boy had cold feet, that's all. If your cousin hadn't interfered, and if you'd behaved as if you had good sense, all of this could have been settled yesterday, and you'd be on your honeymoon instead of standing here dressed like a refugee and smelling like throw-up."

"It wasn't her fault," Roxann said. "Lay off."

They both turned. She was leaning against the doorframe, her arms crossed.

"*You* may leave," Dee said pointedly. "And remove that rattletrap from my driveway."

Roxann pushed away from the door. "Nice to see you again, Angora. Good luck in Chicago."

Angora watched her leave, feeling as if her last link to freedom were slipping away. She couldn't even eke out a goodbye. When the front door closed, hot tears sprang to her eyes. She turned back to Dee. "Mother, I really am sorry. I know you and Daddy spent a lot of money on the wedding—"

"It's not the money," Dee said, waving impatiently. "I took out an insurance policy."

Angora blinked. "What?"

"I took out an insurance policy on the wedding expenditures in case something like this happened."

"In case I was jilted?" Angora asked, incredulous.

Dee sighed. "Well, I was right, wasn't I?"

Angora's body went completely cold, but somehow her feet moved, carrying her back into the foyer where she'd seen her purse sitting on the table among boxes of embossed napkins and little bags of unused birdseed. She shoved her life list inside the Prada bag—thank goodness black crocodile went with everything, including flannel—then slung it over her shoulder.

"Where are you going, young lady?"

"Away from here." She jogged to the front door, yanked it open, and ran outside, taking the stairs as fast as she could in her heels. "Roxann! Roxann, wait!"

The van was pulling away from the sidewalk, but to her immense relief, the brake lights came on.

She ran up to the passenger side door and tugged until it opened.

"What's wrong?" Roxann asked.

"I can't stay here. Take me with you."

"Angora—"

"Please, Roxann?" She blinked up a few desperate tears. *"Please."*

CHAPTER TEN

ROXANN STUDIED ANGORA'S tearful face. She could imagine the insensitive things Dee had said—the woman was a shrew. With the possibility of Frank Cape on her tail, though, the last thing she needed was to have Angora slowing her down, and she didn't want to involve her cousin in her dilemma.

"Oh, God, here comes Mother. Please, Roxann?"

She sighed. On the other hand, Angora was the only relative she had who actually wanted to spend time with her, and even her cousin's too-chatty company would be a respite from the loneliness that had seized her lately. Plus if Frank Cape found her, he might be less likely to confront her with a witness along. In the side mirror, she could see Dee bearing down the sidewalk, muumuu flying.

"Okay, get in."

Angora squealed, sprang into the seat, and slammed the door. *"Go."*

Roxann gunned the engine, which backfired and left a cloud of blue smoke that obscured her aunt. She'd definitely sealed her fate as far as Dee's will was concerned.

Angora laughed like a child. "Thank you, thank you, thank you! I couldn't stay in that house one more second." She sighed. "I've dug my grave with Mother this time."

If Angora had made it to the Miss America pageant, her talent could have been passive-aggressivism, which she had down to an art. Play Miss Goody Two-shoes until she was ready to burst, then misbehave, wallow in remorse, tearfully confess, beg forgiveness, and start all over again. Roxann slowed. "Do you want me to take you back?"

"No."

Impressed, Roxann accelerated. "Give Dee time, she'll come around."

Angora snorted. "Mother will never change. When I die, she'll stand over my casket and bemoan my laugh lines."

Yesterday she herself had turned up a radio commercial for a new anti-wrinkle cream, so she couldn't cast stones. "She means well." Actually, Dee was just plain mean, but there was no use fanning the flame.

Angora shifted in her seat, filling in the silence by arranging bulky flannel around the seat belt. "It's funny—I don't remember much about your mother," she murmured. "Except that she smelled like lemon furniture polish."

Roxann blinked—they'd never discussed her own mother, not even when they roomed together. "She...Mom was always cleaning. Back then, Dad liked an orderly house." Because someone else was doing the cleaning. And the cooking. And the fetching.

"Do you miss her?"

Her eyes burned unexpectedly. "Of course."

"I don't think I'd miss Dee at all—how sad is that?"

"Sad," she agreed. "But I don't think you mean it."

Angora made a noncommittal noise in her throat. "Roxann, why did your folks divorce?"

She concentrated hard on the road. "Incompatibility. Dad was an ogre. Controlling. Jealous. Mother tired of it, I suppose."

"Your dad seems like such a sweetheart."

"I have some good memories of us all together," she conceded. "But Dad was no sweetheart. And when Mom...when they split up, he turned bitter."

"Was there another person involved?"

Every fiber in her body rallied to her mother's defense. "Mother had a male friend, but she was not having an affair."

"Although your dad thought so?"

She pursed her mouth and nodded slowly. "So he kept me from her—not because he wanted to raise me, but to punish her."

"Your dad is crazy for you. At Christmas, every other sentence out of his mouth is 'Roxann is so intelligent.' "

She smirked. "Just to aggravate Dee." Besides, only she knew that he'd been talking in code—how many times had her father said he'd rather have a child who was "smart" than "intelligent"? She was certain he'd framed her diploma as a mocking reminder of how she'd wasted her education.

"Where are we going?" Angora asked, as if she suddenly cared.

"To South Bend."

Her eyes lit up. "For Homecoming?"

"Well...I guess the timing is right. I'm actually going to stay with Nell Oney for a few days—do you remember Dr. Oney?"

Angora frowned. "Yeah. Didn't she teach philosophy?"

Roxann nodded. "And she got me involved in the Rescue program." Roxann didn't need a shrink to tell her Nell had been the mother figure she'd craved—wise, calm, attentive. She'd wanted to stay in touch with the woman who had taken a special interest in her, but the university and the people connected to it represented too many bittersweet memories.

"Do you two have business to take care of?" Angora asked.

"Sort of."

"Do you think she'll mind if I'm along?"

"No, but you can't discuss any of the things I've told you about the program with anyone."

"You of all people know I can keep a secret."

Roxann glanced over, her stomach knotted. "Don't, Angora."

For the split second, a spark of defiance shone in Angora's wide blue eyes, and Roxann had the horrible feeling that Angora would lash out at her parents and the world by divulging their secret. There was nothing more dangerous than a person who felt as if they had nothing left to lose. She swallowed.

"Roxann, have you ever wanted to kill someone?"

At the eerily serious note in her cousin's voice, warning bells chimed in her head. "Everyone has moments of extreme anger," she said carefully.

"No," Angora said, her gaze locked on Roxann's, her pupils dilated. "I mean really kill someone." In her lap, her hands convulsed. "I think I could kill Trenton and not feel a bit guilty."

A chill tickled the back of Roxann's neck as she recalled moments in college when she'd questioned Angora's stability. "Passion is a powerful emotion. Sometimes it can feel like hate instead of love."

But Angora seemed to be somewhere else. "All I know is that I put my life on hold too many times because of promises men made to me." Her voice had taken on a bitter tone. "What makes the beasts think they can use a woman and then toss her aside when she becomes inconvenient?"

Roxann used her most soothing tone. "You're hurting right now, but you'll feel better by the time we get to South Bend."

Angora's eyes welled up, and her mouth tightened. "I swear on my crown, the next man who jerks me around is going to wish he hadn't."

Her cousin wouldn't be the first repressed woman to snap and retaliate, ergo all those news interviews with wide-eyed neighbors in their robes saying, "She seemed like such a nice woman."

Then as quickly as it came, the glimmer in her cousin's eyes vanished, replaced by a contrite expression. "I don't know what I would have done if you hadn't shown up yesterday, Roxann. Or if you hadn't let me come with you on this trip. Seems like you're always saving me."

Unexpectedly moved, Roxann couldn't respond.

"I know, I know—it seems like I always need saving."

"I didn't say that."

"You were thinking it." Angora inhaled, then exhaled musically. "But that's okay, because from now on, I'm going to take charge of my life."

Roxann bit her tongue—the only thing Angora had ever taken charge of was Visa, Mastercard, and American Express.

Angora lifted her chin. "I don't need Trenton—I can get a man any time I want one."

With her golden good looks, her cousin never had a problem attracting men, but inevitably, her insecurities manifested in some way to have them running in the opposite direction: too prim, too needy, too snobby, too virginal. "Getting" a man was not Angora's problem, nor any other woman's for that matter. Keeping him—now there was the rub.

"In fact," Angora continued. "I can find someone better looking, someone who's great in bed."

"And you would know?" Roxann asked gently.

"Yes." Angora twirled her hair around her index finger—a dead giveaway that she was lying. Then she sighed. "No."

"Don't sound so forlorn."

"Roxann, how many thirty-two-year-old virgins do you know?"

Roxann swerved, then corrected. "You're still a virgin?"

"I knew I shouldn't have said anything."

"No, no...I'm surprised, that's all, since you're so pretty and since you've been engaged."

"And since I'm so old?"

"We're the same age."

"You didn't answer my question. How many thirty-two-year-old virgins do you know?"

"Well...I don't have many close female friends, but I'm sure..." She trailed off helplessly. "Okay, I don't know any thirty-two-year-old virgins."

She pulled a small pink packet from her purse. "A wedding-night gift from Mother—condoms."

"Not ready to be a grandmother just yet, is she?"

"No." She pulled one out and read the label. "These things are made of lambskin."

"Sheep intestines."

"Huh?"

"They're made of sheep intestines. But 'lambskin' is more marketable."

"Oh, that's gross."

She shrugged. "They're the best, as far as sensation is concerned. My hat's off to Dee."

"For knowing?"

"For letting you know that she knows."

"Ah. Well, the only thing that Mother harped on more than my laugh lines and my waistline is sex—she said she'd cut me out of her will if she found out

I didn't wait until my wedding night." She stuffed the condom grab bag back into her purse.

"How would she know?"

"My gynecologist."

"What?"

"I've been going to the same gynecologist since I was fifteen, and she told me he would tell her if ever...you know."

Roxann ground her teeth. "Angora, that's not only immoral, it's illegal. Your physician can't reveal your...*status* to anyone, not even to Dee. Surely you know that."

"Mother's laws supersede all others."

How could she rationalize with a woman whose world had been skewed by a selfish, overbearing mother? "Angora, there's nothing wrong with being a virgin at your age, but it should be because of your own convictions, not your mother's."

Angora angled her chin. "You're so right. I think it's high time I change gynecologists. And broaden my sexual horizons."

"You're entitled," Roxann agreed, simply because Angora couldn't carry off the label of "promiscuous" if she wore it on a sash.

"Maybe I'll sleep with someone scandalous," she murmured. "Maybe...a bad boy. Or an older man." Angora produced a foxy smile. "Maybe I'll sleep with Dr. Seger. Cross another item off my life list."

Roxann's stomach jumped, but she attributed it to last night's unfortunate choice of drink. "That's an interesting possibility."

"Are you going to bid on him at the bachelor auction?"

"I hadn't thought about it." Liar, liar.

"Let's go and buy ourselves a man."

"On my budget, the man would have to be made out of rubber."

But Angora was warming to her plan. "How long will it take for us to get to campus?"

"Driving straight through, I figure around fifteen hours."

She bounced up and down in the seat, dislodging her crown. "Let's take our time and cross off a few items on our life lists along the way!"

Roxann tried to conjure up some enthusiasm, but failed. "Angora, we don't have to abide by some silly list we made when we were little more than children." Besides, it was too disconcerting to see how many of the things that had once been important to her had been left undone.

"Oh, come on—it'll be fun," Angora coaxed. "Just like old times."

Except as she recalled, the "old times" weren't that fun for either of them. She squinted. "What did you have in mind?"

Angora lifted the collar of the faded flannel shirt. "The first order of the day is to go shopping, of course."

Of course.

Her cousin waved vaguely toward the map lying on the seat between them. "So find a route that will take us by a mall, preferably one with a Saks."

She groaned.

"Hey, you could use a few new duds yourself, kiddo. You look exactly the same as you did in college."

Roxann craned to critically study her reflection in the rearview mirror. "I don't look exactly the same." Those little creases around her eyes, for instance. And five gray hairs that congregated in her side part.

"Are you kidding? You're frozen in time." Angora tsk-tsked at Roxann's faded jeans. "And that's not always a good thing."

Shopping—a grueling experience. Despite her stint in the dress shop in high school, she didn't have Angora's eye for color or style. "We should be in Jackson by noon, maybe we can find a Wal-Mart."

"This is serious." Angora was gaining momentum. "You could have your eyebrows waxed."

"I prefer having them singed by a roaring gas flame."

"And have you ever thought about letting your hair grow out?"

She rolled her eyes up to stare at the fringe of bangs tickling her brow. "No. In fact, it's time for a trim."

"Long straight hair is back in. You'd be absolutely exotic." She snapped her fingers. "I've got it—hair extensions!"

"You always were determined to make me over."

"And you always were determined to shop at the campus Goodwill."

It was what she could afford. Plus the vintage, boyish clothes boosted her image of rebellious coed. Indeed, she'd stuck out when most young women were going over the top with big, feminine hair and look-at-me clothing. Carl had admired her individuality, but maybe she was getting too old for jeans and T-shirts. Besides, since almost everyone was going out of the way to dress down these days, she was in danger of falling into a trend—*argh*.

Angora yawned and laid her head back. "So, cuz, do you have a boyfriend?"

Roxann watched the road signs in the dark and headed toward the interstate. "No. I don't date much." Even she and Richard hadn't really dated when she lived in Birmingham. If she was lonely, she'd drop by the bar or coffeehouse where he happened to be playing, and he'd go home with her. If he was lonely, he'd show up on her doorstep with Thai food.

"What are the men like in Biloxi?"

Capistrano's face came to her. "Like the weather—thick and predictable." He probably hated Thai food.

"Don't you get lonely?"

"I stay pretty busy." A definite meat-and-potatoes man.

"Have you ever come close to getting married?"

"Not that I know of." In fact, he probably wrestled his meat to the ground and killed it with his bare hands.

Angora groaned. "Men are such pigs—why do we want one?"

She scowled. "Who says I do?"

"You don't want a family of your own?"

"Maybe. Someday." The last two items on her life list came to mind, but that little part about the sperm contribution posed a bit of a problem.

"Someday? Roxann, do you realize that at our age we're already considered high-risk for pregnancy?"

Her own gynecologist had said the same thing on her last annual visit. Blah, blah, blah.

"The way I see it, we have another good year left to find a husband, then one year of decent sex before getting pregnant. If we can get pregnant at our age. Our eggs are getting old, you know. With every month that passes, we're becoming more barren."

"Stop."

Angora sniffled. "Maybe it's not important to you, but I always pictured myself with a little boy and a little girl. I'd never want an only child because it's just too much..."

"Pressure," Roxann supplied.

"Right. But Uncle Walt never pressured you."

"No." That would've required being attentive. "But I think most only children realize that the expectations of the family ride on their shoulders." If she didn't make her life matter for something, the Beadleman name would be remembered as a flirtatious mother who'd met an untimely end and a drunkard father who would probably meet his Maker while stretched out in his recliner.

Angora sighed. "That kind of pressure can make you do crazy things, all right."

"Like marrying a man just to make your mother happy?"

She hadn't meant to hurt her, but Angora closed her eyes and pressed her lips together. "Or turning your back on men to become a martyr for abused women?"

Roxann was so astounded at how closely Angora's assessment had matched her own, that she had no choice but to lie. "That's ridiculous."

"Really? So you're open to having a man in your life? To getting married?"

Suddenly she was reminded of the upside of traveling alone—you didn't have to answer irrelevant questions. "I, uh...suppose. I really don't think about it much. If it happens, it happens."

"Oh, now see—that's a myth. Nothing 'just happens.' You have to help things along."

"To what end?"

"Well...to happily-ever-after, of course."

"You were jilted at the altar yesterday, and you still believe in happily-ever-after?"

"Well, sure. What else is there?"

"How about 'contentedly-ever-after'?"

"Can you be content without a man?"

Roxann nodded. "I *am* content without a man." Eighty-four percent true.

Angora sighed. "Then you're a stronger woman than I am. I couldn't stand it, working with scared women all the time, moving around, changing jobs, having no money, being alone." Another sigh. "You're so brave."

She frowned. "Thanks."

"I mean it. It takes guts to chuck your education and go out on a limb for people you don't know and might never see again."

She frowned harder.

"To sacrifice your own happiness so that—"

"Okay, Angora. You're making me blush."

She sighed again, with more drama. "I thought by now I would have done something with my life, and now I'm starting over."

"Have you been working for the museum all these years?"

"Yes, and it's dreadful. They treat me like I'm an idiot."

"So why do you work there?"

"Well, Ms. Valedictorian, after graduation, I didn't have as many options as you did. Not much I could do with a degree in art history—even Daddy couldn't find a place for me in the hotel business—so the museum job seemed promising. By the time I realized it was a dead end, I had met Trenton and wanted to be near him and his family." Her laugh was hollow. "I guess I am an idiot. I was never smart, like you. Of course you know that."

Except a high IQ did not a smart person make. If she was so smart, for instance, why had she brought Angora with her on the lam? Right now the woman was sitting there waiting for a nugget of brilliant advice.

"You can't make someone love you," Roxann said slowly. "You're only responsible for your own feelings and actions." She'd counseled hundreds of women with those same lines.

Angora lifted her head. "You know, you're absolutely right."

Encouraged, she continued. "Isn't there some small part of you that's relieved you didn't marry Trenton?"

"No, I was really looking forward to marrying a rich man and living hundreds of miles from my parents."

So much for magic words.

"I'm not like you, Roxann. I want it all—a husband, a home, kids. I can't be happy helping other people live their lives."

It was a good thing that Angora withdrew a foot-long emery board from her purse and began sawing on her nails, because Roxann was speechless over the backhanded compliment. Everything Angora had said was true—she did chuck her education, work with scared women, move around, change jobs, live frugally, and was, for the most part, alone. And she did help other people live their lives. So why did a lifestyle that had once seemed noble and romantic sound downright bleak when someone else described it?

And worse, Angora truly believed that her cousin had sacrificed a man, a home, and a family so that she could devote her life to others. But in truth, she was starting to feel resentful of her thankless job, and of the string of needy women who stood between her and her own happily-ever-after.

Roxann went cold remembering the eerie message on her computer screen. She was a fake, going through the motions of benevolence with an empty heart. She was counting on the gratitude of the forlorn women she aided to fill the void in her gypsy life, which wasn't fair, or even reasonable.

"Are you okay?" Angora asked. "You look a little green."

"Still a little hung over," she lied.

"Would you like for me to drive?"

It had taken Angora eight attempts to get her driver's license. "No, I'm fine. Why don't you take a nap?" Now that the confrontation with Dee was over, Angora was limp, and yawning between every sentence. Plus Roxann wanted to be alone with her own thoughts—not a good sign ten miles down the highway on a proposed two-week road trip.

"No...I want to stay awake," Angora said, but her voice was groggy. She put her purse behind her head and leaned back. Her eyelids fluttered. "So you don't fall asleep...at the—"

The nose job took over and the snoring set in. Roxann shook her head and wondered again what she'd gotten herself into. And at the worst possible time. She adjusted the rearview mirror, alert for a tail, but few cars were on the neighborhood roads of Baton Rouge at this hour. Besides, even if Frank Cape followed her, he'd probably give up when he didn't find her at her father's.

Her father...

She'd never forgive herself if something happened to him because of her sleazy associations. She pulled into a drive-through and bought a large coffee, then punched in her father's number on her cell phone in the event he had cut his fishing trip short. But as she expected, his answering machine picked up, and she felt compelled to talk to him in person.

When the teenager handed her coffee through the window, the hot liquid sloshed over the side, and the incident in the diner with Capistrano came to mind. If he hadn't come in that day, and if she hadn't been fired, she would've taken her normal lunch break to run home and drop off groceries or something, and might have been at the apartment when Frank Cape dropped by. She shivered. Not that she owed the detective anything for his interference.

She sipped the coffee, checked the rearview mirror, and steered Goldie onto the access road leading to the interstate. Angora hadn't moved a muscle, unless you counted her snoring muscles. NPR was the best she could get on the old AM radio, so she settled in for a lively discussion on growing herbs. And after an hour's education on soil, sun, and plant selection, she was tempted to give up Rescue to grow rosemary and sage in her spare time. In fact, the placid announcers made it seem as if world peace could be achieved if everyone just pruned their peppermint periodically.

At mid-morning her father finally answered his phone. Roxann hadn't realized just how worried she'd been until his telltale rasp rattled out over the line.

"Hello?" He sounded winded, as if he had just walked in.

Her heart swelled with a dozen emotions. "Hi, Dad."

"Roxann—where are you? There's a policeman sitting in my driveway."

"Did he tell you his name?"

"Capistrano. Said you were in some kind of trouble."

She rolled her eyes. "I'm fine, Dad."

"Then why is he here?"

"It's complicated, but he was out of line for following me."

"Sherwood said you had somebody with you last night."

"Angora."

At the mention of her name, her cousin's snoring stopped and she lifted her head. *Great.*

"I thought your cousin was getting married this weekend."

"She was. I mean, she was supposed to." She cleared her throat and lowered her voice. "It's a long story. I'll call you in a few days and explain everything."

Angora squinted at Roxann.

"Meanwhile, tell Detective Capistrano that I've gone back to Biloxi."

"Are you in danger?" her father asked.

"I'll be fine. Really."

He sighed heavily. "This is how you use your education? Play cat and mouse with unsavory characters?"

She swallowed hard, trying not to feel like a little girl who'd misbehaved. "I'll call you, Dad." With much remorse, she pushed the disconnect button and turned a cheerful smile in Angora's direction. "Feeling rested?"

"Yes." Angora stretched. "What was that all about?"

"I called my father to let him know we'd stayed at his house last night."

"Who is Detective Capistrano?"

"Nobody. Hey, is that a mall?"

Angora was nothing if not easily distracted. "Yes! Take this exit—we're going to spend some money."

"I don't have much cash," Roxann warned. Actually, she had fourteen dollars and twenty-two cents in her purse, which wasn't even leather.

Angora pshawed. "Who needs cash when I have Trenton's gold card?"

"I didn't hear you say that."

CHAPTER ELEVEN

ANGORA STOOD BEHIND Roxann and stared at her cousin's reflection. Envy threatened to surface, but pride over the wardrobe makeover she'd supervised won out. "You look marvelous."

Roxann's brown eyes cut to her in the mirror. "I look ridiculous."

Angora sighed—nothing was more exasperating than a beautiful woman who failed to recognize her physical potential. How many times had she heard Dee say that the family cheekbones had been wasted on Roxann? And one of her most mortifying memories was having the plastic surgeon draw on her God-given piggish nose with a black marker based on a picture of Roxann that Dee had produced.

"It's my mother's nose," Dee had insisted, "and it should have been yours."

After her jaw had been broken and reset, and her teeth straightened, she and Roxann could have passed for sisters, except for the hips and the hair. Her own true color was a mousy brown, but Dee had been so determined that everyone think she was a natural blonde, Angora's hair had been lightened since kindergarten.

"You just need time to adjust to your new look," Angora assured Roxann. "You're going to knock his socks off."

"Who?"

"Whoever."

Roxann scoffed, but Angora noticed the subtle change in her demeanor as she turned sideways and perused her whip-slim figure in brown leather pants, pink blouse, and high-heeled ankle boots. She was thinking about someone.

Roxann tugged at the waistband. "These pants are tighter on me than on the animal that wore the hide."

Angora grinned and turned to the clerk hovering in the background. "We'll take this outfit, and all the rest."

"Angora, I can't let you buy all these things for me."

"Why not? After all, you rescued me." She waved Trenton's gold American Express card. "No limit."

She handed over the card with a flourish. Bankruptcy was too good for Trenton after what he'd done to her. Although now with Darma Walker's money, along with her dead husband's, it would take more than a shopping spree at a sub-par department store to make an impression on him. Or to relieve her own anguish.

The rage that had hovered just beneath the surface since yesterday made her skin prickly and hot. She hated Trenton all the more for giving her what was probably a permanent nerve rash. Unable to restrain herself, she clawed at the itchy skin on her neck with the frenzy of a lapdog. Trenton didn't deserve to live happily ever after, not after destroying her life, the miserable, lying beast. And to think she'd saved herself for him, had been willing to dedicate her life to him, all because Dee had promised that he was the one for her.

"We can get some ointment for your hives."

She stopped mid-scratch at Roxann's voice, feeling like a ten-year-old. "I'll be fine," she said, straightening, but panicked for a few seconds, trying to remember where she was—sometimes her mind took her to another place.

"Angora?"

Racks of clothing, bad carpet, three-way mirrors—oh, yes, the department store. She manufactured a smile for Roxann, then disguised her raw neck with a quick flip of the collar of her new silk blouse. "Next stop—hair and makeup."

Roxann blanched. "Huh?"

Instantly cheered, Angora hooked her arm around her cousin's shoulder. "When we're finished, no one will be able to recognize you." At the sudden serious expression on Roxann's face, she added, "Not that you look bad now."

"No, you're right," Roxann said slowly, smoothing a strand of hair behind her ear. "I could use a new look, at least for a little while."

Ah, so Roxann did want to impress someone—Dr. Carl? She couldn't blame her—the man was outrageously male. She had harbored a crush on him, too, but things hadn't turned out quite the way she'd hoped. Still, it hadn't stopped her from fantasizing about him, wondering what it would be like to lose her virginity to him. Keeping her knees closed for the frat boys she dated had posed no problem because none of their fumbling kisses had piqued her interest.

But her senior year she had found a tree-shaded bench across from the building that housed Dr. Carl's office. From her shielded vantage point, she munched on celery and cauliflower and watched him eat lunch on the steps of his building every day that the weather permitted. His routine never varied. At noon he would emerge with a brown bag, then eat a delicious-looking sandwich, a little bag of chips, and a bottle of juice, all while reading the newspaper. Not that he ever got much reading done, since every girl who walked by stopped to chat, or at least said hello. He would smile politely and nod while chewing, seemingly unaware that he had them all in a lather.

Okay, so she had been in love with him. Every night she would mentally rehearse crossing the street and engaging Dr. Carl in a conversation so witty and entertaining that he would instantly realize they were destined for each other. Except the next day she would sit munching her Dee-directed baggie of raw vegetables, paralyzed in self-loathing while braver and more slender girls were rewarded with his magnificent smile.

Then one day Roxann had happened by Dr. Carl's eating place, with a paper or something for him to look at. Angora had watched, burning with jealousy, as he had actually invited her cousin to sit. His delicious-looking sandwich had gone uneaten while they discussed the paper, heads together. He had talked and gestured with animation, and Roxann had hung on to every word, scribbling notes.

After that, Roxann had appeared with more regularity, producing one paper after another that seemed to need his input. He had tolerated her cousin's company like the good and kind man he was, but surely he knew that Roxann had slept with many men, that she wasn't wholesome like Angora.

She and Roxann hadn't lived together for a couple of years at that point, but still saw each other when she needed help with an assignment, or studying for an exam. Angora never mentioned the lunches she witnessed, or that she knew Roxann was in love with him. She couldn't afford to alienate her cousin—she needed her help to graduate. So as always, she'd kept her mouth shut and pondered why good girls finished last.

Angora ground her perfect teeth. She was soooo tired of being a good girl.

"Earth to Angora."

She blinked Roxann into view. "Um, sorry."

Roxann angled her head. "Are you okay? Maybe we should find a hotel and relax, watch a movie. You had a rough day yesterday."

She wanted to scream, *My life is one long rough day*, but the genuine concern in Roxann's eyes stopped her, and a familiar push-pull of emotions churned in her chest. One minute she wished Roxann had never been born, the next minute she coveted her approval. God, it would be so easy to hate Roxann—seemingly the source of all her problems, yet seemingly the solution to all her problems. Absent for long stretches of time, but there when Angora needed her most. Affection surged in her throat, and the fierce animosity ebbed as quickly as it had flowed. "You're just trying to get out of having your colors done."

"My colors done? What's that?"

Angora rolled her eyes. "Let me take care of everything."

To her surprise, Roxann was like an obedient, if wary, child, submitting to her ministrations at the makeup counter, and later, as Angora helped Steve the hairdresser select shoulder-length extensions to match the blue-black strands of Roxann's stick-straight hair. She did complain that everything was taking too long, and yelped when her eyebrows were tidied with hot wax, but otherwise acquiesced. An hour later when Steve turned Roxann around in the chair, the transformation was truly remarkable, and this time, Angora couldn't stem the flood of envy.

Smooth, dark skin, enormous brown eyes surrounded by long, long lashes. Those patented cheekbones and a straight, slender nose. Naturally red lips, full and curvy, a small, strong chin. Features so clear and elegant, framed by thick short bangs and a fall of dark hair. She might have been a movie star from the fifties.

"You're...gorgeous," Angora murmured.

Roxann laughed sardonically and stood to brush her clothes. "Thanks for all the goodies, Angora, but we'd better hit the road."

Her cousin was oblivious to her looks, always had been. Frustration clogged Angora's throat. If she had been blessed with chiseled features and a willowy figure, she would have been Miss America for sure. She reached up to touch her crown, then remembered she had left it in the van. Roxann probably thought she was vain, but she couldn't help it—the crowns were markers of her few accomplishments. Sometimes at night when demons kept her awake, she would remove one of the sparkling tiaras from the revolving case her mother had had specially built and wear it to bed, propping herself up on pillows so she wouldn't damage the delicate stones. She never failed to dream good dreams with the weight of winning on her head.

"You're welcome," she said as she paid Steve for their treatments, plus makeup kits, skin-care regimes, perfumes, lotions, shampoos, hairspray, blow dryer, diffuser, hot rollers, curling iron, and a half-dozen other beauty necessities with the borrowed AmEx card. Take that, Trenton. "Do you think we'll make it to South Bend by Wednesday?"

Roxann startled her by pulling her away from the counter rather urgently. "Lower your voice," she whispered.

Angora frowned. "Why?"

"Because—" Her cousin seemed flustered. "Because we're traveling alone—we can't be too careful."

Excitement bubbled in her chest. "Does this have anything to do with the detective who's looking for you?"

"No. Let's go."

"Okay," she said in response to Roxann's sharp tone, then followed her back to the counter where they collected their many bags. But Roxann seemed nervous, glancing at her watch, then out the window into the parking lot. She must really be getting worked up about seeing Dr. Carl again. Then an amazing thought struck her—was he the reason Roxann had never married?

She stared at Roxann's preoccupied profile and pursed her mouth—she'd found her cousin's weakness. Wonder of wonders...Roxann was human after all.

CHAPTER TWELVE

ROXANN TRIED TO KEEP the passage between her throat and nose closed to duplicate the speaker's pronunciation on the tape. *"Un, deux, trois, quatre, cinq, six, sept, huit, neuf, dix."*

"You'll be fluent in no time," Angora offered through a mouthful of Fritos. She'd been on a junk food binge since this morning's McDonald's biscuit-and-gravy breakfast. With Frito-greasy fingers, she turned pages of a faded copy of *How to Make Love to a Man* that she'd fished out of Roxann's box of mementos.

Roxann switched off the tape, then rolled her tight shoulders. She hadn't slept very well last night, even though Angora had spared no expense in securing a luxurious room. The fact that she was unaccustomed to a good mattress and down pillows probably contributed to her sleeplessness, and her conscience didn't seem to have an off switch. If she gave up her work with Rescue, wouldn't she be no better than people who murmured about social problems over crab puffs at dinner parties, but thought the solutions lay with politicians or organized religion, or something else that had nothing whatsoever to do with them? And worse, wouldn't she be admitting that her father was right?

Good grief, she was tired of thinking. Maybe that's why Angora didn't mind letting other people make decisions for her—it was less stressful than knowing you had no one to blame but yourself if your life turned out dismally. Roxann bit into her lower lip. Or perhaps her expectations were simply too high. No one was entitled to happiness every waking moment, were they?

"Did you say something?" Angora asked.

Had she spoken aloud? "No."

"I thought you said something. Where are we?"

"A few miles outside Little Rock."

"Arkansas?"

"Right." She was taking a rather winding route toward South Bend under the guise of humoring Angora on her life-list quest. This morning they had stopped at a YMCA so she could give Angora a crash swimming lesson. Considering the fact that Angora was afraid of putting her head under, didn't want to get her hair wet, and refused to hold her breath, the session went well, meaning neither of them drowned. But because of her generous curves, Angora bobbed like a cork; when she finally mastered the dead man's float, Roxann declared her graduated.

In truth, she was driving off the beaten path in the unlikely event that Frank Cape or Detective Capistrano had picked up her trail. From Jackson, Mississippi, she'd veered left, stopping every forty miles so Angora could pee and buy another Coke and candy bar. The scenery was stunning, though. The farther north they drove, the more dramatic the flaming fall foliage, stirring memories of cozy autumns in Indiana. Maintaining a leisurely pace, they would be in Springfield, Missouri, by nightfall, Bloomington, Illinois, by Tuesday night, and South Bend, Indiana, by Wednesday afternoon.

At the moment, however, they were both weary of sitting, and she was light-headed from mimicking the tape. Ticking off some of the items on her life list gave her a tiny sense of accomplishment, but mostly was a diversion from the rearview mirror. Tucked inside a box on the backseat was a leather-bound copy of three Shakespearean plays—a splurge on her budget, but Angora's shopping spree had been contagious, as well as her frivolity, because the one purchase Roxann was most excited about was a long lime-green silk scarf that had spoken to her. Of course now she was feeling guilty—DNA that Angora seemed to have missed out on.

She had to admit her cousin knew how to live large. That kind of spending used to revolt her, but for a few hours yesterday she conceded that while money didn't necessarily guarantee happiness, it certainly afforded a person more coping tools. She still didn't condone spending for the sake of spending, but she was beginning to realize that people who had money weren't necessarily evil.

Dee notwithstanding.

"Roxann, have you ever used a vibrator?"

She blinked.

Angora folded down a page of the naughty book and closed the cover. "You're the only person I can ask these things. Have you?"

"Um, sure."

"So if I were to use one, would that mean I wouldn't be a virgin anymore?"

"I...perhaps medically, but...there's more to losing your virginity than... penetration." This conversation was not happening.

Angora laid her head back on the seat. "My first orgasm was in the laundry room of our dorm."

"I don't think I want to hear this."

"It was a Friday night, and I didn't have a date, so I thought I'd wash a few towels while the laundry room was empty."

Roxann steeled herself for graphic details.

"I climbed up on the washer to sit and read, and suddenly, I started feeling really weird and warm. Then in the middle of the spin cycle, whammo!"

A few seconds passed before her words fully sank in. "You mean..."

Angora nodded. "I still do laundry every Saturday night. The smell of a dryer vent turns me on."

"Um...wow."

"You think I'm nuts."

"No, I think you're...resourceful."

"You and I are in our sexual peak right now, you know."

"Whatever that means."

"If you don't have a boyfriend, what do you do for sex?"

Roxann squirmed. "Let's just say I do my laundry about once a month."

"So is everyone in the world doing laundry?"

"Less risky, I suppose. Physically and emotionally."

"But why are relationships with men so hard?"

"Relationships in general are hard, but throw sex into the pot, and it's a recipe for disaster."

"But women want sex, and men want sex."

"But not at the same time, or for the same reasons."

"So it's all a game."

Roxann shrugged. "Life is a game."

"Don't you believe there's a perfect man out there for you?"

"I'd settle for an imperfect man with a small measure of nobility."

"And will you know him when you find him?"

"I'd like to think so, although I haven't been actively looking."

"But what if he's not looking, either?"

"Huh?"

"If he's not looking, and you're not looking, then how will you find each other?"

"Angora, I'm not losing sleep over a manhunt." There were too many other things to lose sleep over. "When it comes right down to it, you have to be happy with yourself before you can be happy with someone else."

"The reason we're alone is that we're not happy with ourselves?"

Roxann squinted. Did she say that?

Angora reached behind the seat and dug an item out of the box of junk on the floorboard. "Let's consult the Magic 8 Ball." She held the toy reverently and closed her eyes tight. "Will Roxann and I find the person who fulfills us?" She turned over the toy and squealed. "Yes, definitely."

Roxann laughed. "I told you that thing is broken."

"Maybe not—maybe we're just coming up 'Yes, definitelys.' What would be so bad about meeting the person who fulfills us?"

"I...need to focus on the road signs."

Angora pointed to a banner strung across the road ahead of them, swaying in the waning daylight. "Little Rock Fall Festival, October tenth through the twenty-first. Oh, can we stop?"

"Sure. I could stand to stretch my legs a little."

"And I'm starving."

"You have Frito crumbs on your chin."

Several miles down the road, they entered the commercial and residential outskirts of Little Rock.

“There’s a sign for parking up ahead,” Angora said, bouncing. “Oh, look at the crowd—and there’s a carnival going on!”

Tomorrow she was limiting Angora’s sugar intake. Roxann pulled Goldie into the parking lot and backed into the space a parking attendant indicated. When she jumped down from the van, she found herself smiling in spite of the worries nagging the back of her brain. The scent of buttered popcorn floated on the warm night air, and organ music danced on a breeze. Families were chained together by their hands, with children straining in every direction. Roxann could feel the tension draining away. The snug black jeans and silky red tee felt alien, as well as the new hair and makeup, but she was enjoying the “disguise”—it made her feel freer somehow. Freer to have fun. With a jolt she realized she’d forgotten what it was like to have fun.

Corn dogs and beer were first on Angora’s list. Roxann indulged, too, even though she knew she’d probably regret it later. Next they rode the carousel and the Tilt-A-Whirl. Then Angora spotted a flight simulator and talked Roxann into going a round for the sake of the “piloting” item of her life list. Angora was so dizzy afterward she needed to be helped from the ride. Still, she insisted she was going to learn to fly a plane someday.

Roxann couldn’t help but notice that Angora’s confidence grew in relation to their distance from Dee. God only knew what evil things that woman had done to her daughter, and how the trauma would manifest itself. It was good to see her cousin smiling and laughing, playing children’s games and buying silly souvenirs. She fairly glowed. It helped that because of her crown, the locals thought she was some kind of celebrity. When the buxom lady at the cotton-candy booth discovered that Angora was titled, she asked her to help judge the Little Miss pageant that was being held on the festival grounds. Angora was ecstatic. Roxann took advantage of the opportunity to break away and make a few phone calls. They agreed to meet back at the van in an hour.

Roxann first suspected that she was being followed as she passed the Ferris wheel. Call it a hunch, but a set of heavy footsteps behind her were too measured, too purposeful. She stopped to buy a small fountain drink, and the footsteps she’d isolated stopped, too. All her defenses went on alert. She turned quickly and scanned the area over the top of her cup, but saw nothing suspicious. She exhaled in relief—her imagination was getting the better of her.

The fairgrounds were thick with teenagers and the air smoky from firecrackers. Blinking colored lights on the rides cast a fluorescent glow on the faces of onlookers. Thrilling screams from the roller coaster overhead reached a crescendo, then faded as the machine roared past. The funnel-cake booth was doing a brisk business, emitting sticky-sweet aromas. A child's laugh pierced the air, and Roxann couldn't help but smile. When had she turned into a suspicious, cynical woman?

She headed toward a group of picnic tables near the exit where the noise level would be low enough to make phone calls. She wanted to check in with her supervisor, and call her father again. And she'd been thinking that even Dreadful Dee deserved to know that Angora was safe. A couple of young rednecks walked by and whistled at her appreciatively. She didn't react, but at the ridiculous lift of her spirits, realized that she'd never, ever been whistled at. In fact, in college she probably would have belted the guys. Age changed a person's viewfinder.

She selected an empty picnic table, used a napkin to brush off leftover popcorn, and sat down facing the crowd. The winner of the turkey-calling contest was announced, and Billy Conley's mother could pick him up at the Lost and Found tent at her earliest convenience, please. Roxann rummaged in her purse for her cell phone, dreading the call to her father. He would be—

"Alone at last."

Her heart froze at the menacing tone. She lifted her head slowly while moving her hand blindly in her purse in search of the pepper spray. The stranger was tall and wiry with thin blond hair that hung to the shoulders of his camouflage jacket. His face was raw-boned and gaunt, his eyes too close together. Frank Cape was not an attractive man.

"Do I know you?" she asked, stalling.

"No, but I know you," he said, wrapping his bony hand around her forearm like a vise. "Now don't get any ideas about bringing a weapon out of that purse. You tell me what I want to know, missy, and no one has to get hurt."

Her wrist and fingers were already numb from the pressure. “I don’t know what you’re talking about.” Her mind raced for an escape route—the bench seat attached to the table made her feel trapped.

His laugh boomed out, and anyone close to them might have thought they were sharing a friendly chat. “Of course you do—you took Melissa and Renita away from me, and I mean to have them back.”

“I only dropped them off at the airport. I don’t know where they are.”

“Liar.” His grip tightened. “You’d better start talking. I want an address and a phone number.”

“The police are looking for you—they know you broke into my apartment,” she bluffed.

He scoffed. “Your crummy apartment was torn up when I got there. I figured somebody else got fed up with your meddling.”

She swallowed. “Did you leave the message on my computer?”

“Do I look like Bill Gates?” Leaning closer, he revealed sharp eyeteeth. “Where are they?”

“I can’t help you.”

“Yes you can,” he hissed. “Or the people around you will start dropping like flies.”

The blood drained from her face, leaving her lips cold.

A lascivious smile made his eyes even smaller. “Maybe I’ll just take you with me and make you talk.”

“That won’t be necessary,” a calm voice sounded behind him.

Roxann looked up to see Detective Capistrano standing wide-legged, munching a caramel apple. As much as she hated to admit it, she was sort of happy to see the brute.

“Let her go, Cape.”

“Who are you?”

He took another bite. “The man who’s going to shoot you if you don’t let her go.”

Cape let her go. “This ain’t none of your concern.”

“You’re a suspect in a Biloxi armed robbery that put a friend of mine in a coma.” He swallowed and angled his head at Cape. “Everything you do concerns me.”

Cape straightened. "You some kind of cop?"

"Yep. The unpredictable kind." He tossed the apple into a nearby trash can and wiped his hand on his jeans. "Give me a reason to bury you."

The hoodlum threw up his hands casually and produced a charming smile. "I was just leaving."

Capistrano smiled back. "You'll find your piece-of-shit car in the city impound lot."

The man's face darkened. "You had my car towed?"

"Expired tags and missing taillight." Capistrano tsk-tsked. "Safety first."

Cape's mouth tightened, but he remained silent. After he strode past Capistrano, though, he turned and made an air gun out of his thumb and forefinger, aimed it at Roxann, and pulled the trigger in a warning that couldn't be misinterpreted. She shivered and stood up, stumbling back in her haste to get away from the table. Capistrano was there for a steadying arm. She pulled away a little more vehemently than she intended.

"You're welcome," he said dryly.

"Where did you come from?"

"Akens, a little swamp town south of Biloxi."

She sighed. "How did you find me?"

"Driving that eyesore of a death trap is like a beacon in the night."

"But how did you know which direction I was going?"

"Your father said you were going back to Biloxi, but knowing you, I just started driving in the opposite direction."

What had he thought of her father? What had her father thought of him? "You don't know me."

"Then your cousin started racking up charges on a stolen credit card—"

"It isn't stolen."

"It isn't *hers*."

"Her fiancé gave it to her."

"The guy who jilted her at the altar?"

"How do you know about that?"

"Your dad said according to you, the woman his neighbor saw was your cousin. I called your aunt to check your story. She filled in the details."

She just bet she did.

"No offense, but your aunt's a real bitch."

Okay, so he nailed that one. "Who did you think I had with me?"

"Melissa Cape."

"That would be pretty stupid."

He simply shrugged, which irked her beyond words.

"When did you meet up with Cape?" she asked.

"I spotted him at a gas station this morning. I figured he was following you, so I followed him."

"So he spoke to my father, too?"

"Your dad said he hadn't been there."

"But Cape might have threatened him."

He shrugged as if to say it was likely.

She had to sit down again. The thought of Frank Cape bullying her father sent that corn dog spinning in her stomach. Rummaging for her phone gave her a few seconds to blink away quick tears. "I need to call him." She punched the power button, but nothing happened. "Dammit!" And to her mortification, the tears welled again. She gave her eyes a quick swipe.

"Here."

She glanced up and took the tiny phone he extended. "Thanks." After punching in the number, she breathed shallowly while the phone rang. His recorder picked up and the tone sounded. "Dad, it's me. Roxann." She tried to sound cheerful. "I was just checking in to make sure that you're...that everything is okay. I'm fine, and I'll call back soon." She disconnected the call with a heavy heart and handed the phone back.

"He seemed like the kind of man who could take care of himself," Capistrano offered.

"Did he look...healthy?"

His thick eyebrows went up.

"I don't get home very often."

"He looked spry enough to me. We talked about fishing lures over a cup of coffee. He's worried about you."

"He doesn't approve of my lifestyle."

"He thinks you should do something with that diploma of yours he has hanging on the wall."

She grimaced. "I hope he didn't bore you."

"Nope." Capistrano sat down opposite her. "You look different."

Better? Worse? Heat flooded her face, and she tugged on a hank of hair extension. "It's my cousin's doing. I'm her project."

"Where is your cousin?"

Roxann gestured vaguely, then bolted upright. "Cape."

He swung one leg over the bench. "Let's go."

Fear hurried her feet. After stopping three vendors to ask for directions, they finally located the blue-and-white-striped tent where the Little Miss Something or Other pageant was being held. The contest appeared to be near an end, with all the coiffed little girls lined up on a makeshift stage—well, one rebel was lying on her back and spinning around. The seats were filled with overweight women wearing hopeful expressions, and lots of spectators stood around the perimeter. She scanned the judges' table, but Angora wasn't there. One chair was glaringly empty.

"She's not here. Do you see Cape?"

"No. She wouldn't just leave with him, would she?" he whispered.

"I don't think so, unless he tricked her." Not a gargantuan feat.

"You didn't warn her?"

Roxann bristled. "I thought it would be better if she didn't know...anything." Like normal.

He frowned. "What does she look like?"

"Blond, pretty, curvy."

"Hmm."

At his tone, she cut her gaze to him. He'd probably fall head over heels for Angora and all her femaleness.

At the sudden applause, Roxann looked to the stage, where to her surprise, Angora emerged, all smiles and holding a clipboard.

"Is that your cousin?" he asked, staring.

"Yes, that's Angora," she murmured.

"She's pretty, all right."

Roxann bit into her lower lip.

He turned his head slightly. "She looks like you."

Her pulse quickened and she studied his profile, oddly comforted by the sheer immobility of his features. But on the heels of the warm fuzzies came the awareness that immobility was not always a favorable characteristic, and she'd had her fill of domineering men. Besides, she knew little about this particular man. He could have a wife and eight kids. He certainly struck her as the kind of man who would want to replicate himself.

"You don't have to stick around," she said cheerfully, and stuck out her hand. "But thanks for your help with Cape."

He looked at her hand until she dropped it. "Where are you two headed?"

"That's none of your business."

He crossed his arms. "Fair enough. Just tell me where I can find Melissa Cape and you'll never have to see me again."

"I'm supposed to be so grateful for what you did that I spill my guts?"

He shrugged. "Whatever label you want to put on it."

"Gee, and I thought you were just being nice."

"Nobody ever accused me of being a nice guy."

"Goodbye, Detective."

He turned back to the stage. "I think I'll stick around to meet your cousin."

Roxann poked her tongue into her cheek.

Angora, in her element, proceeded to hold the audience captive while she announced Little Miss Photogenic, Little Miss Congeniality, Little Miss Talent, Little Miss Best Hair (the one rolling on the floor), and finally, Little Miss Little Rock Fall Festival. When the crowd began to break up, Roxann walked to the bottom of the stairs that Angora was descending.

"Wasn't that fun?" she squealed, touching her crown.

"Uh, yeah. Listen, something's come up—we need to get going."

Angora's gaze landed somewhere behind Roxann's shoulder and her face went absolutely feline. "Hel-lo."

"Hello," Capistrano said, then elbowed Roxann none too discreetly.

She frowned. "Angora meet, um, Mr. Capistrano. And this is my cousin, Angora Ryder."

Angora purred. "Do you have a first name, Mr. Capistrano?"

He extended his hand, along with a dopey smile. "Joe."

Joe. Roxann pursed her mouth. A nice enough name.

"And it's *Detective* Capistrano."

"Oooh, detective." Then Angora stopped. "Detective? Are we in trouble?"

Roxann just hated to burst the bubble. "Detective Joe says you're using a stolen credit card."

Angora jerked her hand back. "Trenton gave me that credit card."

"Yeah, I know," he said sympathetically. "It's just sour grapes on his part. If you give me the card, I'll try to have this misunderstanding cleared up. Where are you headed?"

"Sou—"

"Angora," she cut in with a warning glare. "Give the detective the card."

Angora found the card and handed it over with a long face. "Your name sounds familiar."

He looked amused. "Your cousin must have been talking about me. We're working on a case together."

Roxann rolled her eyes. "Let's go, Angora."

"What happened? Why are you in such a hurry?"

"A dangerous man is following the two of you," Capistrano said, "because your cousin won't cooperate with the police."

Angora's eyes went round. "Is that true, Roxann?"

She narrowed her eyes at Capistrano. "One person's cooperation is another person's sell-out."

He scowled. "Look, I have to go back to Biloxi tonight. I can't protect you if Cape decides to follow you again. Go back with me and we'll talk about Melissa. I'll let you be involved in contacting her if it makes you feel better."

Roxann hesitated.

"My partner has a wife and two little girls," he added. "Cape deserves to pay for what he did to that family, and for what he did to his own family."

She sighed and nodded slowly. "Okay...you've convinced me."

He straightened. "Well. I'm glad to hear you've come to your senses."

Gesturing for Angora to follow her, she turned in the direction of the exit and began weaving through the crowd.

Angora leaned in close. "So we're not going to Sou—"

"No," Roxann said with a jerk on her arm. "I'm sorry, but we'll have to finish our vacation some other time."

"But what about Dr. Carl?"

"Later, Angora."

Capistrano stayed close at their heels as they tramped through the flattened grass. Fireworks started going off overhead, blue and purple and gold. Another time, she would have slowed to enjoy them. Instead, she just wanted to get on the road as soon as possible. But as they approached the concrete-block building that housed the restrooms, she turned to Capistrano. "Do you mind if we stop here before we hit the road?"

He suddenly looked weary. "Fine. I'll wait here." He turned his back and leaned against a gate, reaching into his shirt to withdraw a crushed pack of cigarettes.

Roxann grabbed Angora's elbow, waited to make sure he was occupied, then steered her around the side of the building and across the back through wet weeds.

"What are you doing?" Angora whispered.

"Be quiet and walk fast. No way I'm going back to Biloxi with that man."

Angora squealed. "Oh, this is so exciting!"

Roxann jogged all the way to the van, then vaulted into the driver's seat and slammed the door. Angora was a few seconds behind her, huffing and puffing.

"It'll take him at least another five minutes to figure out that we're gone," Roxann said, then flipped on the lights and cranked the engine. Like a faithful servant, Goldie turned over.

"Will he come after us?"

"Maybe, maybe not," she said, finding a gear and sending the van lurching forward. "If he has to be in Biloxi tomorrow, he can't spend much time chasing us." She pulled out onto the paved road and nudged the speedometer needle up to the limit. "Angora, I think I should take you back to Baton Rouge."

"No way, this is just starting to get good." She leaned closer. "Who's Frank Cape? And Melissa?"

Roxann hesitated. "I don't want to involve you."

Angora's bottom lip came out. "You don't think I can handle it."

"I don't want to put you in danger."

"You think I'm dumb."

"I don't want to put you in danger."

She teared up. "Just because I'm not as smart as you, Roxann, doesn't mean I'm stupid."

"I don't think you're stupid, Angora." Roxann sighed. "Melissa Cape is a woman I helped to relocate away from her ex-husband, Frank."

The tears evaporated. "And Capistrano wants to send her back?"

"He wants her to testify against her ex, who shot Capistrano's partner and put him in a coma. Meanwhile, Frank Cape is on my ass because he's trying to find her, too."

"To prevent her from testifying."

"Right"

"Wowee. You're the only one who knows where she is?"

"Yes."

"Omigod, this is so much better than my job."

Roxann glanced in the side mirror, perplexed to see no headlights behind her.

Capistrano had given up the chase? "The story gets a little more complicated."

"Okay, but talk slow."

Roxann counted to three. "I left Biloxi because someone broke into my duplex and typed a threat on my computer screen."

"So you weren't planning to come to my wedding all along?"

All roads led back to Angora. "I only received the invitation that day."

"Oh. Was it the freaky Cape guy who broke into your place?"

"I thought so, but just now when he confronted me at the carnival—"

"He was here? Did he hurt you?"

She shook her head. "He was only trying to scare me. Capistrano got there before anything happened."

"So Joe saved your life?"

"I wouldn't go that far."

"He's really dreamy."

"Can I finish?"

"Well, he is."

"*Anyway*, when I accused Cape of breaking into my place, he denied it."

"So he lied."

"No, he truly seemed surprised."

"But who else could have done it?"

"Well, there are other ex-husbands, I suppose, who might have found out where I live, but that would take some doing. Cape is a PI, so he has resources."

"What did the message say?"

Roxann exhaled. "It said, 'I've got your number, you fake.'"

"What does that mean?"

"I honestly don't know."

"It sounds personal."

"I had a problem with a roommate, so she might have come back."

"She?"

"Elise James—she was a grad student at Notre Dame when we were freshmen, but I didn't know her then. Did you?"

Angora squinted. "I...don't believe so."

"The Rescue program paired us up when I moved to Biloxi."

"What kind of problem did you have with her?"

Roxann sighed. "It's personal."

"Ooh, tell me."

"Elise...made a pass at me."

The whites of Angora's eyes shone clear in the semi-darkness of the cab. "She's a lesbian?"

"Actually, I think she might be experimenting."

"And you weren't interested in experimenting?"

"No, Angora, I wasn't."

"Don't get so testy. Can you find out if this woman broke into your place?"

"I don't know how to contact her. Elise left the program and they don't know where she is."

"Are there any other suspects?"

She quirked a brow—Angora was getting into this. "An old boyfriend from Birmingham crossed my mind. He and I parted on bad terms several months ago."

"Was he violent?"

"No, but he had an attitude. And a drinking problem, so anything's possible."

"You have bad taste in men."

Roxann checked the side mirror—no Capistrano. "We have bad taste in men."

"Except for Dr. Carl."

Roxann had to admit that he seemed to be pulling her toward South Bend, but part of that, she acknowledged, was wanting to escape her current problems. "Capistrano had Frank Cape's car impounded, and he won't be able to pick it up until morning. So to get a jump on him, we'll have to drive all night."

"Okay."

"And no more credit cards—the charges are too easy to trace. Whatever cash you need, get it from an ATM while we're here."

Angora sighed. "Without Trenton's card, I don't have any money."

"What about your own bank account?"

"Overdrawn—there were too many wedding expenses."

Roxann slowed the van. "Angora, I have a little money, but we're going to have to be very frugal for the rest of the trip." An alien notion to her cousin.

But Angora held her left hand out in front of her. Her enormous engagement ring caught the light. "No we won't."

CHAPTER THIRTEEN

"WELCOME HOME, my dear."

Roxann walked into Dr. Nell Oney's sweatered embrace, inhaling the woman's signature vanilla scent, grateful beyond words that she hadn't changed over the years. But when she felt the woman's frail bones through the heavy clothing, she realized how much her mentor had aged—more gray in her soft brown hair, more lines around her gentle mouth. Still, she remained an attractive woman, aging gracefully.

"You look wonderful," Dr. Oney said, squeezing her hands.

"So do you," she said, applying light pressure to the woman's cold hands. Dr. Oney was a bit past fifty, Roxann calculated. And no family, save the cats she took in. She had once told Roxann that the people at Rescue were her family. With a start, Roxann acknowledged that she was looking at herself in twenty years. And while living in a patio home just off campus wearing hand-knit sweaters covered with cat hair held a certain literary appeal, it seemed fantastically lonely.

"Meet Angora Ryder, my cousin. We graduated in the same class. Angora, I'm sure you remember Dr. Nell Oney."

"It's nice to see you," the professor said, shaking Angora's hand. Then she squinted and looked back and forth. "You two do bear a striking resemblance—except for the coloring, of course."

"And the crown," Roxann added dryly.

"Dr. Oney, I hope you don't mind me tagging along," Angora said. "Roxann rescued me from a little scrape."

"I don't mind," she said. "And call me 'Nell.' Let me show you girls where you can put your things. The guest room has twin beds."

They traipsed after her, dodging four—no, five—cats. Angora sneezed a thousand times before they set their things down on outdated red comforters in the tiny guest room. The walls were lined with shelves of worn paperbacks—proof positive, Roxann conceded, of those long, lonely years stretching ahead of her. In fact, didn't she immediately upon relocating to a new city acquire a library card?

"I have two classes to teach this afternoon, so I'd better be off," Nell said from the doorway. "Do you need anything before I go?"

Roxann wanted to ask about Carl, but bit her tongue and shook her head. "We can't thank you enough."

"No need, really. But just so that I know, this Cape fellow who's been following you, what does he look like?"

"Tall, thin, rednecky. He was wearing camouflage when he caught up with me in Little Rock."

"Do you have a weapon?"

"Pepper spray. But hopefully he's given up by now."

Nell nodded. "Still, you can't be too careful. Do you two have plans tonight?"

She exchanged looks with Angora, and her cheeks grew warm. "Well, uh—"

"We're going to the bachelor auction," Angora cut in. "Want to come?"

Nell laughed and shrugged. "I hadn't thought about it, but maybe I will. Just to watch."

They made plans to meet back at the house, then Nell left.

"Did she seem old to you?" Angora asked.

"We seem old to me."

"I remember her looking more, I don't know—more liberated. Cool. Braless."

"People change, buy underwear." She rummaged in her purse, then frowned. "Have you seen my life list?"

Angora wasn't paying attention. "Do you think she's happy?"

"I suppose so. Have you seen my list?"

"She doesn't even drive a car—don't you think that's kind of backward?"

"She marches to the beat of a different drum. Angora, have you seen my list?"

"No. When did you have it last?"

"I can't remember—maybe when we were in Springfield?" Where Angora had blown the afternoon with a travel agent planning the round-the-world cruise on her life list as if she were launching next week. Sometimes the woman seemed to be on another plane of reality. "Or Bloomington?" Where they'd forgone the tattoo artist's needle in favor of ornate henna tattoos around their ankles so Angora could strike another item from her list.

"I thought you didn't care about that silly old list," Angora teased.

"I...don't." But there was something bothersome about misplacing a list that had outstanding items on it. Since you couldn't possibly remember everything on it, you were, of course, relieved of the obligation. Still, it seemed like... cheating.

I'VE GOT YOUR NUMBER, YOU FAKE.

She shivered. Knowing that someone was looking over your shoulder had a way of making you evaluate your life, your decisions. Had she made good ones? Bad ones? She checked her watch—it was 6 p.m. in London.

"Come on," Angora said. "Let's unpack later—I want to cruise campus."

"I don't think people use that phrase anymore."

Angora grabbed her arm and tugged her toward the door. "You look a little peaked—are you more worried about that Cape guy than you're letting on?"

She didn't answer, because in truth, she was more worried about seeing Carl again—how petty was that? A dangerous criminal wanted to extract information out of her, and she was concerned about how her old flame would react to seeing her again. What if he didn't recognize her?

"Don't worry—that cute hunky detective probably scared the crap out of Cape."

At the mention of Capistrano, she scowled. He wasn't cute, he was...*noticeable*. And he wasn't hunky, he was...*bulky*. But he did have an uncanny sense of timing. And maybe he had scared Cape—for now. But Frank Cape would be back. Or he'd just wait until she returned to Biloxi.

Then she pursed her mouth—perhaps she wouldn't return to Biloxi. It wasn't as if she had a gaggle of friends waiting for her, or even a job, for that matter. In fact, she'd bet that no one even noticed she was gone. Once Capistrano's partner recovered, she'd certainly drop off his radar.

"I'd like to check my voice recorder first," she said, padding to the living room. She found a base unit for a cordless phone on a glass table, but no handset there, or in the tidy, but cramped blue kitchen. Nell's bedroom and office were across the hall, but Roxann didn't want to pry behind the closed door, opting to wait until her cell phone recharged. The highly processed foods she'd been sharing with Angora had made her thirsty, though, so she peeked into a kitchen cabinet in search of a water glass. Instead, she stumbled onto a stash of medical supplies. A few prescription bottles rolled out onto the counter. Antibiotics. Antivirals. She recalled suddenly that Nell was a bit of a hypochondriac—another manifestation of loneliness.

From out of nowhere, a cough emerged from her throat, and her future hit her like a ton of bricks. She had to get out of there. "Let's go, Angora."

They walked the short distance to the campus entrance. The exercise felt good to her unused muscles, but her new boots still weren't broken in. Considering her new duds and hairstyle, she thought she'd feel young again when they reached the university grounds. Instead she felt exposed as a middle-aged has-been, and downright light-headed from the deluge of forgotten impressions: the pleasing mix of period architecture, the throngs of majestic trees, and the wind barreling down the streets as if propelled by the energy of the young bodies. Although the chance that she'd see Carl on the sidewalk was remote, her gaze darted over each face, poised to see him at every turn. Perhaps she should have called him...

"It looks smaller than I remember," Angora offered, pivoting her head.

Roxann agreed. Even the students seemed smaller, compact and waiflike. And so impossibly young. It was a warm Wednesday afternoon, and the little people streamed in all directions over sidewalks and grassy banks with purpose and synchronization. They looked so happy and so unburdened. Had she ever been that happy?

"Let's go this way," Angora said, pointing to a sidewalk that would take them up and away from the direction Roxann wanted to take—through the oldest part of campus, and coincidentally, past the building where Carl's office was still housed, according to the address in the alumni newsletter.

"Okay," she agreed, chastising herself. She'd see him in due time.

As they walked, Angora pointed to a nondescript redbrick building on the crest of a wooded hill. "There's our old dorm."

"Uh-huh. Probably coed now."

"You think? Wow, I bet no one leaves here a virgin anymore."

Roxann smiled her agreement. Students surged by them, laughing and poking each other, lopsided from the bulging backpacks on their shoulders. Earbuds bounded. Despite the brisk temperature, lots of skin was on display—navels, thighs, and oh, the cleavage. And from all the touching that was going on, hormones did indeed appear to be running amuck. A tall athletic guy winked at Angora and turned around to walk backward as he perused her up and down.

"It's the crown," Angora insisted as she gave him a little finger-wave. "This is going to be fun."

"He thinks you're a teacher."

But from the glow on Angora's face, she definitely had plans for her virginity to die a quick death. Roxann bit her lower lip—she hoped the event would be all her cousin thought it would be. And that the lucky guy was of legal age.

Yellow banners on every lamppost announced Homecoming week and shouted, "Be there!" in frantic letters.

She was there, but feeling a little out of sorts. Didn't someone say you could never go home? South Bend was as close to home as she'd ever felt. To realize that her four years here had been replaced by thousands of other footprints and term papers and first loves made her feel very insignificant. They walked higher and higher, where the foot traffic thinned and the fall leaves thickened.

"Will your sorority be doing something special for Homecoming?" she asked Angora.

She shrugged. "I suppose."

"You don't keep up with your sisters?"

Angora's face went odd, and she looked off in the distance. "I quit the DZs."

"I didn't know that. Why?"

She shrugged again. "Some of the girls started being mean to me, calling me 'Church' because I wouldn't sleep with their creepy brothers. Tammy Paulen—" She stopped walking.

Roxann swung her head around. "What about Tammy Paulen?"

Angora seemed dazed.

"Angora, what about Tammy Paulen?"

"She...was the worst."

She wet her lips and spoke carefully. "I thought you said you didn't know Tammy very well."

"I didn't. I don't even think she knew my name."

"But she teased you?"

Angora nodded. "Her brother heard I was a virgin, and she...wanted to give me to him for his birthday."

Roxann's stomach convulsed. "That's sick."

"Well, she got hers, didn't she?"

A chill went through Roxann that had nothing to do with the breeze. "Angora—"

"Hey, is that who I think it is?" Angora pointed like a bird dog across the street.

Roxann followed her finger, and her heart vaulted. She hadn't realized it, but the path led them high above and opposite Carl's office building, leveling off in front of the humanities building for a splendid view through an opening in the trees the distance of a football field. Without knowing, Angora had led them to a perfect vantage point.

It was Carl, all right. Sitting on the steps of the building, munching a sandwich and reading a book in the sunshine. Still broad-shouldered and lean, he was wearing a soccer coaching jacket over chinos, T-shirt, and V-neck sweater. The sunlight picked up the silver in his hair, and the glare from his small wire-framed glasses. Years fell away, and Roxann's tongue was glued to the roof of her mouth. No man had affected her the way Carl had, not before and not since.

"I was thinking barbecue for lunch," Angora said, nodding to a concession stand below them on the street mere paces from where Carl sat.

"Sounds good," she murmured.

Concrete steps took them down to street level. Thank goodness there was a handrail for stability—the heeled boots were making her legs wobbly. Scenes about how she might approach him, and what he might say flashed through her mind, but suddenly they were on the sidewalk across the two-lane street and he looked at her. He stopped chewing and wiped his mouth, then squinted. She smiled, and when he set aside his book and lunch and stood, her heart lifted. She waved over passing cars. He removed his glasses, then jaywalked through slow-moving cars toward them.

"Roxann?" he said, jogging up to her. "Roxann, is that you?"

He was more handsome than ever, pale, pale blue eyes surrounded by black lashes. His eyebrows were jet black, thrown into relief against the silvery shock of hair that fell over his wide forehead. His chiseled nose and wide forehead were the same, along with his strong chin. And his smile—how could she have forgotten the gift of his incredible smile? It lit his entire face, and animated his body. That smile was the energy bank that he and people around him drew upon.

The sights and sounds around them receded. "Yes, Carl, it's me."

CHAPTER FOURTEEN

"I HOPE YOUR COUSIN doesn't mind that I stole you away," Carl said, holding open the door to his office.

"She said there were a few places on campus she wanted to visit," Roxann said, passing under his arm. She was assailed by that big-person-in-a-small-person-place feeling again. As if all the things around her were props, and Carl was the leading man on stage. Very surreal.

He stepped in, closed the door, and hung their coats on a hook on the back. When he turned, they simply stood and smiled at each other for a long moment, just as a script might call for. He was divine—longish silvery hair, flattering glasses, chiseled features, sparkling blue eyes, clean-shaven jaw. *Action.*

"You haven't changed," he murmured. "Still so beautiful."

She blushed. "I have changed, but thank you."

"God, I've missed you." He clasped her shoulders. "Did you get my message about the award? Are you married? How long are you staying?"

She laughed, and he looked sheepish.

"Where are my manners? Please sit down. Would you like some coffee or tea?"

"No, thank you." She sat in the cane-bottomed chair he proffered, comforted by the clichéd clutter of books and papers in the crowded office. How many times had they worked here, shoulder to shoulder, knee to knee? "Yes, I received your message about the award, and while I'm flattered, I'll pass. That's why I didn't call you back."

"I understand."

"And no, I'm not married."

He smiled. "I never married, either."

She was certain her pleasure showed all over her face. "And I'm not sure how long we'll be here. We're staying at Dr. Oney's."

"Oh. I was hoping..." Then he shook his head. "Never mind. I guess that means you're still working with the women's advocacy program that Nell coordinated?"

She nodded. "Full-time. More or less."

He steepled his hands and struck a solemn pose. "I'm so proud of what you've done with your life—the youth of today just don't seem as interested in social responsibility."

She hooked her hands around her knee, compelled to move past polite platitudes. "I wish I could say I entered the program with pure intentions, but looking back, I think I was only killing time until I heard from you."

He did have the good grace to squirm before offering up a remorseful noise from his throat. "The board's inquiry came at an unfortunate time."

She nodded slowly. "I wonder how they knew about us."

He shrugged. "Someone must have told them, although it didn't seem important at the time to ask who—the damage was done. I assumed you had shared our relationship with another student."

Roxann bristled. "I didn't."

He didn't believe her, she could tell. "Well, it's neither here nor there."

An awkward silence fell, which Roxann stubbornly refused to break. She waited, for what she wasn't sure—perhaps a bended-knee apology for not having defended their nonsexual relationship?

"So...you're happy?" he inquired.

She nodded. "I haven't regretted the path my life has taken."

"I'm glad."

Roxann surveyed the numerous awards on his wall, including a shelf of soccer trophies. It struck her as a bit juvenile for anyone other than a ten-year-old or a professional athlete to display his trophies, but she wondered how much of her resentment came from the glaring proof that his life had gone on, seemingly un-fazed, after she left. "I see you've been successful."

He smiled. “Thank you.”

They spoke at the same time.

“I saw—”

“—your photo—”

“—in the alumni—”

“—newsletter.”

They both laughed.

“You’ve been on my mind ever since,” he said. “I kept wondering where you were, what you were doing, how your life had turned out. When your name came up for the award, it gave me a chance to look you up.”

“Who nominated me?”

His grin was sheepish. “I did. And Nell agreed wholeheartedly.”

“So why didn’t you look me up before?”

He gestured vaguely, seeming flustered. “I didn’t think you’d want to hear from me.”

“I didn’t, for a while.”

“And now?”

Good question. She was still drawn to him, no doubt, like a crippled moth to a flame. But could she ever forgive him for the furrow he’d plowed through her heart? “I’m not a naive coed anymore, Carl.” Her voice sounded stronger than she felt—at least the coed part was true.

He left his chair to stand in front of her. “I can see that.” He reached for her hands and pulled her up against him. His body was lean and firm, proof that he still followed a strict vegetarian diet and exercise regime. She remembered his penchant for nice cologne as she inhaled a complex aroma. He held her loosely and lowered his mouth to hers for a gentle, exploratory kiss.

Very...nice. Had his kisses always been so sweet? He really needed to change that flickering light bulb overhead. And when was the last time the crown moldings had been dusted?

A rap on the door sent them flying apart—that part came back to her pretty easily. Along with the guilty flush.

A beaming young redhead stood with her hand on the doorknob. "Dr. Seger—oh, I'm sorry." Her smile vanished, which did little to diminish her beauty. "I didn't realize you had a...visitor."

"Kelly," he boomed with a little laugh. "Do you have those papers you need for me to sign?"

"Yes," she said, staring at Roxann. "But I can bring them back later."

"I think that would be best," he said. "I'll see you in class."

"Okay. Bye."

When the door closed, he turned an apologetic smile in her direction. "I should know better than to leave the door unlocked—students just barge in whenever they please."

Roxann pressed her just-kissed lips together, thinking that any woman in Carl's life would have to learn to share him with the student body—professors were practically public domain. "Dr. Oney said you weren't teaching as many classes as you used to."

"That's right—although I'm doing more counseling and advising."

One-on-one with those lovely student bodies. Immediately she felt contrite—Carl couldn't help it if the female students were infatuated with him. And she certainly couldn't blame the girls—that would be the pot calling the kettle black. "Well, I'd better let you get back to work," she said, suddenly anxious to escape and do some heavy thinking.

"When can I see you again?"

She smiled as she slipped into her coat. "I hear you're on the auction block tonight."

His face reddened. "I don't know how I got talked into that."

"Maybe I'll come and drum up your bids."

"That would make the evening tolerable."

"Except I don't have much cash," she warned with a laugh.

He pulled her into a loose hug. "You don't have to pay me to spend time with you. Let's have a romantic dinner tomorrow night at my place."

She hesitated, but only for effect. "Do you still live at the same address?"

He nodded. "Do you remember how to get there?"

"I think so." Although she'd only been there a couple of times for student cookouts—never alone with Carl. Too tempting.

"Meanwhile—" He kissed her lightly. "I'll see you tonight?"

"Yes," she said, feeling better. When she left the building, her step was lighter. The whole heebie-jeebie thing was just because she was accustomed to her association with Carl being furtive, clandestine. Almost delicate. The fact that they didn't have carnal knowledge of each other had made their relationship seem like the stuff that classic novels were made of—a bond that transcended a physical union. This *freedom* would take some getting used to.

"Roxann?"

She turned in the direction of the shout and balked at the woman jogging across the lawn, dodging students. "*Elise.*" Since Elise had been a track star, she quelled the urge to make a run for it.

Her former roommate came to a bouncing stop in front of her, copper curls springing wildly about her elfin face. She wore spandex shorts and a sports bra with sweat stains. "I thought that was you. I didn't know you were coming up for Homecoming."

"It...was a last-minute decision. I'm staying with Dr. Oney for a few days." The woman's eyes were glassy, and her mouth loose—she was on something, probably one of those "performance enhancers" she bought from a guy named Sid who buzzed the Biloxi Y in a Firebird. "Elise, you dropped off the face of the earth—Tom is going crazy wondering where you are."

Elise started cracking her knuckles one at a time—a nervous habit that had always driven Roxann nuts. The woman's hands were enormous. "I just couldn't take it anymore, Roxann. Dealing with all those people, all those problems. I know I should call Tom. I will. I really will." Her gaze darted all around, and she was still cracking.

"Where are you living?" Roxann asked.

"In Biloxi, with a friend I met over the Internet."

Surprise, surprise. "How long have you been here in South Bend?"

"Since Saturday. I ran a marathon to raise money for the new counseling center." Now she was cracking her neck—repeatedly.

"Elise, someone broke into the duplex Friday. Do you know anything about it?"

"No. No, I don't." But without eye contact, she couldn't tell if the woman was being truthful. "Roxann, I'm sorry about the way I handled...things."

"Neither one of us handled the situation well," Roxann said carefully.

Elise shifted from foot to foot, bouncing on the toes of her running shoes. "I realized that the reason I've been so unhappy all these years is because of a relationship I had in college that I never quite got over."

Get in line.

"But I'm working through things," she said, nodding with shaky confidence. Suddenly she laughed, a wild, artificial noise. "Too bad that counseling center wasn't here ten years ago." She started to shiver, and rubbed her hands up and down her arms.

Roxann slipped off her jacket and hung it over the woman's shoulders. "Elise, you don't look well—let's walk down to the clinic."

"No!" She yanked off the coat. "I'm f-fine, I just need to finish my run." She jogged away a few paces, then turned around as if she suddenly remembered Roxann was still standing there. "I hope we can be friends someday," she shouted. Then she jogged away, and not in a straight line.

She watched Elise until she was out of sight to make sure she didn't run out into the street, or collapse. Another lost soul, with an affinity for self-destruction. Or just plain destruction?

Roxann went in search of a water fountain, and spotted Angora lounging on a bench, sharing her potato chips with the pigeons. She'd been crying. "How was it?" she mumbled.

"How was what?"

"Dr. Seger. Did you do it on his desk?"

"Are you insane? Of course we didn't!"

Angora tossed the foil bag into a nearby garbage can and licked her fingers. "The way you were fawning all over him, I wouldn't have been surprised."

Roxann frowned. "That's not true, and that's not fair. What's wrong with you?"

Angora leaned forward, resting her elbows on her knees, and stared at the ground. "What's wrong with me? I'm supposed to be on my honeymoon right now."

Roxann's heart squeezed for her and she sat down. "You'll love Chicago. And a year from now you won't even remember Trenton's name."

"I can't go to Chicago," Angora sobbed. "I'm not qualified to work for that art agency. I wouldn't last a week."

"They wouldn't have offered you the job if you weren't qualified."

"I only got the job because I graduated from Notre Dame."

"I don't think you give yourself enough credit."

She wiped her cheeks. "No. Mother is right—Trenton was my best chance for a good life, and I let him get away."

"Well, I hate to tell you this, but I think he sort of cut bait all on his own."

"I might as well join a convent."

"They don't have laundry rooms in convents."

Angora finally cracked a tiny smile. "I wish I were you."

Roxann sighed. "I wish you were me, too. But we're sort of stuck with ourselves, aren't we?" Then she stood and jerked her thumb over her shoulder. "If you're ready to go, I need to rinse my tie-dyed shirt to wear to the auction tonight."

Angora sprang up and began walking back the way they'd come. "You are *not* wearing that shirt tonight."

Roxann smiled into her hand. "Wait up."

CHAPTER FIFTEEN

ANGORA SWALLOWED a half-glass of wine in one drink. Intermission. Six bachelors down, and not one worthy of her virginity. Not one held a candle to Dr. Carl Seger. She cast a sideways glance at Roxann and tightened the grip on her glass—why did all things come so easily for her cousin? *She* had been the one who loved Dr. Carl from a distance for the better part of her time at the university. *She* had been the one who had memorized his features and mannerisms while watching him eat lunch every day. *She* had been the one to sit through his Intro to Theology class for four semesters, convinced he would one day notice her.

And he had, at long last. Her final semester, April twenty-first. Third period. She'd "left" a notebook at her desk, then waited until the room emptied of students before going back inside. Dr. Carl had been erasing the chalkboard in long, powerful strokes and hadn't heard her at first. Until she "dropped" the notebook. Then he'd turned and smiled, offering a hello.

"I forgot my notebook," she'd said, holding it up.

"Are you in my class?" he'd asked.

"Yes."

"That's why you look so familiar."

"Yes." She'd waited while he finished the board, then descended from the dais carrying his own books. He seemed surprised that she was still standing there, but now that she had his attention, she wasn't about to budge.

"Four times."

"Pardon me?"

"I've taken this class four times."

His eyebrows had gone up, then his gaze had traveled to her snug sweater. "You must like theology."

"Not really." His gaze on her had made her feel bold, womanly. Just thinking about it now sent a heaviness to her midsection.

He'd checked his watch. "What's your name?"

"Angora Ryder."

"Well, Angora Ryder, where is your next class?"

"I don't have one."

He had looked her up and down again, then pursed his mouth. "I was just going back to straighten up my office. I could use a hand."

She had smiled and followed him to his office, where he'd locked the frosted-glass door.

"Students are always popping in," he'd explained. "Which is why I can never get my files in order."

"Where should I start?" she'd asked, fairly trembling at the sexual charge in the air.

He'd sat down in his office chair and pulled her to his lap for a long, hard kiss that had steamed up his glasses. When he pulled back to take them off, he'd looked at her. "Is this what you wanted?"

She had nodded, too far gone now.

His eyes were hooded as he'd fumbled with her sweater, pulling it up along with her bra to free her breasts. He had been all lips and teeth, making little wanting noises, and she'd felt flush with power. Then he was pushing her head down, down to his fly, which had somehow come undone. She didn't have time to think about the techniques Roxann had taught her on the tube of toothpaste—it all happened too quickly. One minute she was on the verge of suffocating while he gasped and moved her head up and down on him, and the next minute she was gagging. He had gone so limp and so quiet, she was afraid he'd had a heart attack. But when she'd spit out the offending goo, and it landed on his expensive shoe, he had recovered rather quickly.

"You'll get your passing grade," he'd said brusquely, then stood and helped her straighten her clothes.

Shocked, she realized he thought she'd taken his class four times because she was too dumb to pass it, not because she wanted to be near him. She'd opened her mouth to explain, but he'd shushed her.

"This must be our little secret, yours and mine, or you could get into a lot of trouble." Like a sheep, she'd nodded. Then he'd opened the office door, given her a little shove through it, and closed it behind her. That night in her bed she'd suddenly remembered one of the things he'd murmured during the deed.

"Roxann."

He'd noticed the resemblance, and although he had no idea they were related, he'd been thinking about Roxann the entire time. After that, Carl had ignored her completely. But the real slap in the face had been the C she'd received in the class.

Angora blinked and drained the glass of sour chardonnay. She'd given the man a blowjob in his office, and he hadn't even recognized her today. He'd only had eyes for Roxann, and if her cousin was telling the truth, they'd never even fooled around. Once again, the spoils went to Roxann.

She returned to the bar for another drink. While she stood in line, the audience suddenly burst into applause. She turned to see Dr. Carl Seger himself at the microphone, waving for quiet. The man was splendid.

"There is a person in the room," he said, "whose name came up for the Distinguished Alumni award for dedicating her life to helping others. But her volunteer work is of such a confidential nature, the board decided to forgo the honor lest the nomination attract publicity that would be detrimental to the programs she serves."

He sought Roxann in the audience, and Angora knew what was coming next.

"But to our great delight, the nominee in question found her way back to South Bend this week. Without further ado, the board would like to recognize Roxann Beadleman for a decade of selfless work with abused women. Please come forward, Roxann, and accept this token of our admiration for your many good deeds. You truly embody the spirit of an Alumni Homecoming Queen."

Angora couldn't believe her ears. She watched as Dr. Carl lifted a tiara from a wooden box—a large, magnificent crown with dangling crystals and a point in the front. It made the one she was wearing look like a toy. She drank deeply.

She had to hand it to her cousin, though—she knew how to work the crowd. Roxann protested until the audience of a thousand or so were whipped into a frenzy. By the time she got on stage, they were riveted to every word. Worse, she looked great, passing over the short red dress that Angora had picked out for her in favor of a plain long black skirt, black tank, and a long lime-green scarf around her neck. A perfect foil for the crown, which Dr. Carl set on her head like an adoring king.

"Thank you," Roxann said, holding the crown with one hand.

It was probably heavy, Angora thought miserably. Crowns were supposed to be of a weight symbolic to the responsibility of the title. All of hers were about as heavy as a potato.

"I'm stunned and honored," Roxann said. "And I don't deserve this recognition..."

Angora smirked into her glass and watched her cousin wrap the entire room around her little finger. Good, sweet, honest Roxann who had dedicated her life to others—not because it made her feel good, but because it made her feel superior. Yep, that was why. Dee had been right about Roxann all along. Everyone had a price, and she'd found Roxann's when they were eighteen. Wonder what the audience would think if she jumped up on stage and made that little revelation? And while she was up there, she'd announce that Dr. Carl had a botched circumcision.

But she couldn't very well do either without incriminating herself. And she needed that job in Chicago now more than ever. It was her ticket out of Deeville. Why the hell had she come back? Angora took another drink and tried to focus on Roxann's speech.

."..and I'm humbled by your recognition."

The audience burst into applause and, to add insult to Angora's injury, gave Roxann a standing ovation. She hadn't even gotten a standing ovation when she hit the high end note in "When Whoever's in New England's Through With You" at the Louisiana state fair karaoke competition. She watched as Roxann made her way back to her seat next to Dr. Oney. When Roxann scanned the room, probably looking for her, Angora stepped behind the bartender. She needed time to conjure up congratulations for her cousin, the fake.

The lights dimmed, and the auction resumed. Another dud presented himself and strutted around the stage—where did they find these guys? Bad haircut, and too-short pants. She continued to drink, despite the fact that she could feel herself being pulled into a funk.

Then Dr. Carl appeared on stage again, this time as the prize. She swished the wine in her mouth like Listerine, and swallowed noisily. Why not? For as long as she could remember, she'd wanted something of Roxann's—anything of Roxann's. Dr. Carl would do nicely. Besides...the man owed her big-time for that humiliating encounter in his office ten years ago. Even if the cad didn't remember it.

"Do I hear one hundred?" the auctioneer asked. A hand went up near the stage.

"One hundred from the lady in the yellow. Do I hear one fifty?"

Roxann raised her hand tentatively.

"One hundred fifty from the queen! Do I hear one seventy-five?"

The lady in yellow raised her hand.

"One seventy-five! Do I hear two hundred?"

"Two thousand," Angora said loudly.

A stunned silence ensued, then all eyes swung to her. The attorney had garnered the top bid of the night at eight hundred, from a bridge foursome who looked as if they needed to have their wills done, pronto.

"Did you say two *thousand*?" the auctioneer asked, arcing his arm in her direction. Dr. Carl looked smug.

"Yes," she said, stepping forward carefully because the carpet was moving. "Two thousand dollars." It was nearly all she had left from hocking the ring, but moments like these only came around once in a lifetime.

"Two thousand from the lady in the back! Do I hear twenty-one hundred?"

The crowd tittered.

"Sold to the lady for two thousand dollars!"

This time the applause was for her as she walked forward to claim her prize and say her name. She managed a little wave in Roxann's direction, who returned a watery smile, but Angora directed all her attention to Dr. Carl, who escorted her up the stairs and off the side of the stage.

"Aren't you Roxann's cousin?" he asked.

"Uh-huh."

"I'm sorry, I don't remember your name."

"Angora. Angora Ryder."

"Right." He smiled, a glorious display that stole her breath. "Did you buy me as a date for Roxann?"

She frowned. "No. I bought you as a date for myself."

He looked her up and down, lingering on her breasts and legs, highlighted nicely in the blue Diane Von Furstenberg dress. "Did you go to school here?"

"Yeth." Her tongue felt thick.

"Did I ever have you?"

"Once, but it wasn't very memorable."

His eyebrows went up. "Have you been drinking?"

"Absolutely."

He laughed. "Well, a bite to eat will sober you up. I thought we'd have dinner, then go dancing."

"Thounds nithe."

"Should we say goodbye to Roxann?"

"Nope."

He looked disappointed, but shrugged. "Okay, then off we go. Two thousand dollars is a lot of money. I hope you don't regret this in the morning, um—"

"Angora."

"Right. Angora."

She tucked her hand under his arm and melted into his shoulder. "I won't."

CHAPTER SIXTEEN

ROXANN TRIED TO KEEP a smile on her face for the rest of the auction, and eagerly accepted Nell's invitation to dinner afterward, although she had to admit she was hoping she'd see Carl, if for only a few minutes. And Angora's behavior was puzzling, to say the least. If she didn't know better, she'd think her cousin was planning to follow through on her joking comment about losing her virginity to Carl.

"My treat," Nell insisted as they were seated in a booth at a restaurant called Utopia a few blocks away. "For the Alumni Homecoming Queen."

She blushed and smiled down at the box holding the crown they'd presented to her. "That was incredibly embarrassing, considering..."

"Considering?"

She pressed her lips together, then sighed. "Considering I've been thinking about giving my notice to the organization."

Nell's smile faded. "I see."

"Are you disappointed?"

Nell shook her head. "This is your decision, Roxann. May I ask why?"

She sipped from her water glass and shrugged slowly. "I'm tired of the schedule. Ready for a change."

Her mentor arched an eyebrow. "Ready to settle down?"

Another sip. "Maybe. Someday."

"Ah, your biological clock is ticking."

Items for her life list flashed before her eyes. *Have a daughter. Be a good mother.* "I still haven't decided about the mothering gig."

"But you'd like to get married."

"Maybe. Someday."

She lifted her glass and smiled over the top. "Do you have someone in mind?"

"No."

"I wondered if you were still carrying a torch for Carl after all these years. You two parted on such a bittersweet note."

"I'd be lying if I said I hadn't thought of him often over the years."

"I could tell tonight that he was glad to see you."

"He seemed surprised when I saw him today. You didn't tell him I was coming?" '

She shook her head. "Carl's path and mine rarely cross these days. He's so involved with the administration and with the church, he does very little teaching."

"That's what he said." Roxann toyed with her napkin. "He also said that he's never married all these years."

"No." Nell laughed. "Why is it that men who don't marry are even more intriguing, while women who don't marry are simply old maids?"

"I don't think of you as an old maid."

The professor shrugged. "I don't mind, really. But it isn't nearly as fulfilling as the feminists made it sound thirty years ago."

"You have your career."

"Yes, I do. But my career can't keep me warm at night, can it?"

Roxann blinked. She'd always thought of Nell as an asexual person, uninterested in base pastimes like romantic love.

"Oh, yes, I'm a woman." Nell laughed, but her laugh turned into a cough, which grew in severity until people around them stared. "I'm sorry." She gasped into a handkerchief.

"You're ill. We should go."

She shook her head and drank from her glass. "I'm fine. Just a cold from the change of weather." But her hand trembled violently.

The waiter arrived with flat bread and hummus. They ordered soup and salads. Nell still looked a tad blue, and Roxann wondered if one of the woman's imagined ailments had truly materialized. She was trying to think of a diplomatic way to inquire when Nell spoke.

"Roxann, how well do you know Angora?"

Roxann frowned. "She's my cousin."

"Yes, but how well do you know her? Is she always so unpredictable?"

She splayed her hands. "If you're talking about her behavior at the auction tonight, I think she was feeling a little upstaged by the award they gave me." She smiled. "If you hadn't noticed, she has a thing for tiaras. And throwing money around is her way of getting attention. Besides, she was drinking."

"You're being generous, don't you think?"

Roxann tamped down the spark of anger at Nell's uncharacteristic sarcasm. Besides, the woman had tapped into some of her own concerns. "Four days ago she was dumped at the altar."

"Oh? Yes, that's tragic. Still, she seems...unstable."

"If you knew her mother, you'd know why."

"Does Angora have psychological problems?"

Roxann frowned. "You're serious."

Nell nodded.

"Not that I know of. Why?"

"I shouldn't say anything, it's been so long ago."

"What?"

Nell glanced around them, then leaned closer, her mouth pinched. "Did you know Angora was a suspect when that girl was killed on campus years ago in a hit-and-run?"

The hummus turned to sawdust in Roxann's mouth, and she swallowed painfully. "Tammy Paulen?"

"You remember her?"

"Yes." She was still digesting Nell's words, and replaying snatches of troubling conversations with her cousin. "We were talking about her the other night when we found my annual. Angora was a suspect?"

Nell nodded.

Now was probably not a good time to mention that Tammy had taunted Angora, or Angora's comment that the girl had gotten what she deserved. "Did the police ever make an arrest in the case?"

"No."

"Well...there were probably lots of suspects, weren't there?"

"Three. The two boys who called in the report, and Angora."

She put her fingers on her temples. "Why didn't I know this?"

"The investigation was kept under wraps because the president was afraid of a scandal. I was brought in to assist because I was Tammy's faculty advisor."

"I can see why the police would suspect the guys who reported the incident, but why was Angora a suspect?"

"I understand that her name kept coming up when Tammy's friends were questioned."

"But all of Tammy's friends were her sorority sisters. Angora quit the sorority because they gave her such a hard time."

"The sorority mother told me that Angora was forced out."

Angora did have a habit of adjusting the truth until it reflected well on her. Still, Roxann's head was spinning. "But...but there must not have been enough evidence to warrant an arrest."

"No. There were no witnesses. But I watched the videotape of the police interviewing Angora, and it was clear to me that she had issues with the Paulen girl."

"I heard the Paulen girl wasn't the nicest person."

"I heard the same thing," Nell conceded. "And Tammy's friends admitted that she treated Angora badly. They said she had something on your cousin, was holding it over her head."

"What?"

"No one knew, although one girl said she thought it had something to do with a blond wig."

Roxann went completely still. "A blond wig?" She managed a little laugh. "That's...strange."

"You don't know what they might have been referring to?"

She tried to speak, but could only shake her head.

Nell shrugged her thin shoulders. "You know how girls are—maybe she found out that Angora wasn't a natural blonde, or something superficial like that."

"Right," Roxann said, recovering. "No connection to the accident. Besides, I just can't see Angora being involved."

"Roxann—" The professor looked down, sighed, then looked up. "Do you think you're a good judge of character?"

She pulled back. "I'd like to believe so."

"That came out wrong—I meant where your cousin is concerned."

Words of defense gathered in her throat, then Roxann swallowed them. Hadn't Angora always been able to evoke her sympathy? To convince her to do things against her better judgment? Was it possible that instead of being a poor little rich girl, her cousin was a grand manipulator? After all, she had a master tutor in Dee.

"Angora and I will get a hotel room tonight."

"Don't be silly, you're staying with me."

"I don't want you to feel uncomfortable about Angora sleeping under your roof."

"I don't, and I didn't mean to upset you. Please don't leave." The woman looked a little desperate—she was indeed lonely.

Roxann touched Nell's hand. "Thank you for telling me the truth. I'll keep an eye on Angora. By the way, I ran into Elise James on campus today."

"I know that name, but I can't place her."

"She went to grad school here, and she joined the Rescue program about a year ago. I thought you might know her."

Nell sighed. "Unfortunately, the memory is the first thing to go. Is she nice?"

"Nice and troubled. We were paired up to live together in Biloxi, but I don't think Elise ever had her heart in the work. She suffered some personal problems and a few weeks ago she just took off." No need to go too much into detail, lest Nell start to think she was some kind of lesbian siren.

"This kind of volunteer work isn't for everyone. And if a person already has problems, the stress can sometimes exacerbate those problems."

Roxann nodded. "I think she was on something when I saw her today. She was rambling, incoherent."

Nell broke off a small piece of the flat bread. "What was she rambling about?"

"Something about a college relationship that had screwed her up."

"Sounds like whatever she's on has her screwed up."

Their food arrived, but Roxann's appetite had vanished, and nature was calling. She excused herself and went to the ladies' room, grateful for the moment alone. She hadn't been alone, not really, since leaving Baton Rouge. And now she had a sick, heavy feeling that returning to South Bend would simply reopen old wounds. Carl had drawn her back, but why on earth would Angora want to come back to a place where she had so many bad memories?

Roxann stared in a mirror over the sink and let the revelation sink in. *Carl.* Angora had been drawn back to Carl, too. She had made light of the fact that sleeping with him was on her life list, when she'd probably been in love with him just as much as Roxann. Why hadn't she seen it?

And Angora had probably been devastated earlier today when he'd recognized Roxann and not her. Roxann winced. No wonder Angora had acted so strangely the rest of the afternoon, and had bid so outrageously for his attention. On the heels of being jilted, her cousin was starved for validation.

She leaned into the cold porcelain sink and tried to remember the last day her life had had any semblance of normalcy. As is, a mushrooming cloud of doom was dogging her and the people she came into contact with—she didn't even want to think about what can of worms would spring open tomorrow. Plagued with warring thoughts and emotions, Roxann left the restroom before Nell began to think she'd been abandoned. But just outside the restroom was a pay phone, and she was struck with the longing to hear a comforting voice. Or at least a familiar one. Her cell phone was at Nell's on a charger. Before she could change her mind, she dialed her father's number. He answered on the third ring.

"Hello."

His rough-hewn voice scraped over the line, rugged and reassuring. She smiled into the phone. "Dad, it's me."

"Roxann, honey—are you okay?"

"I'm fine, Dad. Has anyone else been around asking about me?"

"No. Where are you?"

"I'm in South Bend, with Angora, We came up for Homecoming, but we'll be back to Baton Rouge soon."

He sighed. "Dee has been driving me nuts. Since that cop talked to her, she's sure Angora is in some kind of trouble."

"Well, she isn't." She chewed on the inside of her cheek. Yet. "Listen, Dad, is there a history of psychological problems in your family?"

"What kind of fool question is that?"

"It's important, Dad."

"Well...my mother's sister died in an asylum."

Roxann inhaled sharply. "What was wrong with her?"

"Schizophrenia. When she was twenty-five she pushed another woman out of a tenth-story window."

Her eyes bugged. "Why haven't you ever told me?"

"You never asked. Are you seeing that Detective Capistrano?"

Her eyes bugged wider. *"What?"*

"Are you seeing—"

"No, I'm not seeing him! What makes you think I'm seeing him?"

"He seemed to know an awful lot about you."

"Dad, he's a detective."

"He told me you were working together on a case."

"Well, we're not."

"He told me you could be in real trouble with the police."

"Well, I'm not."

"He told me about his partner. I think you should help him."

She closed her eyes. "Dad, I have to go. Keep the doors and windows locked, and don't talk to Detective Capistrano. I'll call you before I leave South Bend."

Roxann returned the phone to its cradle, trying to assimilate the bits of the conversation—discounting the absurd line of questioning about the infuriating detective. Schizophrenia was hereditary—was it possible that...no, Angora was a little flighty, but she wasn't a murderer. Heck, on any given day she had reservations about her own sanity.

Still, it might be a good idea to take Angora back to Baton Rouge as soon as possible, lest rumors about the Paulen girl resurface and disturb her further. They would leave first thing in the morning. As for Carl...

She sighed. Maybe after she tied up loose ends in Biloxi, she'd return to South Bend for that romantic dinner and...see what developed.

Remembering she hadn't yet checked her voice recorder at home, she quickly dialed the access number. Two messages.

"Hello, Roxann, this is Mr. Nealy. Your old boyfriend was hanging around the back door today—Richard, I think you said his name was? Anyway, if he gives you any guff, you just let me know."

So maybe it was Richard who'd broken in and left the message. Creep. She'd left town for nothing because she could have handled him with a kick to the groin.

The second message was a hang-up, so she quickly rejoined Nell at the table. "Sorry it took so long—I decided to check in with my dad."

"That's nice. How are you and your father?"

"We're fine."

Nell angled her head. "Something's wrong."

Roxann was drawn into the warmth of Nell's eyes, compelled to unburden herself just a little. "You were right. There is a history of mental illness in our family. Angora's and my great-aunt was schizophrenic."

Nell nodded sadly, then lapsed into another coughing seizure, this one more fierce than the last.

"I think I'd better take you home," Roxann murmured, rising.

"But you haven't eaten."

"I'm not hungry, and you need to rest." Nell didn't protest as Roxann helped her to her feet "I don't suppose the chances of getting a cab are any better than they used to be."

"Afraid not," Nell whispered with a smile. "But I'll be fine—my medication is wearing off, that's all."

"Still, I wish I had driven so you wouldn't have to walk."

"Can I offer you ladies a ride?"

Roxann closed her eyes and thought a very bad word. When she opened them, Capistrano was standing before them, cleverly disguised as a Good Samaritan.

CHAPTER SEVENTEEN

"WHAT ARE YOU DOING HERE?" Roxann asked him through clenched teeth.

"Having dinner—the scampi was great."

Nell's hand tightened around Roxann's arm. "Is this the man you told me about?"

She frowned. "No, this isn't Frank Cape. This is...an acquaintance of mine from Biloxi."

"Oh." Nell looked back and forth between them.

"Dr. Oney, meet Detective Capistrano."

"Nice to meet you, ma'am."

She nodded, then looked back to Roxann, as if waiting for a cue.

Roxann surveyed his innocent expression, then sighed. "He's harmless. Where are you parked, Capistrano?"

During the short drive to Nell's, Roxann sat in the middle of the front seat of his Dooley truck and exchanged glares with him in the rearview mirror. She was half furious at him for following her, half furious at herself for assuming he wouldn't.

"Thank you," she said to him as he helped Nell down from the passenger side. He dwarfed the small woman, but seemed to handle her gently. At the porch, Roxann said, "I'll take it from here. Goodbye."

"I need to talk to you." His head was so big, it obscured the moon behind him.

"This isn't a good time."

"It's important."

She hesitated, then gave Nell an apologetic glance.

"Take as long as you need," Nell said. "I'm going to bed. I'll see you girls at breakfast."

When the door closed, Roxann turned, arms crossed.

He gestured to her outfit. "You look plumb girly tonight."

"Forgive me if I don't swoon."

"I'm not crazy about black, though. You should wear white."

"You are harassing me."

"Funny, the last time I saw you, I saved your scrawny ass."

"My ass isn't—" She scowled. "I thought you had to get back to Biloxi."

He shrugged. "After you gave me the slip, I nearly said to hell with it and did."

Her smug smile came easily.

"But I had some time off coming to me and thought now was as good a time as any to take it." He leaned on the porch rail, as if he were planning to loiter.

"How did you know where we were?"

"Your cousin practically blurted it at the carnival, and when she said something about seeing a Dr. Carl, I figured it was either a medical doctor or a professor. I saw your diploma when I was at your dad's. Notre Dame is in South Bend. I just put two and two together. You'd make a terrible criminal."

"When did you get here?"

"I saw your crowning—very nice. Too bad your cousin outbid you for your old boyfriend."

She gasped.

"That's why you came back, isn't it? To see this Dr. Carl guy?"

"You don't know what you're talking about."

"Well, it doesn't take a detective to see the way you two were making eyes at each other. But he's a little ripe on the vine, don't you think?"

She poked her tongue into her cheek. "What's the important thing that you wanted to talk about?"

"Pistachio."

"What?"

"Pistachio ice cream. It's a weakness of mine, and I was hoping I could persuade you to join me." He splayed his hands. "Unlike Dr. Grandpa, I'm free of charge."

"You're certifiable."

"And you're hungry because you didn't get to eat dinner."

"No I'm not." But her brain conjured up a picture of a big bowl of green ice cream and sent a prompt to her traitorous stomach, which howled into the silence.

His laugh rode on the light breeze. "Liar. Come on, you don't have anything else to do tonight."

She hesitated. "I'm not going to talk about Melissa Cape."

He held up his hands in an off-limits gesture.

She relented and stalked to the truck, but only because she couldn't bear the thought of spending an evening with Boots, Chester, Pumpkin, Buttermilk, and Pansy. She resisted his help climbing up, closed her own door, sat as far away from him as possible, and stared straight ahead.

"Brrrr." He shook with an animated shiver. "There is a definite draft coming off you."

"Go," she said. "Before I change my mind."

He went, and soon they were seated at the crowded bar of an ice-cream parlor that brought memories flooding back.

"This place used to be called Duck's," she said, mostly to herself.

He handed her the chocolate malt she'd requested. He looked fair to middling in a black sport coat over dark jeans and a white dress shirt. "Used to come here a lot, did you?"

"I worked here."

He grinned. "No kidding."

She surrendered a smile. "No kidding. Smock and apron and paper hat. The work was easy, and the tips were good."

"Were you at Notre Dame on scholarship?"

"No." She sipped her malt.

"No offense, but how do you pay back school loans on the kind of money you make?"

She glanced over. "That's absolutely none of your concern."

"Hm. Well, is there anything we can talk about?"

"Have you seen Frank Cape?"

"No. I suspect he hightailed it back to Biloxi."

The best news she'd heard all day. "I checked my voice messages. My neighbor said he'd seen a former boyfriend of mine lurking around—I suspect he's the one who broke in. If so, he's all bark."

"You have a lot of former boyfriends."

"Not so many."

Capistrano pulled out a pad. "What's Romeo's name?"

"Richard Funderburk."

"Is he old, too?"

She frowned. "Around thirty-five."

He wrote it down. "Anything else I need to know?"

She shook her head and sipped, noting the knuckles on his right hand still hadn't healed. "Who did you hit?"

"Hm? Oh." He looked down at his hand and made a fist, then opened it again, stretching his fingers. "Some bum resisting arrest. I lose count." He made a rueful noise in his throat. "You and I, we've seen our share of bums, eh?"

She nodded and sipped.

He shifted on the tiny seat that had to be killing him. "Roxann, I don't agree with what you're doing, but I do admire your commitment to something you believe in."

YOU FAKE. She couldn't look at him.

"What I'm trying to say is that even if you haven't been honest with me about—"

She shot him a warning look.

"—about...you know, I still think you're an honorable person."

She lifted her gaze and studied his brown eyes, made boyish by the spiky blond lashes, made wise by his line of work. Honorable? What would he think if she told him that she'd joined Rescue not out of any heartfelt commitment, but because a woman she respected asked her to? Because she needed a place to recuperate from Carl's rejection? And because after she'd recovered, it simply had been easier to stay and hide out? "Thank you, but like I said before, you don't know me."

"I'm trying to."

Roxann scoffed inwardly. He was trying all right—trying to work her. "You're wasting your time, Detective. You'll never find Melissa Cape through me."

One dark eyebrow went up. "I thought that was off-limits conversation."

"But it's why you brought me here, what you want to know."

"No." His mouth tightened. "What I want to know is that you prefer chocolate malts over ice-cream cones—"

"It was just a craving."

"And that you have a great tattoo on your ankle—"

"It's temporary."

"And that you travel to so many exotic places that you need a special watch—"

"It's for work." She gave him a wry smile. "See? You don't know me." She looked away and toyed with the straw, twirling it in the thick malt. *Honorable?* Yeah, right.

He didn't intrude on her silence, but she could feel his gaze on her, leaving her itchy and raw. Goose bumps skittered over her shoulders and arms, and she suddenly remembered how cold they always kept the ice-cream parlor. A shiver took hold of her, and her teeth chattered. Her chest tightened and her throat ached. Either she was coming down with a case of the flu, or a case of the guilts.

He shrugged out of his coat and settled it around her shoulders. She stiffened before conceding that the silky fabric felt good against her skin. When she was young and her parents happy, they would come in from parties, her mother wearing her father's sport coat over her pretty dress. It had seemed so intimate to her, and so grown-up.

Roxann sunk her teeth into her bottom lip—Capistrano was certainly playing the knight-in-shining-armor bit to the hilt. Still, he'd chased away her chill.

Conjuring up a smile, she turned toward him. "Thank you. I'm sorry. I was rude."

He shrugged enormous shoulders. "You're entitled not to trust me."

She signaled the waitress for a glass of water. "Don't take it personally—I don't trust anyone."

He dipped back into his ice-cream bowl. "Your dad told me about your mother—I'm sorry."

She bristled. "What did he tell you?"

He studied her. "That she died in a car accident."

"Oh." She looked down at the counter. "She did."

"How old were you?"

"Eleven."

"That's tough. Are you an only child?"

"Yes. You?"

"Nope. Six besides me, three brothers, three sisters."

Large families fascinated her. "Are you close?"

He pursed his lips and nodded. "Yeah, even though we're spread all over. It's nice."

"And rare."

"Your job has made you cynical."

"Yours hasn't?"

"Maybe," he admitted, then turned his spoon over and licked it clean. "But I'm always on the lookout for a reason to be optimistic."

"How's your partner?"

His expression turned rueful. "Same. But thanks for asking."

A family of six bustled in and ordered cones all around, the smallest ones barely able to see into the display case of forty-two flavors. A smile pulled at her mouth as she remembered the joy of handing a cone of blue or pink ice cream to a toddler. Ice cream could cajole anyone out of a bad mood—except her, it seemed.

"So, Detective, what does your family think about your being on the road like this?"

He scratched his head. "My parents haven't kept tabs on me for a while now." Then he smiled, which caught her off guard. "Oh, wait, you're asking if I'm married."

"Just making conversation."

"No, never been. You?"

"No."

"Not all men are as bad as the thugs you've dealt with in the Rescue program."

She pursed her mouth.

"That subject is off-limits, too, I suppose. Okay. So what do you plan to do once you get back to Biloxi? For a living, I mean."

"Why do you want to know?"

He spooned up a last hefty mound of pistachio ice cream. "I feel bad about getting you fired, thought I might help you find a job. Something in law enforcement, or maybe in the courthouse."

Courthouse? "You've been talking to my father."

"Did he want you to go to law school?"

She nodded.

"Why didn't you?"

She shrugged. "It seemed like an indirect route to contributing to society."

"You don't strike me as someone who would have chased ambulances." He cocked his head. "Maybe a...prosecuting attorney."

She stopped mid-sip. One item on her life list that she'd written under the influence of cheap marijuana. She managed a laugh. "I don't think so. Thanks for the offer to help, Detective, but I'm not going back to Biloxi."

"Oh." He mulled the news, then pushed the ice-cream bowl away. "Where are you moving?"

She shrugged.

"Here? With that Dr. Carl guy that you're so ga-ga over?"

Roxann lifted an eyebrow. "Ga-ga. Now there's a word I would have bet wasn't in your vocabulary."

Suddenly his face turned serious. "The guy's a player, Roxann."

"What?"

"Your professor—he's a dirty old man who likes to nail young women."

Roxann went still. "That's a filthy thing to say. You don't even know him."

"I don't have to—there's one in every college in this country, from the Ivy Leagues down to the rinky-dinks."

"One what?"

"One horndog professor who makes it with all the busty girls in his classes."

Disgusted, Roxann shook her head. "You don't know what you're talking about."

"Oh, no? I overheard two girls at the bachelor auction trading stories about the man, and they weren't G-rated."

"You're making that up."

"No, ma'am."

She gestured helplessly in the air. "Then they were lying."

"Did you think you were the only girl he was doing when you were here?"

She lunged to her feet, and his jacket fell to the tiled floor. "Take me back."

"Look, I shouldn't have said that—"

"*Now*, Detective. Or I'll walk."

He wiped his mouth with a napkin, then slowly pushed himself to his feet and retrieved his jacket. "Whatever you say."

She walked out ahead of him, back straight. The ugly things he'd said kept going through her mind. Sure, Carl had lots of admirers, but he would never... he hadn't tried to take advantage of her, and heaven knows she was so crazy about him, she would have been easy pickings.

No, it wasn't true. He was a deacon, and a decent man whose job and position meant everything to him. He was human, and she assumed he wasn't a monk, but if he wanted girlfriends, he wouldn't have to dip into the student population.

Capistrano opened the door and offered her a hand up. She ignored him and struggled, finally falling into the seat. He closed the door, and walked around the front of the truck. Big, slow, confident. The man was too arrogant for words.

He opened the door and swung up into his seat, then closed the door and sat in silence while the clock in the dashboard ticked off several loud seconds. "I'm sorry. Everyone has someone in their past they put on a pedestal. I didn't mean to insult you. I could be wrong."

"You are."

"I hope so," he said, then cranked the engine. They didn't speak on the way back. He found a country radio station and occasionally whistled under his breath. She couldn't wait to get away from him.

When he pulled up to Nell's, he reached over to open the door for her, then hesitated. "I guess I've blown any chance I had with you."

She stared, incredulous. "You *never* had a chance with me."

He sighed. "It's the scampi, isn't it? I knew I should have stayed away from the garlic."

She fumbled for the handle. "You're a raving lunatic, and if you ever come around me again, I'll file a complaint."

"I'm leaving in the morning," he said. "But tonight I'm staying at the Holiday Inn if you need anything."

She grimaced. "Why, you gutter-minded—"

"I mean in the unlikely event that Cape shows up."

"Oh."

"And in the unlikely event you change your mind about...anything else, here's my number."

I've got your number.

The plain white card with simple black lettering glowed in the dim cab light. She snatched it, then opened the door and slid down, twisting her ankle. She cursed under her breath, then limped around the front of the truck to the sidewalk.

The window zoomed down. "Oh, and one more thing, Roxann."

She sighed and didn't bother turning around. "What?"

"Good luck on number thirty-three."

She whirled and gaped. He held up a sheet of paper between forefinger and thumb. Her life list. Mortification flooded her chest.

"Give me that." She lunged for the window, but he snatched the list out of reach and had the nerve to grin.

"Maybe I'll hang on to this little gem as collateral."

She ground her teeth. "You can't possibly think I'd give you information in return for some stupid list I made in college."

He pursed his mouth. "I don't know—it has some pretty juicy stuff on it."

"You're despicable."

"And you're very ambitious." He looked at the list. "At least you used to be."

"Just immature musings," she said through clenched teeth. "*Private* immature musings."

"If they were so private, you should've been more careful than to lose it outside the ladies' room at the carnival."

She must have pulled it out of her purse when she removed her keys as they were making their escape. Anger and frustration clogged her throat when she pictured him reading her list, laughing at her. "You...you—"

"Here." He held the handwritten list out the window. It whipped and curled in the breeze at the end of his long arm. "Take it. I don't know why I thought you'd have a sense of humor about this."

Another slap in the face. She yanked the list from his fingers and wadded it into a ball.

"Goodbye," he said, with one arm hooked around the steering wheel. "Maybe I'll see you around." When she didn't answer, he shrugged. "Or not."

He pulled away from the curb, and she watched until his taillights disappeared. She set her jaw and growled in lieu of screeching at the top of her lungs. As her anger swelled, every muscle contracted, and she stiffened in juvenile frustration, gearing up for an all-out tantrum before she realized how ridiculous she must look. So she settled for banging her fists against her head until she saw stars. Finally, she marched to the house, already cursing Capistrano for the sleep she wouldn't get tonight. He had a lot of nerve saying those horrible things about Carl. And laughing at her dreams.

The house was dark when she stepped inside except for a night-light Nell had graciously left on near the hallway. She stood in the shadows and listened for signs that Nell was still awake, but didn't hear anything. A touch on her leg sent terror bolting through her until she realized that it was just one of the cats copping a nib. Chester, the one that Nell doted on. Roxann indulged him for a few seconds, then tiptoed into the room she shared with Angora, not sure how she would handle the conversation about Carl. Now that she realized Angora had a crush on him, things could get awkward.

But the awkward conversation would have to wait because Angora wasn't there. A quick glance at the clock revealed it was only midnight, and the clubs didn't close until one, so she wasn't concerned.

And she wasn't about to let her imagination take hold of the dirty things Capistrano had said about Carl and run with them. Even if Angora was hell-bent on losing her virginity, Carl was much too noble to take advantage of her, especially considering the girls were related. Roxann lay down on top of the covers, replaying her conversations with Nell and Capistrano. Both of them had hinted that her character judgment was skewed. Was it possible that...no. Carl wasn't a philanderer any more than Angora was a murderer.

The phone on the nightstand rang, startling her. She picked it up automatically, then remembered she was a guest in someone else's house. "Dr. Oney's residence."

"Roxann? I...I need to see you."

Her first thought was that it was Angora, but the voice was wrong, and the wording strange. "Who is this?"

"Elise." She sighed, the dramatic sigh of someone under the influence trying to gather their thoughts. "I have to tell you...everything."

"What, Elise?"

"Not now, I'm not thinking very good. *Well.* I'm not thinking very *well.* Tomorrow...meet me at the chapel tomorrow at noon. And don't tell *anyone.*"

The woman had trouble hanging up, but finally the dial tone sounded. Roxann hung up slowly, wondering if her ex-roommate would even remember making the call. It was just like her, staging a theatrical apology. Elise lived for drama. Her stories about confronting married men who had dated and dumped her were hair-raising. Elise had issues.

But then, didn't everyone?

She must have dozed because she was awakened by a small rough tongue licking her chin—lapping up traces of the chocolate malt, no doubt. She shooed Chester and sat up, noting that Angora still hadn't returned. The clock radio read 2:15 a.m. Plenty of time to get home after the clubs closed. Frustration and anxiety plucked at her—she didn't want to think about what her cousin might be doing with Carl. What if Capistrano was right—what if Carl was a philanderer? She doubted if Angora was equipped to lose her virginity on a one-night stand.

She rubbed her face and made a quick decision. Carl's house was only a twenty-minute walk—she could go there and put her mind to rest and be back before anyone noticed.

She undressed in the dark and changed into the jeans she had on earlier, and tennis shoes. A black hooded sweatshirt would keep her from being too noticeable. At the last minute, she remembered her pepper spray and stuffed the can into the front pocket of her sweatshirt. Feeling like a criminal, she slipped out the back door and stole around the side of the house. The streets were busier than she'd expected—Homecoming had brought out the rowdy in everyone, it seemed. She decided to kill two birds with one stone and jog, which would also help explain why she was out at this time of night in case anyone saw her. She felt like an idiot. She was an idiot. They weren't at Carl's house, and Angora wasn't doing things to him that she'd marked with a highlighter pen in that making-love-to-a-man book.

A half-mile later, she was cursing herself for forgetting a flashlight. The ground was uneven and muddy, the streets dark and sinister. Lord, if Frank Cape wanted her, he could have her now and no one would be the wiser. Thoroughly spooked, she kept looking over her shoulder, but no one emerged from the shadows to gobble her up. The road conditions forced her to slow her pace, but she reached the street Carl lived on in fifteen minutes. The trees were taller and the houses more crowded than she remembered, and the cars parked in the driveways were dated. She stopped at the end of the quiet street to catch her breath, then walked on the sidewalk until Carl's ranch-style home came into sight. His old boxy black Volvo was recognizable in the shadows, still in good shape.

The lights were on in at least two rooms, meaning someone was home, unless Carl had left them on. She crept closer, keeping an eye on her surroundings, and feeling a little nauseous. But her need to prove Capistrano wrong kept her moving forward, coupled with her need to prove to herself that Carl was the man she thought he was.

CHAPTER EIGHTEEN

ANGORA CLAWED AT THE RASH on her neck and chest—at this rate she'd never get laid. After plying her with good food and working her up with close-body dancing, Carl Seger had brought her back to his home to show her every first edition of every boring book in his stupid library. She knew he found her attractive because he'd been touching her all night. At the moment, though, he was stroking the cover of a green leather-bound volume.

"And this one I bought at a garage sale while I was vacationing in the Hamptons—"

"Carl," she said with a seductive smile. "I've seen every room in your house except the bedroom."

His eyebrows shot up. "Well, I...didn't think this was that kind of date. After all, the auction was for charity."

She squinted, trying to figure out if she'd just been insulted. "I didn't pay two thousand dollars for a lecture on old books."

He smiled. "You didn't?"

"No. I paid two thousand dollars to lose my virginity."

The book fell to the floor with a thud. "You're a virgin?"

She nodded, glad to finally have his attention.

He moved closer to her and gave her a deep, grinding kiss that allowed all the important parts to make contact. When he lifted his head, he was breathing hard and his glasses were steamed up. "Why me?"

She could tell he was torn between behaving himself and ripping her clothes off. "Take me to your bedroom, and I'll tell you why."

They kissed and rubbed their way to his bedroom, which was an unfortunate attempt at Japanese-style decorating—lots of black and red and gold. She carefully removed her crown and placed it on his dresser. Then they fell onto the bed, which undulated beneath them. Ugh—a waterbed. He tugged on her dress and bra until she was naked from the waist up.

"So why me?" he whispered, kissing her breasts.

At last it was starting to feel good. "Because we have history."

His head came up. "Huh?"

"I gave you a blowjob in your office when I was a student."

"You did?"

She frowned. "You don't remember?"

"You'll have to be more specific."

"I spit come on your Cole Haan loafers."

"That was you?"

"That was me."

He pulled on his chin and smiled. "It must have been pretty good if you saved your cherry for me after all these years."

"I figured you would know what you were doing." And the thrill of losing her cherry to the man Roxann wanted was absolutely delicious. She knew she was being evil, but she couldn't help it—she deserved something for all her bad luck lately, not to mention her two thousand dollars.

Suddenly he sat up and ran his hand through his hair. "Wait a minute—how do I know this won't be on the front page of a tabloid tomorrow? And how do I know you won't tell Roxann?"

She frowned. "Roxann?"

He looked away. "She's special."

Hurt expanded her lungs—she was special, too. Why couldn't anyone in the world see that she was special, too? She manufactured a coy smile and rubbed her bare breasts against his arm. "I won't tell anyone, Carl. I didn't tell anyone all those years ago."

"Because you would have gotten in trouble," he said. "No, it's too risky." He started to rebutton her dress. "I'm taking you home."

Angora sat up. "You can't, not yet."

"I can, and I will. Get dressed."

She swallowed, feeling desperate. "I know a secret."

He shrugged, unimpressed. "What kind of secret?"

She bit into her lip, wavering.

"What kind of secret?"

"It's about Tammy Paulen."

He stopped. "What about her?"

"I know...what you did."

His Adam's apple bobbed. "What are you talking about?"

Snuggling closer, she murmured, "I saw your car that night."

He stiffened. "What?"

"I saw your black Volvo that night speeding away." She kissed his neck. "But don't worry—I never told anyone. I know it was an accident. You wouldn't have hurt her on purpose."

He seemed a little dazed. "No, I wouldn't have. But...you never told anyone?"

"Not a soul. Because I loved you, Carl." She kissed him until he kissed her back, feeling closer to him. Only lovers shared intimate secrets. And sure enough, his enthusiasm seemed to explode. They tore at each other's clothes until they were naked. He hadn't bothered to have that circumcision redone.

"Are you on the pill?" he gasped.

"No, but I have...things." She retrieved her purse from the floor—Dee would have an aneurysm if she knew her precious birth-control first aid kit was being used to have hot sex with a former teacher.

When she handed him a condom, he pursed his mouth. "Nice quality." He opened the package, then directed her to roll it on. Her hands shook, but he yelped only twice before she finished. At last he slid his body on top of hers and stared down.

"God, you look so much like her." He kissed her breasts and moved to lie between her knees. He was panting, his eyes glazed over. "Angora, how adventurous are you?"

She hadn't been the most flexible person in PE class, but she could probably accommodate a unique position or two. "What did you have in mind?"

He rose over her and smiled wickedly—he'd taken off his glasses, and his silvery hair fell over his forehead. Angora arched her back in anticipation of their bodies joining. He slid both hands over her stomach, then up to pinch her breasts, then up to caress her neck. Embarrassment flooded her—he'd surely noticed her nerve rash.

He thumbed the area under her chin slowly at first, then applied more pressure. But she was so distracted by his erection moving against her, she didn't realize how tight his grip was getting until she tried to swallow, and couldn't. She gulped air and gasped his name, but no sound came out. Wouldn't you know it—the one time she'd taken Roxann's place, and she was going to die for it.

Everything faded to brown, then black.

CHAPTER NINETEEN

CAPISTRANO WAVED HER life list and laughed at her. "Your professor is a dirty old man...a dirty old man...a dirty old man."

Roxann woke with a start and sat straight up in the dark. Her hairline was moist and clammy. The air in the small guest room was chilly because she'd closed the door, but she was sweating because she'd fallen asleep in the clothes she'd worn on her shameful errand. Thank goodness sanity had kicked in at the last moment—Angora and Carl were consenting adults, and if they wanted to engage in a physical relationship, she had no hold on either one of them.

She glanced over at Angora's unslept-in bed. And it appeared they had done just that.

The digital clock read five forty-five, and the house was quiet. Dragging her hand down her face, she swung her leg over the edge of the bed, and switched on the nightstand lamp. Mud spattered the legs of her jeans, and a few feet away sat her caked gym shoes. She winced, and stood, brushing bits of dried dirt from the aged comforter. Thank goodness Nell's floors were hardwood, but she wanted to get any tracks cleaned up before her host awakened. She picked up the mucky shoes and slipped out the door into the dim hallway. Dawn was breaking, sending fingers of light into the house. She moved silently toward the kitchen. Nell's bedroom door was closed, and Roxann suspected she was sleeping more these days, especially since she wasn't feeling well.

To save Nell the trouble, Roxann started the coffeemaker. Chester startled her when he appeared from nowhere to do a quick figure eight around her ankles. She stood at the counter for a few seconds wondering what she would say to Angora when she returned from Carl's. Should she chastise her or congratulate her? She certainly couldn't blame her for being attracted to him. Funny, but this morning she didn't feel as betrayed as she might have expected. But she did feel foolish for thinking that she and Carl would simply pick up where they'd left off. How pathetically naive.

She unrolled a wad of paper towels and stole out to the back porch to clean her shoes, holding the storm door until the latch caught so it wouldn't wake Nell. Chester joined her. It was a beautiful October morning, dewy and brisk. The smooth floorboards of the covered porch were cold beneath her bare feet, but she didn't mind. Nell had quite a little garden going in the back, and Roxann was reminded of the radio program on herb gardening—another hobby she had to look forward to in her spinsterhood. She sat down on the steps to clean her shoes, then froze when a groan sounded behind her.

Roxann stood and whirled in one motion. A few feet away on the porch, Angora lay asleep on a chaise, curled up in a rug and covered with dew.

Roxann rolled her eyes and walked over to shake her. "Angora. Angora, wake up."

Angora's eyes flew open, and she cried out.

"Shhh! Nell's still asleep. What are you doing out here?"

Angora burst into tears.

"What on earth is wrong with you?" Roxann peeled back the stiff rug and helped her to sit up. Her blond hair and red dress were disheveled, her stockings torn, and her shoes missing.

"Oh, Roxann, it was awful," she sobbed.

Dark bruises covered her pale skin from jawline to collarbone. Alarm rocketed through Roxann. "What happened to your neck?"

Angora touched the discolored area. "He—" Her sobs escalated until Roxann shook her—hard.

"Angora, calm down and tell me what happened."

"C-Carl. He was ch-choking me."

"*What?* Why was he choking you?"

She shook her head. "I don't know—we were going to have sex, and—I'm sorry, Roxann, I shouldn't have done it." More tears and finally, hiccups.

She inhaled deeply to calm her own thumping heart. "It's okay, Angora. Did he hurt you?"

"I...think I passed out. I don't remember anything until I woke up alone in his bed." She swallowed hard and wiped her nose with her hand. "I just got out of there as fast as I could."

Roxann put her hands to her temples in an effort to assimilate the bits of information. The thought of Carl hurting anyone or anything was incomprehensible, but Angora, flighty as she was, wasn't faking her terror, or those dreadful bruises. Had she somehow provoked him to attack her? It didn't matter—the authorities had to be notified.

"Come inside," she said. "We're calling the police."

"No," Angora pleaded, her hands fisted in Roxann's shirt. "If anyone finds out, I'll just die."

How many times had she seen abused women retreat out of embarrassment? "Be sensible, Angora. If Carl hurt you, he has to answer for it." In fact, she might have to take a swing at him herself. Capistrano's warning rang in her ears.

"But I said something to make him angry."

"What?"

"I can't tell you," she shrieked, thrashing her head back and forth.

Roxann studied her cousin's tearful face, the wild-eyed borderline hysteria. Now wasn't the time to talk. "Come on, let's get you cleaned up."

Angora relented tearfully, gathering her purse and leaning heavily on Roxann while they maneuvered through the back door. "I want to go home," she sobbed.

"I'll take you home today," Roxann promised. "As soon as we get this mess straightened out. Let me get my phone so I can take pictures."

"Pictures?"

"For court, if it goes that far."

Angora's eyes flew wide. "I can't have my picture taken looking like this."

"Angora, this isn't a contest for Most Photogenic. This is serious. I know what I'm doing." For once.

Suddenly she became aware of voices from the living room, male and female. Nell's? When a scream rang out, Roxann released Angora and ran to the living room. Two policemen stood in the doorway, and Nell sat on the couch in her robe, a stricken expression on her face.

"Nell, what's wrong?"

"Are you—" one of the policemen asked, then consulted a small notebook. "Roxann Beadleman and Angora Ryder?"

"Yes," she said. Angora hung back, looking like a caged animal.

"Then you'll both need to come with us down to the station."

Roxann squinted. "If this is about what Carl did to Angora—"

"Carl's dead," Nell cried.

Horror oozed over Roxann. She shook her head at the policemen. "There must be some kind of mistake."

"No mistake, miss. Dr. Seger was found dead in his home this morning by the paper boy."

She reached for the back of the couch for support. "Was it some kind of accident? Heart attack?"

"Murder," the cop said curtly.

Her knees buckled, and behind her, Angora whimpered.

"Which is why," the policeman said, unsmiling, "you ladies need to come down to the station."

She closed her eyes at the obvious implication—everyone at the auction last night knew Angora had won the date with Carl. They wouldn't have had to make too many inquiries to track down her cousin. Snatches of recent troubling conversations with Angora raced through her head, along with her father's revelation that their great-aunt was schizophrenic. Angora had admitted that Carl had choked her—could she have killed him in self-defense? It was too much for Roxann's shell-shocked brain to process at the moment.

"Don't say a word, Angora," she warned. "Not until you've spoken with a lawyer."

One of the cops angled his head. "You might want to call one for yourself, Ms. Beadleman."

She frowned. "Why?"

"Because Dr. Seger was strangled with a lime-green scarf. Sound familiar?"

CHAPTER TWENTY

"HELLO?"

She'd obviously awakened Capistrano from a dead sleep. "Um, hi. This is Roxann. Beadleman."

He grunted and sheets rustled in the background. "Did Cape show up?"

"No. At least not that I know of."

He sighed in relief. "Did you change your mind about something?"

The drowsy amusement in his voice irritated her—the man thought she was calling to invite herself over for a little early-morning tryst? "No, Detective, I didn't change my mind about anything." She winced and forced the words from her throat. "I n-need your help."

His rusty laugh rumbled over the line. "Oh, now you need my help. What is it—car trouble? Low on cash?"

"Carl Seger was murdered last night. I'm at the police station."

More sheet rustling. "What? Are you a suspect?"

"He was strangled with my scarf. Will you come?" She counted to three, prepared for him to tell her he didn't want to get involved.

"I'm already there."

The resolute click was comforting—the man was an arrogant ass, but right now, with four police officers staring at her, she needed an arrogant ass who was on her side.

"Was that your lawyer?" one of them asked. Detective Warner, she recalled. Good cop.

"I don't need a lawyer," she told him. "Where's my cousin?"

"In the next room," another officer said—Jaffey, bad cop. "Bawling her eyes out."

"Can I go to her?"

"Why, so you can synch up your stories?"

She frowned. "No, because she's scared out of her wits."

"She should be." He leaned forward, his eyes menacing. "Both of you should be."

Roxann chewed on her lip, trying not to think about Carl lying dead with her scarf around his neck—it was simply too incredible. "I have nothing to hide, but I want to wait until my friend—er, acquaintance arrives. He's a police detective from Biloxi."

"And can he give you an alibi?"

"I was with him for some of the evening, yes."

"Boyfriend?"

"No." She and Jaffey held a staring contest, and he finally looked away. She prayed that Angora would keep her mouth shut until the lawyer Nell recommended arrived. Angora had forbidden her to call Dee, and she'd relented—for now. But she had a bad, bad feeling that Angora was going to need as much defense as Jackson and Dee Ryder could afford.

"Cup of coffee?" Warner asked.

"Yes, thank you." Actually, scotch sounded better, but she needed to keep her wits about her if she was going to figure out what had happened to her scarf. Her initial reaction that the scarf found at the scene couldn't be hers was quickly refuted by the fact that she couldn't find it, and that the "weapon" matched a confiscated receipt for the lime-green scarf she'd purchased when they stopped outside Baton Rouge. Not the kind of thing she normally bought, but the filmy piece of silk had caught her eye and Angora commented that it looked nice against her hair.

One estrogenic impulse, and look where it had gotten her.

Now she couldn't even remember if she'd been wearing it last night when she changed clothes. Nell seemed sure she was still wearing it at the restaurant, but maybe she'd lost it afterward, while fussing and feuding with Capistrano?

She craned her neck to see if she could catch a glimpse of Angora, but the view from the interrogation room was limited—windows from the waist up on one wall only. The remaining walls were padded with the same low-nap gray carpet that was on the floor—either perps regularly flung themselves around the room, or the cops did it for them.

The chair was as uncomfortable as possible, naturally. Molded plastic. The overhead lighting was intense and unflattering, the wooden table was bolted to the floor. A pad of paper and a pencil lay nearby, just in case she felt compelled to confess, she assumed. The bizarre urge to laugh seized her, but she covered her mouth with her hand and swallowed hard. The entire atmosphere had a strange, cartoonish quality. Quite remarkable, and quite terrifying.

"Here." Warner handed her a paper cup of strong coffee that scalded her tongue, and, unfortunately, she still didn't wake up as she'd hoped, to find Angora asleep in the twin bed next to her in Nell's guest room. Carl was dead. No, worse—Carl was *murdered.*

A rap on the window caught her attention, and when she saw Capistrano's mug peering in, her heart lifted crazily. She hated to admit it, but there was something reassuring about having the big lug around.

"Is that your boyfriend?" Jaffey asked.

"Acquaintance," she corrected.

He gestured for Capistrano to come in and the men introduced themselves. Capistrano flashed his badge, for professional courtesy, she assumed. He was a good head taller than anyone in the room. And he looked remarkably put together to have rolled out of bed fifteen minutes ago. She didn't want to think about how she looked.

"You look like hell," he said.

"Nice to see you, too."

"Has she been charged?" he asked the room in general.

"Not yet," Jaffey said.

Capistrano walked around to lean on the wall facing her. "What happened?" he asked Jaffey.

But Warner took the lead. "Paper boy noticed Seger's door was open this morning around five o'clock, and went to investigate. Found him dead in the library, strangled by a scarf that belongs to your girlfriend here."

Roxann pursed her mouth. "Except I don't know how it got there. Was I wearing it last night when we"—she frowned—"said goodbye?" The cops gave each other knowing looks that infuriated her.

"I don't remember," Capistrano said. "I wasn't looking at the scarf."

How did he *do* that? Make it seem as if there was something between them? In fact, why the devil had she even called him?

He looked back to Warner. "The scarf is purely circumstantial evidence anyway. What else do you have?"

"Mud on her jeans," he said, pointing. "And a pair of running shoes, caked with dried mud."

Capistrano looked back to her with a raised eyebrow.

"I...couldn't sleep last night, so I went jogging."

"Where?" Jaffey asked.

She closed her eyes. "To Dr. Seger's house and back."

Capistrano averted his gaze.

"That's all I need to hear," Jaffey said, reaching for his cuffs.

"No, wait," she said, holding up her hand. "I jogged to his house because..."

"Because?" one of the other cops prompted.

She inhaled. "Because someone told me that Carl was a philanderer, and I was worried about my cousin being with him."

"She outbid you for a date with the professor," Jaffey said.

"It was for charity." A dumb argument, even to her own ears.

"What time did you *jog* over to Seger's house?"

"Around two-thirty a.m."

"And what happened when you got there?"

"Nothing. I realized how stupid it was of me to be concerned, so I simply turned around and ran back to the house where I was staying."

"Right," Jaffey said, his sarcasm thick.

She leaned forward. "I could have lied just now. Why would I tell you I jogged over there unless I was innocent?"

"Did anyone see you?"

She turned to Capistrano. "I don't guess you could have been following me *then*?"

He shook his head. "I gave up." His gaze was pointed.

She looked back to Jaffey. "I didn't see anyone else, although someone could have noticed me, maybe someone driving."

The cop gestured to her black sweatshirt. "You weren't exactly dressed to be noticed, now were you?"

She didn't answer—her humiliation was complete.

"Do you have a history with Carl Seger?" Warner asked.

She sat back. "He was my professor when I went to school here from ninety-two through ninety-six, and I had a work-study under Dr. Seger my senior year."

"Let me rephrase. Do you have a personal history with Carl Seger?"

Roxann inhaled and exhaled, wondering how much to tell. But really, how much was there to tell? "We were fond of each other, but we didn't have a sexual relationship." Out of the corner of her eye, she saw Capistrano straighten, edge closer.

"Did you see him after you graduated?" Warner continued.

"No. Just before I graduated, Carl was accused of having an improper relationship with a student. I left campus and...I didn't see him again until this week."

"Did the two of you stay in touch?"

"He called twice—once a few months after I left to say he was sorry how things had ended, and a few weeks ago he left a message on my phone in Biloxi asking if I would consider accepting a Distinguished Alumni award. But I didn't return his call."

"Because you were still angry over how things had ended?"

She frowned. "No. Because I wasn't interested in receiving the award."

"So there was nothing personal in the message?"

"He said that he missed me."

"But you didn't call him back?"

"I said that already."

Warner sat down to her left. "Ms. Beadleman, were you the student that Dr. Seger was accused of having an improper relationship with?"

She blinked. "Yes...I always assumed."

“Did you ever hear of him being involved with other students?”

She shook her head. “All the girls were crazy about him, but Carl was a gentleman around me.”

“Who told you he was a philanderer?”

“I did,” Capistrano said. When all eyes turned in his direction, he shrugged. “Just a hunch. Plus last night at the auction I overheard a couple of coeds talking about his technique outside the classroom.”

“You never said why you were in town, Detective,” Jaffey said.

“You never asked. I followed Ms. Beadleman here from Biloxi. She’s involved in a case I’m working on, and a thug named Frank Cape was on her tail.”

“That’s why I came to South Bend,” she added. “To stay with Dr. Nell Oney for a few days until Cape lost interest.”

“When was the last time you saw this Cape fellow?”

“Little Rock,” she said, then looked to Capistrano, who nodded agreement.

“Why is he following you?”

She looked at Capistrano, then back to them and sighed. “Frank Cape is an abusive man. I work for a women’s advocacy group, and I helped his ex-wife and daughter relocate. He thinks he can threaten me into telling him where they are.”

“He threatened you?”

“And my family.” Suddenly she stopped and looked at Capistrano. “In Little Rock he said if I didn’t tell him where Melissa was, the people I cared about would start dropping like flies.”

“The guy’s no honor student,” Capistrano offered. “He put my partner in a coma.”

All the cops straightened and fingered their weapons involuntarily. Then Jaffey scoffed. “You’re saying that this Cape fellow stole your scarf and used it to strangle Carl Seger so you would tell him where his wife and kid are?”

“I didn’t say that, but right now it makes as much sense as anything. Officer, don’t you think if I were going to kill Carl, that I would have chosen something a little less obvious than the scarf that at least a thousand people saw me wearing last night?”

He chewed on his tongue, then retrieved the pencil and pad of paper. "Ms. Beadleman, I think you'd better tell us exactly where you were last night, when, and who you were with."

She recited her schedule and timetable as best as she could remember. Capistrano corroborated her story until the time he dropped her off. Then she was on her own.

"Nell was asleep when I came home, so that's when I decided to go to Carl's. No wait—I lay down first, and received a phone call."

"From?"

"From an ex-roommate of mine in Biloxi, Elise James. She went to grad school here and came up for Homecoming."

"What time was that?"

"Around midnight."

"What did she want?"

"It was a strange conversation. She was stoned, I think. She said something about wanting to tell me everything and asked me to meet her at the chapel today at noon."

"Do you know what she was referring to?"

"We had a falling-out when she lived with me, after which she moved out. I assumed she wanted to apologize. Elise can be dramatic."

"What did the two of you argue about?"

"It's personal."

"We can always ask her," Jaffey said.

She sighed. "Elise got it into her head that she was...attracted to me."

All the men smiled, even Capistrano, the lout.

"She's a lesbian?" Jaffey again.

You'll have to ask her."

"Are you a lesbian?"

"No."

"Bisexual?"

"No."

"So this girl hit on you and you threw her out?"'

"What does this have to do with Carl being murdered?"

"Just amusing myself," Jaffey said with a nasty little smile.

"Let's get back to the subject," Capistrano said.

She smirked at him—he could pester her, but no one else could?

"What happened after the phone call?"

"I dozed off for a couple of hours, then I woke up and couldn't get back to sleep. I changed into these clothes and my tennis shoes, ran over to Dr. Seger's and back, then went to bed."

"Dr. Oney said she didn't hear you leave or return."

"I tried to be quiet. And the bedrooms are on opposite ends of the house."

"What did you see when you got to Seger's house?"

She shrugged. "Nothing. I saw his car sitting out front."

"A black Volvo."

"Right."

"What else?"

"Some lights were on, in maybe two or three rooms."

"You didn't see anyone inside?"

"No. I didn't get close enough."

Jaffey sneered. "Are you sure you didn't see your old flame boinking your cousin?"

She bit down on the inside of her cheek and maintained eye contact. "I'm positive."

"So where does she come into all this?"

"Angora?"

"Yes."

"We went to school here at the same time."

"Did she know Dr. Seger?"

"Everyone knew him."

"Did she know him in the biblical sense?"

"No."

He looked at his notes. "She lives in Baton Rouge?"

Roxann nodded.

"Why did she come back to South Bend?"

"I stopped in Baton Rouge for her wedding, then she decided to come with me. She didn't know about Cape following me."

"What happened to her groom?"

"He changed his mind at the altar."

Jaffey made an amused sound. "A jilted bride might just be mad enough to nail the first guy she meets."

"I wouldn't know." Although the same thought had crossed her mind last night.

"When did your cousin return from her evening with Dr. Seger?" Warner asked.

"I don't know. When I woke up this morning and went outside—"

"To clean your incriminating shoes," Jaffey cut in. "We saw the roll of paper towels."

"When I went out on the back porch to clean my running shoes," she continued, "Angora was asleep on the chaise."

"Did you notice the bruises on her neck?"

"Immediately."

"How did she say they got there?"

She took a drink of the coffee.

"Ms. Beadleman?"

"She said that Carl put them there."

"How?"

"She said they were getting ready to...have sex and he started choking her."

"Did she say why?"

"She said she'd told him something that made him angry, but she wouldn't tell me what."

"Can you make a guess?"

"No, I can't."

"What else?"

"Angora said she passed out, and when she came to, she was alone in his bed. Then she left."

"Did she walk back to the house you're staying in?"

"I assume so—her dress was a mess, and she was barefoot. I didn't see her shoes."

"We found them on the porch. Muddy, same as yours. And we found a tiara on the dresser in his bedroom. Someone told us you got a crown last night for some kind of award?"

"Yes, but the tiara is Angora's. Mine is—" She stopped. Where was that thing?

"In my truck," Capistrano supplied.

Good grief, she'd misplaced everything last night. Including her good sense. Why else would she have run over to Carl's like some lovestruck stalker? She froze. Years of working with obsessive people had rubbed off. Dear God.

Jaffey toyed with the pencil. "Here's what I think—I think you jogged over there for a peek and found Dr. Seger choking your cousin for whatever reason. You pulled your scarf out of your pocket and killed him. Maybe you didn't mean to, but it happened."

"That's absurd," she said, shaking her head. "I didn't kill Carl." She choked on the last word, then recovered. "I couldn't have."

"Will you take a lie detector test?"

"Absolutely."

"So if we believe your story," Warner said, "you didn't kill him, but your cousin certainly could have."

He had vocalized her own fears—especially considering what Nell had told her about the Tammy Paulen incident—but she tried to keep a poker face. "I have a difficult time believing that Angora could do something like that." But Capistrano was looking at her strangely.

"Do you know anyone else who could have killed him?" Jaffey asked.

"No, but I don't know much about Carl's life. Talk to Nell Oney and some of the other professors."

"We did. By the way, she had access to your scarf, didn't she?"

Roxann narrowed her eyes. "Since I don't know where I lost it, I couldn't say. But Nell Oney is one of the few truly good people I know. She and Carl were friends. She would never hurt anyone."

"The woman is ill," Capistrano said. "Barely strong enough to turn a deadbolt, let alone bring down a man the size of Seger."

"The same for Angora," she added.

A knock on the door interrupted them, and a female officer stuck her head in. "The Ryder woman's lawyer is here."

"I'll be right there," Jaffey said. When the door closed, he shook his finger at Roxann. "We'll need your clothes and your fingerprints. And don't leave town." He looked at Capistrano. "Can I trust you to keep an eye on her?"

"Sure thing."

The detective looked at her and she had the distinct feeling of a hen being handed over to a chicken hawk.

CHAPTER TWENTY-ONE

ANGORA LOOKED UP and dubiously shook hands with the man who introduced himself as her lawyer. Mike Brown was a short chunky man with curly brown hair and glasses that wouldn't stay up on his nose. He looked all of nineteen and was dressed like a farmer—smelled like one, too.

"Please excuse my appearance," he said in a boyish voice as he sat down heavily. "I was working my compost pile when my phone rang."

She had no idea what compost was, but the man must have some means if he had a pile of it. At the moment, however, she had more pressing matters on her mind. Carl was dead. Dead. Dead. The more the word revolved in her head, the less it even seemed like a word, much less one that was so...final. Dead, just like Tammy Paulen. And these visions of her strangling Carl—were they real? Or had hearing the graphic details of his death put them there? Her head was too full to think.

Her lawyer pulled out a pad of paper and went through three pens from his briefcase before he found one with ink. "Here we go. Now Ms. Ryder, have you spoken with anyone about the murder?"

She shook her head and massaged the pain just beneath her breastbone. A foul-tasting blend of indigestion and grief and guilt. She'd already been sick twice, once before they left Dr. Oney's and once on the ride over in the police car. Good God Almighty, when Dee found out what had happened, she'd have her birth certificate changed. And if everything unraveled, then she might as well go to prison for all the life she'd have.

"Ms. Ryder?"

"Yes?"

"I asked if you'd like something—coffee, soda?"

What she wanted was to sit on the floor and cry like a baby. "N-no, thank you."

He cleared his throat. "Ms. Ryder, do you understand that you're a suspect in the murder of Carl Seger?"

She squinted. "How old are you?"

He blushed. "Thirty-five. I know I look young, and I did just pass the bar, but I got a late start."

Boy, did she know all about that. "How do you know Dr. Oney?"

"She's an old friend of the family, encouraged me to go to law school."

"Mr. Brown, I don't have a lot of money." She doubted if she could get a refund on the money she'd bid for Carl, and she couldn't go to her parents.

"That's okay," he said cheerfully. "I'm doing pro bono work on the side until I get my soybean crop harvested."

Her attorney was a soybean farmer? What *were* soybeans, exactly? Her doubt must have been apparent because he smiled.

"I'm not a trial lawyer, Ms. Ryder. I'll only advise you through the police interviews." Then he frowned. "How did you get those bruises on your neck?"

"Carl Seger choked me."

His face darkened. "Do you need medical attention?"

She shook her head. "I just want to get this over with and go back to Baton Rouge."

"Is that where you live?"

"Yes."

He wrote it down. "Are you married?"

A lump formed in her throat, forcing her to swallow. "No."

He took down a few more vitals, then withdrew a limp blue bandana and wiped his shiny forehead. "Ms. Ryder, I read the police report, and I have to tell you it doesn't look good."

"But I didn't murder Carl."

He nodded as if he didn't believe her. "It isn't murder if you killed him in self-defense."

A rap on the door preceded the entry of two plainclothes cops. Mike told them his name, and they identified themselves as Detectives Jaffey and Warner.

Jaffey looked at her as if she were a snack. "Are you ready to talk, Ms. Ryder?"

She looked at Mike, who remained quiet, as if he wanted her to make the decision. Hm. She nodded.

"No tape recorder," Mike said. "And I'll stop Ms. Ryder if I think the questioning is going against her best interests."

The detectives shrugged. Jaffey leaned over and planted his hands on the table. "Ms. Ryder, did you kill Carl Seger?"

"Stop," Mike said, placing his hand on her arm. His big fingers looked a bit grubby. "Let's start again, gentlemen."

Jaffey sighed and pulled up a chair. "All right. Ms. Ryder, how do you know Carl Seger?"

Mike removed his hand and nodded for her to answer.

"He was a theology professor when I attended college at Notre Dame." Jaffey asked for the years and she told him.

"Were you a student of his?"

"Yes, for a few classes."

"Were you ever involved with him sexually?"

She shifted on the uncomfortable plastic seat. "Not involved, no."

"Was there ever an encounter?"

She glanced to Mike, but he only pushed his glasses higher. "Once," she murmured.

"What happened?"

"He invited me back to his office. I...gave him oral sex."

"And that was it?"

She nodded, hot from shame. "He barely acknowledged me after that."

"Did that make you feel worthless? Angry?"

Angora bit her tongue. "No one likes to be rejected, Officer."

"Did Dr. Seger invite a lot of female students back to his office?"

"I don't know."

"Why didn't you report Dr. Seger to the school authorities?"

She concentrated on the ugly fingerprint ink around her nails. "I don't know."

"Is it because you were in love with Dr. Seger and were a willing participant?"

Angora looked up. "I was young and stupid. Afterward I was so humiliated, I never told anyone what happened." She'd simply pretended it hadn't happened.

"Were you in contact with Dr. Seger after you graduated?"

"No."

"But you never forgot him."

"I sometimes read about him in the alumni newsletter."

"Your cousin told us you were recently jilted at the altar."

Tears stung her eyes. "So?"

"So that would make a woman mighty angry. Angry enough to get even with the next man in her life that crossed her."

Why had she told Roxann about her nasty urges? A feeling of betrayal flooded her chest, magnifying the odd pain radiating there. "Did Roxann tell you I said that?"

"*Did* you say that?" Jaffey asked.

"Don't answer," Mike warned her. "Next question."

"When did you become reacquainted with Dr. Seger?"

"When my cousin and I arrived in South Bend yesterday."

"And you bid on a date with him at the bachelor auction last night?"

"You know I did."

Jaffey whistled. "Two thousand dollars is hefty sum for a little food and conversation. Did you have something else in mind?"

"I don't know what you mean."

"Maybe a little revenge for the way he treated you all those years ago."

"Is that a question?" Mike asked.

Jaffey frowned. "What happened after you and Dr. Seger left the auction?"

"We went to Utopia for dinner, then dancing at a place called DeSoto's."

Warner held up his hand and checked written notes he'd brought in. "Utopia? That's where your cousin and Dr. Oney had dinner last night."

"I didn't see them there. We were in a private dining room."

"Ms. Beadleman says she lost her scarf sometime during the evening. You didn't by chance find it at the restaurant, and decide to return it to her later?"

"No. And it was a cheap scarf."

Jaffey's eyebrow went up. "Cheap scarf—I'll make a note of that. What time did you leave the restaurant?"

"Eleven o'clock, maybe? I'm not sure."

"What about the dance place—DeSoto's?"

"Closing time—maybe one in the morning?"

"Then what happened?"

"We went back to his place."

"To have sex?"

She squirmed. "That was the idea, I suppose."

"And did you?"

"No."

"Why not?"

"We...were going to, but then Carl started choking me." Her voice broke and she touched the tender skin on her neck. "I thought he was trying to kill me."

"So you killed him?"

"Don't answer that," Mike warned.

She ignored him. "I passed out. When I woke up, I was alone. I left the house and ran all the way back to Dr. Oney's."

Warner made a noise in his throat. "Ms. Ryder, why do you think Dr. Seger was choking you?"

"I...said something that made him angry."

"What was that?"

She glanced at Mike, who nodded. "When I was going to school here, there was a girl named Tammy Paulen who was killed on campus in a hit-and-run."

Neither man seemed surprised. "Go on," Warner urged.

"I was driving back to my dorm room that night, and I had my window down. I heard a scream, and when I turned the corner, she was lying in the road and a black Volvo was speeding away."

"Dr. Seger's car?"

"Yes."

"What did you do?"

"I didn't know what to do—I was in shock. I kept driving, then pulled over and parked my car. When I walked back, a car had stopped and two guys were bending over her. I knew they would help her, so I went back to my room." She swallowed. "I didn't know she was dead."

"Why didn't you tell the police what you saw?"

"Because...I didn't see it happen. I only heard her scream and saw the car. And the more I thought about it, the more I thought I might be mistaken."

"You couldn't put two and two together?"

They thought she was dumb. "Even if Dr. Seger had hit her, it was an accident. Tammy was...dead, and I couldn't see how destroying Dr. Seger's career would help anything."

The men exchanged doubtful glances, then Jaffey gave her a tight smile. "Ms. Ryder, we know that you were questioned in the hit-and-run of Tammy Paulen. Nell Oney was the girl's academic advisor and filled us in on the details. She said that Tammy Paulen knew something that she was holding over your head."

Her heart fell to her stomach—she thought her secret had died with that horrible girl, but could Tammy have told Nell?

"What does this have to do with Carl Seger's murder?" Mike asked.

Jaffey gave her the evil eye. "I think it's mighty convenient for Ms. Ryder to suddenly say that she saw Dr. Seger's car leaving the scene of a hit-and-run when he's not alive to defend himself." He pointed his finger at her. "Maybe you ran Tammy Paulen down in the street and now see your chance to pawn it off on Dr. Seger and claim self-defense for murdering him."

She shook her head. "No, you're wrong. Besides, my car was examined."

"But not until three days after the accident. It had been washed."

She didn't respond.

Jaffey slammed his hand on the table. "Did Tammy Paulen know you got on your knees for Dr. Seger? Was she threatening to tell?"

"N-no. Tammy died when I was a freshman, and the thing with Dr. Seger didn't happen until I was a senior."

"So you say. Then what was the big secret Tammy was holding over your head?"

"You don't have to answer," Mike said. "She's already told you what happened with Dr. Seger. You can see by her bruises that the man nearly killed her."

Jaffey shrugged. "Maybe she's into erotic asphyxiation."

Angora's eyes bugged. She'd read about that kind of thing—is that what Carl had been trying to do?

"Ms. Ryder, did you know your cousin went to Dr. Seger's house last night?"

She frowned. "What?"

"She jogged over there to see what was going on." He angled his head. "What do you suppose she saw when she looked in the window?"

Angora's stomach twisted. Roxann had spied on them? Had she seen Carl fondling her? Choking her?

Roxann had seemed so concerned this morning on the back porch, but was she covering up her own sins? If jealousy had propelled her to follow them, maybe she had seen them together and snapped. Maybe Roxann had killed Carl with her scarf while she lay passed out on his bed. And now she was letting Angora take the rap.

A sudden sharp pain in her chest took her breath away. She clutched the top of her dress, and fell forward in her chair.

"Ms. Ryder," Mike said, his voice elevated. "Ms. Ryder, are you okay?"

She was having a heart attack. She was going to die and everyone would say she was a murderer and Dee would have her cremated so she wouldn't have to bother with tending a grave.

The pain grew so intense her stomach heaved. Bright lights exploded behind her eyes. Someone grabbed her, but it was Carl, and he had his hands around her neck, squeezing the life out of her. She gasped for breath and clawed the air. God, what a waste her entire life had been. No one would even miss her.

CHAPTER TWENTY-TWO

"SHE'LL BE FINE," Capistrano said for the tenth time.

Roxann threw back the last mouthful of her hospital-vending-machine coffee. The emergency waiting room was packed with old people and mothers bouncing crying babies, which was why Jaffey and Warner had vamoosed two hours ago after giving orders for Angora to come back as soon as she was physically able. Meanwhile, she and Capistrano were holed up on a thinly padded bench in a corner. "I hope so."

"Is there a history of heart disease in your family?"

"No." She tossed the cup into an overflowing trash can sitting at her knee. "Just schizophrenia."

He smiled, but when she didn't smile back, he sobered. "Seriously?"

She nodded. "My dad told me the other day that our great-aunt was committed to an asylum after she pushed someone out of a window."

"Did the person die?"

"Yes."

He leaned forward to rest his elbows on his knees. "So what triggered that revelation?"

"I asked him."

"Why?"

"Because Nell told me that Angora was a suspect in a hit-and-run that occurred when we were students here."

"Who was the victim?"

"A girl named Tammy Paulen. She was a sorority sister of Angora's."

"Why was she considered a suspect?"

"Because she and the girl didn't get along. Apparently Tammy was holding something over Angora's head."

"Do you know what it was?"

She didn't look at him. "Yes. But I can't say."

"Was it enough for her to want to kill the girl over?"

"Of course not."

"But you think she might have?"

Roxann leaned back against the wall. "I don't know. It's hard to explain—Angora has always lived in a bit of a fantasy world. She would make up stories to convince people—and maybe herself—that her life was exciting."

"What kinds of stories?"

"Oh, the places she'd been and the people she'd met. It was funny because Angora would lie about little things that didn't matter."

"I guess they mattered to her."

She nodded. "Angora was a small-town beauty queen and carried herself as if she were better than everyone else. If truth be told, though, she was one of the most insecure people I ever met."

"But capable of running down a girl who was tormenting her?"

She sighed. "Maybe. Angora has a way of blocking out things—I guess that's her coping mechanism. You talked to her mother, I'm sure you can imagine what her childhood was like."

He nodded.

"Anyway, I remember the night we went to Tammy's memorial service. Everyone was upset, but Angora was inconsolable. We were living together in a dorm at the time, and I was worried about her state of mind."

"Did she ever talk about the accident?"

"Not then. I didn't know the Paulen girl was hassling her. But the night we spent at my father's she made some curious comments about the incident, and the other day she told me that Tammy knew she was a virgin and wanted to give Angora to her brother as a birthday gift."

He grimaced.

"Sick, huh? Anyway, then Angora said something about Tammy 'getting hers,' and she had this strange, faraway expression. She just zones out sometimes."

"So that was what you were holding back at the station?"

"You could tell?"

"I knew something was bothering you. What was your cousin's relationship with Seger?"

She closed her eyes briefly—*was*, as in past tense. "She was infatuated with him, like everyone else, although I didn't realize it. After being jilted at the altar, she was hell-bent on losing her virginity. I guess she picked Carl."

He lifted his eyebrow. "She's a virgin?"

A tiny sliver of jealousy cut through her at the tone of his voice. She remembered the way he'd looked at Angora. "Yes."

He pursed his mouth. "Does that particular characteristic run in the family, too?"

"You are so out of line."

One side of his mouth climbed. "Oh, so Miss Principled and Uptight is human, after all."

Roxann spoke through clenched teeth. "Just when I think you might be tolerable, you blow it by opening your mouth."

"I have to grow on a person."

"Like fungus?" She stood and stalked over to the receptionist's desk. "Can you give me an update on Angora Ryder, please?"

The moon-faced woman looked at her suspiciously. "Is she the lady the police brought in?"

"Yes, but she's not under arrest."

"Just a moment." The woman picked up the phone and lazily punched in a number, punctuating every movement with a sigh. Roxann wanted to strangle her, then quickly amended her thought in light of the circumstances. Poor Carl. God, what a mess they'd stepped into—maybe even created, although she couldn't quite get her mind around the idea of Angora murdering Carl. Still, his handprints were on her neck, so even if he hadn't planned to hurt her, he might have triggered a violent response in her.

She'd give anything to have stayed in Biloxi after the break-in, maybe hid out in a hotel. Instead, she'd allowed that message on her computer to unleash old worries that had hovered just under the surface for years. What was the saying about liars—their punishment was not that they couldn't be believed, but that they couldn't believe anyone else. The deception that she and Angora had created years ago had affected them both more than they could ever have imagined, shaping relationships with people they should have been close to, but couldn't be.

Roxann turned her head and looked at Capistrano, jammed into a space half his size. A little girl with sagging pigtails walked over and handed him a doll. He smiled and pretended to have a conversation with the doll before handing it back to her. The child gave him a shy grin and galloped off.

His smile lingered even after he made eye contact with Roxann across the room. She expected him to be embarrassed that she'd caught him in such an unguarded moment, but he didn't look away. In fact, his gaze traveled down her body in a leisurely fashion, combing over the clothes he'd loaned her to replace the ones the police sealed in a plastic bag. Beneath the huge white dress shirt and cavernous sweatpants, her skin tingled, as if she had donned his clothes the morning after a night of scrupulous lovemaking.

It was the stress, the proximity, and the deprivation. Why else would she be experiencing a sudden physical attraction to a hulking detective who was only hanging around because he expected her to eventually betray the whereabouts of his witness? He completed his inspection of her assets and met her gaze again in spite of bodies moving between them.

He was rather good-looking in a rugged sort of way. Who had Helen compared him to—Steve McQueen? Quite a change from the slender soft-handed men she had dated in the past. He stared and shifted his big body forward on the bench, an unmistakable gesture of invitation. She wet her lips involuntarily.

"Ma'am?"

She turned back to the receptionist. "Yes?"

"Ms. Ryder is in X-ray, but the technician says it's backed up. It'll be at least an hour if you'd like to get something to eat."

"Can I see her?"

The woman frowned, but relented and pointed the way.

Roxann followed a winding path through hallways and curtained areas. Angora lay in a corner bed with her eyes closed, pale, with golden hair fanned against the pillow. The bruises on her neck had turned pale purple. To Roxann's surprise, Angora's lawyer sat next to her bed.

"I didn't realize you were still here, Mr. um—"

"Brown," he whispered, standing. "I'm not supposed to be, but I didn't want the cops bothering Ms. Ryder."

The man was short and well-fed, with honest light brown eyes behind thick spectacles. He smelled faintly of manure. "How is she?" she asked.

"They think it might be her gallbladder. Something to do with a crash diet, followed by a binge?"

Not good, but at least not a heart attack. "Will she have to have surgery?"

"They won't know until they do more tests."

"As if you care," Angora said.

Roxann turned to see Angora had awakened. She was surprised at the venom in her cousin's voice. "How are you feeling?"

"Lousy. And I don't want you here."

She pulled back. "Why?"

"I'll step out into the hall," Mr. Brown offered, then skedaddled.

Angora's mouth tightened. "Are you happy now that I'm on my deathbed and accused of murder?"

"You're not on your deathbed, and how can you think that I'd be happy about any of this?"

"You told the police things I said." Angora sat up, her red eyes welling. "Things I told you in confidence. They think I murdered Carl because of you and your jealousy."

She frowned. "Jealousy?"

Angora leaned forward, her eyes wide and glazed. "You couldn't stand the thought of Carl and me together, so you sneaked over to spy on us."

"You're wrong." Roxann crossed her arms. "I had heard some bad things about Carl, and I was worried about you. But when I got there, I realized it was wrong and that you're old enough to take care of yourself."

"That's right," Angora flung back. "Haven't you interfered enough in my life?"

Roxann gaped. "Interfered? If you recall, I've gotten you out of more than one jam."

Angora narrowed her eyes. "And if I recall, you were rewarded nicely."

Her stomach leaped. "Angora, don't do this. You're upset."

She flailed against the sheets, eyes wild. "And why shouldn't I be? My cousin is framing me for murder. I knew everyone else was out to get me, but I thought I could trust you."

Roxann eased down to sit on the end of the bed, maintaining level eye contact. It was the best way to calm an unstable person. "Angora," she said softly. "No one is out to get you—we all want to help. If you killed Carl in self-defense, you'll be acquitted."

But Angora became even more agitated. "I told you, and I told the police—I passed out!"

"And I believe you," Roxann assured her. At least she believed that *Angora* believed she'd passed out.

"No you don't," Angora said, pulling up her legs and hunkering against her pillow. "I think you did it, and you're setting me up. You've made my life miserable since we were kids—you had everything. You were prettier and smarter." Her face contorted and she assumed a "Dee" pose. "Angora, why can't you be more like Roxann?"

Roxann swallowed hard. "You're not being fair."

"Fair? Don't talk to me about fair." She laughed, a high-pitched screech. "My mother wanted you instead of me. She wanted you more than your own mother wanted you."

"That's not true."

"Oh, yes it is." Angora stabbed the air with an ink-stained finger. "The reason your father got custody of you after the divorce wasn't because he was trying to keep you from your mother—your mother didn't want you."

Her lungs shrank. "That's an ugly thing to say."

But Angora was triumphant. "It's true. Your mother didn't want you. And everyone in the family knew except you."

Roxann stood and stumbled back, shaking her head, replaying snatches of long-forgotten memories in her head—the custody hearing that had seemed so lopsided, plans to see her mother that always seemed to dissolve at the last minute. She thought her father had thwarted the visits, but had he been covering up for her mother all these years? Her heart thumped wildly in her chest, a mild reaction considering the fact that the foundation of her childhood beliefs had just been rocked. She whirled and ran smack into Capistrano, who, by the look on his face, had heard at least the end of their conversation. Face flaming, she charged around him. "I'm leaving."

But he captured her with one arm. "Dr. Oney just called. Frank Cape came to see her."

Alarm zigzagged through her limbs. "Is she okay?"

He nodded. "Just shaken up. She'd like to see you."

She puffed out her cheeks in an exhausted sigh. "Will you take me?"

"Of course." He waved a uniformed security officer forward. "I notified the police to be on the lookout for Cape, and I thought I'd have someone posted near your cousin in case he made an appearance here."

He'd thought of everything, and God, it was nice to be looked after, instead of doing the looking aftering. "Thank you."

He nodded, taking it all in stride, this being-in-charge thing. "Let's get out of here," he said, his eyes sympathetic.

"Roxann," Angora said behind them, her voice contrite. "Roxann, don't leave me here alone with a madman on the loose. I'm sorry for what I said. Roxann?"

But she was over Angora's tantrums, and tired of making excuses for her. At the doorway she turned back. "I never thought I'd say this, Angora, but you're your mother's daughter."

From the blanched look on Angora's face, the comment had hit its mark.

CHAPTER TWENTY-THREE

ROXANN SLUMPED IN THE SEAT of Capistrano's truck and wondered what all the sane people in the world were doing. And to think a week ago she'd believed her life was complicated. Ha.

She glanced at her watch—six o'clock in the evening, and the longest day of her life seemed far from over. If she were in England, she'd be getting ready for bed about now. A memory stirred and she cursed.

"Was that meant for me?"

She sighed. "No. With all the commotion, I completely forgot about meeting Elise at the chapel."

"So call her. The police might want to question her anyway."

"I don't know where she's staying, but I guess I could check the local motels." In her mind she replayed the scene when she had spoken to Elise. "She said something interesting yesterday when I ran into her."

He grinned. "That you have a good bod?"

"You are so unfunny. She said she realized that all of her troubles stemmed from a relationship she had in college."

"Are you thinking she had a relationship with Dr. Seger?"

"That's making a pretty big leap."

"But since the man is dead, it's worth mentioning to the police." Then he grinned. "But it's still not as interesting as it would've been if she'd said you have a good bod."

"Shut. Up." She sighed. "When did Cape show up at Nell's?"

"Around four-thirty, but it took a while for Dr. Oney to track us down at the hospital."

"Poor Nell," she murmured. "First Carl's death, and now this."

"Maybe it isn't a coincidence. Maybe Frank Cape was making good on his threat to hurt people you were close to."

"But how did he know I was in South Bend?"

"Have you been using credit cards?"

"I don't have any."

"Your cell phone?"

"No, only pay phones. Besides, why would Cape think that I was close to Carl Seger? I hadn't seen Carl in years."

His shrug was a little too casual. "But you were in love with him?"

Love—another word she would have bet wasn't in the man's vocabulary. "Carl was the first man who listened to me, the first man who made me feel important."

"And the first man to break your heart?"

Roxann gave a self-deprecating laugh. "I was devastated when he didn't come for me after the scandal, but I thought it was out of some lofty sense of nobility." She waved her hand dramatically. "It somehow seemed even more poignant."

"And you've been pining for him ever since?"

"No, not pining. Wondering, maybe. It was pretty strong stuff for a young heart."

"Sounds like it," he said in a dubious tone.

"You've never been in love, Detective?"

He shifted in his seat, then fiddled with the radio knob. "Can't get a station worth a damn up here."

"I thought not." She smirked, then laid her head back. But she acknowledged a bit of a tingle at managing to put him on the spot.

Capistrano cleared his throat. "Listen, I couldn't help but overhear what your cousin said back there. It was probably the medication talking."

"No it wasn't." She pushed herself up and stared out the window at clumps of Homecoming visitors, most of them probably oblivious to last night's murder, or immune because they hadn't known Carl personally. "A couple of years before my mother was killed in a car accident, she left me and my father for another man. Deep down, I've always known, but I've never admitted it to anyone. He drove a blue car."

He looked at her, his gaze straight and void of pity. It gave her the courage to forge ahead.

"And on some level, I guess I sensed my mother didn't want me after the divorce, but it was easier to believe that Dad was keeping me away from her."

"He never told you?"

"No."

"To protect you."

She nodded slowly. "Yes." For years her father had silently borne the brunt of her resentment, all the while knowing that her mother hadn't cared enough to stay. Or visit. Or even call. She wiped a tear from the corner of her eye and sniffed mightily. How she'd underestimated her father. And how she'd overestimated Carl. Who else? She glanced sideways at Capistrano. He hadn't mentioned Melissa Cape recently...was it possible that he was sticking around out of the goodness of his heart?

Nah. He'd said so himself—no one had ever accused him of being a nice guy.

He slowed to pull into Nell's narrow driveway. "Where's your van?"

"Around back."

"Well, I guess we know why Cape thought you were here."

She frowned. "Why didn't you put him out of everyone's misery back in Little Rock?"

"Nothing I would've liked better, except he wasn't doing anything."

"He was harassing me."

He brought the truck to a stop. "You said I was harassing you."

She unhooked her seat belt. "Well, next time, shoot him in the foot or something."

"I wouldn't waste a bullet there," he said, then turned off the ignition.

A locksmith was installing a new dead bolt on the door. Nell didn't answer their call right away, but when she did, her red eyes belied her welcoming smile.

"I'm so sorry," Roxann said, squeezing Nell's hands. "It's my fault that Frank Cape was here—did he hurt you?"

"No," she said, then motioned for them to sit in the living room. "Forgive me, it's just...everything. Carl's d-death, you girls being questioned, then that awful man showing up."

"How did he get in?" Capistrano asked.

"I don't know," she said. "The doors were locked. I was in the kitchen and he was suddenly standing there."

"What did he say?"

Nell's tongue darted in and out, and she scooped Chester from the floor to hold in her lap. She stroked his coat in a manner that was, hopefully, as soothing to her as to the purring animal. "He said he was looking for Roxann, said she could lead him to his wife and daughter. Said that no cop was going to scare him off."

Capistrano shifted in his chair. "Did he say anything that might make you think he was involved in Dr. Seger's murder?"

Her eyes widened. "Do you think he could have killed Carl? I thought Angora—"

"The police aren't sure," he cut in. "Cape did make threats on people who were close to Roxann. Please try to remember."

Her brow furrowed. "He just said to tell Roxann that he'd show up when she least expected it. Then he took a knife out of my butcher block and plunged it into a cutting board." She shivered. "Roxann, I know it goes against Rescue program policy, but maybe you could contact his wife and see if a reconciliation is possible. Or see if she would at least talk to the man."

Roxann gaped. "Nell, it required every ounce of strength that poor woman had to take her daughter away and start a new life. I can't just call her up now and encourage her to contact him." She looked at Capistrano. "You did not hear that."

He averted his eyes.

But her mentor was undaunted. "It was never the intent of the program to put the lives of the facilitators at risk. Frank Cape is a dangerous man, and there's been enough bloodshed around here. Perhaps I can intervene and get you out of the middle?"

"Maybe that's not a bad idea," Capistrano said.

Roxann glared at him. "It's a terrible idea."

"Dr. Oney," he said, "were you aware that if Cape's ex-wife comes forward to testify in a crime that Frank committed, we could put him away and she wouldn't have to worry?"

Nell glanced at Roxann. "Is this true?"

Roxann stuck her tongue in her cheek, still glaring at Capistrano. "Everything except the 'she wouldn't have to worry' part. You know how often these thugs get off on a technicality or are granted early release from prison."

Nell looked at Capistrano. "Can the police protect her?"

"Yes."

"Where is she?" Nell asked Roxann.

Roxann sprang up. "That's privileged information, Nell."

"And as a founder of this program, I'm making an executive decision to override policy for the good of everyone concerned." She set Chester down and he scampered away. "Roxann," Nell said, her voice breaking, "I don't want to see you get hurt."

"I'll...think about it."

Nell nodded, satisfied.

"Did Cape leave on his own?" the detective asked.

"After he made the threat, I was afraid he might hurt me, but there was a knock on the front door, and he went out the back." She turned a sad smile toward Roxann. "It was the university chancellor. He asked if I would help arrange a memorial service for Carl."

Just like Tammy Paulen. "Does he have family nearby?" If he had ever spoken of his family when they were together, she couldn't recall.

Nell shook her head. "Carl didn't have any family living. I heard him say several times that he wanted to be cremated and his ashes spread over the campus. I suggested to the chancellor that it would be best to wait until next week, after Homecoming. Maybe by then the police will have made an arrest." She looked at Roxann. "I know she's your cousin, Roxann, but I don't want to see Angora get away with murder again."

This morning Roxann had been willing to defend Angora, but now she was beginning to wonder if her cousin teetered on the edge of stability, and if returning to campus on the heels of her jilting simply had been too much for her. She said nothing.

Capistrano stood. "Dr. Oney, do you have somewhere safe to stay for a few days?"

She nodded slowly. "My sister lives in Indy. I can take the bus."

"Pack a bag and we'll take you to the station," he said. "Stay there until I can track down Frank Cape."

Nell didn't argue—she seemed relieved to be escaping the melee. "What about Roxann?"

"She'll stay with me."

Roxann blinked. She would? "I will?"

"Relax," he said. "My room has two double beds. But at least I can keep an eye on you."

Relax, he said.

CHAPTER TWENTY-FOUR

ROXANN RETURNED THE PHONE to its cradle. "Angora is having surgery in the morning." They were sequestered in his hotel room on separate "islands," she on one bed with the phone, Capistrano on the other mulling over a manila file of papers. He'd already blown the fully clothed rule she'd laid down by shucking his shirt, while she, on the other hand, still wore her jacket over the shirt he'd loaned her. Zipped.

And as far as shirtless went, he didn't look half bad. She'd never been attracted to a man with a hairy chest—not that she was attracted to this one. But it was...curious, all that dark hair lying close to his skin. And the muscles...

"Roxann?"

She jerked her head up. "Yes?"

"I asked how long she'll be in the hospital?"

Her cheeks warmed. "At least overnight, but I encouraged her attorney to consider a psych consult while she's there."

"The guy seemed like a greenhorn to me."

She bit her bottom lip. "I thought so, too, but he's nice. And he's staying with her at the hospital."

"Racking up those hourly charges."

"No, he took the case for practically nothing. For the experience, I suppose."

"Cape hasn't shown up?"

"No. What are you working on?"

He scratched his head and leaned back against the headboard. His jean-clad legs extended almost the length of the bed. "Just trying to piece together elements of the murder. Sometimes if I keep going over the details, something new will spring out at me."

She swung her legs over the side of her bed to face him. "You know, you never once asked if I did it."

He looked up. "If you did what?"

"Killed Carl. I admitted that I went to his house that night, and he was found with my scarf around his neck, but you never asked."

Capistrano shrugged his massive shoulders. "Didn't have to. You're not wired to be dishonest. If you'd done it, you would've confessed, especially since your cousin is being accused." He turned back to his folder.

It piqued her, his pat psychoanalysis of her, even if it were true. The dishonest pact that she'd made with Angora years ago had eaten at her and she hadn't realized it, not even after her insides were gone. She'd avoided relationships of any kind, pawning it off on her schedule, her obligations, her commitments, when in reality, the Rescue program had been a handy emotional hideout. The sad part was that she still couldn't bring herself to come clean—everyone would be so disappointed in her. Nell. Her father. Capistrano. And wouldn't she then have to face the lie herself?

"Maybe you're biased," she offered.

He looked up again. "Because I'm attracted to you?"

She squirmed and zipped her jacket higher on her neck. He laughed, a big booming noise that made her frown. "How can you even think of sex when my life is such a nightmare?"

He shrugged. "You look sexy in my clothes. Besides, it might take your mind off things."

She sputtered. "Someone who once played an important role in my life was just murdered. I am a suspect, and my cousin, who is also a suspect, is in the hospital. Then there's that little matter of being dogged by a maniac."

"So you're saying you're not in the mood?"

She gave him the finger.

"Okay, okay," he said, seemingly unfazed, then looked back to his notes. "We'll have the medical examiner's report tomorrow. And they're checking for Cape's fingerprints at the scene of the crime."

Roxann marveled at the man's ability to move from subject to subject seamlessly—as if neither one mattered more than the other. She inhaled deeply to calm her frustration. He'd love knowing he irritated her. "Can I have a restraining order issued on Cape?"

"Sure. We'll do it first thing in the morning. Then at least we'll be able to hold him for something if he comes near you again. And maybe by then we'll be able to tie him to the murder."

As much as she hoped that Frank Cape was guilty, the thought of him killing Carl to get back at her was nauseating. If the man was that crazy, then she was seriously glad she'd helped Melissa and her daughter get away from him. And even more disturbed that Nell would suggest that she appease the bully.

In an attempt to look somewhere other than Capistrano's bare chest, she glanced at the sound-muted television, surprised when a picture of Carl appeared over the shoulder of the newscaster. She dove for the remote next to Capistrano's leg and turned up the volume.

"—Seger was a theology professor at the University of Notre Dame, and a coach on the varsity soccer team. Fifty-two-year-old Seger was found dead in his home early this morning in a South Bend neighborhood, a few miles from campus. Police are releasing few details, but a source tells us that Seger, a bachelor and a deacon of the university church, was strangled by a woman's scarf. The mystery comes in the middle of the university's Homecoming activities, when the city's population increases by half. The police have questioned suspects, including some of Dr. Seger's former students, but an arrest has not yet been made. School officials will hold a memorial service for Dr. Seger next week."

She lowered the volume. "It still doesn't seem real."

"Much of life is like that," he said, then stretched tall in a yawn. "Do you want to hit the shower first, or should I?"

"Um, go ahead. I need to make a few phone calls."

He stood and gestured to his gun lying in a holster on the TV cabinet. "Do you know how to use old Pete here?"

She nodded. "I've been to the firing range a few times."

"The safety is on. Don't answer the door."

"Duh."

He moved his body like an animal, slow and measured, and sure of himself. Comfortable. Sexy. Male. The smooth skin of his wide back was broken by a four-inch-long scar, fully healed, but red and perhaps less than a year old. She was torn between asking its origin and not wanting him to know she noticed.

"Steak knife," he said, standing with his back to her.

"What?"

He turned. "The scar. I was stabbed with a steak knife by a woman trying to keep me from arresting her boyfriend who had just broken her jaw." His smile was wry. "My partner told me that's what I got for turning my back on a woman."

"Looks like it was a serious wound."

"Serious enough. Made me start appreciating the things that are important."

"Like?"

"Like family and friends and pistachio ice cream."

She relinquished a small smile. "You're lucky. Most people spend their entire lives trying to figure out what makes them happy." The voice of experience.

"I'm no expert," he said, folding thick arms over his chest, "but it seems to me that people complicate their lives either by trying to be something they're not, or by trying to fix things they can't."

I'VE GOT YOUR NUMBER, YOU FAKE.

Some things just can't be fixed, Roxann, no matter how much glue you put on 'em.

She swallowed and gestured to the phone. "I really should make those calls."

He leaned over to pull off his boots and tall thick socks. She watched beneath her lashes, mesmerized. Bare feet were not typically the sexiest part of the body, but just the fact that she was seeing them reminded her of the intimacy of their sleeping arrangement. He rifled through a drawer and removed pale blue boxers, navy pajama pants, and a white T-shirt. He walked toward the bathroom, then stopped short of the door and grinned. "If you happen to change your mind—"

"I won't, Detective."

He sighed and disappeared behind the closed door. The water came on, then the shower, and she tried to think about something else. Oh, yes—the phone calls.

Not a pleasant task. First to her father, who would've probably heard about the murder by now. He had, and he was worried.

"Yes, Dad, Angora and I both know—knew—Dr. Seger. And we were both questioned because we saw him last night at a campus event." True enough. "The police haven't made any arrests yet."

"When are you coming back?" he asked, suddenly sounding old.

"Soon," she promised. "Angora had a gallbladder attack this morning and is in the hospital. She's having surgery tomorrow and we'll stay until she's able to travel, probably a few more days."

"Does Dixie know?"

"I thought I'd leave it up to Angora whether she wanted to contact her mother."

"I don't like the idea of you being there alone with a murderer on the loose."

"I'm not alone." She hesitated. "Officer Capistrano is...around."

"Oh. Well, I guess that makes me feel a little better."

The bathroom door opened and Capistrano yelled, "Roxann, can you hand me a bar of soap?" Then the door closed again.

She covered the mouth of the phone, sending curses through the wall.

"So you are seeing him?" her dad asked.

"No, I'm not seeing him. He just happens to be—never mind. One thing before I go, Dad." She took a deep breath. "Angora told me about Mother...that she didn't want custody of me when you divorced."

After a few seconds of silence, he said, "Dixie has a big mouth."

"Why didn't you tell me?"

He sighed. "Your heart was already broken like that sad little teacup you carried around. I couldn't bear for you to know that your mother was so wrapped up in her new boyfriend that she didn't have time for you. After she died, well...what was the point?"

She blinked back tears and smiled into the phone, "Dad, when I get back, can we talk?"

"Sure. For as long as you want."

"Roxann?" bellowed Capistrano.

"I'll call you soon," she promised, then hung up and stalked to the closed door. "How dare you yell for me when I was on the phone! That was my father."

"Your father liked me." His voice was muffled, but amused.

"That was before he knew you were taking a shower within earshot of the phone I'm using."

The doorknob moved and she whirled, turning her back just as the door opened. Steam rolled out around her, but she stared stubbornly at the opposite wall.

"Soap?" he asked. "It's in my toiletry bag. You can get it, or I can."

"I'll get it," she snapped, then stalked over to his bag.

"Side pocket, green bar."

"I see it." A big block that smelled like pine needles. She backed up to the door, holding the soap behind her. "Here."

"Thanks," he said, then took the soap and closed the door.

She sighed and wiped her wet hand on her—no, *his* sweatpants, feeling like an idiot. She had no business being attracted to Capistrano, not when so many other things demanded her concentration.

She called Nell's sister next, just to make sure she'd arrived safely. Nell was resting, her sister assured her. As was Chester, the one cat that Nell insisted on taking with her. At least she was safe, and there was one less person to worry about.

Roxann spotted Capistrano's file and shot a glance toward the bathroom. His electric razor was buzzing, so she had time for a peek. His handwriting was large, but neat—not surprising. Behind the first page was the police report of Carl's murder. Abbreviated and barely readable. *Oct 18, 5:05 a.m. Wht Male found on floor of home libr, apparnt vic of strnglat. Wearing shrt. pants, one shoe. Grn woman's scrf arnd neck. Signs of rigor.*

She swallowed hard and thumbed through the file, coming across a manila envelope marked "crime scene photos." Her heart raced, but she felt compelled to slide her finger under the flap. At least a dozen black-and-white photos slipped out into her hand. The first was a wide-angle shot of the library and Carl's body lying on the floor near an ottoman, his limbs sprawled, his head at an odd angle, looking away from the camera. She inhaled sharply and covered her mouth. He looked like a mannequin, a prop in a weekend murder-mystery game.

Another photo was taken standing over his body, this one clearly showing the scarf wrapped around his neck. Her scarf. Roxann gulped air.

Close-ups of different parts of his body and clothing—his hands, his feet, his shirt, his house shoes—one on, one off.

And then his face. Unrecognizable as the handsome, confident man she had known. He was cartoonish and swollen, his cheeks and forehead puffy. His head was turned to the left, his eyes slightly open. Just enough that if she looked hard enough, she could imagine their bright blue color. The photos slid from her fingers and bounced on the carpet. She choked on a sob.

"Hey, hey," Capistrano chided, his arms going around her from behind. "You shouldn't be looking at those."

She turned into his chest and nodded, inhaling a clean, evergreen scent. His skin was damp, and he wore only the pajama pants. She felt petite against his frame and safe in his arms. God, was it good to feel safe. Everything female in her reared its head, and her arms went around his neck. His kiss took ownership of her fear and anxiety, offering comfort and refuge in return. When she moaned into his mouth, he pulled her up and against him, deepening the kiss. But he let her take the lead, let her decide when and if the kiss would go from comforting to carnal. A few skipped heartbeats later, she lifted her leg and hooked it around the back of his knee—an unmistakable signal, she figured.

His hands moved down over her back and inside the baggy sweatpants to mold her into him. When he encountered the thong underwear, a groan of pure male appreciation moved through his body, and she laughed. He grinned and lifted her off the floor to set her on the edge of the bed. The outline of his arousal against the thin fabric of his pajamas sent moisture to her thighs.

He knelt before her, cupped her face in his hands and kissed her again, with more intensity and a probing tongue that hinted of other intimacies. Her neck loosened and her bones turned elastic. She kneaded the skin on his shoulders and back, reveling in the solid maleness, the stability of his body.

"Let me see you," he murmured, his hands already undoing the ridiculous jacket she wore. She allowed her silence to be her acquiescence. The slide of the zipper sent chills over her shoulders. It would be good for them to get each other out of their systems, she decided. Good to get it over with so they could go their separate ways when this mess ended.

Her jacket fell to the floor, then the shirt of his she wore. He never took his eyes from her, drinking her in and smiling with pleasure. He kissed her neck and collarbone before wrapping his arms around her waist, nudging down the straps of the filmy white bra and kissing her breasts. His lovemaking had an edge, a restrained power that seemed instinctual to him. Even the guttural whispers and moans he breathed over her skin were animalistic. She had always presumed that big, macho men used their strength to threaten and intimidate—she'd certainly been exposed to enough of them through the Rescue program—but the detective's determined mouth pushed her closer to the edge than she'd imagined was possible while still wearing panties.

He certainly knew what he was doing, she noted as she gasped for air. But did *she*? He was so different from any man she'd been intimate with, she felt almost virginal. Maybe she should have given that making-love-to-a-man book a refresher read.

But once the underwear came off, it was amazing how quickly everything came back to her. In fact, things were going quite well until a knock sounded at the door.

Capistrano stopped what he was doing—much to her chagrin—and walked to the door, grabbing his gun on the way. There was something so...*arresting* about a naked man wielding a gun. She scrambled for something to cover up.

"Who's there?" Capistrano asked, pointing his weapon in the air.

"Officers Jaffey and Warner, Detective. Open up."

Capistrano mouthed a curse, lowered the gun, and retrieved his pajama bottoms from the floor. He waited until she was haphazardly clothed before he unlocked the door.

They charged past Capistrano into the room. "Roxann Beadleman, you're under arrest for the murder of Carl Seger."

Okay, so *arresting* had been an unfortunate word choice.

CHAPTER TWENTY-FIVE

IT HURT TO BREATHE. Angora pushed the nurses' call button several times in succession, but she knew they wouldn't come. They hated her. "Nurse!" she yelled, although it came out a hoarse whisper. "Nurse!"

The door to her private room opened, and Mike Brown peeked around the corner. She rolled her eyes—the man was undoubtedly the most annoying little boy she'd ever met. And although she was grateful for his legal advice, the hayseed act was wearing a bit thin. She'd heard more about running a "soybean-slash-corn" farm than she ever wanted to know. Tractors. Tillers. Pickers. Plows. *Ugh.*

"I brought you magazines," he said, holding up a bulging plastic bag.

She gave him a begrudged smile—she had requested magazines, after all. "Thanks."

He walked in, wearing overalls of all things. And not Tommy Hilfiger. "*Progressive Farmer*," he said, plopping the bag down on the bed next to her. "I had a year's worth saved up."

"Er, thanks."

"Is there anything else I can get for you? I have to go home for the evening milking, so I can't stay long." His baby fat made him look young and shiny. "But I'll be back tomorrow."

She batted her lashes. "Can you find a nurse to add painkiller to my IV so I can get some sleep tonight?"

He dimpled. "I'll see what I can do." He left the room, landing heavily on his workbooted feet.

Laying her head back, she stared at the ceiling tiles and wondered what Trenton was doing and if he'd heard of her major illness. If she'd known how much attention a hospital stay would get her, she would've landed this gig sooner. A gallbladder was a small price to pay to have rattled even Dee, who had sounded almost motherly on the phone when she'd called to break the grim news about the operation she needed. And the secondary infection she'd contracted was a bonus. "Complications," her chart read. It had at least kept the police at bay, and the get-well bouquets coming—from her parents, her former boss at the art museum, Mike Brown, and Roxann.

Roxann. She sighed, This entire situation surrounding Carl's death was a big fat mess. At least the bruises were fading. She wanted to act as if it hadn't even happened, and Mike was eager to go along. He'd had her tested by a sandal-wearing talk-doctor from the university and seemed satisfied with whatever the woman had told him. She, on the other hand, found it hard to put faith in a woman who didn't shave her legs.

But back to Carl—the perv deserved it, she'd decided. Maybe a few female students would be spared her humiliation and heartache. The universe was in balance, as far as she was concerned.

She heard footsteps, which gave her just enough time to fan her hair out on the pillow. But it was only Mike, smiling and mopping at his forehead, which was perpetually moist. "You're not due another painkiller for two hours, Angora."

"That's unacceptable," she croaked, clutching at her midsection. He disappeared again, then returned in a few minutes. "One hour. I made the nurse promise she'd give you another in one hour."

She smiled prettily. "Thank you."

His eyes shone. "You're welcome."

"Is the guard still at my door?"

"Yes, but he said he hadn't seen anyone who matched the description of the Cape fellow that your cousin is so worried about."

A commotion sounded in the hall, and they exchanged wide-eyed glances. Angora hunkered against her pillow and Mike armed himself at the door with a vase of roses.

"No, get the one with the carnations in it," she hissed.

He switched the vases, then stood poised in the doorway to wallop the bad guy. The handle turned and he pulled back, coming close to whopping Dee in the mouth.

"Mother!" she whispered, truly surprised. She held out her arms weakly, but didn't lift her head because it was more pitiful, and she didn't want to mess up her hair.

Dee glared at Mike and his weapon, then swept into the room. "Darling, your father and I came as soon as our tennis tournament ended."

Angora conjured up a weak smile. "You shouldn't have come all this way just to see me."

"And why not?" her father boomed, then shot a pointed glance toward Dee. "We should have been here sooner."

"Why is there a guard outside your door?" Dee asked.

"Um, it's a long story."

Her mother pursed her heavily coated mouth. "Make it short."

Angora's mind raced furiously. "Well...there is a murderer on the loose."

"Of that professor you told me about on the phone."

"Right. I, um, bid for a date with him at a charity b-bachelor auction."

Disapproval darkened Dee's eyes.

"So I was...the last person to see him alive—other than the person who killed him, of course." There.

Her mother's eyes flew wide. "You're in danger?"

She sighed dramatically. "The police seem to think so."

"Honey," her father said, leaning into her. "We had no idea."

"I didn't want to alarm you."

Dee's eyes narrowed. "Your cousin has something to do with this, doesn't she?"

She lifted her chin. "The world doesn't revolve around Roxann, Mother. And I'm feeling fine, thanks for asking." She manufactured a little cough, which really did hurt, and lolled her head to the side. "I'm having complications, you know."

"When can we take you home?" her father asked.

"The doctors haven't told me when they're planning to release me—those complications are really complicating matters."

"Will you have an ugly scar?" Dee asked.

Of course that would be high on her mother's list. "I don't know."

Dee sighed. "Well, with those hips, you're past wearing a bikini anyway." Her mother hefted her Donna Karan purse onto the bed, sending a tremor throughout the mattress.

Her father said he needed to repark the rental car—Dee had made him pull into a handicapped spot so she wouldn't have to walk. When he left, Angora realized that when the going got tough, her father did something automotive. She braced herself for whatever bomb Dee was going to drop.

"Surprise—I brought your wedding pictures with me!"

She squinted. "Mom, I didn't get married, remember?"

"Well, almost, dear. I told the photographer to develop the pictures he took before the ceremony. Here are the proofs of the ones with your eyes open." She handed them over. "You have a peculiar look on your face in most of them, but your bridesmaids look splendid."

Her mother was right—she did, and they did. Instead of glowing with nuptial bliss, she had a pinched look about her face, as if something sharp were in her shoe. But the bridesmaids wore their best fake I'm-so-happy-for-her smiles. In the photos of herself alone, she seemed almost incidental to the shot. A great picture of the fountain with a bride in the foreground. A great picture of the church with a bride entering right.

"Here's the one of you and me," Dee said, then wiped at an imaginary tear. "I look so sad."

In the photo, Dee looked the same as always. Sad, happy, surprised—who knew? She'd had the plastic surgeon sever most of the muscles that affected expression, although the "angry" muscles had somehow managed to regenerate.

"And this one of me and your father is grand. I already ordered a sixteen-by-twenty."

It was a good photo—her mother looked slim and pleased at the prospect of being rid of her.

"I ordered you a photo album—one of every shot," Dee said.

"But I don't want a photo album," she whispered.

"And good news—almost everyone I contacted said you should keep their gift, that you deserved it."

"Mother, did you hear me?"

"Except for Lilly Barkin, but she only sent a Pyrex dish, for heaven's sake. As if you could cook anyway."

"Mother, I don't want any photos, and I don't want any gifts." Well, maybe the silver tea service, but the rest of it was going back.

"Don't be difficult, Angora."

"I just want to pretend as if that day never happened."

"Well, it did happen, young lady, and I had to do all the explaining." Dee fanned herself. "Have some sympathy for me—after all, I was humiliated in front of my entire social circle."

"*You* were humiliated?"

"That's right. That church wasn't packed to see Angora Ryder be married, missy—it was packed to see Dee Ryder's daughter be married." Her mouth flattened. "And you couldn't even do that right. God, Angora, you are a colossal screw-up."

"I think you'd better leave."

Angora and her mother both looked up. She had forgotten that Mike Brown was still in the room. He sort of blended in with the drab walls.

Dee lifted one eyebrow. "Excuse me?"

"You're upsetting her. I think it's time for you to leave."

Angora blinked—no one ordered her mother around.

"*Who* are you?" Dee asked in the voice she saved for the gardener.

"Ms. Ryder's attorney."

Dee scoffed. "And why would my daughter need an attorney?"

"I told you," Angora broke in hurriedly. "I was the last person to see Dr. Seger alive." She sent Mike a warning glance—if her parents thought she was a suspect in a murder case, they'd stroke out. "Mr. Brown is handling the police for me."

Dee looked him up and down. "Looks to me as if he's handling the livestock." She shook her head. "No, this person will never do. I'll call Bennett and he'll fly up to take care of everything. You may go," she said to him, punctuated with a shooing motion.

"Mrs. Ryder, this is your daughter's decision." He hooked his thumbs in his suspenders and boldly stared at Dee.

Dee stared back for a few seconds, then faltered. "Angora?" she chirped.

Angora gawked. Any man who could face down her mother was someone she needed on her side. "I choose Mr. Brown," she murmured in renewed appreciation.

"And you should be going, Mrs. Ryder," he said. "Angora needs her rest. She's had complications, you know."

Angora coughed to bolster his argument. And in truth, she was growing tired.

Then the door burst open and those two plainclothes police officers strode in. The hateful one, Jaffey, leveled his gaze on her. "Angora Ryder, you're under arrest for the murders of Tammy Paulen and Dr. Carl Seger. You have the right to remain silent—"

Her mother swayed, then hit the floor face first. The cop didn't miss a beat, shouting her rights while the three men wrestled Dee into a chair. She roused and began to screech hysterically, something about the Junior League and being blackballed.

"Do you understand your rights?" Jaffey yelled over the fracas.

Angora nodded, then sighed. Only Dee could turn the spotlight on herself while her daughter was being handcuffed to a hospital bed.

CHAPTER TWENTY-SIX

AFTER A NIGHT IN THE COUNTY JAIL, the next-to-last thing Roxann needed was a gauntlet of reporters in the hall of the district attorney's office. But the very last thing she needed was a confrontation with her Aunt Dee in front of said reporters. Her aunt was coming out of the restroom, and when she saw Roxann, her face screwed up.

"This is all your fault!" Jackson held his wife back by the shoulders as security guards circled. "If you hadn't interfered, Angora wouldn't be in this mess."

Roxann bit her tongue to keep from pointing out that she was in the same mess, and her daughter wasn't exactly blameless.

"You talked her into it, I know! Angora is a good girl—she would never do anything to disgrace me and her father on her own."

Roxann stopped. Cameras flashed. "Angora was arrested for murder, and you're worried about the family name? God, you're such a bitch." They'd probably bleep that part out on the local news.

Dee's face went scarlet. "Peasant. Just like your father."

"I take that as a compliment." She stepped up her pace and caught up with her white-faced attorney. Phyllis Troy had the most impressive ad in the Yellow Pages but was more nervous than Roxann at the prospect of a conference with the DA. Not a good sign.

The meeting-room door stood open. Roxann held back until her aunt and uncle passed through, then closed the door behind Phyllis, who was now visibly shaking.

"Come on in and have a seat." District Attorney Robert Mason waved them in. He was a big blond-haired man in his fifties who had the voice and demeanor of a Baptist preacher. He lorded over a dark wood conference table surrounded by padded chairs. One of the chairs was occupied by a young woman whom he introduced as an assistant DA. Angora's attorney, the round-faced Mr. Brown, occupied another. He had dressed up, sporting a new denim shirt, and his curly hair was slicked back with something shiny. Angora herself looked frail and victimized sitting in a wheelchair and wearing a paper gown. A blanket covered her legs. She refused to make eye contact, which suited Roxann just fine. Dee and Jackson moved their chairs to sit on either side of Angora and hold her hands. Sadly, it was probably the most of their undivided attention she'd ever received.

"How was jail?" Mason asked Roxann without preliminary.

"Unpleasant," she answered. In a single night the institutional funk of the place had permeated her skin, hair, and clothing. Thanks to a doctor's note, Angora had been spared the same treatment and confined to a guarded hospital room until her arraignment, which had taken place this morning moments before Roxann's. They both had pleaded "not guilty." Roxann tried not to let the fact that Capistrano hadn't shown up in court, or since, bother her. The episode in the hotel room was a manifestation of mixed emotions, none of them grounded. She had thought of a way to get rid of him, but first things first.

Mason opened a file on top of the stack in front of him. "This wasn't your first time in our jail."

"No. I was arrested twice during protest rallies when I attended the university."

Dee made an indignant noise in her throat. "I'm not a bit surprised."

Mason swung his gaze in her direction. "They were peaceful protests."

"Roxann has always been a troublemaker," Dee said, her head bobbing. "She's a bad influence on Angora." From the tone of her voice one might have thought Angora to be a six-year-old.

The DA cleared his throat loudly, indicating he wanted silence, but Dee was never good at taking a hint.

"My daughter would do something illegal or immoral only if Roxann talked her into it."

Angora's attorney turned his slick head. "Mrs. Ryder, would you kindly shut your pie hole?"

Roxann blinked, and her estimation of the greenhorn rose a couple of notches. Not only was he astute enough to realize that Dee wasn't doing Angora any favors, but he didn't mind telling her. Wow.

Her own attorney, meanwhile, leaned over and puked something brown on the beige carpet. She was hustled to the ladies' room and the goop temporarily covered with an upended trash can. When Phyllis returned, apologetic and pastel, everyone reconvened at the opposite end of the table. Roxann was getting sick to her stomach, not because of the throw-up, but because this Troy woman was probably making ten times her salary.

"Let's get right to it," the DA said. "Ms. Beadleman, Ms. Ryder, as you can imagine, this is a high-profile case with all the trappings of a scandal, which the university could do without. So we'd like to take care of this matter as expeditiously as possible." He paused and looked back and forth between them for effect. "Basically, we think you're both involved in the murder of Dr. Seger." He let the words sink in. "But whichever one of you talks first gets to walk."

Roxann chanced a glance at Angora, who was chewing on her lower lip. Dee was massaging her hand and whispering low, with a pleading look on her face. Panic blipped through her—Angora wouldn't lie to save her own skin, would she? Her heart thudded. Of course she would.

Since her own attorney was useless, Roxann leaned forward and clasped her hands on the table. "Face it, Mr. Mason. You have nothing but circumstantial evidence, or you wouldn't have arrested both of us. You need an eyewitness, which you don't have. But you and I know that if you put us both on trial, it'll be easy to generate doubt among the jurors. If that's not enough, we'll throw in the fact that I'm being stalked by a man who threatened to hurt people around me, and who, by the way, is still unaccounted for. If you think we're lying, then give us a lie detector test, but don't try to bribe us into making up something to incriminate the other just so you can dangle someone in front of the press and the public."

He lifted an eyebrow. "Maybe you should have been a lawyer, Ms. Beadleman." Then his smile vanished. "But the way we see it, you two could have been in cahoots to get rid of the man. We found these lists that the two of you made where Dr. Seger seems to be the target of some kind of sexual fantasy."

She set her jaw. "Those were harmless ramblings of youth."

"We were smoking dope," Angora offered.

Roxann closed her eyes, and Dee said, "See, see, I told you—Roxann is a bad influence."

"Maybe," Mason said, "the two of you went over to his house for a threesome, and things got out of hand. The medical examiner's report said that the alcohol level in Dr. Seger's blood was near the legal limit. And he was already unconscious when he was strangled."

"He had passed out?"

"No—hit from behind with a blunt object on the base of the skull."

Roxann digested this new bit of information. "But if we had hit him, then strangled him, why would we incriminate ourselves by leaving behind a very identifiable scarf?"

Mason shrugged. "Some killers get a kick out of leaving a souvenir. It's not my job to look into your psyche, Ms. Beadleman. It's my job to prove that you have motive, means, and opportunity." He looked back and forth between them. "The offer is on the table for two more minutes, then you both can take your chances."

"What about the other murder charge?" Mr. Brown asked and looked at his notes. "A student named Tammy Paulen?"

Mason looked at his assistant, who offered Brown a flat smile. "We're willing to drop those charges if your client cooperates."

Roxann's eyes bugged. If she cooperates? They might as well have said if she hands them Roxann's head on a platter. "Why?" she pressed. "Why would you drop the charges if you have evidence of a crime?"

The lady DA fidgeted, then said, "Some of the files from the Paulen case seem to be missing. So...we'll be dropping those charges, regardless."

Mason tapped his watch. "One minute, ladies."

Angora looked at her from across the room, and Roxann saw thirty years of hurt, jealousy, and disappointment in her eyes. Angora's lips parted and she started to say something, then stopped. She shifted in her wheelchair, and tears glistened in her eyes. Dee was pumping her hand.

Angora could do it all in one fell swoop, Roxann realized—pin the blame on the cousin she saw as competition, and exonerate herself in the eyes of the parents she so wanted to please. Roxann swallowed. And if Angora was guilty, then she had even more incentive to fabricate a story. And when it suited her, Angora could lie like a Persian rug.

She maintained eye contact as the seconds ticked away and the tension mounted. The faint odor of the throw-up had found its way out from under the trash can. A fly buzzed lazily on the light fixture above the table. The assistant DA clicked the end of her pen in slow, steady succession.

Dee whispered furiously in Angora's ear. When her cousin looked away, Roxann began to nurse a bad, bad feeling. Angora suddenly shoved at her mother and cleared her throat.

"Mr. Mason...if you had an eyewitness to the crime, what would the charge be?"

Oh, God.

Mason bounced the tips of his fingers together. "Since Dr. Seger was already unconscious when he was strangled, it clearly was not accidental, nor a crime of passion, nor of self-defense. We'd be charging first-degree murder."

"And the sentence?" Angora asked.

"Life in prison."

Roxann knew Angora well enough to know when she was terrified—the question was, was she terrified that Roxann had seen something through the window? If so, was she contemplating turning on Roxann first?

"Angora—" she began, but Mason stopped her.

"No conferring, Ms. Beadleman, unless it's with your attorney. My watch says fifteen seconds."

She wet her lips and willed Angora to look at her, but she wouldn't. *Don't do it*, she pleaded silently.

"I—" Angora said, and all eyes went to her.

"Yes?" Mason prompted.

She looked at Roxann, desperation on her face. "I...don't have anything to add to my story."

Roxann exhaled slowly.

Mason's mouth went flat and he closed the folder, smacking it back on top of the pile. "All right, then, we're finished here. By the way, we're going to try you ladies at the same time." He stood and gathered his things, then strode from the room with his assistant on his heels.

Roxann's attorney had fallen asleep during the commotion. The woman obviously shut down in the face of stress. Roxann scribbled "You're fired" on a sheet of paper, stuck it on Troy's briefcase, then wheeled her out in the hall in the rolling chair.

When she came back in the room, she looked at Angora. "Can I talk to you—alone?"

"Stay away from her," Dee said to Roxann. "Angora should have turned you in when she had the chance."

But Roxann was still looking at Angora, who nodded. "Wait for me in the hall," she said to her parents, and to her attorney. When the door closed, Roxann eased into a chair in front of her cousin. "How are you feeling?"

"Not great," she said. "I feel like I've been turned inside out, and those crabby nurses aren't giving me as many painkillers as before."

Roxann smiled. "They must not realize they have a celebrity on their hands—Miss Northwestern Baton Rouge."

Angora smiled back, then her eyes filled with tears. "The police won't give me back my crown."

"Isn't that a coincidence—you lost a crown and I have a spare one lying around somewhere."

She lit up. "You mean it?"

Roxann sighed. "Angora, you know better than anyone that I didn't deserve that Distinguished Alumni award. So cheer me up a little by taking that thing off my hands."

She looked back, bit into her lip, and smiled. "Okay." Then she teared up again. "Roxann, I'm sorry I said those terrible things about your mother."

She squeezed Angora's hand. "It's okay. I'm grateful to you for telling me—now I realize what my dad was going through." She smiled. "And now I understand why you were so lenient on him."

Angora nodded. "Your dad's great."

"Yeah. It was nice of your parents to come up."

"I suppose. Is your dad coming?"

"No, I asked him not to. I hope I convinced him that this is one big misunderstanding that will unravel in a few days."

"Is it?" Angora asked. "Is it one big misunderstanding?"

Roxann inhaled and looked into Angora's eyes. "Angora, I'm going to ask you a question, and you have to be honest with me. I swear, whatever the answer is, I'll help you get through it, okay?"

Angora nodded.

"Did you do any of those things to Carl that the DA said happened—did you hit him, or strangle him with my scarf?"

Her lower lip began to tremble. "I didn't hit him, but..."

Roxann's stomach pitched. "But?"

"But I keep having these terrible visions of him lying on the floor with that green scarf around his neck. And I don't know if they're real, or if it's something that's gotten in my head. I do that sometimes—think about something so hard that I can't remember if I made it up, or if it really happened."

"Did you find my scarf somewhere?"

"No. I'm sure about that part."

Roxann smiled. "Well, then, don't you see? If you didn't find my scarf, then you couldn't have done it."

Angora hiccupped. "Unless Carl found your scarf. We were at the same restaurant that night."

Roxann stared. "Utopia?"

"Yes. I didn't see you, but the police told me you and Nell were there."

"We were."

"Is that where you lost your scarf?"

"It's possible," she murmured, trying to think back. "I remember going to the ladies' room, and...and I made some calls at the pay phone."

Angora's eyes widened. "Carl made a call, too."

Roxann grinned. "Angora, you're a genius."

"I am?"

"Yes—I'll bet that's what happened. I assumed that the killer found my scarf and used it, but maybe Carl found it and was keeping it to give back to me later. Maybe it was just there, and the killer used it."

"Wow, I am a genius."

She laughed. "And now that one mystery is solved, we can start looking for other clues."

"But what about my...visions?"

Roxann angled her head. "Angora, in these visions, what does Carl look like?"

"He's lying on the floor, looking straight up at me, with his eyes wide open, staring through his glasses."

"That's definitely not how Carl looked in the crime-scene photos—and he wasn't even wearing his glasses."

Angora exhaled in relief. "Then I didn't do it."

Roxann smiled. "I'd say that's a safe assumption."

"Well, if you didn't do it, and I didn't do it, then who did?"

"I don't know, but I intend to find out. But Angora, you have to tell me everything, and I mean everything you know that might be relevant."

"Everything?"

"Everything."

Angora sighed. "Okay. Do you remember when you taught me how to give a blowjob on a tube of Crest?"

CHAPTER TWENTY-SEVEN

"HELLO, MELISSA?"

"Yes," the woman answered, her voice laced with suspicion. "This is Melissa Morgan."

Her new last name—of course. "Melissa, this is Roxann from the Rescue program."

"Roxann? I didn't think I'd ever hear from you again."

"How are you and Renita getting along?"

"Wonderfully. She loves Kansas City, and her new school. She's like a different child, so happy."

"I'm so glad for you."

"Is something wrong, Roxann?"

"Actually, Melissa, I'm in a bit of a bind, and I was hoping you could help me out."

"I will if I can."

She took a deep breath and made her request, explaining the ramifications if Melissa did or didn't decide to help. Twenty minutes later, she had her yes. She thanked Melissa, then hung up and dialed Nell's sister on the pay phone. The sister had obviously heard news of the arrest, because when Roxann identified herself, she was hesitant to let her speak to Nell. But when Nell heard, she took the call right away.

"Roxann, dear, are you all right?"

She spent the next few minutes assuring her mentor that everything was fine, despite the news sound bites and grim newspaper reports. "I think the DA was pressured into making an arrest."

"Do you still think that Frank Cape might have had something to do with the murder?"

"It's possible. Or..."

"Or what, dear?"

"Dr. Oney, when Carl was being investigated by the regents for having an improper relationship with a student, was I that student?"

"Yes, what did you think?"

"Well, I've been hearing some pretty unflattering things about Carl—that he traded sexual favors for grades, things like that."

Dr. Oney gasped. "Carl would never do that. Never."

She smiled into the phone. "I knew you'd say that."

"When do you think I can come back to South Bend?"

"Not yet, not until Cape is tracked down."

"But in time for the memorial service next week?"

"I hope so. I'm going over to your house to pick up my van—can I check on anything for you? Feed the cats? Water the flower garden maybe?"

"I left food and water for the cats, but bless you, yes, my rosemary will need a drink."

"Will do."

"Roxann, I've been giving more thought to that Frank Cape predicament, and I think you should let me contact the ex-wife and offer counsel. I just can't bear it if you're hurt."

"It's already taken care of. I talked to his ex-wife a few minutes ago, and she agreed to help."

"That's wonderful. Maybe it will help flush out Cape—and if he's the one who killed Carl, I want to see him punished."

"So do I."

"Is Melissa happy in her new location?"

"Yes."

"And Renita?"

"Oh, yes. Very."

Nell sighed in satisfaction. "It's good to know the program is working the way it's supposed to."

"You have a lot to be proud of." A checkered car caught her eye. "There's a taxi, so I have to run. I'll call you soon."

"Bye, dear."

If Roxann had any doubts that her picture had been plastered all over the news, all she needed was the wide-eyed stare in the rearview mirror from the taxi driver to clear things up. The guy was so spooked, he drove off before she could pay him. But considering how low she was running on cash, she didn't mind. She didn't even want to think about the hole the ten-thousand-dollar bail bond had left in her IRA.

Nell's place seemed melancholy, and she noticed for the first time how run-down the outside had become. Peeling paint, overgrown shrubs, and rocks missing from the stone steps. She might have blamed it on not having a man around the house, but her father's house looked the same. It said something about the feeling of home, she supposed, and that having people around made a house worth maintaining.

She found the outside hose and watered the flower beds and herbs, hoping she wasn't somehow killing them in the process. Afterward she sat on the cool stone steps to return her supervisor's frantic phone message. Apparently, he'd heard.

"Jesus, Joseph, and Mary, what's going on in South Bend?"

"A man I knew was murdered, and I've been arrested."

"You sound pretty calm for someone charged with murder."

"Funny how a person adapts," she said wryly. "Don't worry about me. I figure as long as the real killer thinks the heat is off, he might make a mistake."

"He?"

"It could be Frank Cape, although I can't be sure. He followed me to South Bend."

"Oh, my God. So that's why Nell left a message asking questions about the Cape case. She's afraid for you."

She smiled. "Yes, but I just spoke with her, so don't worry about calling her back. Besides, the murder could also be a random crime, or any number of things. Obviously, I'm going to need a few days off." Then she puffed out her cheeks in an exhale. "Actually, Tom, I'm giving my notice."

"What? Why?"

"Well, it might be tricky trying to facilitate from the state pen."

"Don't even joke about that."

"Seriously, Tom, I've run my course. This thing with Cape makes me see that."

"All right, you know this is a freewill organization, both the people we help, and the ones doing the helping. But if you ever want to come back, just call."

"I will. Thanks, Tom. Listen, I ran into Elise James on campus—have you heard from her?"

"No, and I've left several messages on her cell phone. I have a check for her for a couple of hundred dollars, and I don't know where to send it."

"She said she was going to call you, but to be honest, she was pretty messed up."

"Understood. Thanks for letting me know."

She pushed down the antenna and returned the phone to her purse, suddenly remembering a curious detail about Elise—the woman had such large hands. Large and strong enough for strangling? She pursed her mouth, wondering if Capistrano had given the woman's name to his counterparts in town as he'd promised. Of course, since he was diddling one of their prime suspects, they might find his leads questionable at best. Every time she thought about her stupid, stupid lapse in judgment, she wanted to swallow something jagged.

Oh, well, enough about her sorry sex life—she needed to get to the hotel and retrieve her clothes. She'd book a room under another name, then maybe throw on a wig and start doing some poking around on her own.

She rounded the corner of the house to retrieve Goldie, then stopped. The van's tires had been slashed. Not just by some prankster kid looking for a place to stick his new Case pocketknife—the rubber had literally been shredded by a sharp instrument, and by someone with considerable strength. Or anger. The violated feeling that coursed through her reminded her of when her apartment had been rifled.

I'VE GOT YOUR NUMBER, YOU FAKE.

Frank Cape? She reached into her purse and put her finger on the trigger of her pepper-spray can, for comfort rather than purpose. Judging from the lack of footprints in the grass, he was probably long gone. Then she froze as heavy footsteps sounded behind her.

"There you are."

She wheeled and aimed the spray at Frank Cape's face, and instead hit Joe Capistrano square in the chest. The effects were instantaneous—he yowled and spun like a helicopter crashing. Roxann dropped the can and ran for the water hose, which she turned on him full force. He tore off the long-sleeved T-shirt and stood in the water stream, running his hands over the red areas of his torso again and again. All of that hair was good for something after all. Otherwise, he'd be nursing third-degree burns.

He didn't talk, and since she wasn't exactly looking forward to the conversation, she concentrated on the task at hand, which was holding the hose and trying not to laugh.

After a fifteen-minute shower, he yanked the hose away from her. "That's enough," he barked, then turned off the spigot and wound up the hose, muttering under his breath. His jeans were soaked and plastered to his legs—they had to weigh a ton.

Roxann pressed her finger to her mouth. "I'm sorry."

"Dammit, you should be. I feel like I've been barbecued."

"I thought you were Cape."

"Didn't anyone tell you to make damn sure where you're aiming that stuff before you hit the trigger?"

"Didn't anyone tell you not to sneak up on people?"

"I wasn't sneaking."

"You were sneaking."

"I wasn't sneaking."

"Oh, yes, you were sneaking."

He lifted both hands and slung off the water. "Forget it." Then he saw the van tires. "Cape?"

"I assume so."

He walked over and examined a slashed tire. "The poor thing might have committed suicide."

"Funny. How did you know I was here?"

"I called and you'd already left the courthouse, so I took a chance." He quirked an eyebrow. "You weren't fixin' to leave town, were you?"

"No. Just wanted to get my things from the hotel and book a room."

"You have a room."

"And book a private room."

"Look, about what happened between us, I'm sorry—"

"I'm sorry, too," she cut in with a glib smile. "And we need never to talk about it again."

He frowned. "I was going to say I'm sorry we were interrupted."

Oh. "Well, considering I was taken from the hotel in handcuffs, so am I."

He sighed and ran his hands through his auburn hair, displacing more water. "Do you think I could dry off before we continue our one long argument?"

She dug her keys out of her purse. "I might have a towel in the van. I want to take a look inside anyway."

Big mistake.

The seats had been slashed, including the bench behind the driver's seat. The items from her box of mementos were strewn. She found the crushed box and slowly started putting things in as she found them—a keychain, a charm bracelet, the Magic 8 Ball. All of the personal items she kept stashed in the back had been ransacked and scattered—blankets to cover cold, fleeing bodies, nonperishable snacks to feed hungry little bellies, and her relic of a suitcase filled with disguise clothing. This was most apparent in the form of a blond wig that had been singled out and attached to the dashboard with a wicked-looking buck knife.

A blond wig.

They said Tammy had something on your cousin, was holding it over her head...something to do with a blond wig.

Her lungs squeezed, and she gulped for air. It was all connected somehow, her past and her present.

"What is it?" Capistrano demanded. "Roxann, what's wrong?"

YOU FAKE. I'VE GOT YOUR NUMBER, YOU FAKE.

CHAPTER TWENTY-EIGHT

IT WAS A PITIFUL collection of memories, Roxann decided, looking over the contents of the battered box jostling on her lap. She picked up the Magic 8 Ball and silently posed the question "Is my life a national disaster?" She turned over the toy.

Yes, definitely.

Capistrano thumped his hand on the steering wheel of the Dooley. "Dammit, Roxann, if you don't tell me what's wrong, I can't help you."

"What's wrong? What isn't wrong?"

"Something spooked you back there."

"Isn't it enough to find Goldie destroyed?"

"You named your van?"

"You named your gun."

He frowned. "All those clothes and wigs—do you use them when you move women from place to place?"

"Sometimes."

"Is there some significance to that blond wig?"

She swallowed. "It had a knife through it."

"I mean the wig itself—or the color. Is Melissa Cape blond?"

"Brunette."

"Do you think it was a threat against Angora?"

"Maybe."

"You know something you're not telling me."

"Give it a rest, Detective. I've had a bad day."

He sighed and shifted on the towel he'd spread over the seat of his truck. Another towel was draped over his bare shoulders. "How did it go today at the courthouse?"

"Fine and dandy."

"I'm serious."

She fingered her green and white Notre Dame tassel, with the little '96 gold-tone charm attached. "After the arraignment, the DA offered me and Angora a deal if we'd serve up the other one."

"And your cousin didn't jump on it?"

"No." She frowned. "I thought you liked Angora."

"Like?"

"Well, the way you look at her—" She stopped before he got the impression that she was jealous or something stupid like that.

He grinned. "You're jealous."

"You're delusional. And I thought we were talking about the meeting."

"Did you tell the DA about Angora—the possible mental problems, the comments she made?"

"No. She underwent a psych consult at the hospital."

"And?"

"And, according to her attorney, she's a pathological liar and fantastically spoiled, but she wouldn't harm anyone. I had a private heart-to-heart with her—she didn't do it."

"I hope you're right." He checked the rearview mirror, ever alert.

"But she did tell me a couple of things that could be important."

"Like?"

She dropped the tassel back into the box. "Like she went down on Dr. Seger in his office once when she was a student."

He emitted a low whistle. "I thought you said she was a virgin."

"Do I have to give you a definition of 'virgin'?"

"No, but that's not exactly virginal behavior."

Roxann shrugged. "She must've been crazy about him is all I can say."

"So chances are, Dr. Seger was participating in extracurricular activities with his students?"

She squirmed. "Chances are."

"But he never hit on you?"

"No."

"He must've liked you."

She cut her gaze to him. "Are you saying that guys don't make passes at women they like?"

"No. I mean that a guy like Seger who was exploiting young girls probably had a line in his head separating the girls he respected."

She simply stared.

"I'm shutting up."

"Thank you."

He kept his word for about thirty seconds. "Did she tell you anything else you didn't know?"

She nodded. "The night Tammy Paulen was run down, she was driving nearby. She heard a scream, then saw a black Volvo driving away."

"Seger?"

She looked out the window. "He has—had—a black Volvo." Her voice cracked, and she cleared her throat of the sudden emotion that welled. Okay, maybe she could believe that Carl engaged in dalliances with his pretty students, but the thought that he would actually leave the scene of a crime was incomprehensible. He taught ethics, for heaven's sake.

He made a rueful noise in his throat. "It's not your fault that Seger wasn't the man you thought he was."

"It makes me feel foolish that I could be so blind, though."

"Maybe the way he acted around you was the way he wanted to be."

"You're being generous all of a sudden."

He shrugged. "Nobody is all good or all bad. Even some of the worst criminals love their mother, or tell bedtime stories to their kids, or buy cream for their cats."

Okay, he'd managed to surprise her—and make her feel a tad better.

"So we know he wasn't a saint. And that it's entirely possible one of his students could've dropped by and done him in."

She told him their theory on how the scarf had made its way to the crime scene.

"Not bad," he said. "Maybe we can find someone at the restaurant who saw him pick it up. One thing is sure—if the DA is relying on one of you to turn on the other, he doesn't have enough evidence to convict."

"That's what I told him."

"You or your lawyer?"

"My lawyer is a narcoleptic idiot with a good ad agency. I handled everything."

He pursed his mouth. "You know an awful lot about the law for someone determined not to have anything to do with it."

She smirked.

"Listen, I'm sorry I wasn't at the arraignment, but I thought my time would be better spent looking for Cape."

"I guess you didn't find him?"

His mouth twisted. "No. He probably changed vehicles, maybe his appearance." He looked over. "No offense, but you should've stayed in jail. You'd be safer."

"I filed a restraining order on Cape this morning, since I was already at the courthouse," she said wryly. "And I have my pepper spray."

"Don't remind me."

"Is it possible Cape could've wrecked my van when he threatened Nell? I didn't check it."

He shook his head. "Surely Nell would have noticed, or the police when they came to make the report."

Her laugh was dry. "I'm not overly impressed with the South Bend detectives, although Warner seems okay. But I don't think they're going to go out of their way to find another suspect. Did you tell them about Elise?"

He nodded. "Last night when they were, um, taking you in. But you're right—they didn't seem very excited about the prospect of a new lead."

"Yet the more I think about it, the more I think she might be involved somehow."

"Why?"

She wet her lips.

"Dammit, Roxann, tell me."

She sighed—she did need a sounding board, and Capistrano was the most solid surface around. "Remember that Nell told me Tammy Paulen was holding something over Angora's head? Well, it has something to do with a blond wig."

"What is it?"

She waved her hand. "That's not important, but whoever trashed the van knew about it, and knew that I knew about it. And it makes me think that Frank Cape isn't in this alone."

"So you know what this girl had on your cousin?"

She looked away. Too painful to think about—she never allowed the memories to fully materialize. Angora probably felt the same, which explained why they always skated around the topic.

"You were involved in it, too, weren't you?"

She kept looking away.

He dragged his hand over his face. "Okay, whatever it is—would Elise know?"

"Possibly. If Tammy told her."

"They were friends?"

"I don't know, but she was going to school here when Tammy died."

"But how could Elise get hooked up with Frank Cape?"

"I have no idea."

"Okay, then we need to find Elise."

"That's what I was planning to do today."

He pulled into the hotel lot and parked. "Oh, you're working alone now?"

She nodded and handed him a slip of paper.

"What's this?"

"An e-mail address where you can reach Melissa Cape. She's willing to go to a local courthouse, be sworn in, and answer questions over a videocam about what she knows regarding the robbery. In return, though, she wants her ex-husband's custody and visitation rights rescinded."

He looked up, his mouth parted. She'd succeeded in surprising him.

"She's expecting to hear from you," she said.

"This is breaking some kind of rule, isn't it?"

"Only all of them."

He folded the piece of paper in his hand. "Thank you, Roxann. Thank you for Officer Lafferty and his family. We'll get Cape one way or another." Then he angled his head and leaned closer. "But if I didn't know better, I'd think you were trying to get rid of me."

She met his gaze squarely. "You got what you wanted, now you're off the hook."

He sat back and a little laugh escaped him. "You don't think very highly of yourself, do you?"

"What's that supposed to mean?"

"It means that in the beginning, yeah, I wanted information on Melissa Cape, but now...hell, I'm interested."

"In the case?"

"In you, since I have to spell it out."

She chewed on her tongue and studied his eyes, the set of his jaw. He was sincere...at the moment. And God, it was tempting to fall for him. But men like Detective Joe Capistrano needed a damsel in distress to whisk off the railroad tracks as the train was barreling down. And when she was out of harm's way, he'd move on to another case, another damsel. Besides, even if this nightmare ended right now, she had too many issues to work out to be tying herself to a person or a place. Or a...situation.

"I'm flattered," she said. "But I don't think so."

One dark eyebrow went up. "You don't think so? That's your answer?"

"Yep," she said, then lifted the door handle, climbed down, and slammed the door.

His door slammed and he was right behind her. "Hey." Then he caught her arm and stopped her. "Hey, I'm sorry. I have lousy timing."

"That, too," she agreed.

He took the box of junk from her. "But like it or not, I'm not leaving while Cape is still on the loose."

She turned and walked toward the hotel. "Suit yourself. As long as you know where I stand. Right now, I want to get a room and take the world's longest shower."

"You're not going to be able to find a room," he said. "Not with so many people in town. I had to pull out my badge to get mine."

"Will you pull out your badge to get me one?"

He sighed. "So I can camp outside your door in case our man shows? Look, your clothes are already in my room, and I can keep an eye on you there."

She stared.

"And I won't...anything."

She worked her mouth back and forth. "On one condition."

"What?"

"Help me break into Carl's house."

CHAPTER TWENTY-NINE

"I CAN'T BELIEVE I'm doing this," he muttered, pulling next to the curb a few yards away from Dr. Seger's house. The weather had taken a nasty turn—cold and a steady drizzle of freezing rain. The truck's antenna was coated with ice, as were the parked cars.

Roxann pulled on knit gloves and tugged a wool hat down over her ears. "We couldn't find Elise, so she's probably long gone. The only way we'll be able to connect her to Dr. Seger is if we find something in his files—a letter, a picture...something."

"I could lose my badge over this."

"Stop exaggerating and look small." She opened the door quietly and slipped out into the frigid darkness. She heard a click, then Capistrano was next to her. The murder had obviously frightened the neighbors because outside security lights blazed, which didn't help their cause. They moved carefully to the cover of the shadows cast by the trees between the sidewalk and the leaf-covered lawns, then walked in the ice-encrusted grass rather than taking a chance on the slick sidewalk. They passed a bundled woman walking a dog, but avoided eye contact.

"Which door?" she asked as they neared the house, which stood out because it was the only residence in total darkness.

"Front door," he murmured. "The trick to breaking and entering is to act as if you're supposed to be there." Then he frowned. "Scratch that—I forget who I'm talking to."

When they approached the steps, a motion-activated light came on and she practically wet herself.

"Relax," he whispered.

Her heart beat double-time and an uncontrollable shiver traveled through her body. The front door was plastered with yellow "crime scene" stickers. Capistrano was through the ornamental brass lock in less than thirty seconds, then pushed open the door.

"What if there's a security alarm?" she whispered.

"The police wouldn't bother setting it." Then he frowned. "Scratch that, too. And stop asking questions."

After he closed the door, they stood in the darkness until their vision adjusted, then slipped off their shoes. The air in the house was deadly quiet and cold, with a chemical tang, probably left by forensics. Creepy stuff.

"His office used to be in the library," she whispered. "If I remember correctly, it's ahead and to the left."

They found the room, and Capistrano gently removed the police tape across the door. Then he walked the perimeter with a penlight, closing doors and shutters before turning on a desk lamp. She scanned the room, skimming over the carpet where white tape crudely outlined the shape of Carl's body where it had fallen next to the ottoman. The disturbing crime scene photos flashed in her mind, but she inhaled and chased them away.

The room was lined with bookshelves, and studded with nice furniture—a mohair couch, a leather club chair, a massive cherrywood desk. She thought she detected the faintest scent of Carl's cologne, but she might have imagined it. To think that only two days ago he was alive.

"You take the desk drawers," Capistrano said, "and I'll start on the bookshelves. Leave your gloves on."

She nodded, removed her hat, and set to work before she could think about the ethics of rooting through the personal papers of an ethics professor. The bottom drawer was filled with CDs and headphones, so she moved to the next drawer. Receipts and check registers, a calculator, and files for bills—nothing special, unless you counted the sizable charges on his phone bill to 900 numbers. The thought of Carl dialing for sex on top of exploiting female students put a rock in her stomach.

The other drawers revealed nothing of import—files of class grades and minutes of faculty meetings. She closed the last drawer with a sigh. "Nothing here."

"Nothing here yet, either," he said from the bookshelf. "Why don't you start on the other end?"

She did, experiencing a pang of sadness that Carl's carefully collected volumes would have to be moved to a new home—probably the university library.

"He had some nice editions," Capistrano murmured.

Roxann lifted an eyebrow at his broad back. So his reading repertoire extended beyond commercial thrillers. The man had layers.

Systematically, she removed each book and flipped through pages to see if Carl had hidden anything inside. For thirty minutes they flipped and shook and reshelved. Then she reached a collection of Shakespeare with spectacular navy spines. She pulled out the first volume and stopped. "Detective. I think I've found something."

He joined her. "False books?"

She held the book-inside-the-book she'd removed up to the light. "It's a journal—1980 to 1985."

"More than one," he said, removing another falsie. "Nineteen eighty-six to 1990."

She thumbed through the pages, scanning entries, and realized quickly that some of Carl's literary efforts were bent toward erotica. She skipped the body-part words to look for names—would he be so bold? Apparently so.

Janeese L...Carlo B...Marie A.

"Are there any for 1992 and up?"

He pulled out the last two volumes. "Yeah. Let's take these with us."

"Isn't that stealing?"

"Technically, it's called burglary. Let's go."

They returned the false books, extinguished the lamp, then opened the shutters and doors. Replacing tape where necessary, they retraced their steps to the front door. He locked the door from the inside, then pulled it shut with a click.

"Wait," she said, wincing. "I left my hat."

To his credit, Capistrano only sighed. "Stay here, I'll get it." He handed her the journals, then broke in for the second time and disappeared inside.

The bitter cold reminded her why she lived in the south. She shivered and moved from foot to foot to keep the blood flowing.

She smelled him before she saw him. Then the motion-detector light came on, revealing Frank Cape, his menacing face framed by a black knit cap. Her pepper spray, she realized miserably, was safely tucked in her purse inside the Dooley.

"Capis—"

Cape clapped his hand over her mouth, then stuffed a cloth in her mouth. "This is good," he said, jerking her forward and down the steps. "Thought I was going to have to shoot that guard of yours and leave another body here for the police to find."

Her eyes flew wide.

"Oh, yeah, I killed the teacher man—lot of good it did me. Nobody keeps their word these days."

She grunted and fought to release one hand, kicking at his knees with as much leverage as she could gain on the icy ground. "Be still," he hissed, then slapped her hard. "We're going to see my wife."

Stars burst in her head, and tears streamed down her cheek from repeatedly gagging on the foul-tasting cloth. Her next strategy was to go totally limp, which wasn't exactly brilliant because then she was easier to drag. She lost a shoe and was fairly certain her shoulder had been dislocated. Though disoriented, she grasped that they were approaching a car with its engine running. He yanked her upright and released one arm long enough for her to pull out the gag and scream, although it came out a weak gurgle. She elbowed him in the nose, and he emitted a gratifying grunt. But then he cursed and pulled out an automatic handgun. "You just don't learn, do you?"

For one terrifying second, she thought he was going to shoot her, but he raised it over her head for a knockout blow.

Then Cape flew sideways, as if he'd been hit by a locomotive. Capistrano landed on top of him, and Roxann figured that would pretty much kill anyone.

But Cape lived and had even managed to hold on to his gun. Capistrano grabbed the man's wrist and aimed the gun in the air. Cape fired twice.

"Roxann, get in the car!" Capistrano bellowed.

Never one to follow orders, she looked for anything she might use as a weapon. Behind Cape's car seat she found a tire tool. Another shot rang out and she flinched when it ricocheted off the open car door. Okay, she was scared to freaking death, but if she allowed Capistrano to be injured defending her, she'd feel obligated to...take him home or something. So she crept closer and waited for an opportunity to lend a hand.

The men were pounding away at each other, rolling in the rain. She hacked at Cape's legs with the tire iron, but it was so hard to see, she might have hit the detective a few times in the process. The next thing she knew, Cape was on top with his gun pressed against the detective's head. Roxann lifted the tire tool and swung, delivering a striking blow to Cape's back. He roared in pain, and the detective pushed him off. Frank rolled, but still had the wherewithal to raise his gun. Her heart vaulted to her throat. A shot rang out. She screamed and covered her face with her hands.

When she spread her fingers for a peek, Capistrano was kneeling over Cape, feeling for a pulse.

"Is he...?"

"Yeah, he's dead." He pushed himself to his feet, then limped over to her and yanked the tire tool away. "I thought I told you to get in the car."

"I was trying to help."

He tossed her weapon to the ground. "Well, you damn near crippled me, and you could have gotten us both killed."

To her complete mortification, her eyes filled with tears. She blinked furiously. Her face was so cold, her cheeks ached.

He cupped her face in his hands and sighed. Water dripped off his nose and chin. "Are you okay?"

She sniffed. "I guess so. Nothing broken."

He stroked her cheek with his thumb. "He hit you?"

She nodded.

"I should shoot him again."

"He told me he killed Dr. Seger."

He puffed out his cheeks and exhaled. "Well, let's hope he left some physical evidence at the crime scene, because I doubt if the police will take our word."

In the distance, a siren wailed. Capistrano lifted his head. "Speaking of which. Want to bet we're the most popular 911 call tonight?" He looked back to her. "You let me do all the talking when they get here. Pretend you lost your voice."

She frowned.

"I mean it, Roxann. Don't say a word." Two police cars came screeching into the neighborhood. "Hold up your hands and don't move."

Roxann raised her arms and stood shivering, wondering if things had just gotten better...or worse.

CHAPTER THIRTY

"I COULD HAVE YOUR BADGE for this," Jaffey said to Capistrano. "Breaking and entering. Compromising a crime scene." He gestured to the journals, swollen, the ink runny and illegible. "Tampering with evidence."

"It was my idea," she started, then pressed her lips together.

Jaffey looked at her. "Well, Ms. Beadleman, I'm glad to see your voice has returned." Then he looked back to Capistrano. "And on top of everything else, a dead man—*another* dead man. Do you know what this kind of thing does for tourism? For the university's image?"

Capistrano drummed his fingers on the table. "Look, tell the press that the man who killed Dr. Seger was killed by a cop. Little kids can play outside again, the police are heroes, everybody's happy."

Robert Mason, looking none too pleased to have been dragged down to the police station late at night, scoffed. "Oh, yeah, especially Ms. Beadleman and Ms. Ryder—they get to pin Dr. Seger's murder on a dead man."

"Did you find Cape's prints on the scene?" Capistrano demanded.

Jaffey pulled on his chin, then looked to Mason and back. "Yeah," he finally admitted. "We matched three partial prints lifted from the library to Cape. But that doesn't mean he killed Seger. In fact, Officer, I think it's pretty coincidental that you happened to kill the man who's accused of shooting your partner."

"I wanted Cape punished," Capistrano said flatly, "not dead. If you check the butt of Cape's gun to the wound on the back of Seger's head, I think you'll get a match."

Jaffey's expression told him they'd already done just that—and it had matched. "Why wouldn't he just shoot Seger?" he asked, playing devil's advocate.

Capistrano shrugged. "Maybe he didn't want to alert the neighbors, maybe that cheap gun jammed on him—we'll never know."

"Because you shot him," Jaffey said.

"In self-defense. He admitted to Roxann that he killed Seger."

Jaffey turned to her. "He killed Seger to scare you into revealing the whereabouts of his wife and daughter?"

"That's my understanding."

"Will you take a polygraph test?"

"Yes. I offered to take one before. Detective Jaffey, if you don't believe us and you don't think that Cape did it, fine." She pointed to the ruined books. "The journals prove that my cousin was telling the truth about what Dr. Seger was doing to and with his students."

"Thanks to you and Detective Capistrano," Jaffey said, "these journals will tell us very little."

"But there are others," Roxann said, then looked at Mason. "And I read enough of those pages to know that you suddenly have dozens, maybe hundreds of suspects, old students and new, any of whom might have been in town for Homecoming. So, I can understand why you'd suddenly have doubts that Frank Cape committed the murder—there are so many other possibilities."

Mason rubbed his eyes as if when he opened them, they might all be gone. Then he blinked bleary eyes and nodded to Jaffey. "Can we have a word outside?"

The men left, and Roxann pulled the blanket she'd been given tighter around her shoulders. She didn't think she'd ever be warm again. "What do you think?"

Capistrano sighed. "I think they don't want to believe us, but they don't have a choice. The DA and Jaffey's boss just want this mess to go away."

She gave him a rueful smile. "That makes all of us." She sipped the coffee sitting in front of her. "Detective, I'm sorry."

He seemed surprised. "For?"

"For dragging you into this tonight. I got this crazy idea in my head and went off half-cocked."

"But you were right."

"And you had to kill a man because of me."

He leaned forward. "I had to kill a man because of the man. Which never feels good, but at least I know Cape was guilty of some pretty crummy things. End of story."

Roxann glanced to the window—both men had their backs turned, their heads close in discussion. She reached for the journal that covered 1996 and flipped through the distorted pages.

"What are you doing?"

"Just let me know when they're coming back."

Depending on what kind of pen he'd used, the words were sometimes blurred, sometimes merged, sometimes gone. She recalled that, unfortunately, Carl had preferred to use a fountain pen, which ran easily. The entry on the date Angora had given her—April 21, 1996—was blurred, but she was able to make out the shadows of some pertinent words: *blonde...theology class... office...fellatio...shoes.* Bile backed up in her mouth—he hadn't even mentioned Angora's name. He probably hadn't even known her name, or hadn't bothered to remember it.

"Bastard," she muttered.

"Was that meant for me?" he asked wryly.

"No, keep watching."

Another volume covered 1992. Thanks to the date on their life lists, she knew the date of Tammy Paulen's memorial service. The girl had died two days prior, so Roxann quickly found the relevant pages, but they were a soggy mess. She thought she made out the capital letter T on a couple of pages, but she couldn't be sure.

"Better wrap it up," Capistrano said. "I think they're finished."

A few seconds later, Mason and Jaffey returned, neither one of them looking fulfilled.

"I'll drop the charges pending against you and your cousin," Mason said, "but only if you two pass polygraphs, and I mean with flying colors."

The best news she'd heard in what seemed like years. She swallowed and nodded gratefully.

"You and Ms. Ryder be in my office Monday afternoon, prepared to tell the truth."

She nodded again.

"As for you," Detective Jaffey said to Capistrano. "Since you were in South Bend on police business, we're going to pretend that you were actually invited to help us on this case while you were here. As far as the public is concerned, you were acting on behalf of our police department when you shot Cape. When you return to Biloxi, you'll be placed on desk duty for the minimum time required by *our* department after a shooting, which is forty-five days."

Capistrano nodded and rose to shake Jaffey's hand. "Sounds fair."

"It's a goddamn gift," the man said, returning a brief shake. "I also want you to get the hell out of my town first thing in the morning."

"Agreed."

"All right, both of you, get out of here before we change our minds."

Roxann bolted to her feet and headed for the door. Capistrano thanked the men again and led the way out of the station. They didn't speak until they were in the Dooley, shivering and waiting for the engine to warm up and the windshield to de-ice. "That was close," he said.

The understatement of the century, she thought, utterly weak with relief that Carl's murderer had been caught and Melissa Cape had been let off the hook—the woman would probably be relieved when she discovered her ex-husband was dead.

But deep down, Roxann harbored a selfish little flame—the secret she and Angora had maintained for years hadn't come to light after all. It had been a fluke that Cape had chosen a blond wig to attach to the dashboard of her van. She had simply overreacted, reading more into the deed than was warranted. She was safe from everything but herself.

"About the hotel room," Capistrano said, putting the truck into gear.

"Don't worry—I'm too tired and too cold to argue."

He didn't argue with her not arguing, but the drive to the hotel took a long time since he had to watch for icy spots. "What was it like going to school here?" he asked.

"It was heaven," she said. "I loved every minute of it. The campus is so beautiful, and the atmosphere...I can't explain it—everyone was so hungry to learn and experience things. I'd never known intellectual freedom like that before. I know it's a huge campus, but it seemed intimate when I was here. Like we were in a little world of our own. I didn't want to leave." She smiled. "I know that sounds silly. Did you go to college?"

He nodded. "Criminology, Mississippi State. But I couldn't wait to get out and go to the police academy."

"Do you like what you do?"

"Most days I love what I do. And even on off days, I can't imagine anything I'd like better."

"That must be nice, to have found your calling."

"Haven't you found yours?"

She shook her head. "I resigned from the Rescue program."

"Why?"

"Because I'm not convinced that my contribution is making a difference. I sort of feel like a stick in a bucket of water—if you took it out, no one would know it had ever been there."

"Ah, but you're concentrating on how the water was affected, and not the stick."

She digested his response, wondering how much psychology a person had to study to earn a criminology degree.

"So you're free to live anywhere?" he asked, wisely changing the subject.

"I suppose."

She waited for his comment, but he offered none, which was even more vexing. They traveled in silence the rest of the way. Her limbs sang with fatigue, and her jaw throbbed where Cape had hit her. Beneath the blanket, her clothes and shoes were still wet. A permanent chill had invaded her skin. She needed to call Angora, but she decided to wait until morning and perhaps deliver the good news in person. For now, she just wanted to be horizontal for several hours.

She started peeling off wet clothes before he even unlocked the hotel room door. He'd already seen everything she had at close range, so modesty seemed pointless. He went into the bathroom and turned on the shower. She sat down on the bed to remove her socks, then unhooked her bra.

He came back out and jerked his thumb toward the open door. "You go first." But his gaze moved over her unabashedly.

Roxann stood and walked to the bathroom door, then turned. "We could share."

He started walking, removing his clothing along the way. She slipped into the shower first, wincing against the stinging needles of the hot water against her cold skin. She washed her hair, dragging her nails over her scalp again and again. She'd rather gotten used to the extensions and was considering letting her hair grow. Angora would be pleased to know she had managed to erode Roxann's aversion to all things inherently feminine.

The door to the glass enclosure opened and he stepped in behind her. With a thick white washcloth, he rubbed her arms, back, and stomach, massaging in the soothing lather of the evergreen soap. Slowly, slowly, she warmed beneath the pressure of his hands. Then she returned the favor, enjoying the way her touch affected him. When her fingers played over the scar on his lower shoulder, and the bruises on his legs, she was reminded of how close he'd come to dying tonight at the hands of Cape. And if he hadn't risked his life, who knew what Cape might have done to her to persuade her to talk?

When Capistrano kissed her breasts, she didn't stop him. When his ministrations intensified, she didn't stop him. And when he lifted her against the tile wall to join their bodies, she opened her knees to receive him. He rocked his hips into hers, taking her breath away. They found their rhythm to the song of mingled moans and mutual words of encouragement. The exquisite synchronization of their stroke obliterated the anger and fear and frustration of the past several days. She came explosively, a full-body contraction that depleted him seconds later. They recovered slowly, then cut off the water, wrapped themselves in towels, and fell into bed.

"That didn't mean anything," she murmured against his arm.

"I know," he whispered back.

Her dreams were profound and troubling, disjointed and colorful. Carl, Elise, Richard, Dee, Cape. Everyone wanted a piece of her. Worse—they'd found out her secret and were holding it over her head.

Roxann started awake. The room was dark, but slivers of daylight shone between the drawn curtains. She turned her head to look at the clock—ten-thirty on Sunday morning. She would try to make it to evening mass at the university cathedral. She had plenty to be grateful for today.

But meanwhile, she was wrapped around Capistrano like a beer huggy. Their towels had become tangled with the bedcovers, and she couldn't tell whose legs were whose. He sighed heavily, as if resetting his breathing tempo. Lifting her head, she took advantage of the opportunity to study him.

His profile remained rigid, even in repose. But his brow was more relaxed and his jaw unclenched, shaving years from his face. His beard, darker than his auburn hair, hovered just below the surface of his skin. His tousled hair gave him a boyish appearance, and she could easily imagine him at twenty-five, eighteen, twelve, six years old.

Capistrano stirred and his arm tightened around her involuntarily. Not an unpleasant feeling. His head was propped up on two pillows, and the sheet rode down to his waist. Massive shoulders and arms, impressive pecs, and a narrow waist. She decided she liked the hairy chest after all—it was... insulating. His morning call tented the sheet and sent a twinge to her thighs.

This was the kind of man, she realized, that incited career women to trade in their navy pumps for a breast pump—being around a man so male couldn't help but make you feel vigorously female. Her ovaries were probably straining against her birth control at this very moment.

Across the room, a phone pealed—his cell phone. Since he was immediately awake and across the room in three strides, she imagined he'd been awakened similarly many times before.

"Yeah?" he said, rubbing his eyes with thumb and forefinger. His hair stuck out at odd angles. Seconds later, he smiled—whoever was on the other end was someone he was glad to hear from. "Oh, hi, Betty...no, it's fine. Just a late night is all."

She sat up and swung her legs over the side of the bed and covered herself with a towel. Her limbs ached.

"Really? That's *great.* I'm headed home today, so I'll stop by tomorrow... sure thing, see you then." He disconnected the call, his sleepy face wreathed in smiles. "That was my partner's wife—Lafferty came out of the coma this morning. The doctors say he has a good chance of a full recovery."

Roxann's smile mirrored his. "That is good news." And a fitting close to their time together. From the rueful look on his face, she knew he was thinking the same thing.

"I thought I'd go to the hospital early this morning to see Angora," she said with forced animation. "And I need to call Melissa, and Nell, and Dad and...Triple-A."

He nodded. "I guess I need to get on the road myself."

She hadn't had a one-night stand in so long, she'd forgotten how awkward the morning after could be. After a strained silence, he turned and disappeared into the bathroom—a strategy she'd used herself a few times. Taking her cue, she dressed hurriedly and tamed her hair, then straightened the covers—an unmade bed seemed so...*reproachful.* Then she called her road-service club and arranged to have Goldie towed to a nearby tire place.

The call to Melissa was difficult, but since she'd witnessed Frank's death, she felt obligated to tell her. Melissa cried, but Roxann wondered how much of the emotion was relief that she was finally rid of the man.

And she was talking to her father when Capistrano emerged, shaved and combed. There was something very disconcerting about talking to your father on the phone when there was a naked man in the room.

She averted her eyes. "So I should be in Baton Rouge by Wednesday."

"Are you bringing Angora home?"

"I suspect she'll go home with her parents once we get things wrapped up."

"Will you be able to stay here for a while?"

"If you...don't mind."

"That would be nice," he said. "Now that the case is solved, will you still be seeing that Capistrano fellow?"

She looked at Capistrano, who had donned jeans and was pulling a T-shirt over his head. She cupped her hand over the mouthpiece. "Dad, I was never seeing him."

"Tell him I said thank you for keeping an eye on my best girl."

She blinked. "O...kay." Her father had never called her his best anything. "I'll be there in a couple of days, all right?" She hung up the phone, marveling.

"I'm sure your father's relieved," Capistrano offered, then pulled on a dark green sweatshirt over the T-shirt.

"He said to give you his thanks for...taking care of me."

He pursed his mouth and sat down on the opposite bed to pull on socks and athletic shoes. "It was my pleasure," he said without looking up. He finished tying, then stood. "Did you call someone about your van?"

She bristled at his insinuation that she needed to be reminded. "Contrary to popular belief, Detective, I've been taking care of myself for a long time. And outside of maniacal stalkers, I think I've done pretty well."

His eyebrows rose. "I'm getting the hint that you don't want anyone to care about you."

"That's not true."

"Okay, then you don't want *me* to care about you."

She crossed her arms and shook her head. "Don't do this, Detective. Last night was...what it was—two people who needed each other. For last night."

"Whatever you say." He stuffed clothes into a duffel bag, then zipped it. "Do you need a ride to the hospital?"

She shook her head. "Thanks, but I have more calls to make."

"The room is paid for until the end of the week."

"That's not necessary," she protested.

"It's already done," he said, exasperated. "Christ, Roxann, why won't you let anyone help you? Are you afraid you might have to get close to someone?"

She set her jaw. "Don't talk to me like that—you don't know me."

He slung the duffel to his shoulder and gathered the stack of files. "As you've informed me several times." A small laugh escaped him. "I hope you get past whatever is keeping you from living." He walked to the door and yanked it open. "If you do...you've got my number."

CHAPTER THIRTY-ONE

THE CLICK OF THE DOOR closing might as well have been a slam. Roxann sat rigid on the bed, fighting ridiculous tears. She was not about to be goaded into a relationship with no foundation other than sex, because she suspected she could get used to his company. And right now she needed to concentrate on getting her life back together—finding a new job and place to live, reconciling with her father. It was just like a man to expect a woman to make room for him in her life just because he was—how did he put it—*interested*? What a crock.

She sniffed mightily and leaned over to pull the broken Magic 8 Ball out of the junk box on the floor. She smirked, conceding that she was chasing a thrill by asking, "Is Detective Joe Capistrano madly in love with me?" She turned over the toy.

Don't count on it.

And there she had it—her love life in a nutshell. She had run out of Yes, definitelys.

She called the hospital and asked for Angora's room, thinking she'd give her the basics of Mason's deal until she could get there and explain everything fully.

"Hello?" Angora asked.

"Hi, it's Roxann."

"There you are—no one knew how to get in touch with you. Have you heard the good news? We're not murderers."

Roxann laughed. "That's a relief. So you heard about Cape?"

"The police held a press conference a couple of hours ago. We've been celebrating with red Jell-O."

"We?"

"Mother and Dad and Mike and me. Oh, and Nell is coming by."

Roxann frowned. "Nell?"

"She's looking for you, and I told her to come on over because I was sure you'd call or drop by."

"When did she get back in town?"

"Overnight bus. She said the chancellor of the university called her at two o'clock this morning to give her the good news about Cape. Are you coming?"

"Yes. Mason still wants us to take a polygraph—tomorrow afternoon."

"Then can we go home?"

"As soon as you're up to it."

"I'm still plenty sore, but I'm ready to get out of here."

"Me, too. I'll see you in a few minutes. Oh...is Dee there?"

"Nope. She and Father went out for brunch. They promised to sneak me in a mimosa."

"Do you need anything else?"

"A box of Ho Hos would be nice."

She grinned. "I'll see what I can do." She gave Angora the number at the hotel and her room number, then hung up, feeling better than in weeks, maybe months. It was scary to think how close they'd come to being tried for a crime they didn't commit. She picked up the Magic 8 Ball and turned it over several times.

Yes, definitely.

Yes, definitely.

Yes, definitely.

"Oh, now you say yes," she muttered.

The phone rang, startling her so badly she dropped the ball and watched it roll under the credenza as she picked up the receiver. It was probably Angora getting in her order for a supersized bag of Cheetos. "Hello?"

"Is this Roxann Beadleman?" a woman asked.

"Yes. Who's this?"

"My name is Tanya Chasen—you called the alumni office yesterday asking for help locating Elise James."

"Yes, I know she participated in a couple of fund-raising events—I thought the office might have a record of where she's staying while she's in town."

"Are you a friend of Elise's?"

"Yes. We were roommates until about two months ago."

"Oh. Well, I hate to be the one to tell you this, but Elise is...dead."

Her throat closed. "Wh-what happened?"

"Drug overdose. Her body was found in the bathroom of a local club a couple of nights ago, with no ID. The morgue was holding her as a Jane Doe until someone thought to bring her picture to our office. We identified her from a photo taken during a marathon last weekend." The woman's voice broke. "She came in second place."

Overdose. Roxann was shocked, but not surprised—Elise seemed determined to play Russian roulette with every known vice, yet push herself to the limit as an athlete. She thanked the woman and hung up slowly. Carl, dead. Elise, dead. It was almost too much to absorb. She allowed the news to sink in, then sent a prayer to the ceiling for Elise, remorseful that she had suspected the woman of ransacking her apartment, and far worse—of killing Carl. Poor Elise was a mixed-up soul, searching for an excuse and a panacea, and she'd found neither in her short life.

She sighed, then chased down the Magic 8 Ball, deciding she'd feel much better once she saw Angora and Nell. She lay on her stomach, and reached under the credenza, feeling for the toy, trying not to think about what else might be under there.

Her hand met paper, and she pulled out a copy of the first page of the medical examiner's report on Carl's death. It must have fallen out of Capistrano's file. She scanned the sheet, reminded once again that Carl had died so needlessly. If she had only listened to Capistrano and set up the video meeting with Melissa earlier, this entire tragedy could have been avoided. Frank Cape needed never to have set foot in South Bend. She pressed her lips together, feeling a good cry coming on, then stopped at the sight of Carl's full name. She remembered seeing his middle initial stenciled on the glass door of his office, but she'd never asked him what it stood for.

As Roxann stared at the name, a hot flush climbed her face. At first the implication seemed too outrageous, but as her mind sifted clues and conversations and observations, her hazy theory began to take on a shape, and a face. Her insides heaved, and sweat broke out on her temples.

Angora.

CHAPTER THIRTY-TWO

HER INCISIONS WERE ITCHING AGAIN. Angora wiggled in the hospital bed and tried to think the twinges away, then went back to reading the *Slim Down Now!* magazine her mother had forced upon her.

"If you eat a frozen mashed banana instead of a cup of ice cream, you would save two hundred twenty calories. If you normally indulge in ice cream once a week, you would lose a whopping four pounds a year."

Four lousy pounds? In an entire year? Who did these people think they were kidding—a frozen banana wasn't ice cream, it was a freaking frozen banana. She took a bite out of a chocolate Moon Pie, then slapped the magazine shut and rooted around for something more interesting. It was all pretty much the same crap, though—eat less, exercise more, blah, blah, blah.

Mike Brown's stack of *Progressive Farmer* lay untouched. Out of sheer boredom, she opened the cover and wrinkled her nose: "To Fertilize or Not to Fertilize," "Pasture Rotation," "Liquid Swine Waste." But one item in the table of contents caught her eye: "Marvelous Meat Loaf."

When she was around six years old, her mother had hired a little old woman named Liza who made the most incredible meat loaf and mashed potatoes with gravy. But even at six her cheeks were a bit on the chubby side, so her mother restricted her portions to mere spoonfuls no matter how much she pleaded for more. Dear Liza would sneak a plateful to her room after dinner. But when Dee caught Angora under the covers sopping gravy with a piece of white bread, she'd fired Liza on the spot and hired a bony woman who considered spinach a staple. Ugh.

With mouth watering, she turned to the recipe. Knowing how to make meat loaf seemed like a good basic skill to have. Oooh, there was a picture—a nice juicy hunk of meat with a drizzle of red sauce baked on top, served up with creamy mashed potatoes swimming in brown gravy. Heaven. On. Earth.

A knock on the door sent her scrambling—her parents were back. "Come in," she sang, shoving the Moon Pie and the magazine under her pillow. She wiped her mouth with the sleeve of her gown and pasted on a sublime smile.

But the last person in the world she expected to walk in was Trenton, impeccably dressed in tan slacks and a mint-green cashmere sweater she had bought him for his birthday.

"Hello, Angora."

Her jaw dropped and her mind raced, searching for all those vile things she'd imagined saying to him if and when she ever saw him. "Uh, hi."

"Guess you're surprised to see me."

She nodded, speechless.

He walked to the end of her bed. "I heard about all your trouble and wanted to come and see for myself that you were okay."

So he did care. "Wh-when did you get here?"

"I flew in about an hour ago."

"Where's Darma?"

"We're not together anymore."

Her heart surged. "Why not?" Because he'd come to his senses and realized that Angora was the love of his life.

"She wanted me to sign a prenup, and that was that." He gestured to her stomach. "How are you feeling?"

"Better. I had my gallbladder removed, and a cup of gallstones."

"Your mother and I warned you about eating like a garbage pail."

If she hadn't gone on that diet before the wedding, she would've been fine. "Then I developed complications. An infection—doctor said he'd never seen one so bad."

"Yeah, that can be serious. Did they have you on an IV?"

"Until yesterday."

"That explains why you're so bloated."

She frowned. "Did you hear I was arrested for murder?"

"Your mother said the charges were being dropped."

"They are, but for a while, I was a primary suspect."

He laughed. "Yeah, the police up here must be a bunch of clowns if they thought you were capable of murder. Everybody at the club had a big hoot over that one." He laughed again, dabbing at his eyes. What might have been a compliment was canceled out by his sarcasm—as if she weren't smart enough to pull off a murder.

"I was the last person who saw the professor alive. We were on a date."

He put his hands in his pockets. "Did the two of you, um...you know?"

"Have sex? That's none of your business."

Trenton cleared his throat. "The papers said you bought him at a bachelor auction or something."

She finally smiled. "I hocked my engagement ring, so I had a little extra cash lying around."

He pulled on his collar. "Okay, I deserve that. But I'll get you a bigger ring."

"Huh?"

"I made a big mistake, Angora, and I wouldn't blame you if you don't forgive me, but I want us to get back together."

Mixed emotions filled her chest—hadn't she fantasized that he'd come crawling back to her?

"We're perfect for each other, Angora. You know me, you know what I'm thinking."

"I didn't know what you were thinking last Saturday."

"After all these years of waiting, you didn't sleep with that man, did you?"

She shook her head.

He exhaled in relief. "See? Deep down you couldn't. You knew you were meant for me. We could have a small ceremony, then go on to Hawaii for say, ten days, and have a huge reception when we get back."

"But I don't have a dress—"

"I'll buy you a Versace."

"And the church—"

"Your mom said we could have the ceremony at your house."

"You talked to my parents before you talked to me?"

He sighed. "I knew I had to repair my relationship with the entire family. Your parents were very understanding. What do you say, Angora? We can move to Chicago and start new careers together. You'll love the shopping there."

She lifted her chin. "I could move to Chicago all by myself."

"But you'd have to rely on your allowance to get by."

He was right, darn it. The job at the art agency was mostly commission, and it would take her a while to build a client list.

"Marry me, Angora, and you'll live like a queen."

"But Trenton...do you love me?"

He scoffed. "Of course I love you. We're so much alike, not loving you would be like not loving myself."

She bit into her lip and studied his face—he was so handsome, so smart, so well connected. And he had such good taste. She might look the rest of her life and not find anyone as wonderful as Trenton. And so what if he'd humiliated her—wouldn't she have the last laugh once they were married? *She won him back*, they would say at the club.

Another knock sounded, and her parents appeared. Dee wore a hopeful expression. "Aren't you glad to see Trenton, darling?"

She conjured up a smile.

"And isn't it wonderful that the two of you will be able to work things out after all?"

Marrying Trenton would make her mother so happy—it would certainly make up for all the trouble she'd caused them lately. That whole arrest scene had hit her father hard—he was looking old these days.

And wasn't Chicago the chance to do something with her life? Okay, so the art world wasn't as glamorous as she'd imagined—most of the artists finger-painted to support their body-piercing addictions—but the Chicago job was a great opportunity and what else was she halfway qualified to do?

"Yes," she said to her mother. "It's wonderful."

Trenton's shoulders fell in relief and his smile did lift her spirits. "You won't regret this, Angora."

Her mother beamed. "Trenton is going to stay until tomorrow evening and we'll all fly home together."

But Angora shook her head. "I'm going to ride back with Roxann."

Dee scowled. "You can't be serious. That tramp is the one who got you into this mess."

"I've made up my mind, Mother. Once I move to Chicago, I might never see Roxann again. I don't expect you to understand, but I want to do this."

"I don't know—"

"Dixie," her father said. "You heard your daughter."

Angora jumped on the momentum. "You all should head back now so Daddy can go into the office tomorrow and so you can start getting things ready for the ceremony. Pick out the dress, the flowers, whatever you want is fine."

Her mother seemed surprised. Granted, they'd argued for hours over the details the first time around. "Well...all right, dear."

"Are you sure the drive won't be too uncomfortable?" her father asked, dear man.

"Roxann will take care of me."

"But I just got here," Trenton said.

She smiled. "And we have the rest of our lives together. Roxann and my attorney will be here soon, and I'd like to rest." Besides, she knew her mother didn't want an encounter with either one of her impending visitors.

The three of them looked at each other, perplexed, but they relented and said goodbye. Her father hugged her carefully. Her mother kissed the air next to her cheek. And Trenton kissed her on the forehead. "I'll see you later this week."

She nodded and held her breath until the door closed. She was so used to being ignored, all the attention was downright suffocating. After rescuing the Moon Pie and the magazine from behind her pillow, she snuggled down in the covers and munched slowly.

So, she was going to marry a doctor after all. Everything would be just the way she'd planned, and she'd live happily ever after with Trenton. They would be fine—she'd forgive him for being infatuated with Darma. After all, she'd been infatuated with Carl.

Things would be...fine.

She scoured the meat loaf recipe and decided it was something she could try on her own, then she checked other issues of the magazine and found a mother lode of wonderful comfort-food recipes—homemade macaroni and cheese, buttermilk biscuits, hot brown, sweet potato pie. When she had her own kitchen, she could make whatever she wanted to eat. And if Trenton didn't like it, she'd simply sneak and eat it alone.

Her phone rang, and Mike Brown was on the other end with the time and place of the polygraph the following day. "I'll drive you," he offered. "I have to dress a couple of hams, but I should be through in plenty of time."

She had the feeling that dressing the hams didn't involve matching shoes and handbags. "Mike, I want to thank you for all your help, and I'd like to pay you for your trouble."

"Ah, forget about it," he said. "Just getting to know you has been a pleasure."

She imagined him pushing up his glasses. "I think you're nice, too," she said.

"See you tomorrow," he said cheerfully. "Call me if you need anything."

Angora hung up the phone thinking that Mike Brown was the kind of man who probably put away a lot of meat loaf and gravy. Heck, he probably *grew* his own meat loaf.

She reached for the remote and turned on the TV. Carl's murder and the death of Frank Cape were all the rage on the local news. She shivered at her brush with danger. Her guardian angel must have senior status to have gotten her through this mess.

A honking noise blared into her room, startling her. The source of the intermittent sound wasn't readily apparent, but she deduced it was some kind of alarm. She sat up, holding one hand against her bandages. The intercom beeped.

"The fire alarm has been sounded. If you're able, please vacate your room and proceed to the nearest exit. Emergency personnel will be around to make sure each room has been evacuated. The fire alarm has been sounded..."

Her heart beat faster as she swung her feet over the edge of the bed. The movement pulled at her incisions, sending burning pain through her abdomen.

She inhaled sharply. Her room was on the eighth floor—how would she ever make it down the stairs?

The door to her room swung open and she sighed in relief at the sight of Nell Oney. "Dr. Oney, thank goodness you're here. Can you help me? Over there are my house shoes, and my coat is in that closet."

But instead, the woman locked the door and walked toward her, smiling. "There is no fire."

CHAPTER THIRTY-THREE

ROXANN SLAMMED DOWN the phone—Angora's line was still busy. Nearing panic, she tore downstairs and outside into the parking lot, praying that Capistrano had been delayed. It would take her forever to flag a taxi. She spotted the Dooley pulling away from her and her immense relief fueled a burst of adrenaline. She ran as fast as her legs would carry her, waving and screaming at the top of her lungs. "Wait! Capistrano, wait!" Just when her fear peaked, the brake lights came on. She stumbled, recovered, and flung herself toward the truck.

He opened the door. "What's wrong?"

She was too winded to talk. "To the hospital...fast." She yanked open the passenger side door and vaulted inside.

Capistrano pulled out, following her hand directions. "Did something happen to Angora?"

"I can't...be sure...but I think...she's in danger."

"From whom?"

"Nell."

"What?"

She took a deep breath and exhaled. "I found a page from the ME report that fell under the credenza in the hotel room. Carl's middle name is Chester."

He frowned. "I don't get it."

"Nell's favorite cat, the one she dotes on, is named Chester."

He scratched his temple. "Okay."

"I think she's been in love with him all these years. I think she put Frank Cape up to killing Carl."

"That's a pretty big leap, Roxann."

"No. I remembered something that Cape said when he told me he killed Carl. He said a lot of good it did him, and that nobody keeps their word. I think Nell struck a bargain with him—kill Carl, and she'd find out where Melissa was living."

"Did she find out?"

"No, but not for lack of trying. She asked me several times, and my supervisor said she'd even been in touch with him about the case. And I distinctly remember a conversation where she asked about Melissa and Renita." She shook her head. "I never mentioned their names."

"But how would she have gotten in touch with Cape?"

"I'm guessing through Elise James—she ran with a pretty bad element." She wet her lips. "Elise is dead, by the way. Overdose on prescription drugs that were laced with something. But I'm starting to wonder..."

"Go on."

"I wonder if Nell was the one who gave her the drugs. She's been ill, and I stumbled across enough prescription painkillers in her cabinet to take out a herd of elephants."

He quirked an eyebrow. "What else do you have?"

"She tried to divert suspicion in the Tammy Paulen case to Angora, tried to convince me that Angora was guilty and unstable. I'll bet she told others the same thing."

"To protect Seger."

"Probably."

He pointed to the file between them. "Do you remember the date the Paulen girl was killed?"

"Yeah, it was December second, 1992."

"Look in that folder for a copy of Dr. Seger's bio. It's four or five pages stapled together."

"Why? What am I looking for?"

"Just a hunch, but check the dates on his list of speaking engagements."

She found the paper, which listed Dr. Seger's accomplishments. A resume of sorts, including an exhaustive list of seminars he'd given. Roxann scanned the dates, then stopped. "November twenty-ninth through December third, Carl was giving a seminar in Philadelphia."

Capistrano whistled low. "Think he loaned his car to anyone to use while he was gone?"

"Someone who doesn't have a car." She closed her eyes. "I can't believe it. Angora said that she told Carl she'd seen his car leaving the scene."

"So he knew that Dr. Oney had done it."

"Right. Maybe he called Nell, threatened to blackmail her. Maybe that's when she contacted Cape and made the deal or sped up the deal they'd already made."

Capistrano's mouth tightened. "If we realized that Seger wasn't around when the Paulen girl was killed, someone else will eventually notice, too. And without Angora around to testify..."

She nodded, reeling. Nell...lonely Nell. Had she stayed holed up in her little house quietly going mad?

He picked up the phone. "What's the name of the hospital?"

"Holy Cross."

He punched in a number and asked directory assistance for a direct connection. "Security please," he said. "This is urgent." Then he frowned. "What?... When?...Thank you."

He disconnected the call. "The hospital has been evacuated for a possible fire. The fire department is on its way."

"Think it's a coincidence?" she asked.

He pulled a blue siren from beneath his seat, rolled down the window, and stuck it to the top of the cab. "Darlin', there are very few coincidences in this world."

CHAPTER THIRTY-FOUR

ANGORA ALLOWED NELL to plump her pillow and brush off the crumbs. "Thank you."

"I brought you something," Nell said, holding up a white bag. "Jelly doughnuts and milk."

Angora smiled—maybe she'd misjudged Dr. Oney. She'd thought for some reason that the woman didn't like her. "Thank you. The food here is terrible."

Nell handed her a doughnut and opened a pint carton of milk. "Go ahead and eat. I had one already."

She frowned at the message still playing over the intercom. "If there's no fire, why don't they turn off the alarm?"

"They probably have to wait for the fire department to reset it."

Angora bit into the doughnut—the food of all foods, in her opinion. Dee wouldn't even allow them in the house. Ooh, and whole milk. Wow. She took a big drink, then winced. "This milk tastes funny."

"It's fresh," Nell assured her. "I just bought it in the cafeteria."

"Oh. I'm used to drinking skim."

"That must be it," Nell agreed.

She took another large bite and swallow of milk, "Roxann said she was coming over."

"I'm sorry I'll miss her. I can't stay very long."

"Roxann really thinks the world of you, you know."

Nell looked sad. "I think the world of her, too." She stood and walked around the room with her hands clasped behind her, as if she were in the classroom giving a lecture. "I hear that you've been spreading lies about Dr. Seger."

She stopped mid-chew and talked through a mouthful of jelly. "Huh?"

"Mike Brown said you told the police that you had a sexual encounter with Carl in his office."

She swallowed and tried to speak, but her throat was dry and tingly. She downed another drink of milk, then laid her head back. "I wasn't lying. It... happened."

"You lying little glutton of a bitch," Nell said in a calm voice.

But Angora wasn't sure she heard her correctly, because something was wrong. Her head felt funny, and her stomach burned—inside and out.

"He also said that you saw Carl driving away from the scene the night that Tammy Paulen was killed."

"I...did." She moaned and clutched her stomach.

"That makes two lies, Angora. *I* was driving Carl's car. I saw that little slut in the road and I ran over her." She laughed. "Not only did I not slow down—I actually sped up. She was pregnant, you know. She told me it was Carl's baby, but she was a liar, too."

Nell walked over and lifted Angora's hand, then dropped several capsule halves from her own gloved hand and closed Angora's fingers over the bits of plastic.

Angora couldn't resist her—she had no control over her limbs. She watched as Nell guided her hand over the tray table and allowed the empty capsules that now had her fingerprints on them to fall out and roll next to the carton of milk.

"But those are our little secrets, Angora. You can take them to your grave. Which should be very shortly considering the amount of painkiller I put in that milk."

Angora's tongue seemed to overflow her mouth. She couldn't talk, but she could hear every word the sick woman was saying.

"I thought they'd lock you up for sure. I set you up with a dim farmer who thinks he's F. Lee Bailey. He told me things because he thought I was trying to help you." She laughed. "I think the poor clod is in love with you."

"Help...me," Angora whispered.

“Oh, but I am. You see, you have the reputation of being unstable. Did you know there’s schizophrenia in your family? It’s hereditary. I know because my mother was schizophrenic.” She laughed. “But I digress. You were depressed, Angora. You were just jilted at the altar, then all this business with Carl, then your surgery. You were so overcome with grief that you took your own life with pills you stole from my kitchen cabinet. I made a point of telling my sister when I went to Indy that someone had been pilfering my medicine.” She sighed. “So you see, everyone will believe you simply gave up.”

Angora fought the urge to give in to sleep. This was the third time in as many days that she’d thought she was dying, and Dee always said that the third time was the charm. Where was that senior guardian angel? Oh, boy, she was a goner this time, taken down by jelly doughnuts.

CHAPTER THIRTY-FIVE

ROXANN RAN DOWN the hall, looking for Angora's room number. The acrid smell of smoke was even stronger on this floor, although she didn't see smoke. Capistrano was behind her, followed by two security guards. She was short of breath from running the eight flights of stairs.

"Here!" she shouted, moving the "room evacuated" door tag to try the handle. "It's locked." She peered through the narrow frosted window, but she couldn't make out anything.

Capistrano threw his weight against the door, but it wouldn't budge. He pulled down the sleeve of his sweatshirt to cover his fist, then rammed it through the glass and looked in. "Angora's in there. Alone." He reached through the window and down to unlock the door from the inside.

Roxann rushed into the room. Angora was deathly pale. Next to her sat an open bag of doughnuts and a small carton of milk, surrounded by a mound of broken capsules. "Call a doctor," she yelled to the guards. "Tell them she's been drugged, maybe poisoned."

"Stay here," Capistrano said to Roxann. "I'm going to look for Oney."

But Roxann was right behind him. He borrowed a two-way radio from one of the guards and stuffed it in his coat pocket. Then he fished a card out of his wallet and punched in a number on his cell phone while he moved down the hall, peering into adjacent rooms.

"This is Detective Capistrano of the Biloxi PD. I have an emergency at Holy Cross Hospital. Possible murder attempt. The suspect is Dr. Nell Oney, Caucasian female, approximately fifty years of age, five feet five, one hundred ten pounds. Suspect may have left the building traveling on foot. Requesting periphery surveillance. Also, inform Detectives Warner and Jaffey."

They found one of the sources of the smoke—a smoldering bin of used linens in a supply closet. The detective used the radio to alert the security guards and closed the door. There were probably similar fires throughout the building. They systematically checked rooms, then moved down one floor, but Roxann was afraid that Nell was long gone. On the seventh floor, however, a gravelly sound reached her ears—coughing. Apparently the smoke from the fires Nell had set was too much for her. Roxann nudged Capistrano and pointed to a women's lounge. He radioed the security guards and told them to notify the police. Then he drew his weapon, which brought tears to her eyes. He gestured for her to stay put, then crept to the door.

"Dr. Oney," he called. "It's Detective Capistrano and Roxann. We know you're in there, and we know what happened. Come out and we'll work through this together." He backed away from the door.

A few seconds later, Nell emerged, her pallor gray, and her eyes red-rimmed. She had her hand to her mouth, coughing so violently, her entire body shook.

She gasped for air, and pointed a bony finger at Roxann. "I tried to protect you," she said. "I loved Carl, too, but I was protecting you when I sent you away."

Roxann swallowed, unable to reconcile the wild-eyed woman before her with the nurturing mentor Nell had once been. "All those years ago...you made up the story about Carl being investigated because you knew I'd leave."

"Yes. He was crazy about you, but I knew he'd never change. The man unzipped his fly for any pretty girl who walked by."

She looked to Capistrano who gestured that she keep Nell talking. "You were sure he wouldn't come after me once I left South Bend?"

"No, I wasn't sure. But I told Carl if he didn't stay away from you, I'd reveal that Tammy Paulen was pregnant with his baby when she died."

Roxann blinked as another piece of the puzzle fell into place. "You killed Tammy, didn't you?" she asked softly.

She smiled. "You're smarter than Carl."

"He didn't know until Angora told him."

Nell lapsed into another coughing fit and sagged against the door. Roxann started to go to her, but Capistrano held out his arm. "Do you need to sit down, ma'am?"

Her next inhale expanded her frail chest. She shook her head. "No, I want to have my say before they take me away." She swallowed, then wiped her mouth with her hand. "Carl called me the night that Angora was at his house. Said if I even thought about revealing the Paulen girl's pregnancy, he could prove that I'd killed her. He said he was still in love with you, Roxann, and that now I couldn't stop him from pursuing a relationship with you."

A bittersweet revelation. "So you sent over Frank Cape, with the scarf you took from my room?"

Nell made a regretful sound. "That's where things went bad. I told Frank that if he did me a favor, I could find out where Melissa was hiding."

Bile backed up in Roxann's mouth that Nell was willing to betray a woman who took refuge in the program she had created.

"The idiot was supposed to make it look as if Angora killed Carl. Later he told me the scarf was already in the library, and he thought it was hers. I could have killed Frank myself for incriminating you."

"Carl was at the restaurant where you and I dined," Roxann murmured. "I must have lost my scarf and he must have found it."

Nell's smile was rueful. "An unforeseeable mix-up."

"How did you meet up with Cape?" Capistrano asked.

"Elise was screwing him in Biloxi."

Roxann wet her lips. "Elise is dead, you know."

Nell's laugh was punctuated with a hacking cough. "Oh, yes, I know. Elise and I were close when she went to school here. Carl nearly destroyed her, too, so I took her under my wing. She was strung too tightly to cope with any disappointment. Over the years she called me when she was in the midst of one crisis or another. I tried to help her when I could, find jobs for her."

"You sent her to Biloxi," Roxann said in sudden comprehension.

Nell nodded. "When your picture ran in the alumni newsletter, I could tell Carl was getting restless. He asked me to let him off the hook—he wanted to see you again." She smiled sadly. "I told him no, that you were still off-limits. He'd poisoned enough women with his wickedness, me included."

Roxann couldn't believe what she was hearing. "So you sent Elise to *spy* on me?"

"I was trying to protect you, don't you see?" Nell's bottom lip quivered. "I never had a child, Roxann. You're like a daughter to me."

She set her jaw to hold back her emotion. Nell's love was so twisted, it was inconceivable. "B-but why did you kill Elise?"

"I didn't plan to, but I listened in on her call to you at my house. I went to see her, to stop her from telling you everything. She wanted pills in return for her silence. Those pills wouldn't have hurt her if she hadn't taken more than one."

But anyone who knew Elise knew that one of anything was never enough. Anger stirred in Roxann's stomach. "Angora had better live," she whispered. "She's innocent in all of this."

Nell's ghostly face suddenly turned malicious. "Because of her, I had to have Carl killed." Then she narrowed her eyes. "And I finally figured out your little secret. How can you say that Angora is innocent?"

Roxann's heart pumped harder.

"It took me a while," Nell admitted. "But I started thinking about what Tammy had told me—that it had something to do with a blond wig. It suddenly dawned on me while I was at my sister's house. I checked, and it all fit."

The exit door swung open and Detective Jaffey appeared with two uniformed officers, weapons drawn.

"It's okay," Capistrano called. "Dr. Oney isn't going to cause any more trouble." Then he looked back to her. "Are you?"

She shook her head and succumbed to another coughing spasm until blood appeared in her mouth. "I'm dying," she said to Roxann, with tears in her eyes.

"What?"

"Lung cancer. Doctors say I have about three months left to live."

Roxann broke away from Capistrano's restraining arm and went to her. They hugged for several long minutes, and Roxann pretended Nell was the woman they both wanted her to be. Jaffey walked up. "We'll take it from here."

She watched them lead Nell away, the woman's walk little more than a shuffle. Roxann slid down the wall and sat on the floor, weak and spent after the day's revelations. Capistrano was talking to Jaffey, filling him in on the high points of Nell's confession. Then he spoke to someone over the two-way radio, and walked over to sit down by her.

"Your cousin is going to make it."

She closed her eyes and breathed a prayer of thanks. "Is this nightmare finally over?"

He pursed his mouth and nodded. "Unless you have a confession to make?"

He was referring to the secret Nell hinted at. "Nope. I'm done for the day." She pushed herself up and he followed. "I don't know how to thank you," she murmured.

"Yes, you do," he said, his brown eyes serious.

But her head was too full to deal with yet another demand. "Sorry, Detective. That's not on the table." Then she walked toward the exit sign.

CHAPTER THIRTY-SIX

"WE COULD POSTPONE the trip back for another day if you don't feel up to it," Roxann said, pushing the wheelchair down the hall.

Angora craned her head around. "I'm feeling fine. I just want to get out of here and on the road." She wore the crown Roxann had given her, and a blue pashmina shawl around her shoulders. She looked like a celebrity leaving the hospital, and indeed, she had become somewhat of a town icon since news of Dr. Oney's treachery had broken.

Everyone at the nurses' station waved. "Goodbye, Angora."

"Goodbye," she sang, waving at her adoring audience. "Thank you, everyone. Thank you."

Roxann wheeled her to the side entrance where a refurbished Goldie awaited them. And Mike Brown. He was dressed in work clothes, including a John Deere ball cap, but he looked fresh-scrubbed. He smiled at Angora and juggled the items he was holding to take off his hat when they came closer. Without preamble, he thrust a wildflower bouquet into her hands.

"Picked them myself this morning," he said, fiddling with his hat and the large brown paper bundle he held. "When I came back from milking."

"Milking what?" Angora asked, then buried her nose in the flowers.

"Cows," he said, pushing up his glasses. "And a couple of goats."

"I didn't know you could milk goats."

"Oh, sure," he said solemnly. Then he thumped the bundle he held—it sounded solid. "And I brought you a ham."

Angora's eyes bulged. "A ham?"

Roxann was pretty impressed herself. The man was scoring big with pork.

"I'll put it in the van for you," he offered.

Roxann slid back the van door and he deposited the ham on the floorboard behind the bench seat where she'd made a bed for Angora. New seat covers hid the damage of Frank Cape's knife—or Nell's. She wasn't sure who had done what anymore. Had Elise broken in to the duplex and left the message on the computer at Nell's instruction? But Nell hadn't known about the secret at the time, so was the word fake an accidental word choice that just happened to push Roxann's buttons? Was her guilt that deep?

So it seemed.

Mike helped Angora out of the wheelchair and practically lifted her into the van, then settled her onto the seat and tucked in covers all around. "You look like a queen," he said a little breathlessly, and Roxann realized that the man had a huge crush on her cousin.

Angora beamed. "Thank you, Mike."

"I'm sorry that Dr. Oney used me to get to you."

He spoke so quickly that it must have been weighing on his mind for some time.

"You couldn't have known," Angora said, touching his arm. "It's not your fault."

"Still, I'm going to stick to farming from now on."

"I think you're a wonderful lawyer," she said, and Roxann was glad to hear the sincerity in her voice. "I appreciate the way you stood up for me." She pulled him forward and gave him a kiss on the cheek.

He blushed furiously and turned his hat inside out. Then he withdrew his wallet and extracted a business card. "You probably never want to see this place again, but if you're ever up this way, I'd be proud to show you my farm."

She took the card and nodded. "I'd be proud to see it."

"Goodbye, ma'am." Then he shoved his hat on his head and strode off, climbing into a white Suburban parked nearby.

Roxann smiled. "Ready?"

Angora looked up. "Yeah, I'm ready. Let's go home."

She shoved the door closed, then climbed into the driver's seat and adjusted the rearview mirror so they could see each other. "What a trip this has been."

"I'll say. Honestly, Roxann, I had no idea this much sorrow and...evil existed in the world. Or maybe I knew, but I didn't think it could get to me. I've led such a charmed life."

"Are you sorry you came?"

Angora thought for a moment, then shook her head. "I don't know how to explain it, but it's as if the last couple of weeks had to happen, as if I've been holding my breath all my life waiting for it to unfold." She frowned. "Of course, I had no idea it would be so tragic." Her eyes were pinched, sorrowful. "Roxann, not a day goes by that I don't feel terrible about the deal we made."

She leaned on the steering wheel, her pulse elevated. "Same here."

"Do you think it had anything to do with what we just went through?"

"You mean some kind of penance? I don't think all those people died just to jump-start our conscience, but maybe something good can come out of all of this."

Angora bit into her bottom lip. "Is there anything we can do about it now?"

Roxann turned around in her seat so they could speak face-to-face. "We could always come clean." How many times had she almost picked up a pay phone to make an anonymous tip on herself, just to get everything out in the open? But they'd promised each other sacred silence and she'd kept her end of the bargain.

"What would happen to us?"

"That's hard to say. Worst-case scenario, we could be brought up on criminal charges."

"Not again."

"But that's not likely, especially in light of the publicity the university has just suffered." She sighed. "And there would be personal consequences."

"Mother would never forgive me. Trenton would be scandalized. The job in Chicago would be out." Then she gave a little laugh. "But I'm not so sure all of that would be a bad thing."

"You don't want to go to Chicago?"

"I don't want to marry Trenton."

Roxann agreed with her wholeheartedly, but had kept her opinion in check.

"I'm tired of doing and being what everyone expects of me. Sometimes I wish Mother had left my face the way it was so I could just...*be*. Be plain, be fat, be happy. You know—a simple life with a good man and a few kids." She burst into tears. "I think I'm in love with M-Mike B-Brown."

Roxann's eyebrows skyrocketed. "What?"

"He's so good to me—I've never had a man take his hat off for me, bring me flowers, a ham." She sniffled. "Mike makes me laugh, and he makes me feel good about myself."

At first the idea of Angora the debutante being the wife of a plump Midwestern farmer was comical, but after Roxann tried it on for size, the image seemed to...no, actually it still seemed far-fetched.

"Angora, you have to do whatever will make you happy. But I'd hate to see you run from Trenton and your parents just so you won't have to face them."

"Oh, no, I'm going to face them. I'm going to tell them the truth, then break it off with Trenton."

"We could take care of this while we're here, but we both have to agree."

"I...think we should," Angora said. "Don't you?"

Roxann nodded. "Yes, I do." Even though she could imagine the disappointment on her father's face, she could also imagine the relief of a clear conscience. "Are you sure you're up for this?"

"No, but I'll live. Do you think that Mike will still be interested in me after he finds out?"

"I suspect so." She smiled and started the engine, then turned in the direction of campus. Her stomach pitched and her neck muscles tightened. "This is going to change everything, you know."

"I know."

CHAPTER THIRTY-SEVEN

ROXANN CLUNG TO THE BACK of an aged wing chair in her father's living room. Her knees were practically knocking and her mouth couldn't seem to produce enough moisture to say what she had to say.

"Go on," her father urged from his La-Z-Boy, unreclined for the serious discussion they'd been having. "It can't be that bad, Roxann."

She inhaled deeply. "Dad, when Angora and I were eighteen, we made a deal. I took the ACT test, and the Notre Dame entrance exam for her." She swallowed hard. "And while we were there, I took tests for her whenever she was afraid she wouldn't pass."

He closed his eyes briefly, and his grizzled mouth pulled down. "In return for what?"

"She paid me enough to cover most of my tuition."

"You didn't get a scholarship?"

"No, my grades in high school weren't good enough."

He shook his head, his eyes wide and disbelieving.

"But you made straight As in college—you were a valedictorian."

She walked around and sat down in the chair. "I studied hard because I was trying to prove something to myself, maybe trying to punish myself for what I was doing."

Her father's hand shook while her heart broke. "How did you do it? Don't the instructors even know who's in their class?"

So far, the conversation was meeting her worst expectations. Roxann sighed. "Everyone was always telling me and Angora how much we looked alike. I...wore a blond wig on the days I took her exams." She leaned forward.

"Dad, I felt awful the entire time I was doing it, and ever since. I wanted to go to law school when I graduated, but I felt too guilty—like the degree I'd earned was the fruit of a poisonous tree."

"Well, it was." He got up and walked over to stand in front of the old cabinet-model TV, looking out into the yard that, she suspected, he'd tidied for her homecoming. The sun highlighted his sparse hair and the stoop of his shoulders. Then, to her dismay, she realized his shoulders were shaking. Her father hadn't cried at her mother's funeral, but she'd managed to make him cry on a sunny Wednesday in late October.

Swallowing her emotion she went to stand behind him and touched his shoulders. "Dad, I did a dishonest, horrible thing, and I'm so, so sorry that I let you down."

"No," he said, his voice breaking. "I'm the one who let you down, Roxann. I was a hateful, distant father who saw the woman I loved and lost every time I looked at you. I expected you to live your life the way I had it planned, and when you didn't, I thought it was out of spite."

She turned him around and looked into the face of remorse and regret. "Dad, it wasn't out of spite. It was out of shame. I couldn't face you, I couldn't face the world after I graduated. I hated myself for what I'd done."

His chin wobbled. "I should've been there for you."

She hugged him close. "We're here for each other now."

He pulled back, his face creased with worry. "Roxann, I have to ask—does the cheating have anything to do with all those murders?"

"No." Then she managed a rueful smile. "Except for the fact that I mistook a message that someone left on my computer as a threat, that they somehow knew what I'd done. My guilt surfaced and I panicked. That's why I was on the run, even before I knew Frank Cape was after me."

"You mean this Cape fellow didn't leave the message?"

"He said he didn't, although lying would have been one of his better character traits. Or it's possible that my ex-roommate left it."

"The girl who died?"

"Right. Maybe she thought it was amusing, I don't know."

"What did the message say?"

"It said, 'I've got your number, you fake.' "

He scratched his temple and scoffed. "I think that's a line from a book."

"Really?"

He walked around the room, poking into different piles of books. "Where did I read that line? Somewhere...oh, this is the book." He held up a hardcover with a torn jacket. *Mac Tomlin, Gumshoe.* He flipped through the pages, scanning for several seconds. "Here's the scene, page one twenty-four. The suspect tells Tomlin that he'll never prove that he killed his wife. Tomlin says, 'I've got your number, you fake.' "

She was inclined to pass it off as a coincidence, but what had Capistrano said—there are very few coincidences in this world? Darlin'. Once she got past the irritation of remembering something he'd said, she thought that quoting a line from a book was just the sort of thing that Richard Funderburk might have done, to be clever. And Cape was a PI—maybe Mac Tomlin was an idol of his. Assuming the man could read.

"I'll probably never know who left that message," she said.

Her father returned the book to a shelf, then sat down in his recliner. "I'm glad you told me about the deception, Roxann, but it has to be put right."

She nodded. "Angora and I talked to the dean of admissions and several regents before we left South Bend about our punishment. Since she didn't meet the entrance qualifications, Angora's diploma was rescinded. I was stripped of honors."

"But they're not pressing charges of fraud?"

"No. They said we'd been through enough at the hands of university personnel. I think they were relieved we weren't going to sue them."

"So you get to keep your degree?"

"Yes."

He exhaled. "Was Angora devastated? Poor girl, shackled with that piranha of a mother. Never had a chance."

"Actually, I think she was relieved. Angora has her faults, but deep down she's an honest person."

"Except Dixie will throw this up to her for the rest of her life."

Roxann smiled. "I have a feeling Angora is going back to South Bend to live, and that her visits to and from her mother will be few and far between."

"Oh?"

"She met a guy—her attorney. A soybean farmer. He told Dixie to shut her pie hole."

Her father grinned. "I like the sound of that boy." He pressed his thin lips together, his eyes still troubled. "What are you going to do now, sweetheart?"

She sat back in her chair and looked around the room. "I was hoping you'd let me camp out here for a while. I could cook and clean in return for my room and board. And I might need your help studying."

"Studying?"

"For the LSAT."

His eyes sparkled. "You're going to law school?"

"If I can pass the entrance exam."

He waved his hand. "Just a formality." He stood up, his body animated. "How about some coffee? No—sit still, I'll make it."

Roxann sat back and, for the first time in years, truly relaxed. She closed her eyes and, starting with the top of her head, allowed every muscle in her body to loosen and expand. The last time she'd felt so light and carefree was the morning of the day she walked home and her mother wasn't waiting for her on the porch. It was the last day, she realized, that she'd felt safe and loved. But it wasn't too late to make amends with her father, and she did have people in the world who cared about her—Helen at the diner, Mr. Nealy next door, Angora, and lots of folks in the Rescue program, even if they didn't remember her name, or hadn't known it to begin with.

"What happened to that Capistrano fellow?" her dad called from the kitchen.

At the sound of the man's name, her entire body contracted involuntarily. "He went back to Biloxi."

"Are you still seeing him?"

She sighed. "Dad, I was never seeing him."

"Are you going to *be* seeing him?"

She opened her mouth to say no, then stopped. Why was it so hard to admit that she'd fallen for Joe Capistrano? Because of the way he made her question her life choices, and her motives? Carl Seger had spouted platitudes about social consciousness while exploiting hordes of female students. But Capistrano was out on the streets every day catching bad guys so that people could sleep a little easier at night. He had made her see that she wanted to help improve domestic and custodial laws instead of evade them.

So maybe he wasn't offering her forever. Maybe they could have now, and just... *be.*

I hope you get past whatever is keeping you from living...if you do, you've got my number.

"Roxann?" her father said from the doorway. "I asked if you're going to be seeing the young man?"

She sat up and reached for her purse. "Dad...do you mind if I make a long-distance call?"

"Be my guest."

The card Capistrano had given her was a little worse for time spent in the bottom of her purse, but the number for his cell phone was readable. She dialed the number, heart pounding. When it rang once, she hung up. After a quick pep talk, she dialed again. It rang, and she hung up again. Cursing her cowardice, she dialed the number again. It rang once, twice, three times before he picked up.

"I thought I'd wait to see if you were going to hang up again," he said, sounding amused.

She frowned—a pox on caller ID. "It could have been my father calling. Besides, I might just hang up now."

"Oh, don't do that. I've missed you."

She swallowed. "I've missed you, too."

"See, that didn't hurt, did it?"

"I'm coming to see you."

"If you weren't, I was coming to get you."

"Is this going to work, Capistrano?"

"I didn't get scalded, pepper-sprayed, and tire-ironed for it not to."

She smiled into the phone…and relaxed.

EPILOGUE

ROXANN CLIMBED into the passenger seat of the Dooley with an armful of mail.

"Popular lady," Capistrano said.

"I haven't picked up my mail in ages."

"Does this mean I have to let you go outside every weekend you visit?"

She shook her head at his foolishness, then flipped through the pile, discarding junk mail and sorting bills. A letter from Richard with a Birmingham postmark evoked a rueful noise from her throat.

"What's that?"

"A letter from an old boyfriend."

He made a hurt face. "What if he wants you back?"

"I'm not available," she sang, then opened the letter. A fifty-dollar bill floated out.

Dear Roxann,

I hope this note finds you well. I thought you'd like to know that I'm in AA and have been sober for almost five months. One of the steps to recovery requires us to seek forgiveness from people we've wronged and try to repair the damage we've done. I probably owe you my life for orchestrating that intervention, so thank you from the bottom of my heart. And I remembered that I owe you fifty bucks.

Fondly,

Richard

“Is your old flame buying us dinner?” he asked.

“Nope. You’re buying dinner, he’s buying a study guide that I need.”

She pulled out another envelope, this one forwarded to her through the Rescue program. “Another boyfriend?”

“No, but your petty jealousy is turning me on.” The letter was from Melissa Cape Morgan.

Dear Roxann,

Funny that I don’t even know your last name, yet I owe you so much. Renita and I have never been happier—you are in our prayers every night. Enclosed is a picture that Renita drew for her “lady hero.” Thank you.

xoxoxoxo

Melissa and Renita

Renita had drawn a crayon version of their “rescue” to the airport. She’d portrayed Roxann wearing a long red cape and tall red boots. Roxann smiled, and her heart expanded. Maybe she had done some good all these years. She would call Tom Atlas tomorrow to see what she could do for the Rescue program on a part-time basis.

The next card was a heartfelt message from Nell Oney’s sister, thanking Roxann for attending the memorial service. So sad—Nell had suffered tremendously in the end. Roxann swallowed the lump in her throat and hoped Nell was in a better place.

Finally she pulled out a thick, square envelope and grinned. “It’s from Angora.” She ripped it open and pictures fell into her lap.

Dear Roxann,

Thought I’d let you see what life on the farm is like. I really love it here, especially the animals. And of course, Mike is wonderful. We were married last Wednesday night at the Justice of the Peace. I was thinking about you during the ceremony. Mike and I are expecting a baby in the summer—we’re both thrilled. Mother is less thrilled, but resigned.

Much love, Angora

P.S. Mike also runs a crop-dusting business on the side, so he's teaching me to fly a plane.

The pictures showed a round-cheeked Angora, nearly unrecognizable because her hair was now a light brown—her natural color? She wore sensible clothes and shoes, and she was holding a baby goat. Another picture was of her in the kitchen, elbow-deep in flour and smiling into the camera. The third picture was a snapshot of her and Mike at the Justice of the Peace. Angora wore a knee-length white dress and a white hat, and held a bouquet of dried wildflowers, beaming. Mike wore a suit and bow tie, and looked as if he'd just won the lottery. The last photo showed Angora sitting in the cockpit of a crop-dusting plane, waving.

"What's so funny?" Capistrano asked.

"Angora is amazing. Who would have dreamed that she'd enjoy living on a farm?"

He laughed. "I'll bet it has more to do with the farmer than the farm."

"They're expecting a baby."

"Wow, that didn't take long."

"Angora wanted to have kids right away. She said our eggs are getting old."

He pursed his mouth. "Hm. Might have to do something about that 'being a mother and having a daughter' thing on that list you made."

"If that's a proposal," she said dryly, "think of a better delivery."

He pulled in front of the duplex and parked at the curb. "You know I love you," he said. "I'm helping you move, for Christ's sake."

She jumped down from the truck. "Nope, you'll have to do better than that."

He caught up with her and grabbed her around the waist. He kissed her thoroughly, then lifted his head. "Okay, how about, 'Let's get married and have a bunch of kids'?"

She grinned. "Is that a hypothetical question?"

He scratched his head as if he just realized what he'd done. "Er, no. No it is not."

She shrugged. "Okay." Then she turned and walked toward the back entrance.

"Okay?" he asked, on her heels. "That's all you have to say?"

"Okay, *Detective*."

"That's better," he said, lowering another kiss on her mouth. At the sound of a throat being cleared, they pulled apart.

Mr. Nealy stood on his front porch, broom at the ready. "Nice day," he said, but his mouth was pulled down in a disapproving frown.

"Hi, Mr. Nealy—you remember Joe Capistrano?"

"Yes," he chirped. "Hello, young man."

"Hello, sir." He leaned close to her ear. "He hates me."

"Shut up," she whispered. "Mr. Nealy, I have a table that I'd like to give to you—can I bring it over?"

"Sure," he said, a bit more cheerfully.

Inside her kitchen, boxes were stacked on the floor, packed with the few clothes, dishes, and other belongings she owned. She walked over to a wooden telephone stand with claw-and-ball feet. "I found it in an antique shop," she said. "I think Mr. Nealy will like it."

"Want me to carry it over?"

"No, I got it."

Her neighbor was holding open the back door of his duplex when she went out. She held up the table. "What do you think?"

He finally smiled. "I'm sure I can find some use for it in here. Thank you, Roxann."

She stepped inside, immediately assailed with the smell of cedar and mothballs and loneliness. His belongings were meager, but neat.

"Just set it down over there by the bookcase."

She did and complimented his book collection. "My dad is a bit of a collector, too," she said, then stopped when a familiar spine caught her eye.

Anger sparked in her stomach. She slid out a copy of *Mac Tomlin, Gumshoe* and gave Mr. Nealy a pointed look. She turned to page 124 and read, " 'I've got your number, you fake.' " Then she closed the book with a thud and looked up. "Sound familiar, Mr. Nealy?"

"N-no," he stammered, red-faced.

She planted her hands on her hips. "You broke into my place and left that message?"

He held up his hands. "I didn't break in—I used the key you gave me for emergencies."

"You ransacked my stuff!"

"I only moved things around a little, and I was careful not to break anything."

"I was frightened to death!"

He looked long-faced and apologetic. "I just wanted to scare you a teensy bit, just so you might come over and..."

"Ask you for help?"

"Well, yes."

She shook her head. "I don't believe this."

"Please don't tell the police," he begged. "I was just so lonely, Roxann."

"And you're going to stay lonely if you don't stop manipulating people—what you did was a terrible thing." She stuck out her hand. "Give me back my key."

He removed it from his front shirt pocket and placed it in her palm. She poked her tongue into her cheek, not even wanting to think about how often he'd been over there when she wasn't.

"I'm sorry," he said. "I just wanted a friend."

She sighed. "Mr. Nealy, you need a *friend* who's a little closer to your age."

"I don't know anyone."

She drew mightily on her patience. "Go down to Rigby's Diner and ask to sit in Helen's section. And be *nice*. If you're lucky, she *might* go out with you." She shook her finger. "But don't you ever do anything like this again."

"I won't," he said.

She slowly walked back to her duplex, marveling that the antics of one old man could have unleashed such pandemonium in her life. Proof, she realized, of the power her deep-seated guilt had had over her life.

Capistrano was leaning over the counter when she walked in. "You're not going to believe—" She stopped when she saw he was marking through something on a piece of yellow legal paper. "What are you doing?"

He grinned and held up the life list she'd once crumpled. It had been ironed flat. "I found this in the items the police returned and thought you should keep it."

He had discreetly crossed through number thirty-three with a black marker. She smiled. "Thank you." Then she stopped. "Hey, wait, someone crossed off number one—backpack across Europe."

"Sounds like a great honeymoon to me."

She vaulted into his arms and checked her watch. "Right now, it's seven p.m. in London."

"Wait a minute," he said with a frown. "You did agree to marry me, didn't you?"

She pulled away and rummaged in one of the boxes until she came up with her Magic 8 Ball. She closed her eyes and held the toy reverently. "Should I marry the great Detective Joe Capistrano and live as his sex slave for the next forty—"

"Fifty."

"—fifty years?" She opened her eyes and turned over the toy.

Yes, definitely.

The End

A NOTE FROM THE AUTHOR

Thank you so very much for taking the time to read my romantic mystery GOT YOUR NUMBER. I hope you enjoyed it! I'm a big believer in life lists, so I was happy to incorporate them into a novel. (If you're interested in creating your own life list, see the next section.)

Every book is fun to write in its own way, but for this book, I confess that Angora made it fun. Sure, Roxann was my main character, but Angora was a pure delight to write. Most authors will tell you, the most emotional, the most dysfunctional characters are the most interesting...just like actors will say that playing a villain or an unstable character is far more interesting than playing the good guy!

And the men were a joy to write in this book—Capistrano was just so alpha, and lawyer-farmer Mike was such a hero to me when he stood up to Angora's mother! I love that scene. (I can say that because I didn't so much write it as Mike *made* me write it.)

Anyway, every book and cast of characters is a different, wonderful writing experience. If you enjoyed GOT YOUR NUMBER and feel inclined to leave a review at your favorite online book retailer, I would appreciate it very much. Reviews are the lifeblood of authors and our books, and help us to find new readers.

And are you signed up to receive notices of my future book releases? If not, please drop by www.stephaniebond.com and enter your email address. I promise not to flood you with emails and I will never share or sell your address. And you can unsubscribe at any time.

Also, although I can't count the times this book has been edited and proofed, I'm human, so if you do spot a typo, please email me at stephanie@stephaniebond.com to let me know! Thanks again for your time and interest, and for telling your friends about my books. If you'd like to know more about some of my other books, please see the next section and/or visit my website.

Happy reading!
Stephanie Bond

OTHER WORKS BY STEPHANIE BOND

Humorous romantic mysteries:

TWO GUYS DETECTIVE AGENCY—*Even Victoria can't keep a secret from us...*
OUR HUSBAND—*Hell hath no fury like three women scorned!*
KILL THE COMPETITION—*There's only one sure way to the top...*
I THINK I LOVE YOU—*Sisters share everything in their closets...including the skeletons.*
GOT YOUR NUMBER—*You can run, but your past will eventually catch up with you.*
WHOLE LOTTA TROUBLE—*They didn't plan on getting caught...*
IN DEEP VOODOO—*A woman stabs a voodoo doll of her ex, and then he's found murdered!*
VOODOO OR DIE—*Another voodoo doll, another untimely demise...*
BUMP IN THE NIGHT—*a short mystery*

***Body Movers* series:**

PARTY CRASHERS (full-length prequel)
BODY MOVERS
2 BODIES FOR THE PRICE OF 1
3 MEN AND A BODY

4 BODIES AND A FUNERAL
5 BODIES TO DIE FOR
6 KILLER BODIES
6 ½ BODY PARTS (novella)
7 BRIDES FOR SEVEN BODIES

Romances:

ALMOST A FAMILY—*Fate gave them a second chance at love...*
LICENSE TO THRILL—*She's between a rock and a hard body...*
STOP THE WEDDING!—*If anyone objects to this wedding, speak now...*
THREE WISHES—*Be careful what you wish for!*
TEMPORARY ARRANGEMENT—*Friends become lovers...what could possibly go wrong?*

Nonfiction:

GET A LIFE! 8 STEPS TO CREATE YOUR OWN LIFE LIST—*a short how-to for mapping out your personal life list!*

CPSIA information can be obtained at www.ICGtesting.com
Printed in the USA
LVOW11s1623080216

474190LV00009B/1180/P